RYAN COPELAND

THE SPIRIT OF THE WARRIOR

The Axton Empire
Book 1

This is a work of fiction. All the characters, organizations, and events portrayed in this novel are either the product of the author's imagination or are used fictitiously. Any resemblance to individuals living or dead is entirely coincidental and the product of the author's imagination.

Cover design by Clayton P. King Design
Composited cover images:
© Andrey Kiselev | Dreamstime.com
© Luis Louro | Dreamstime.com
© Joseph Golby | Dreamstime.com
© Dimitar Gorgev | Dreamstime.com

Edited by Liz Reddick and Clayton King

DEDICATION

For my dad who showed me a love of reading

CONTENTS

PROLOGUE

The air was rich with the taste of copper and salt. Pools of dark crimson dotted the ground, sending thick clouds of steam into the black night air. Scattered all around the large wooded clearing laid the mangled, broken, and lifeless bodies of his Magi brothers and sisters. Their traditional robes of silver and white were stained a deep dark red from sword, spear, and arrow wounds. Their bodies contorted into inhuman ragdoll shapes, horror and pain etched into their faces. No sound pierced the dead of night save for his hard panting and the occasional breaking twig far off in the distance.

He thrust his eyes open with a great shock and began darting them around the night sky above, unsure if he was still asleep or succumbing to death's awaiting embrace. The cold air was biting at his face and hands, and his breath was ragged and unsteady. He laid in the clearing for what felt like a lifetime trying to recall any detail about their attack, but no image or sound would come to his mind.

Gathering his wits, and with his muscles screaming in protest, he slowly sat up. But as he did, he let out a shrill cry as pain like no other he had ever felt in his life shot from his belly down to his groin and thighs. The deep dark of night obscured his vision, forcing him to pat around his abdomen slowly until he felt a wet foreign stickiness near his naval.

Panic took root deep inside him. His already ragged breath now quickened faster than horses in the summer races. A chill ran the length of his spine. Sweat began to pour from his body despite the freezing air that permeated his surroundings. He knew, without ever having experienced it before, that he was severely wounded, and without immediate help would bleed out on the frozen forest floor.

He steadied his breathing and quieted his mind of all fear for the present situation. Closing his eyes, he fixed his mind on one goal: healing his wound and getting home. He slowly raised his hand to his chest but was met with more pain from the stretching of his abdomen.

He pressed on through sheer determination and began reciting in the ancient tongue of the Magi the incantation to summon the healing magic. In his mind, he saw the healing magic's light burst into his hands. He saw himself healed and, on the move back to the city. But the light never came. Just empty words echoing into the empty black sky.

Panic set in again. Panic and renewed pain from the struggle of simply holding his hand up. He had said the words correctly, he focused as hard as he ever did, yet the power to heal never came.

What is happening? he thought.

Again, he recited the words. And again, nothing came. He had trained these past four years to touch magic, but now it was out his reach. He had mastered the words and summoned the spell before, yet now when the need was most dire, nothing came to him. Perhaps he had been foolish not to believe the rumors concerning magic. He, along with all of his now-dead compatriots, had no desire to believe in such a wild idea. He cursed himself, and felt his heart start to beat faster than a drum during the spring festivals.

Is this why my brothers died? Am I going to die? I am going to die. And no one will ever know why.

He pressed on, reciting the incantation unceasing for what felt like hours. He visualized the white light leaping to his hands. He envisioned himself going home and him sleeping soundly in his bed. All the thoughts of comfort that he needed to calm his mind and lift his moods. Yet after what felt like hours of trying and failing, his arm fell to the snow-covered ground defeated.

Streams of hot tears ran down his face only to freeze upon his cheek. He closed his eyes and fought to clear his mind of all frustrations, and fears, and questions that abound. He focused on the stillness of the forest, the quiet that flooded his ears, and visualized what he desired the most.

He raised his hand slowly back to his chest and continued with his recitation of the words. Just as before, nothing happened. Unbothered, he pressed on and never stopped the words flowing from his mouth. He had to heal himself. He had to look for survivors. He had to make it home to tell the other Magi what had happened. He was determined not to die so far from home and let his brothers' and sisters' deaths be in vain. The thought of betraying their memories and trust sent an overwhelming feeling of rage through his body, and with a sudden jolt, the dazzling light erupted from darkness into his hands.

He held the explosive and beautiful light in his hand for a moment, examining it, ensuring the spell was stable and would not flame out as weak spells are wont to do. He had always found it hard to describe, but the best he could do was to say it looked like the clearest water in the world but bright, and seemingly on fire all at once. The sight of the spell's light was already raising his morale, and after a minute, he pressed the warm glow to his naval and felt the warm, healing light enter his body.

In mere seconds, the pain that had been flooding through his body ceased. Blood that had been slowly flowing receded into his body, and that which did not began to freeze against his skin. He closed his eyes, bathing in the warmth and comfort of the spell's power. He whispered a silent prayer to the gods of his fathers, thanking them for their small mercy. Perhaps their beliefs had not been in vain after all.

While he held the light to his wound, he opened his eyes and surveyed the massacre about him. The light of the spell was dim but enough to illuminate the darkened woods, allowing him to fully realize the immensity of the carnage that had befallen them. Twenty veteran mages laid broken and dead with their blood melting the snow, their once steaming bodies now beginning to freeze in the frigid night air. If he had struggled so hard to summon a simple healing spell, these mages stood no chance in defending themselves against whatever evil had waylaid them.

They were not Imperial Battle-Mages after all, who could defend themselves with swords and axes. They were dedicated mages through and through, who dared not ever carry the weapons of the common man. Such a thing would be blasphemous to such devout practitioners of the power and mystery that was magic. Magic was their weapon and indeed their way of life, though it now appeared to be impossible to reach except with great effort.

He turned and studied one of the many lifeless bodies next to him. Even in the dim light, he could see their skin was already turning a light blue, and their limbs were stiffening. Crude spears and ancient-looking arrows were all that marked the cause of their deaths. He looked at the blackened sky for any sign of the coming dawn, but the night was thick with snow and shadow. He might as well have been staring into the void of death. Suddenly, he regained his senses, and an overwhelming feeling of urgency overtook him. He needed to be gone from there soon, lest the unknown enemy should return.

He knew he would not survive long in his current state and needed to be on the move soon if he had any chance of making it to a safe haven. He looked down at the dimming light as it worked its way through his body, branching out from the center. He had placed it there to create small spider webs of light that seemed to shine bright and then quickly disappeared. It would have been beautiful to behold if it were not for the dead that surrounded him. A few seconds later, the light faded out, leaving a gentle tear in his robes but no sign of injury to his body.

He tried to stand, but his legs started to tremble under the effort, and he plopped down again with a hard thud. Despite the spell having healed his wound, he was sapped of his strength. It had been some time since he had conjured a spell. Even then it had been with one of the practice wands they supplied in the Citadel, let alone from his own hands. He thought for a moment on what to do next, the threat of sleep from sheer exhaustion now threatening his senses. He laid his head back and closed his eyes, welcoming the rest that his body craved.

Without warning, far off in the dark woods beyond, he heard voices speaking in harsh hurried tones cut through the night. He thrust his eyes open, pulled his head upright again, and began trying to locate where the sound originated. Branches and twigs were being snapped off in the distance, and the sound of rushing feet filled him with renewed dread.

Again, he tried to stand, and again his legs failed him. He thought he might have the strength to crawl away, but lying upon the snow-covered ground, he now realized his arms also lacked the power to move his body.

He rolled over, examining the blank night sky, wishing he were back at the Citadel or even in his own home far away in the northwestern edges of their empire. The stars were beautiful there, bright and comforting, always offering light even in the darkest nights. Not like here where the blackness seemed to overtake everything. He fumbled around till he felt the cold iron of an axe. He gripped the rusted iron weapon tight around its wooden handle and brought it to his chest. Whatever was to come, he was prepared to meet it as a man, not as a scared boy.

The footsteps were closer now, maybe within twenty feet of him if he had to guess. He closed his eyes again, and after another quick prayer of mercy to his gods, resolved to meet his doom head-on. He willed himself to sit up again and stared at the oncoming evil that was sure to cut him down. His arms trembled under the weight of the heavy iron axe, his eyes narrowed, and his heart began to pound faster and faster.

The figures were now within ten feet of him. His heart began to feel as though it was going to burst from his chest. He raised the weapon above his head and let out a defiant battle cry, so shrill and angry his voice went hoarse. Now was the hour of his death, and he was prepared to meet it.

CHAPTER 1

THE RANGERS

The snow was beginning to fall the morning they set out on their expedition. From atop his warhorse, his grey eyes searched the tree line in the distance for any sign of impending attack, old habits he had developed over years of fighting. He adjusted the sword at his side before dismounting, removing his pack, and patting the sturdy beast away. He watched the magnificent black warhorse make its way off back home without aid. Such was their training that they needed none. He surveyed the warriors at his back before motioning them to move out and into the rough forests before them.

They each in turn, dismounted their own steeds, secured whatever gear they would need, and began to jog to the tree line in the distance. Not a sound of complaint nor discomfort broke from their lips. His stern face cracked into a smile from the pride he felt, and after a moment, he jogged to the head of their formation to lead them out into the wilderness beyond. The man was named Tiberius, and he was Commander of the Imperial Rangers.

He had the look of a man in his thirties, though none amongst his men knew or cared for his actual age. He was shorter than most men but was powerfully built, and as fast as a fox on the hunt when pressed by a great need. A short full beard, flecked with grey from the stress of war and turmoil framed his face, yet the most telling feature about him was his closely shaved head. The shaved head had been known as the sign throughout the empire of a warrior from the ancient order of rangers.

Indeed, every man, and now woman, that entered their ranks carried it for the rest of their days as a mark of their service and skill.

As they moved through the snow-dusted woods, he would turn now and then to study the rangers who traveled with him. After the five-year war across the sea, the entire Imperial Military had taken a year to rest and retrain. This Imperial decree also held true for the rangers who, though smaller than any other unit, had fought in more battles than all the others. Their modest numbers, fierceness in action, and unique skill set ensured they were needed everywhere at once to fight as many threats as their foes could throw at them. Now, after a year away from the action, they had resumed their regular duties, roaming the empire to bring their Majesty's justice to all people who dwelt within their borders.

It is better this way, he thought as he slogged his way through the packed snow. Warriors were meant to be in the field, not being pampered, and coddled behind castle walls.

After the year of rest and recruitment, he had been ordered to send his rangers north, and organized this journey while the rest of the Imperial Army continued their long break. Even though their comrades in the regular military were down south enjoying the weather and respite, not a single person in his ranks complained about being sent out. A sword left in the ground will rust and wither, but a sword cleaned in blood and sweat will hold its edge, he reminded himself. These rangers will never shirk their duties for an ounce of comfort.

He had ordered his most senior sergeants to select a handful of his newest recruits and marshal them into a small company to join him on this expedition. Not to say that members of the elite rangers were not experienced at all. It had long been known that all those who wished to serve the rangers had to first come from the Imperial Military. That they all have mastery of a standard soldier's fundamental aptitudes before they learn the skills needed for the rangers' mission.

And every man and woman who now called themselves "Ranger," had endured at least half a decade of constant war in the desert kingdom of the Narzeth. Each of them had sought a more significant challenge, and each of them welcomed whatever challenge would greet them. All for the glory and benefit of the people and country they loved so much.

They were as silent as a graveyard as they crept through the woods. Each of them scanning the trees for signs of disturbance, though Tiberius reckoned they were still too close to the main roads and villages for any evil deeds to be revealed. The task given to them was to hunt for any signs of rogue wizards or witches who may have fled north following the Imperial banning of necromancy.

For four hundred years, it was not illegal per se to practice the arcane art of raising the dead. More looked down upon than unlawful. But after the ten kings of the empire and the Magi Brotherhood had petitioned hard to outlaw this form of magic, many practitioners fled to continue their studies away from the Imperial City and the Magi's watchful gaze.

But when the Great War with the Narzeth began in earnest across the sea everything changed. Almost at once, the entirety of the rangers was drawn into the conflict, and the ten's own knights and soldiers were left to guard the empire, leaving the ban against necromancy almost unenforced.

But rumors began to swirl in the northern kingdom. Strange lights and green fires had been reported deep in the woods where only the most skilled hunter and tracker dared roam. An impenetrable veil of darkness seemed to engulf the night, and piercing screams could be heard echoing off the mountain chasms in the distance And because of that, and the restlessness of the rangers, His Majesty Emperor Axton had dispatched his rangers to root out whatever evil there was.

Tiberius had leapt at the chance to finally get back out into the wide-open country. Too long had he been cooped up in Kovaiyemarck, the garrison, and home to the rangers, recruiting and training new members to their order. He needed to be in the dirt and mud. Back on the hunt for whatever villains that may be afoot within his country. And

They pressed on over the hills and under the trees for many hours without a sign of any human-made disturbance before Tiberius called a halt near Bradford Creek. The creek was almost picturesque with its snow-covered ground and towering pine trees. It could have been a beautiful place to live if not for the dangerous business that brought them all so far from home.

Not wanting to tire them out lest they were forced into a sudden fight, he decided now would be as good as any time to rest. He motioned for his First Sergeant Trevin to join him at the head of their formation. He was older and almost six inches taller than Tiberius. Dark-skinned, muscular, and clean-shaven, an old habit left over from his years in the Imperial army where any hair on the face was forbidden.

"Have them bed down and sheltered against the snow," Tiberius ordered in a low voice. "And remind them to keep on their guard and set a watch."

"Aye," Trevin replied, turning to examine the tiring rangers. "Though I expect they would have done so without a word from either of us."

He departed from Tiberius and began passing the orders to the other sergeants and junior rangers in their ranks. None of them argued over their orders, for they were indeed beginning to tire after the long hike up the forest mountain. Yet they know despite their halt, they would always maintain their watch. Their loyalty to their commander and their empire was unbreakable, even against a small matter of snow and darkness. After a half-hour, they were bundled inside their leather-skinned sleeping bags. They lie three to a group with their backs pressed up to one another for warmth.

After the rangers were hunkered down for the night, Tiberius and Trevin proceeded to walk amongst them, inspecting their hastily assembled camp as the sun set over the trees. They would often bend down to whisper some small form of instruction to one of the men before moving on with their inspection.

The tall, ancient pine trees were swaying quietly in the evening breeze, and the full moon was rising now in the east when they saw it.

Over the tree line, some ten miles off, a sickly green light burst high into the night sky so bright it made the darkening forest as bright as midday. Whatever small chatter there had been in the camp was silenced in an instant. Without a sound, each of the rangers were out of their sleeping bags in a flash, swords and bows drawn, preparing for whatever danger was to befall them.

Trevin was first to the front of their formation next to their commander, eyes sharp, bow and arrow ready to fly. Followed behind Trevin were Zachary and Timothy, battle-hardened sergeants of the rangers. Like their First Sergeant, they had been veterans of the rangers and were inseparable from one another.

"What in the hell was that?" Trevin exclaimed, all formality and rank abandoned in favor of decision and action.

Tiberius, however, did not answer right away. He held his gaze to the light source, his mind working through what to do next. After a moment, he instructed Trevin to have the company of rangers withdraw their arms but remain vigilant. He aimed to take the three men himself into the woods and investigate it themselves.

After a few brief orders were issued to the rangers staying behind, the three men prepared their weapons and moved into the woods as silent as wraiths. No torch did they carry to illuminate their path. The moon that had been shining down on them was enveloped in dark, ominous clouds rendering the frozen woods completely black. Yet, despite the lack of light to shine their way, not a single twig or branch was disturbed by their movements. Such was their skill honed from years of training and battle.

A deep sick feeling of dread sprung up within him as they jogged through the woods. The genuine threat of a necromancer with potential droves of undead ahead of them sent his mind and spirit into a frenzy. He had fought scores of undead during the five-year war and knew them to be stupid creatures who could be surprised and killed without much effort. But a wizard was a different matter altogether.

Long ago, he had encountered a necromancer himself when he was apprenticed to the Battle-Mages, and the idea of fighting such an unrelenting force without the skill of magic was not something he wanted to do. But the years of war and loss had tempered his youthful recklessness. He knew his rangers were well trained and would fight to their last breath, but he would not waste their lives, however brave they might be. He needed to approach this with caution, he reasoned. And to make sure he knew what he was getting his soldiers into before they attacked.

After two hours of running, they could see their destination through the snow-covered woods at last. A large black mass of disturbed earth lay inside of a small clearing, not a common sight so far north away from civilized people. They slowed their pace to a stalk, wishing not to give away their presence to anyone who might have lingered. Yet even at their distance, nothing was moving around them save for the slow sway of the branches in the night air and the steady fall of fresh snow

They crept to the edge of the tree line and looked upon what appeared at first glance to be a small rock quarry in the middle of a wide clearing. The smell of decay and dirt was fresh, along with a faint but strange nauseating odor that hung in the air. Tiberius was the first to emerge from the trees, followed by Trevin and Timothy, with Zachary providing watch over them with his bow pulled tight and ready. Tiberius methodically worked his way through the disturbed rocks that littered the ground around him, bending down now and then to check something on the ground.

"Why the hell is a stone quarry this far in the woods?" Timothy asked, breaking the heavy silence.

Tiberius bent low and moved some smaller rocks when he saw the rusted coins and rings on the floor bed. "This wasn't a quarry, sergeant.

The nearest quarry is fifty leagues from here, in the Clastifet's Kingdom," he replied with a low grunt. He stood from where he had knelt and turned to show his comrades the artifacts in his hand, "this was a burial ground."

"Rusty coins?" Timothy whispered in the dark.

Tiberius bid Zachary join them in the clearing. "Aye, rusty coins. Yet these coins are not native to any civilization still in this world."

"They oddly look familiar though," Timothy said, fingering the coins in his leader's hand. "Where did they come from then?"

"They look familiar because they are Narzethian," Tiberius explained, his voice turning grim. "From nearly five hundred years ago, if I had to guess. See here the crossed spears under the spiked shield, the same emblem they carry today."

"Then what is this place?" Trevin asked.

"Reason would tell me that we are standing in what was a burial site of theirs from their first invasions into our homeland."

"They buried their dead above ground?" Zachary asked in disgust. "What kind of heathens would do such a thing? We had known them to burn their dead, not entomb them."

"Ancient beliefs and ancient customs, my friend," Tiberius said, placing the coins in his cloak. "Our land was a land of evil to them and burning their dead would trap their souls here so that they would never pass into the afterlife. Instead, they were interred above it. I'm sure if someone had the time and inclination, they would find many burial sites like this scattered across our land."

Timothy shook his head in confusion. "We didn't even know this was here. How would someone else possibly know?"

Tiberius didn't reply. The mysteries of tonight were weighing him down and would have to wait for another time to be answered. The more pressing matter was not the discovery of this graveyard, but the confirmation in his mind that necromancy was still in practice within their empire. And how many of these twisted wizards or witches were at large in the woods?

Trevin moved out amongst the rocks and stopped to the east of where they stood. "The tracks move out this way, sir," he said, stooping to examine some recently disturbed snow and dirt patch. "They aren't moving fast by the looks of it, but there are probably fifty of them or more. And they have almost a two-hour head start on us. There are also prints here that don't match the others."

Tiberius shifted some rock under his black boots and pulled the shattered remains of a cauldron covered in green sludge up to his face. "That is assuredly the person responsible for tonight's evil deeds. But do not fret, my friends. I don't think this was a wizard," Tiberius declared with a small measure of comfort in his voice. "This was alchemy. Such as I've never seen, but nonetheless not a dark wizard out here in the woods."

"I've never heard of an alchemist to brew something capable of raising the dead," said Trevin.

Tiberius dropped the pieces of the broken cauldron and turned to the three Rangers. "Neither have I, but an alchemist should not present too much of a challenge. It is the undead that goes with him I'm more worried about. We will have to fight them man-to-man, something the three of us are not prepared to do. Timothy, go back and bring the other men here as fast as you can." At this command, Timothy flew into the night, silent and quick.

"Trevin," Tiberius continued, "take Zachary and scout a path ahead." The men nodded and moved off east to scout the area.

Tiberius sat upon a boulder in the makeshift cemetery, contemplating hard as to what his next move should be. *If we move fast, we can overtake them within a day, but what will we find? And even then, what if our opponent is indeed a wizard? And how in the hell did someone know this was here indeed?*

These thoughts brought no comfort to him, but he weighed his apprehensions with his duty, and his duty always won the fight.

He turned to survey the deep night sky. The snow had started falling in steady streams on his face and cloak, small flecks of stars were twinkling behind some ephemeral vale in the heavens above. His mind wandered back to the first time he set out on his first ranging nearly fifteen years after his apprenticeships with the Imperial military had ended.

He remembered the beauty and wonder at seeing so many sights outside of the Imperial City for the first time. He remembered being struck with the notion that all within the borders of the empire was under their protection. Under *his* protection. The weight of such responsibility was foreign and overwhelming to him. Though now, after all he had endured, he carried it heavier than most would.

After an hour, Trevin and Zachary returned from their scouting, breathing heavy but sure minded. "There is a clear path parallel to their movement we can follow. They look like they are moving due east from what we can tell," Zachary reported.

"Any sign of our foe?" Tiberius asked.

"None," Trevin replied. "No sign except for the trampled mess they have made. And the smell of rot and death hangs heavy for miles on end."

"Very well," replied Tiberius. "Take your rest before the company arrives. I expect we'll be off shortly after that."

Without another word, the two men found spots just outside the ring and began eating what little rations they still possessed. Tiberius himself not feeling hungry but needing something to do to take his mind off the impending hunt, allowed himself a little light in the dark and pulled out his pipe for a brief smoke. He looked at Trevin, who had unsheathed his sword and begun cleaning it. His strong hands and dark eyes worked the blade over meticulously for any sign of dullness or imperfection. Tiberius felt the ache in his heart grow

The man is the consummate professional, he thought. I wish we had more time together away from our comrades. More time to talk and be together away from our life of battle and training.

They had barely exchanged a small word of affection since returning from across the ocean. Trevin had promptly returned to his family's home in Uvomor, while Tiberius and his father walked and talked in the forests outside of the Imperial City.

There will be time for love when this is over. When are oaths are finished and our duties are rescinded.

Four hours later, the company of rangers joined their Commander and First Sergeant in the graveyard. A handful of the sergeants were first to Tiberius to learn what had happened. After a quick summary of all that had transpired, Tiberius ordered each sergeant to provide him with five of their troops to accompany him in their hunt. The rest of the rangers were to make for Waterford Village on the edge of the woods where they had first begun their journey.

"We will meet with you in five days. If not, then make for the capital with all haste, and present these to the Emperor and High Sorcerer, and no one else," he instructed, placing a handful of coins into one of his sergeant's hands.

The man stared wide-eyed at the coins and then at his commander. Questions were beginning to form on his young face, but his commander's stern look silenced all uncertainties inside him. Instead, he offered a simple nod and headed off with his fellow sergeants to issue their commander's orders. Tiberius allowed himself a small smile at their discipline and professionalism, traits often aspired to but rarely exhibited outside of his rangers.

Ten minutes later the marching orders were given. The rangers departing for the village offered small hugs and handshakes to their comrades who were to remain behind and began to make their way back the way they had come. Dejection and regret were etched upon their faces as they walked. The lost privilege and honor of flying into combat with their comrades was almost shameful to the proud warriors, but orders would always trump personal pride.

Tiberius watched them go with a melancholic feeling growing in his stomach. He had hoped to have put each of the new rangers to the test on this excursion, yet with all the uncertainty and overwhelming power that could await them, he dared not risk their lives. Besides, if they were to fall in battle, there had to be some to carry the message back to the capital.

A few minutes later, they disappeared down the frozen rolling hill. He bowed his head and offered a silent prayer to The Warrior that his men reached their destination safely. He then turned to face the remaining men who were to follow him onward. Beneath their cloaks, he could see their faces were stern and frozen from the weather, but a spark of strength and determination to follow their commander wherever he may lead was burning bright in their clear eyes.

No words were spoken, for none were needed. Each Ranger there knew their mission and knew their intention was to fight. He examined each of them, and after a nod of approval, he turned and headed along the unknown path that lay ahead of them with a speed and intensity that shocked them. The men wavered for a moment before moving out behind him, fanning wide to cover all paths ahead of them. Only Trevin and Zachary kept his pace, directing him onto the way they had scouted.

Tiberius didn't know how long it would take until they reached their unknown enemy. But none of that mattered. They would arrive and ready to fight and win. And if they didn't win, then they would die in glory. Upholding the laws of their country, and finally fulfilling their oaths and duties.

CHAPTER 2

THE HUNT

A grey, featureless dawn began to break through the black veil of night. The forest around them seemed to spring to life with all manner of deer and birds out for their morning meal. Their wooded path had started to slowly turn down off the mountain they had been climbing, a welcome relief to the Rangers who continued to press their pace. Though they were all veterans of the military, none possessed the same experience that Tiberius and his three companions did. As such, they were not as prepared for the physical exertion they now found themselves forced to endure.

Tiberius began to sense the exhaustion from the men behind him. Deciding now was as good as any time, he called a halt to their grueling march just after noon. The sergeants in his ranks, though beyond exhausted from their commander's pace themselves, immediately went throughout the formation to check on their soldiers. When all of the men were found to still be in relatively good health, they each dropped their packs to rest. And began to form a camp along a small creek bed frozen over from the perpetual winter of the northern realm. They were no longer amongst the sharp inclines of the mountainside but were now seated in a vast valley of dead snow-covered trees. The lush green pines that had covered them all throughout the night were gone now, replaced by gnarled ancient trees that flecked the creek side. In the distance, small birds were tweeting happily after their noontime feasts had finished.

"Who shall have the first watch?" Trevin asked, joining his Commander at the head of the formation.

"I'll take the watch. You're my best fighter, and I need you sharp and focused for tonight." Tiberius replied. Indeed, other than himself, Trevin was the most experienced ranger in their unit.

"Yes, sir," Trevin replied. "Though I wish you would give yourself some rest as well. This march you have pushed us on will surely have taken its toll on you as well."

Tiberius studied his beautiful face, beginning to discern Trevin's spoken words from his intended words. In his mind he could practically hear Trevin say, "I know you are worried about us, but I worry about you too. And if anything evil should befall you because of your pride, I don't know if I could ever forgive myself."

Tiberius allowed himself a sweet smile and nodded. "I'll take a small rest against that tree, I promise."

Trevin nodded and departed to the rest of their company. Soon after fires were started, bedrolls unfurled, food and water were removed from their small rucks, all in complete silence. They encamped in a circle throughout the creek bed, their backs facing just like the last time they had stopped for camp. Some of the men in the small group used this downtime to begin shaving their faces and heads. To their First Sergeant, it was clear these men were raised within the Imperial army. The ladies present, who also started to shave down the fuzz atop their heads, began to laugh at the struggle their male counterparts had in shaving their faces without a mirror to use. Tiberius, who was now seated apart from them on a broken-off tree stump, smiled at their humor. It was always good to keep morale high in the face of the looming battle.

Yet once his rangers had quieted down, and begun to fall asleep one by one, he pulled his old worn pipe from within his cloak and began to smoke and brood over the deeds to soon befall them. A little while later, Zachary, Timothy, and Trevin joined him by his own low burning fire. The four of them had endured many tribulations over the years of war. Yet despite the disparity in their ranks and status, they had formed an unbreakable bond of brotherhood and friendship.

"These kids are a tough bunch of bastards," Timothy said, putting a small pinch of tobacco into his cheek.

"You call them kids, yet forget that you're still the youngest one here," Trevin replied with a chuckle.

Timothy smiled, his youth shining through his hardened face. He had joined the rangers in his twenty-second year, the same day as his best friend and fellow ranger Zachary. Despite his now ten years of service under Tiberius, his face still had the look of a boy barely out of his parents' home. He did not mind it though. The truth was it did wonders at disarming people looking to fight him in the pubs back home and gaining the favor of one or two tavern wenches.

"Even still," Timothy replied, "they marched on without making a sound. Not even a grunt! So, as I said, tough bunch of bastards!"

"That they are. I'm especially impressed by the ladies in our ranks," Zachary replied, also putting in his own chewing tobacco. "Opening up our order to the fairer of the species was a good idea, sir."

"There is nothing fair about the women in our ranks. I'd wager they could take any of you in a fight if you felt like tempting your fates," Tiberius replied with a chuckle.

Traditionally, the rangers had only been exclusive to only the men of the empire. But times change, people change, and Tiberius reasoned he needed all the people he could get to join after the grueling war across the sea. Though he had met resistance from the less forward-thinking members of the Imperial military, it was ultimately not up to them, for he alone held complete authority over his rangers. And if a woman wanted to live and fight and die like a ranger, then gods be damned she would be a ranger. Besides, who was he to deny someone the honor and privilege to defend their homelands if their will compelled them so?

"Do you know what today is, sir?" asked Zachary while he restrung his bow.

"Twenty-first of Golds Harvest," replied Tiberius, his smile melting.

"Aye, sir. I bet down in the capital there are grand parades and feasts to mark this occasion," Zachary continued, thoughts of a warm bed and a belly full of beer and steak flashing before his mind.

"A year of peace after so long a war is reason enough to feast," Tiberius said, dark thoughts and memories appearing before his waking eye.

"Across the ocean, they are probably cursing us as invaders and mourning their dead. Especially at Vermillion Pass," replied Trevin grimly, taking a deep drink of water from his deerskin canteen.

Silence permeated the group. Timothy and Zachary's own smiles began to disappear from their faces in the same manner as their commander's had. The four men began to think about that day at the pass when their lives had irrevocably changed. After many heavy moments of silence, Tiberius's three companions stood in turn and bid him farewell, each wanting to be alone with their thoughts. Tiberius leaned his head against the tree he was propped on, closed his eyes, and stretched his memory back a year ago to the pass.

In his mind's eye, he could see the pass clear as day: the large chasms of red and orange mountains and dirt, the unrelenting sun that beat down on them over a blackened sky. None of the Narzeth dwelt in that land, for they had long believed it to be cursed. Not even flora and fauna native to their country would grow there, leading many in the empire to believe it was, in fact, an unholy land to walk upon. Regardless of the superstitions that were carried, it had long been known that the pass was the most important and strategic piece of terrain in the war. If the empire could take it, then nothing would stop their impending march on the Narzethian capital, Xartel. As predicted, once the empire arrived, it became the site of the largest and bloodiest battle in the Great War.

Both sides had thrown countless soldiers at one another in an effort to secure the pass. Thousands of infantry, cavalry, and artillery rained down all around them from both the empire and their ancient foe. Knights from the empire clashed with the knights of the Narzeth, mangling their bodies inside their steel armors. Spears and arrows flew in every direction, sometimes finding their mark against their own men. It was a bloodbath in the truest sense, but that was not the memory that now plagued Tiberius and his friends. It was what came after. For it was there all the assembled from the empire, and the Narzeth witnessed magic for what it truly was. Witnessed magic at its most powerful, and at its most terrifying.

The High Sorcerer of the Magi Cycret had arrived in the Imperial camp two days into the fevered battle and pleaded with the emperor to use what he had learned in the Library of Beaumont, the ancestral home of the Magi. It was widely known that before the founding of the empire, and the evil of Narzethians had reached its pinnacle, the Magi had called the city of Beaumont their home. And it was in that city that they chose to remove themselves from the affairs of the Narzeth. They had no mind for war, and conquering, and politics, preferring to dedicate themselves to the study and practice of magic.

Over time, the Narzeth's hate and distrust of magic and things beyond their control grew uncontrollable. In the end, they sacked the city and forced all the Magi into hiding and exile from their homes. The ancient tomes and tools were seemingly lost to the desert city for all time until the empire in their wrath invaded and reclaimed the city for the Brotherhood, and ever since the High Sorcerer had been holed himself inside. At first, he was giddy with the prospect of studying and learning all the forgotten knowledge that had long been thought lost to the Magi when they first came to the empire. But over time, he began to realize that the mystery of magic was deeper and more powerful than he could have possibly imagined.

He was determined to stay within that place until the empire had won the war and withdrawn from Narzeth. But it was the intense fighting and bloodshed at the pass that compelled him to leave and join his emperor. For many days, the emperor had resisted using the magic Cycret had learned, yet when all hope for anything other than a stalemate was evident, the emperor finally conceded. The fury and magnitude of magic Tiberius saw that day had rendered him speechless, for nothing of that kind of power had been seen in the world.

Some of those who lived to see the power displayed before them had started to laugh like men possessed. Others openly wept as if mourning the loss of a loved one. Most though, were as silent as the field of death in front of them. As for High Sorcerer of the Magi Cycret, his body and staff were turned to dust along with the enemies of the empire from the sheer magnitude of power he conjured that fateful day. Only his robes of ebony and grey were recovered so as to be returned to the Citadel.

No cheers of victory were heard that day, nor songs and laments for their fallen brothers. The whole of the assembled Imperial military was silent as a graveyard that night while far over the mountains of the pass, a great blood-curdling wail of sorrow could be heard echoing from the Narzeth capital. It was then that Tiberius knew magic was not something to be taken lightly. Not something to be treated as entertainment and spectacle, but as something that should be guarded and revered. The war was officially over two days later, and all men of the empire departed that cursed land, hoping never to see it again. On their return to the shores from which they had disembarked, the emperor ordered the Library of Beaumont razed to the ground lest their enemy scour it for knowledge to use in their revenge.

For longer than Tiberius could remember, he had been fighting in wars and against people who had no value for life and decency. Against people who only wished to destroy the empire and claim the ten kingdoms for their own. His father had taught him about the enemies of their homeland. Over many years from his youth until his assumption of command over the rangers, his father had instructed him in all manners of combat and history and culture. He knew his son would be destined for greater things than he and was determined to ensure his son would not make the same mistakes he had.

"Why is there so much hate in this world?" Tiberius had asked his father one spring nearly twenty years ago. "It would be a much better place if we all put down our swords and reasoned with one another."

"The world would indeed be a much fairer place without the strife of war," his father had said. "Unfortunately, the real world is not like that. There is much beauty and hope around us, yes. But there is also evil and greed and hate, and those are the things we must fight. Remember this: it is easy to take a life, my son. It is much harder to get to know someone's life."

Tiberius slowly opened his eyes and smiled at his father's words. His entire life of fighting and serving the empire had etched unimaginable horrors into his memory, but it was his father and his wisdom and love that always brought him back from the brink of despair. After one last long drag on his pipe, he removed his sword and sharpening stone and set to work on the blade. Over the camp, slow wisps of steam were rising from the rangers' mouths, and the fires around them were beginning to burn low.

It was near dusk when the rangers awoke from their sleep, their tired and worn faces refreshed by the much needed daytime slumber. They each, in turn, pulled rations from their bags and ate in silence. Tiberius observed all this from his perch, his bag already packed and his belly full of his own food. No words were exchanged amongst them, and none needed to be. They all had awakened from their much-needed sleep knowing there was to be a battle that night, and the thought of flying headlong into the unknown was beginning to harden their hearts and sharpen their minds for the deeds to be done.

After their dinner was finished, and the men had begun to pack, Trevin approached Tiberius, his own deep brown eyes refreshed and ready. "The rangers will be ready to march by nightfall, sir," he said.

Tiberius nodded his approval. "Have them leave their packs. We must be swift and silent, and I expect we will be upon our foe in a few hours. We'll come back for our things after." And if not, at least the animals of the forest will have a few snacks from our food, Tiberius thought.

Trevin nodded in understanding and left to relay their commander's orders. Throughout the small camp, Tiberius could hear a few of his men uttering last-minute prayers to their respective gods. Weapons and tools were removed from packs and secured to their bodies, and within a few short minutes the rangers stood ready and proud in front of their commander. Tiberius nodded in approval and finally stood to face his men.

His mind focused on their faces, determined to remember each and every one of them. These men and women had seen true horrors across the sea and yet continued to want to fight on. They were The Spirit of The Warrior, through and through. And the Spirit would always be with them. He was honored to be their leader, and he would lead them as he always did, from the front. He surveyed the assembled men for a moment before bowing his head in humility to them. In one unison movement, they returned his bow. As the night before, words were not needed. The time for words had long passed. Now was the time for action.

He lingered on them for a moment before turning and setting off on a jog through the woods towards his prey. His men were behind him in an instant their own thoughts hardened, and their faces blank. The path of the undead was clearer to them now that they were within striking distance. Soon the hunt would be over, and the fighting would start. He pushed his pace steadily on, determined to meet them unaware and open to attack.

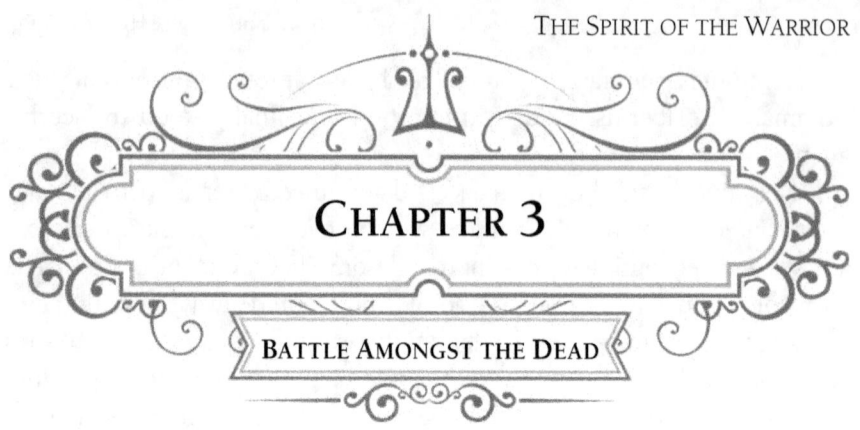

CHAPTER 3

BATTLE AMONGST THE DEAD

The last rays of the sun were barely peeking through the western tree line. Dark clouds were starting to roll in from the north, bringing a small gift of fresh snow. Tiberius could feel the temperature drop several degrees in a short amount of time. He took in a deep breath and quickened his steady pace to a light jog, determined to beat the weather. Though he easily outpaced even the youngest of his warriors at an easy run, he knew they would not falter and fall behind. As always, only his three friends were able to match his pace. Though he knew if he pressed any harder, they too would fall behind. But now was not the time for speed. Now was the time to conserve their strength and prepare their minds and hearts.

"How close are we, you reckon?" asked Trevin from behind him.

"We're still a few miles off," Tiberius replied without taking his eyes off the path. "Probably another hour or so." When no acknowledgment came, he turned to see that Trevin had already fallen back to begin relaying the information to his men. He nodded to himself in approval and turned back to face the path.

The tracks that they had been following were becoming more disjointed and messier, a clear sign that their enemies were not marching at all but rather shuffling in mass. A smart necromancer would have directed their undead to march single file to conceal their numbers. Clearly, this person had no interest in stealth, he thought to himself. A few minutes later, he raised his hand, bringing his group to a sudden stop. He stared ahead in the trees with his nose up in the air, a faint familiar aroma catching his attention. He motioned for his men to take a knee, and in a flash, Trevin and Zachary were beside him.

"What is it?" Zachary whispered.

"A campfire," Trevin answered. "Can you not smell it?"

"No, I can't. How far off do you reckon?"

"A hundred yards or so," Tiberius answered, turning to face them. "Fan out wide and encircle them, we will attack them from all around. Secure the alchemist, but if he gets caught in the fray, so be it."

Trevin and Zachary nodded in understanding before returning to move their men in position. This was one of the many ambush tactics they taught in the ranger training, and his men would execute it flawlessly.

"Well, this ought to be interesting," Zachary said, returning to join his commander at the front of their group.

"Of course, it will," Timothy added, walking beside him. "They will sing glorious melodies about what we do here tonight. Songs of the intrepid Imperial Rangers and how we fought down undead soldiers from our empire's first invasions. Oh, I can already see the ladies when I tell them I was here in the fight."

A wry smile crept up on Tiberius' face, amazed that after all these years, these two fools still managed to make him smile in the face of death. Light snow began to fall on the men's cloaks, a small gift of luck from the unseen forces above. Tiberius pulled his sword, gave it a quick inspection, and readied himself. Victory or death, the glory of enforcing the empire's law, would be theirs, for such glory and honor are all the rangers needed in life.

"Stay with me," he ordered. "Fight fast, defend yourself and your brothers, and victory will be ours." He closed his eyes, steadied his breath, and focused his mind as he never had before.

But before he could move a high pitched, shrill cry rung out piercing the night. The sound of it forced the rangers all around to drop their weapons and cover their ears in pain. In a moment, the shrill cry passed but was replaced by blood-curdling, almost childlike screams of horror and agony such as he had not heard since the war. The sound of swords cutting through flesh, and bones breaking under heavy hammers cut through the cries of anguish. Just as abruptly as the screaming had overtaken them, it suddenly went quiet and still.

Without any thought, Tiberius ran at a full sprint towards where the smell of fire and the sounds of screaming had just been. In a moment, he was in a wide clearing, horror, and anger etched into his face. Dead bodies lay about him. Twisted and contorted in every direction, blood oozing its way out of thousands of cuts and stabs. Blood so thick and hot it melted the snow and raised steam into the frozen night air. Looking on the bodies, he recognized them only by their blue and red and green colored cloaks, all stained by the bloody attack. To his shock and horror, twenty mages were dead at his feet.

He knelt to inspect one nearby, determined to learn whatever he could from their slaughter when more screaming exploded directly in front of him. But this was not the guttural screaming of a dying man, nor the sound of fear. This was the sound he had heard all his life, a warrior's cry. The sound of the clashing of steel against steel. This was the scream of battle. The undead had found his rangers from the other side of where they meant to pounce.

A deep booming bellow emerged from within him, such a sound he had not mustered since that day at the pass. "RANGERS! DEFEND YOUR BROTHERS! WITH ME!" he cried, charging towards the fight.

His body was in motion like a bolt of lightning amongst the trees. Snow from the ground was thrown this way and that under his relentless sprint. The branches nicked and scratched his face as he went yet did not deter him one bit. All thought was on his men and killing the enemy that was attacking them. Such speed and ferocity and anger he had not conjured up in what felt like a lifetime, but his muscles and spirit remembered. In an instant, he was upon them and beheld the most horrifying sight since the war.

To his horror, a black and rotting mass were throwing themselves against the rangers as waves beat upon beach rock. There were at least fifty of the undead, ancient soldiers reeking of putrefaction and soil. Their faces rotted to the bone, with no eyes in their skull, wisps of hair hanging off their heads, and small patches of skin dangling here and there. Their teeth black with rot, and their mouths pulled tight in the corners of their mouths in a twisted devil smile. The stuff of nightmares made real by the deeds of evil. With unchecked anger, he threw himself into that swirling undead nightmare.

Swinging broad to his front, stabbing to his left and right, parrying attacks all around, he was in the thick of the fray before he knew it. His body fluid and changing directions as he went, his sword poetry in motion. It would have been beautiful to see if not for the evil sight surrounding him. The undead swords of ancient iron were no match against his lighter, sharper Imperial steel. He met their frenzied attacks with masterful precision and cut down a swath of them as he went.

Alive, these undead abominations might have proven a match for him. Yet all they could do was try and swarm him without any tactics or thoughts in their mind. Their speed was great, but his was greater as he ducked their blows, cutting a group at their knees. Random spears pierced the cold air, but he effortlessly twirled in place, missing them. The element of surprise with which they had taken the mages was gone. Now they had to fight against a real opponent and one that would not surrender or run.

Arrows began to fly past him, finding their mark against three of the enemy that ran on him. His own group of Rangers had finally caught up to him, Trevin, at the front, followed by Zachary. In an instant, the rangers had the mass of dead surrounded, and were swiftly cutting through them. A new cry of volley went up over the ring as more arrows whistled past the melee finding their targets and dropping them to the snowy ground. Timothy had somehow managed to consolidate his bowmen and was directing their fire against the enemy.

"Trevin!" he yelled above the frenzied battle, "Cut them down! Timothy! Keep firing!" he ordered between attacks.

He pushed forward, cutting, slashing, and dodging as he went until, finally, he reached his men. They were surrounded by a group of the undead who were prodding and almost toying with the battered rangers. They were bloodied and bruised but were nonetheless determined to hold their ground against their foes. A deep guttural cry escaped Tiberius's body, and with a mighty slash, cut down three of the enemy in one great broad stroke of his bastard sword.

"Rangers! Fight!" he cried, drowning out the sounds of death.

With their spirits lifted, the rescued rangers sprang out of their defense. Their swords flew fast and true against their attackers, determined to repel them. Once they were defeated, Tiberius turned back to the larger group and cried out, "All Rangers! To me! To me!"

Trevin and Zachary's men ran through the throng cutting through the undead with ease. Timothy called out over the fray to his archers to draw their swords and collapse in from their ring around the battle. Along with the small group of rangers nearby, Tiberius ran back into the heart of the fight. Swords and spears were no match for his skill as he continued to slay all he approached. No pain or fear entered their bodies. No regret. No doubt. Just anger. Focused, intense, unadulterated anger. They fought on.

Over the fray, Tiberius could see Trevin and Zachary back to back, twirling in a deadly dance around the onslaught. The oncoming swarms of undead were no match for their speed and agility. Timothy and a group of archers were alternating between arrows and their short swords. Their ferocity and speed at which they effortlessly switched between weapons would have been something to stare and marvel at if not for the raging battle around him. A group of female rangers were nearby, ducking and weaving around, slashing and hacking with all their strength. Their training was shining through the chaos, just as he had known it would. Then, all at once, it was over.

Panting to catch his breath in the cold air, he examined the quiet battlefield around him. From what he could see, they were all out of breath but standing tall and firm. Not a single Ranger save himself was unscathed from the melee. Still, none were mortally wounded except those who were already dead at his feet. But in amongst the dead bodies that now covered the ground, he could not find their ultimate quarry. He quickly collected his thoughts and set to work.

"Trevin!" he called out, "Where's the damned alchemist?"

"We'll find him," he replied. "Boys, with me." And with that, he flew into the woods with Zachary and Timothy to find the cause of this mess.

To the rangers, Tiberius ordering them to fan out and take a knee as security was paramount at a time like this. He went to each ranger in the ring to check on them, examining each of their wounds and beginning to patch them himself as he went. His ferocity had subsided with the last of the enemies to fall. His unabated rage now replaced with almost a fatherly tenderness as he cared for each of his wounded rangers.

About half an hour later, the three hunters emerged from the darkness pulling a man along with them as they approached their comrades. When they were upon Tiberius, they threw the man at his feet and backed away, their weapons trained on him. But to Tiberius's surprise, instead of a robed wizard or fastidiously dressed alchemist, there was an old man dressed in rags lying motionless in the snow at his feet.

"Sit yourself up," Tiberius commanded. But the man didn't move from burying his face in the snow.

Trevin grabbed the man and sat him up in one violent motion. "Our leader gave you an order!" he growled.

Tiberius nodded at Trevin and motioned him to retreat away. He squatted down and began to examine the man. By the look him, he had to have been more than eighty years old and covered in boils and blisters over his head and arms. His clothes were ragged and nearly threadbare, his fingers were blue from the frost, his mouth cracked, his shoes broken with bloody scabbed toes that poked out of the sides. A beggar man's shoes, Tiberius reasoned. But the man's eyes are what drew his attention the most. His eyes were on fire.

The sockets where an average person's eyes would have sat was a dark, smoldering, roiling red fire. He knew this magic immediately. "He's been enchanted," he said at last before standing. "Search him."

Timothy was the first to reach out and yank the man to his feet. But as soon as he touched the enchanted beggar, his body turned as limp as a rag. His skin slowly began to fall off his bones, flaking and falling off into small wisps of dust that began to float away in the night air. Timothy released the ragged clothes and stepped away in horror, struck dumb by the sight he had just witnessed.

All the rangers recoiled at the sight save for Tiberius. He alone held his composure and discipline despite the horrid scene in front of them. His mind raced back to Vermillion Pass, where all the enemy of the empire had befallen the same fate. They all stood for a moment processing what had just transpired until finally, after many heavy moments, Tiberius broke the silence.

"How many men did we lose?" he asked Trevin, his face and voice turning grim.

"I'll do a headcount, but at least eight that I know of, sir," came Trevin's reply.

Eight men, he thought. Eight men for a dusty enchanted beggar.

"I'll count the dead, First Sergeant. Take the men and retrieve our gear. No need to rush. We all could use a little respite." Tiberius ordered solemnly.

"Aye. Shall I leave some men to bury the bodies?" Trevin asked.

"No. I'll bury these men when you return," he responded. "They were my rangers, and it was me who led them here. Now, leave me be till you return. I need to look these men over and clear my head."

"Aye, sir. Rangers, with me," Trevin said. And with that, the remaining rangers began to slowly file behind to retrieve their things, leaving Tiberius to tend to their fallen comrades.

A few moments after they departed, Tiberius fell to his knees. The events of the night had finally begun to take their toll on him, and the strength of his legs could not sustain the weight of evil and treachery that had befallen them. He tried to hold his head up but could not muster the strength. His anger was boiling over. His breath quickened, and in a rare instance, he lost control of his discipline and bellowed loudly into the frigid night.

He knelt there for what seemed like hours on end. These men weren't supposed to die out here, he thought as he looked upon the broken and twisted bodies of six men and two women. No one deserves this fate. Regaining his composure, he stood again. His hands had stopped shaking with rage, and his watery eyes were drying in the frigid night air. He buried his sword into the ground, and after finding a flat piece of wood, began to dig a vast grave in the field.

After almost an hour's work, he took a deep breath and prepared the bodies for their burial. These were his men that he had led into combat, and now these eight brave rangers were dead. The task of burying them, of course, fell to him. No songs would be sung of their needless sacrifice, nor poem or rhyme. Just the stories of their bravery, and the memory of their gallantry in fulfilling their sacred oaths to the empire. His mind wandered back to the first time he had seen a ranger's burial. Then, it had been his very father who had performed the funeral of his own fallen men. Of course, he had sent his other men away in the same way Tiberius had. However, on that particular day, his father had ordered Tiberius to stay and witness it for himself.

If a ranger falls in the field far from home, they are to be buried with their brothers, his father had instructed. The ranger's duty was to the empire, and back into the land of the empire they would return. Their weapons are to be plunged into the ground, for where they go, they will not be needed.

Tiberius had asked his father where they were meant to go after their death. In his mind's eye, he could see his father standing tall and proud before him with a broad smile etched into his face. They go to the Warrior in his castle beyond our world, his father had proclaimed. They have carried his spirit into battle and are rewarded by joining his company of heroes.

A soft smile cracked his grim face at the memory of his father. He nodded to himself and began to kneel beside each of his fallen men, examining them. He removed his leather gloves and began to lovingly stroke each of their faces. He would remember each of them and their sacrifices in service of their empire. And as he departed from their bodies, he held his hand to each of their chests and whispered the Rangers' ancient words, "The Spirit of The Warrior will always be with you."

After he finished speaking his words, he began to carry their bodies into the mass grave. He laid all eight of them side by side with their arms crossed over their chest. Their weapons he buried in a ring around their grave, a mark for all who may venture to that place that brave Imperial Rangers had given their lives and lie there at peace. No sound he made while setting to his work, and no rest or pause would he allow himself. These warriors had fought unceasingly to their last, so too shall he in hopes of ensuring their journey to the afterworld was honorable and just.

Once he had finished with them, he turned his attention to the fifty or so undead Narzethians that littered the ground. He piled their bodies together high, determined to burn them as is the way in their home across the ocean. His empire's land was not evil, as they had been raised and trained to believe in Narzeth. No nation in the wide world was evil and cursed, only the people that dwell above it. Though they had been invaders from the past, they did not deserve to have their bodies desecrated by such dark and evil magic.

Trevin and the rest of the rangers returned nearly two hours later, every one of them loaded with their packs, and each of them was grave and quiet. Despite their solemnity, they were now all physically refreshed, and ready to press on if their commander ordered. The thought of combat against dark beings and the astounding magic placed upon the old beggar was fresh in their minds and had renewed their resolve to continue venturing in the wilderness. Tiberius might have continued to press their search if it had not been for the enchanted beggar. This horrible misadventure required better counsel than he could have ever hoped to give.

"How was the trip?" Tiberius asked as they approached.

"Uneventful," Trevin reported, removing his pack and rejoining his men.

Tiberius nodded and turned to approach the mound of undead soldiers. Never in his life could he have imagined he would be lighting a funeral pyre for Narzethians, especially undead Narzethians in the heart of his homeland. Still, he lit a torch, held up both arms, closed his eyes, and said, "May your spirits find rest in your father's homes. May your memory and sacrifice endure in your family's hearts unto the unmaking of the world."

He thrust the torch into the mound and watched as one by one all were consumed by the cleansing fire. He stood rooted in place, watching the fire burn higher and higher before turning to his fallen Rangers.

Standing over them, he studied their faces one last time. Young men and women who had all endured such hardships and war stared up at him. He felt a sharp pang of sadness twitch in his soul for the loss of life during times of peace was hard to swallow. That these men and women had fought valiantly across the sea and lived only to die in their homeland, filled him with overwhelming anger. He clenched his fist as tight as possible, forcing that anger back in the presence of his men. Time enough for tears in private, he reminded himself.

After many heavy minutes, he finally raised both his arms again, held his head up, and spoke with a booming commanding voice, "Rangers! I release you from your service to your country! I bid thee take with you your pride! Take with you, your honor! Take with you each other as you travel into the halls of The Warrior! May you have a seat at his table! May you watch over us and await our arrival! I say to you! All who have given your life for our empire! The Spirit of The Warrior is with you! The Spirit of The Warrior will be with us all as we go forth! For his honor! And for the honor of our empire!"

"The Spirit of The Warrior will always be with you!" his men boomed around him. He looked around him to see his men all standing. Each of their arms was held aloft, all yielding their spirits to the invocation their commander had given for their fallen comrades. He slowly dropped his arms and stood for a moment, looking at his men. His anger and sadness had subsided, replaced with pride for his remaining Rangers.

Finally, he broke the silence. "Trevin, have the men make camp for the night. We have a few hours until sunup, and then we'll travel to the village to collect the rest of our company," he ordered.

"As you wish, sir. But what of the fallen Magi?" Trevin asked.

"We have our customs, and they have theirs," Tiberius responded. "Their bodies will provide nourishment to the animals of the forest as all things do."

"They do not follow the ways of their homelands? Nor of the empire?" Timothy asked.

"No," Tiberius responded. "Their ways are to return to nature that bore them and all of us into existence. The earth is their tomb."

Tiberius knew the Magi's minds and knew the High Sorcerer would approve of his honoring of their order's customs. Long had the Magi held onto their connection to the natural world. Indeed, they were more attuned to nature and the beasts within it than the rangers themselves who walked amongst the forests and mountains of their country. To some, this would seem like sacrilege. But in a land of so many people and so many beliefs and customs, you had to honor every one of them.

The Rangers were busy setting up their camp for the night. None spoke a word, preferring to keep their thoughts and feelings to themselves. They were all finally beginning to tuck in for the night when fiery bright light illuminated the dark forest. Some of the men were on their feet in a flash, swords unsheathed, bewildered by what they had just witnessed. Others were not driven to fear as their comrades were, for the light was not evil but slightly warm and comforting. But just as suddenly as it shone in the darkness, it was gone, and the thick veil of night returned.

Tiberius ran to the edge of their small camp, peering out into the darkened woods. Trevin was beside him in an instant, his own sword drawn. They stood still for a moment, their minds racing, before Tiberius's face lit up in excitement. A healing spell!

He took off into the night, possessed by some small measure of hope that amongst the bodies of the Magi, one had managed to survive. He had not had the time to properly examine them before the fighting with the undead erupted. Even then, the mass of bloodied bodies had given him little hope that any survivors might lie amongst them. But he knew a healing spell anywhere, and that was reason enough to hope beyond all belief that someone was still alive out in the woods.

Nearly ten minutes later, they arrived at the site of the massacre and immediately set to work. The smell of decay and death was still fresh in the air and stung their nose and eyes. Yet the two Rangers pushed past it, turning over body after body in their hunt. Suddenly, a great defiant cry rang out from the opposite corner of where they searched. The two men raised their weapons at once and began to scan for the source of the mighty cry. But after only a few short moments, they eased their swords back down to their sides as their eyes fell on the figure of a small boy sitting amongst the dead mages.

"Have you come to finish your evil work?" the small boy croaked.

The Rangers stared wide-eyed before the boy continued, "I hope you live the rest of your pathetic lives knowing that you couldn't even..." his voice grew weak and trailed off. His eyes rolled in his head, which wavered in the air for a moment before he slumped down to the frozen ground.

The Rangers descended on the boy in an instant. A pulse they found and his chest they could see slowly rose and fell in the blue hue of night. In the middle of his robes, they could see the tear where he had been stabbed and a faint but fresh three-inch scar above his navel.

This lad is made of stronger steel than most men twice his age, Tiberius thought. But how in the name of all the gods above did he survive this slaughter?

CHAPTER 4

THE MAGE

As if emerging from hazy early morning fog, the boy slowly opened his eyes to blinding sunlight that poured on his face. A searing headache burned across his brain and forced his eyes to squint against the dazzling morning light. He ached from head to toe, not wanting to move, but knowing that he needed to face whatever he had gotten himself into. He slowly sat up and was surprised to see he was no longer on a forest floor but resting in a four-post bed in what looked like a rather comfortable room.

A roaring fire burned in a small hearth in the corner of the room. Thick wooden panels adorned the small room with shabby drapes and tapestries hung haphazardly in random places. The smell of hot coffee and frying bacon permeated the room, awakening his senses and turning his stomach over in avarice. He forced his legs over the side of the bed and slowly stood peering out the large circular windows by his bed. He was shocked to find himself in the village he and the Magi had traveled through on their way north. Yet, for the life of him, the name escaped him, lost in the vapors of his memory.

The village was a mass of small stone houses with thatched roofs. Merchants and farmers dressed in thick wool coats and jackets could be seen coming and going with all manner of food and livestock. In the distance, he could see the snowcapped ridges of the Forgotten Mountains. Grey clouds were forming over the mountains' peaks with dim rays of sunlight peeking through like a fisherman's net.

It was a beautiful, picturesque scene that somehow reminded him of home. But not his adopted home at the Citadel of the Magi, where he had spent the last six years of his life dedicated to the study of magic. No, this quaint village on the edge of the Childers Kingdom conjured up a deep longing for his real home. His heart began to ache, and he grew sad at the memories of home, something he had not felt in many years.

He found his robes cleaned and meticulously laid out on a chest at the foot of the bed and slowly began to dress. His muscles screamed in protest, and his abdomen was ginger but healed nonetheless. It was a small blessing he had been found, but now another new mystery to answer. He caught a glimpse of himself in a nearby mirror adorned with dense wood and barely recognized himself. His young face of sixteen looked worn with wrinkles around his eyes. His usual neatly placed hair was disheveled and messed all over, and his eyes were red. He quickly fixed his hair as best he could; and adjusted his robes. They too seemed a lot bigger than he remembered.

He took a deep breath and counted to five before exhaling all of his misgivings. He didn't know where he was, but he knew he was alive. And for the moment, he knew he was safe. For the moment anyway. He took one last look at the wooden bedroom before slowly making his way to the heavy wood door. He took one last deep breath, shut his eyes, and pushed his way out.

To his surprise, outside his quarters, he found himself inside a rather large café filled with all manner of travelers and locals talking busily and digging into their breakfast. As he surveyed the massive wooden walls, he discovered about a dozen other doors like his, no doubt opening into similar rooms such as where he awoke. Above the stone laden hearth in the middle of the room was a sigil on a large wooden shield. A bear with trout in his mouth below a crossed arrow and spear. The sigil of the Childers Kingdom. Wherever he was, he realized he was indeed safe, and in the company of good people of the empire.

He turned again to examine the room, unsure of what to do next when he found four men in dark green and brown cloaks in the middle of the room. They looked tired but alert, a sight he had often seen of his amongst the watchmen back home after a long night of patrolling the streets. He blinked at the sight of them, a distant yet familiar memory forming in his mind. All of a sudden, it dawned on him. These four men in their dirtied cloaks and with their watchful gazes were members of the Imperial

Rangers. The Ranger in the middle noticed him first, stood, and beckoned him to join them. The boy gulped and cautiously began to approach them.

"Good morning, young Mage," the bearded Ranger greeted. "I am Tiberius, commander of the rangers."

"Michael Deerborn, sir. Apprenticed mage to the Magi Order," he replied, somewhat unsure of himself.

Tiberius smiled kindly at the boy and continued, "These are my companions, First Sergeant Trevin Moore, and Sergeants Zachary Trex and Timothy Shepherd. Please, sit."

Michael slowly sat down, turning from side to side to examine the four rangers he now shared a table with. "Master Tiberius," he said, confused, "I, uh, that is to say… have heard many tales of you and your men. And I am, uh, honored, to uh…"

Tiberius chuckled at Michael's words before holding up a hand. "Please, young Mage, it is just Tiberius. No 'master' or anything of that nature."

Michael could only continue to stare at each of the four in turn. He was so shocked by the present and welcomed company, he didn't notice a plate of fried eggs, bacon, and mug of coffee that had almost materialized in front of him. The smell is what grabbed him, and unthinkingly he began digging into his food. The Rangers laughed at the ferociousness with which he seemed to attack his food.

"Hungry?" Timothy asked with a chuckle.

"Very," Michael replied between mouthfuls of food. "I had to cast a rather large healing spell last night, and the side effects make the caster very hungry. Also, it's been at least sixteen hours or so judging by the time of morning since I last ate. Coupled with the effort of summoning magic…"

But the Rangers' renewed laughter cut him off from his rambling. "You sure like to talk for someone with such a huge appetite," said Zachary, sipping his warm coffee. Michael stared at them, growing self-conscious again, half chewing and half unsure of what to do.

"Healing magic draws on your life force to heal another's physical body," said Tiberius to Michael's astonishment. He had never known a person outside the Magi who knew the side effects of casting certain magics.

But Tiberius's mood changed from exchanging pleasantries to coldness in an instant. "What can you tell us about last night, Michael?" he asked. "What do you remember, and why were you and your brothers so far north?"

Michael thought for a moment, trying to bring forth memories that seemed like years ago. He looked hard into Tiberius's penetrating eyes and could tell that any dishonesty would be sussed out in a second. Instead he settled on his trusty default response, honesty. He pushed aside his plate, took a sip of his coffee, and placed his hands flat on the table.

"We were camped in the forest for the night on our way to the Forgotten Mountains. We aimed to cross into the Land Beyond in search of a rumored Dwarven outpost that might have been there," he began. "I was in charge of our group's correspondence with the capital. I was replying to an inquiry from one of our wizards when I heard screaming and yelling from outside my tent. When I ran outside, all I saw was blackness moving around us. And in the blackness, swords and spears were cutting down the other mages, and a high shrill sound rang out over the melee. I stood frozen in place when one of the things came up to me and... and..."

"When it stabbed you in your gut," finished Trevin grimly.

Michael nodded, then continued, "I fell, and I guess I passed out for a while. When I woke up all the other mages were dead, and I was bleeding from my stomach. I summoned a healing spell for myself and, after it was done, I tried to move and get somewhere safe, but my legs were drained, and so were my arms. Then I heard yelling and the sound of footsteps coming. I grabbed whatever I could to defend myself, but I don't remember anything."

The Rangers looked at him for a minute before Tiberius asked, "How is it that twenty fully trained mages died, and one apprentice survived?"

Michael looked at each of them intently as their probing eyes burned holes into his mind and soul. He could see there was no use lying and looked down at his hands that had held the light not a few hours ago. His mind raced back to the frozen forest floor, and all at once, he realized the rumors were indeed true. The fear they had hoped to deny had come to pass. Now, everyone in the empire would have to deal with the immense fallout. In almost a whisper said, "They couldn't summon magic."

Silence filled the group. The bustling cafe's noise was reduced to a small drone under the weight of what Michael had just said. The implications of such a thing occurring were unfathomable to the Rangers and should never be taken lightly. Tiberius weighed this response carefully, trying to determine if this was some clever ruse or perhaps truth. He had heard rumblings of the supposed waning of magical power, but like others in the empire, had brushed it aside as mere nonsense. But he should have known better. You don't call down power as such he saw during the close of the war and not expect some kind of backlash.

"They couldn't summon magic?" asked Timothy, perplexed with an awkward smile on his face. "How is that possible?"

Numbness washed over Michael as he continued to stare at his hand. "Something has happened. Either we can't conjure up magic like so many have had for thousands and thousands of years, or," he replied, unsure if what he was saying would make sense, "magic is leaving our world."

They stared at him, unblinking. The enormity of such a thing happening in their world was undreamt of, and the repercussions it could cause were reason enough to be afraid of what could happen. Magic and its practice had been responsible for virtually every bit of good and prosperity in the empire. From winning the various wars against the Narzeth, and creating the Imperial City, to calling down rain from nothing when the droughts threatened to starve the citizenry. Magic was at the very core of what made the empire powerful and prosperous.

"What makes the Magi believe this?" Zachary asked.

Michael looked up at the men. "None of them know. We first noticed the strain and effort it took about six months ago. Spells that we conjured for years became a struggle, even with a wand or staff. We then switched to simply studying the spells and their usage as opposed to actually performing magic. Soon after that, the High Sorcerer recalled all the wizards and mages in the empire back to the Citadel."

"There are no Magi out in the empire?" Trevin asked. "Not even the in the royal courts of the ten kings?"

Michael shook his head, renewed despair washing over him. "No, sir. High Sorcerer Nightowl ordered all members of the Magi to abandon their posts and return to the Citadel."

Trevin recoiled at Michael's news. "When was this?"

"A month before we set out for the mountains, sir."

Trevin was floored at the news. He turned to Tiberius and asked, "Did you know about this?"

"No," Tiberius replied without taking his eyes off of Michael. "We have been holed up in Kovaiyemarck so long with our own business that the comings and goings of the empire have escaped our sight."

Trevin turned again to face Michael. "If what you say is true, then how were you, an apprentice, able to summon a spell when twenty full mages could not?"

Out of the corner of his eye, Michael could see the First Sergeant's hand unconsciously resting on the hilt of his broadsword. He turned his full attention back to the four rangers and said pleadingly, "I don't know! All I did was focus harder and stronger than I ever have. And I repeated the incantation unceasingly! When all seemed lost, the light leapt from my chest into my hands. But it took me a long time, and I still barely managed to conjure such a simple spell. Considering how long it took me, not to mention the strain it put on me, the other mages didn't stand a chance of summoning their magic!"

"Lower your voice," Tiberius said sternly, his gaze never wandering from Michael. "Why would the emperor authorize a venture so far north and away from Imperial protection if the Magi are unable to use magic?"

But Michael shook his head sadly, "Forgive me, sir. I cannot speak to His Majesty's intent."

"Do you believe him, sir?" Tevin asked Tiberius.

Tiberius's face turned impassive and calm. He surveyed the young man in front of him. His blue eyes were sad and confused, and his small body hung defeated in his chair. At last, Tiberius nodded his approval, and with that, the matter was settled. The three other Rangers seemed to relax and continued to look to their commander. In their minds, Michael had become their friend and companion, and any doubts about his integrity were swiftly extinguished.

Tiberius rose from his seat and said to his men, "Ready the horses. We depart for the capital at once."

The three Rangers were on their feet and out the door without another word spoken. Michael hesitantly stood from his chair, unsure of what was going to happen to him. "What about me, sir?" he whispered.

Tiberius's face broke from its impassivity to a small, warm smile. "You're my companion now, young Mage, and you will join us on our ride to the capital," he replied, beckoning him to join him as he walked to the door. "We both have parts of this misadventure that need to be heard."

"Heard by whom?" Michael asked as he followed the Ranger to the door.

"By the High Sorcerer," Tiberius replied. "And by His Majesty the emperor."

But Michael stopped in his tracks. "I can't go back there, Master Ranger! Not with all I've seen and done and told you. They wouldn't believe anything I have to say, or," he started, but Tiberius held his hand up in silence.

"I'm going to ask you very politely to stop talking, Mr. Deerborn," Tiberius replied as they made their way through the crowded café. "Whatever fears and issues you have are unfounded. We both have parts played out in last night's events. Parts that need to be heard at once. And the longer we delay, the sooner we may all arrive to ruin. We both have our parts in this tale to tell, and together, the truth will be made clear to them that we do not speak lies."

Michael thought this over and decided his new companion was indeed correct. What he knew was important and needed to be heard at once. I can't let my brothers' death be in vain, he said to himself as new-found courage bloomed in him.

"But hang on, I told you what happened to me. What part did you and your rangers play in all this?" Michael asked.

But Tiberius held his hand up again as they reached the door. "That is best not spoken of right now. From what we both experienced last night it is clear there are many seen and unseen forces working towards some evil intent. It is best to hold our tongues until we are good and well on the road."

Michael looked defeated and gloomy. But Tiberius placed his hand on his shoulder and smiled at him. This was the first time he noticed his eyes, grey and haunted as if he had seen too many things in his short life, and still saw them in his waking hours.

"I promise you, my young Mage. All will be revealed. We keep no secrets in the rangers, and now that you are a recognized companion of ours, none shall be kept from you."

Michael nodded in response as Tiberius opened the door for them to depart the inn. These are strange men, Michael thought. To trust each man with their secrets and extend that trust to their friends and comrades is something all men of the empire could do well to practice.

Dusk was a few hours off when they exited the inn. To Michael's surprise, the cold wasn't as harsh as the forest. The hustle and bustle of the busy village folk made the temperature more bearable and to his liking. The Rangers were mounted on their horses in the village's main thoroughfare with two empty steeds at the head of the formation. The men's faces were refreshed and almost excited for the journey. Rangers were meant to be on the road and in the wild, not some fluffy inn. And besides, the good weather and clear skies would be the proper medicine to lift their spirits after the loss they had endured the night before.

Tiberius and Michael mounted the two horses at the front, and with a wave of Tiberius's hand, they moved out from the village at a slow trot. "Why are they moving out so slowly if we carry such important information?" Michael asked.

"We don't know what enemies may be moving against us, my young Mage. Best to not draw any undue attention to ourselves if we can avoid it. Some may think we are returning to our expedition if we go off-road, but many people saw us leave in the company of a Mage. If we speed down the Imperial Road, they will surely become suspicious and report it to whoever may have a desire to know. Therefore, we go slow and deliberate and without a break. We can handle the long journey without rest."

True to his word, they all rode on through the rest of the day with no breaks. What Tiberius had not told Michael was that the rangers were used to being mounted and traveling unceasingly if needed, and their horses were specially bred to endure such hardships. Even Michael found the ride enjoyable though he had barely spent an hour in his entire life atop a horse, let alone atop a horse in the presence of such noble and dangerous warriors.

CHAPTER 5

THE ROAD

The landscapes began to change from the frost-bitten lands and stone construction to greener and greener fields. The people they passed were starting to dress less warmly, and their fields were more plentiful and lush. The snow-covered hills that had been a staple outside of the village gave way to fertile flat plains. In the distance, Michael could see many small mountain ranges here and there that broke up the beautiful vistas that seemed to stretch in all directions. He took all this in with much excitement and wonder. When he and the other Magi had come north, it was under the cover of darkness. And in the back of a wagon with barely any room to stretch. Now, out here in the daylight and fresh air atop a beautiful, strong horse, he began to feel almost peaceful and happy.

Except for the clothes they wore, the Childers Kingdom locals reminded Michael of his boyhood home in White Fyre in the northwest White Kingdom. Like the Childers Kingdom, it was also a land of near-perpetual snow with its own vast forests and small mountains. The scholars had often said that long ago, before the Ten Kingdoms were even thought of, both Childers and White were one unified tribe of people. But unlike the people here, people in the White Kingdom were less welcoming of outsiders to their lands.

The people here in Childers were friendly and kind and waved and smiled at the band of rangers as they passed. The people of his homeland would have sneered and cursed at such a sight. He had often wondered why and had long ago reasoned it was to do with his own king's distaste of the Imperial way of life. He pondered this interesting dichotomy for a moment before turning to Tiberius.

"These people are quite friendly, aren't they?" he asked after passing a group of farmers in an orchard.

Tiberius nodded in agreement. "Have you ever been to the Kingdom of Childers, young Mage?"

Michael shook his head. His only experiences with the empire, outside from his youth in the White Kingdom, had been his training at the Magi Citadel built on the Imperial mansion's grounds. Even then, it was forbidden for them to leave their subterranean homes and classrooms until they reached the apprentice level. Even after attaining the rank of apprentice, Michael remained attentive in his studies and rarely left the confines of his room or library.

"The people of this kingdom are resilient folk," Tiberius explained removing his pipe for his afternoon smoke. "They endure such harsh climate but receive such benevolence from their king. They welcome all who venture into their lands."

So, it did have to do with the love and honor of their king after all, Michael realized. Why would King White hold such disdain for the empire when they have not done anything to him or our people?

Michael pushed these sour thoughts aside and began to reflect on all he had seen in such a short time. Such horrors and evil from the night before. Such warmth and generosity he now felt amongst the rangers. He promised himself that when he was elevated to full mage, he would dedicate more time to traveling and studying the people of this vast empire. The willfully ignorant understand nothing outside of themselves, he told himself.

The day was beginning to grow long. The sun that had hung just past mid-day when they started out was starting to fade into the west. The deep blue sky above them began to turn brilliant pink and purple, the likes of which Michael had only seen in paintings. Small distant twinkling lights began to show in the dusky sky, the faint outline of the veiled full moon was now rising slowly to greet them. Lanterns were being set at the modest homes and inns they passed, and there were fewer and fewer travelers on the road. A renewed cold breeze began to blow softy from the north, and that sent a shock down Michael's back. Tiberius ordered his rangers to halt and to set up camp for the night in a nearby field.

An hour or so later, the Rangers were tucked in for their evening meals, quiet conversations, and shared drink and smoke. The stars shone brightly down on them, and the moon illuminated everything around them. Despite the hazy moonlight that lit up the open pasture they were camped in, Michael still stumbled here and there. In all his young life, he had rarely been outdoors past dusk, and if he had there had always been a fire to light his path. But despite his own small confusion, he couldn't help but notice that the rangers walked around freely as if the darkness didn't matter.

In frustration, he asked, "How can you men see in the darkness?"

"What darkness?" Timothy replied from a nearby fire. "The moon above has lit up the world as if it were the sun."

"Even still, how is it I continue to stumble around like a baby, and you lot walk unhindered?" he asked, joining Timothy and Zachary by their fire.

"We are given the gift of Sight when we become rangers," answered Timothy digging into his mutton and mead.

When Michael didn't reply, he continued, "It lets us see in the dead of night as if it was mid-day, focus intently on the smallest detail, and see over greater distances for a short time."

"I've never heard of this before," Michael admitted. In all his studies of magic and lore, he never came across anything described as the gift of Sight.

Zachary chuckled, and after taking a sip of his mead said, "Very few people in all the history of our realm know about it. All I know is after you complete your training to be a ranger, you receive the blessing of Sight. And the blessing that has yet to leave any Ranger actively serving, retired, or dead who has received it."

"I beg your pardon, Master Rangers, but I don't quite fully understand this Sight you speak of," Michael continued, hoping to learn about this new form of magic. "Where does it come from? Who bestows it upon you? How exactly do you receive it?"

"Come now, my young friend," Timothy cut in. "There are some things we do not speak of to outsiders to our ranks, friends, or otherwise. So please, do not ask how we receive it and from whom. As to where it comes from, I can honestly say none of us know."

"None of you know?"

"Aye, lad. None of us know. I'd reckon not even the High Sorcerer himself has any idea where our power comes from," Timothy said, placing a large piece of tobacco into his cheek.

Michael stared unblinking at the two Rangers. In all his years reading and studying magic, he had never heard of such a power or a 'blessing' as a form of magic. And if the High Sorcerer himself didn't know, then this truly is a power beyond his understanding. Very few things concerning magic were unknown to the highest ranks of magical users in the empire. The very possibility that something remained unknown to even them was very troubling indeed. He had long held those of the upper echelons of his order in such high regard. He had often marveled at the levels of knowledge and power they possessed. Now, he was not as sure.

He bid his new friends goodnight and decided to walk around their camp a bit to clear his head. He found it curious that the rangers slept in bedrolls instead of tents. When he had ventured out with his fellow Magi, each mage had their own tent and small fire within. He had to share a relatively small tent with a fellow apprentice, and the space inside it was barely large enough for one of them. But the rangers were a different breed of man altogether. They preferred being out under the stars and moonlight. After a few contemplative moments, he finally reasoned that it would be easier to rise and fight from a bedroll instead of running out of a tent.

As he neared the edge of the camp, he could begin to make out the vague figure of Tiberius sitting alone on a small boulder looking out into the empty prairie. "Good evening, sir," he said not wanting to startle the commander.

"Good evening, young Mage," he responded, not looking away from the open field.

"What do you see out there?" Michael asked, taking a seat on the ground next to Tiberius.

"I see Timothy and Zachary doing some extra duty for talking out of turn about our gift," Tiberius responded.

A wave of guilt crashed in on Michael. "Did you hear them say that to me? They didn't mean anything by it, I'm sure."

"Our gift extends beyond simply seeing the physical world. It lets us see the unseen, and those of us who've possessed it longer are more sensitive to its true power," Tiberius responded.

"If you please, what is its true power?"

"The Sight lets us discern everything about a person," Tiberius said. "Their soul, their heart, their mind. All of these things are laid bare to us who have the mind to see them. And Timothy and Zachary, brave warriors that they are, have not possessed this blessing as long as I have to truly wield it."

"Please sir," Michael pleaded, "don't punish them for their minor transgression. I thought there were no secrets between rangers and their companions."

Tiberius remained impassive and continued to stare out into the night. "We have no secrets between us. But the secrets that bind us together are ones not shared by any except the Commander of the Order." He turned and smiled at Michael. "And I see nothing out there. But nevertheless, I keep watch. It's my duty to watch over my men."

He beckoned Michael to sit with him. "You've never been around men-of-arms before, have you?" he asked Michael.

The mage shook his head. The closest he had come to seeing soldiers were the knights of his home kingdom riding in the field one summer day as he worked his family's fields.

"Soldiers who've spent any good amount of time together tend to form a bond that is indescribable to those who've never experienced it. Going into battle together makes us closer to one another than our families. And each of these men and women served in the Great War," Tiberius said as he began smoking his well-worn pipe.

Michael thought all this over. Timothy and Zachary had spoken out of turn to tell him about the Sight he decided, but he was glad they did. Learning about new magic was his passion, and this new insight was a small indulgence. Still, the mystery of how the Magi did not know about this power hung heavy on his mind.

After a few minutes of silence, Tiberius turned his full attention to Michael and said, "Seeing as we will be in the capital tomorrow, I guess it's time to let you in on what is going on."

He extinguished his pipe and started his tale of their ranging north. How they discovered the Narzeth graves and gave chase to their foes. How they finally found and fought the undead soldiers, and especially of the enchanted beggar turning to dust in front of him. Michael never interrupted his story. He took it all in and focused intently on the details of the beggar and the power that raised fifty dead soldiers from over five hundred years ago. Tiberius spared no detail in his recount, reasoning that when discussing magic with a Mage, no matter how inexperienced, any insight would prove useful.

When Tiberius finished his story, Michael asked, "That is a fascinating tale, sir. But I do have a few immediate questions. How could an enchanted beggar journey to an unmarked burial site that happened to be so close to where we were camping? And, how could this enchanted beggar seemingly concoct a potion that resurrects the dead, and ultimately lead them to where we were sleeping?"

The question lingered for a moment before Tiberius said, "I was hoping you could help me with some of that. To my knowledge, no potion in the world could mimic the power of necromancy."

Michael shook his head. "There isn't. They can recreate ice and fire and healing, but necromancy takes a special kind of dark magic. Furthermore, an enchantment strong enough to compel a man to walk from the Imperial City to the northern part of Childers is remarkable itself. And enchanting doesn't confer knowledge and direction on a person. It just compels them towards physical action."

"All I know is what I saw, my friend," Tiberius offered.

"I do not doubt the truth of your words," Michael replied. "But what of him turning to dust? Magic like that hasn't been seen since the end of the war. And before that, who knows."

Tiberius was all too familiar with that. The memory of Vermillion Pass and the ending of the war would be a sight he would never forget. How the cries and screams of war were swiftly silenced. As all their enemies were turned to dust in front of their eyes. The very mention of it sent a chill up his spine. It would be something he would carry in his memory for the rest of his days. But as to why the enchanted beggar was turned to dust, he had a guess.

"He had fulfilled his intended purpose. Turning to dust was a way for the true villain to conceal himself," Tiberius said.

"And then there is the greatest mystery in this whole affair," Michael said with his head swimming. "How could a wizard have done any of this with magic disappearing or being unreachable or whatever is happening? The willpower and focus alone would kill him the way things are."

Tiberius swallowed hard and whispered, "Perhaps more so now than ever. I was there that day at Vermillion Pass, and the effort used in turning our enemies to dust killed Cycret."

Michael sat there for a moment, pondering what to say next, but the thoughts escaped him. He appreciated Tiberius's confidence and trust, but the story left him feeling confused and angry. Confused at how any of this could happen, and mad that this evil had befallen him and his fellow Magi.

"Best get some sleep. We leave at first light. We should reach the capital by late noon tomorrow. We'll have to deliver all this information to people who may or may not believe us," Tiberius said, standing and stretching.

Michael followed suit his legs were shaking with the new anticipation. "Do you think the emperor will believe us?" he asked.

"Our emperor was a ranger once, and still possesses the Sight. He will believe us, as will the High Sorcerer. Trust me," Tiberius responded.

He began to remove some rations from his cloak when he noticed the Mage frozen in place as if struck into stone. "Go get some sleep. You'll need it."

Michael bowed and left Tiberius to continue his vigil uninterrupted and headed back to the rangers' encampment, who were all sound asleep but still ready to attack if need be. The safest place in the world is right here, he thought. But somehow, I don't think all these men together could protect me from tomorrow.

CHAPTER 6

THE CITY

They were on the road just before sunrise, determined to arrive in the capital before noon. Tiberius and Michael again rode at the group's head flanked by Trevin and the inseparable Timothy and Zachary. The pair of Rangers, always eager to learn about magic, asked the Mage question after question all morning. As youths, each had hoped to become an Imperial Battle-Mage despite neither having much aptitude for studying nor understanding things beyond the physical world.

Timothy and Zachary each came from separate kingdoms on opposite sides of the empire. Despite their boyhood love of wizards and mages and elves and dwarves and dragon's tales, they remained wild boys who grew into wild men. They lived out their daydreams with their friends in their home's fields and woods, never seeking their studies. It was no surprise to either of their families when they joined the Imperial army. After their acceptance to the Imperial Rangers, both families felt such great pride that all thoughts of neglected studies and education were never spoken of again.

They were held in utter awe listening to Michael recount the first time he summoned fire from nothing into his hand. Or the first time he ever saw a wizard talk to a wild animal and have it heed his command. Though Michael had only summoned a few embers and the wizard never spoke actual words to the beast, but just conveyed feeling and emotion, the two Rangers felt like children again listening to stories at the campfire.

Michael, meanwhile, welcomed the distraction from what felt like an impending journey to the gallows. He was chilled to the core at the idea of facing the High Sorcerer and the emperor himself. Having to explain all that had happened and his conduct throughout was daunting to the young mage, but he trusted Tiberius. The Commander of the Rangers' support would bring the respect and seriousness that his youth could not. Despite all that, he still remained pessimistic, as was his inherent nature.

The countryside rolled on. The lush greenery and forests gave way to open crop fields and vast fruit orchards. The architecture even changed from the stone and wood structures of the north to large concrete buildings filled with merchants and dwellings of assorted people in the empire. A few larger buildings dotted the horizon with great smokestacks emitting vast clouds of steam and smoke. Though he had not seen any of this during his venture north, his reason and logic told him they were close to the Imperial Bridge. And the closer they approached the bridge, and the capital beyond meant he was now within striking distance of his fate.

"Seven years a ranger," Zachary said in between bites of an apple, "and I'm still in awe of all this industry." He was a child of the Huffman Kingdom in the southeast part of the empire and had only dreamed of seeing the Imperial City. "My dad was a hunter, so my life was spent in the woods and streams. Never in a city."

"My dad was a knight, so my childhood was spent serving as a squire to him and learning how to be a fighter," Timothy added. "But we did not have anything close to all this back home."

Timothy's home away in the southeast corner of the empire was populated by vast rolling hills and mountains that seemed to stab the sky. The dense forests and running streams are what he knew, not the urban industrialization he saw around him. Seven years of ranging had opened his eyes to all there was to experience in the world. For that opportunity alone, he was forever grateful.

"How about you, Master Mage? Where do you come from?" Zachary asked, putting a pinch of wet tobacco in his mouth. "Surely a brother of the Magi must come from more than just the humble plains and mountains?"

Michael thought for a moment on how best to answer. No one had ever asked him where he came from. Not a single person he studied with at the Citadel, nor any of the mages and wizards he had ever served under. No one.

"I'm from the Kingdom of White," he said, feeling somewhat uncomfortable. Timothy let out a raucous laugh.

"HA! Then I suppose I should draw my sword on you! I'm from the Black Kingdom." The kingdoms of white and black were long to have held a rivalry based solely on the colored names they each carried and nothing to do with their monarch's quality. Though all people in the empire were very much aware of King White's sternness.

Michael stared at the Ranger wide-eyed, unsure if he was playing a joke at his expense or genuinely meant to draw his sword in anger. But upon seeing the Mage's broad expression, he offered a quick pat on his shoulders. "I'm just joking with you, Mr. Deerborn. There are no petty kingdom rivalries in the Imperial military. All allegiances to our birth homes are broken once you become a true citizen of the empire."

"Forgive my timidity, sir."

"Think nothing of it. Whereabouts in the White Kingdom are you from?"

"My family has lived in White Fyre for as long as we could remember."

"Good fishing down in White Fyre. Lots of sea wenches too, if I remember correctly," Timothy added, fond memories of his time in the Imperial navy flashing in his mind.

"I wouldn't know anything about that, Master Ranger. All of my time was concerned with tending the farm and fisheries with my father and brothers," Michael admitted.

They rode on with Timothy and Zachary trading stories of past conquests and recommending all the best brothels in the city to Michael for his, "research" as they put it. But Michael still felt somewhat out of place in this manner of behavior. His young mind had never entertained thoughts of women, and the pleasures that he had heard were found in their company. His passion was books and study, magic, and the mysteries it held. Still, Michael hoped to one day see and experience all the wonders that other men had already known.

Before long, the party had arrived at the shores of Kings Lake and had begun crossing one of the ten-mile long bridges that connected the surrounding mainland to the Imperial City. The first Emperor Alexander Axton had decreed that all kingdoms of the Axton Empire would have a road and bridge built that connected their lands to the Imperial City. Those roads were guarded night and day by the Imperial army. That was their only jurisdiction outside of the Imperial City.

The bridge was stone and concrete flecked with pebbles of all shapes and colors. The city itself had no gates or any visible tower to provide protection. The Axton Emperors believed that gates were a way to keep people out. Instead, they chose to welcome all citizens of their empire to their city without impeding their travel. The bridge's sides were adorned with the black, grey, and white flags of the Axtons. All manners of merchants, beggars, and holy men lined the edges of the bridge flaunting whatever they had for a few spare coins

The sun was nearly overhead, and no cloud blocked the sky as they started on the final leg of their journey. Children from the city were already congregating at little boat launches to go swimming in the clear blue lake as was the custom to do all year long. The sounds of music and merriment reverberated from the city, bringing the grim Rangers much needed levity. To Michael, however, it might as well have been a funeral march.

In the distance, they could see the great Unity Spire, the home of the Axton Emperors. Nearly two thousand feet tall and made of black steel and glass, the tower had taken the Dwarves and Magi many years to finish and was deemed the greatest wonder in the empire. It was the first and last thing any traveler coming to the city would ever see. Its thick construction and sheer majesty ensured that it and would continue to stand until the end of all things. Seeing the city and the Unity Tower roused in the Rangers the fire of patriotism and duty to their emperor and their undying pledge of protection of all the citizens of their country. Tiberius, however, was feeling very troubled to be back in the city again.

He was born a citizen of the empire itself, as he wasn't from any of the Ten Kingdoms but from the Imperial City itself. He knew all the streets and shops as well as he knew his own family. But he hadn't been to the city in many years. Even after the Great War, he had met his father at the Ranger Garrison, Kovaiyemarck. He had sworn to himself never return to the city except under great need, and no need was more significant than the story he and the Mage had to deliver.

Michael's own trepidation in coming to the city continued to wear on him, though. Every step of the magnificent brown and white horse brought more and more worry and fear. As he continued on, he noticed faint specks hurling through the sky on the edges of the city. Then, as if on cue, a crowd of people near the bridge began pointing in the same direction he looked and talking wildly to themselves. "What's that over there?" he asked Tiberius, pointing into the distance.

Tiberius looked and smiled broadly. "Those are the Dragoons, my young Mage. Fabled dragon knights from across the sea who can cut through the air as their progenitors did long ago."

Michael turned to the veteran Ranger and exclaimed, "They're Narzethians!? In the Imperial City!?"

Tiberius shushed him at once. The very mention of the Narzeth was a sore spot for many people in the empire. The wounds of the five-year war were still fresh to many who had lost countless friends and loved ones.

"The Dragoons were slaves to the enemy for countless generations," he explained, his voice solemn and grave. "Our ancient foe has no mind for creation, only for domination and repurposing things to meet their evil intent. We liberated them early in the campaign, and they swore undying loyalty to the empire. The emperor named them true citizens of the Axton Empire, and they settled here to rebuild and recruit after the war ended."

"Why are they called 'dragon knights'?" Michael asked. "Dragons have been gone from the world for nearly three hundred years. And even then, there is barely any evidence of their existence or behaviors aside from the history books."

"Are you not a student of history and book, Mage?" Tiberius asked. "Believe me, dragons were real once upon a time."

"I do not doubt your words, Sir. But how can you be so sure?"

"Because when I rescued them, they were held captive amongst the bones and graves of dragons," he replied.

"Forgive my ignorance. Please, tell me more about these dragoons," Michael said.

"Long ago, they would ride dragons into battle. Not the large hulking beasts children pretend them to be, but smaller, faster dragons the size of this horse. They would leap into battle with their spears and decimate whole legions of soldiers who had no way to defend from skyward attack. But after the dragons died off, the dragoons gained the ability to leap high into the sky and cover great distances over the enemy's defenses. In this way, they could still fight as much as they had in the days before."

Michael turned again to look closer. Sure enough, he could make out five figures leaping and bounding nearly a hundred feet in the air. *If magic is indeed disappearing from our world, how do they and the rangers have their abilities?* He had more and more questions and almost no answers at all.

They trotted on in silence, observing the children and performers on the road as they went. Trevin had slowly made his way to his commander's side as they neared the city entrance, determined to spend a few fleeting moments with his lover. He had thought long and hard how to talk to Tiberius in such a way to not draw overt attention to themselves. In the end, though, he decided to speak what was on his mind like any ordinary person would.

"The people look happy, Sir," Trevin observed, taking a small red carnation from a child handing out flowers to the passing rangers.

"That they do, First Sergeant. A year of peace and prosperity will do wonders for a person. And children are particularly resilient," noted Tiberius, gazing at the dozens of children who had assembled to greet them. It was uncommon to see rangers in the city, and their presence lifted all the citizens' spirits to know their greatest defenders were coming to their home.

Trevin smiled as he smelled the flower and handed it to his commander. Their eyes met for a moment, each thinking of the other as they often did in their private moments. Tiberius took the flower and smelled it as well. He was reminded of the first time he and Trevin met and placed the flower inside his cloak. It wasn't his physique that had ensnared his heart, nor the kindness with which he spoke. It was Trevin's eyes. Deep and soulful. Eyes that Tiberius would hope to swim in one day when their duties and oaths were fulfilled.

One day, he thought, one day, I'll grow you a garden with every flower in the world. We'll spend our days amongst them reading and talking about other men doing dangerous things in service of their country. But in his bones, he knew that day would be many years off from today. They held one another's gaze for many moments before nodding in understanding to one another and resuming their watch over the vast bridge.

Two hours later, they reached the Imperial City. The Rangers dismounted their horses and stretched as stable hands nearby came to collect their horses.

"Sergeants," Tiberius said, brushing himself off. "The men are given a three-day pass in the city. Have them in formation ready to travel home on the morning of the fourth." At his order, the Sergeants began issuing the command, which was met with great cheer and exuberance.

These men deserve some downtime after all we've been through, he thought, smiling.

"Trevin. Send word to Kovaiyemarck. Tell them we plan to stay here for three days and return after. Have them also issue a four-day pass to all the men there." He knew if his immediate men were given three days of free time in the city, it was equally fair to issue an extra day to the men who could not be with them.

Trevin bowed and headed to the local Bird Post, wishing he could spend a few more minutes in his commander's presence. Zachary and Timothy bid farewell to the Mage. They told him where he could find them that night as they departed together to have some misadventure somewhere in the vast city. Once they were all gone, Michael turned to Tiberius, who stood in place, staring at the spire. After a few moments, Tiberius turned and summoned him to follow as he began making his way through the city.

The city seemed like a maze of cobblestone paths and an assortment of stucco, stone, brick, and wooden homes and buildings. Around every corner, it seemed like there was a garden or park, with different types of trees and animals. He had lived in the Imperial City for two years undergoing his training. Still, he had never ventured outside the Citadel to see all there was in this city.

People from all walks of life could be found wandering the streets and shops, taking in all the metropolis' wonderment. Children from the Black and Huffman Kingdoms were gathered around a street magician, making the most random objects disappear in his hands and reappear behind their ears. Musicians from Zelinka dressed in baggy clothes of many colors were gathered in Axton Plaza. They banged their massive drums and played a bright and happy tune on their horns as dancers twirled around in an exuberant dance. A few times, he passed a group of soldiers dressed in what looked like armor fashioned to resemble a dragon, correctly guessing they were indeed the dragoons.

Tiberius paid none of these sights any mind as he marched towards the tower. As a child, he had often snuck out of his father's house and wandered the streets indulging in all there was for a young person to see and do. He knew at a young age that despite the most excellent education in the world, there was no substitute for seeing and doing things in the world yourself. There was only so much reading and studying about culture and art and war before you had to experience it yourself. Experience, in his opinion, was the best teacher in the world. And he'd had more experience in life than he cared to share.

But age and duty and war had hardened something inside of him, and though he still yearned for peace and love, all childhood wonderment was gone. This realization made him sad that a part of him was dead and buried. But the resolve he felt to ensuring other children would never have to suffer or die quieted his melancholy. In his mind, as in the minds of all servants of the empire, it is better to suffer so that others may always remain shielded from the evil that lurked in the world.

To Michael, the whole city seemed to be alive and spinning with excitement. It was almost overwhelming to the son of a fisherman from White Fyre. His only exposure to music and entertainment as a boy had been King White's royal orchestra playing for the burial of knights and members of the royal family. But here, in the city that seemed to be alive itself, his mind raced with excitement. Never in his entire life did he ever conceive of seeing all there was to see in the Imperial City. If he survived his impending gathering with the emperor and the High Sorcerer, he would have to devote more time to this city.

"This city seems so eclectic and random, Master Ranger," Michael said, trying and failing to keep up with Tiberius's step.

Tiberius nodded in agreement. "Indeed, it is," he replied, "The city has been free and open to all the empire's citizens for some five hundred years. Seeing as the empire has no inherent culture of its own, the people have brought their culture with them. Especially now."

"Why, especially now?" Michael asked, shouting over the banging of drums and the blowing of horns.

"The city is rejoicing the end of the war," the Ranger replied, sidestepping a group of dancers. "We had not the mind to celebrate a year ago. We were all just glad to be home and done with war."

"I hope someday to see all there is in this city," Michael said, observing the dancing and drinking that seemed to permeate every inch of the city.

"You may, indeed, my friend. This city and the merriment within will last as long as our empire."

But Michael still maintained his doubts. Whatever fate awaited him it would be a long time before he could indulge all there was to experience. The thought saddened him but knew the uncertainty before would have to be conquered first. He gave one last fleeting look around him, before turning to continue his hike to the looming spire.

CHAPTER 7

THE TOWER

An hour later, as they arrived at the emperor's mansions gates, they were greeted by two members of the Imperial sentinels under the shadow of the Unity Spire. They were dressed all in a deep navy that was nearly black from a distance with cloaks that ended just below their knees. The hems of their cloaks were embroidered with white and grey. Like the Rangers, each man knew one another by heart without the need for adornment or ranks on their uniforms. In their gloved hands were eight-foot navy and grey spears and round navy shields.

"Halt," called one of the sentinels as Tiberius and Michael approached. "State your business here."

Standing taller and more proudly than Michael had ever seen his companion, Tiberius said, "I am Tiberius, Supreme Commander of the Imperial Rangers. This is Michael Deerborn, apprentice to the Magi. We have journeyed from the Kingdom of Childers with urgent news for His Majesty Emperor Axton."

At this, the guards exchanged confused glances with one another. The ranger commander's presence was curious enough, but one accompanied by a mage was not something they had expected at all. The sentinel finally responded, "Forgive me, Commander Tiberius, but His Majesty is in assembly with the ten kings today and not to be disturbed."

Tiberius took a step forward and raised his body with such confidence and authority he seemed to be towering over the guard. "Stand aside, boy! We have not fled from death and terror to be turned away from a child barely off his mother's teat! My business is of the gravest concern to not only the emperor but to the ten kings as well." His voice boomed with pure authority. "We will pass lest you are determined to doom all the citizens of our country!"

His words hung heavy for a moment before the guards reluctantly accepted his request. They offered a curt nod, turned, and pushed the massive gates to the inner courtyard open. Tiberius motioned for Michael to join him as he swept past the guards without acknowledging their approval. The weight of Tiberius's authority was not lost on Michael. To command the Imperial sentinels to stand down without even a fight left Michael in awe. Not wanting to press his luck, he followed close behind Tiberius through the gate.

The courtyard beyond was littered with people coming and going about their day. Like the spire the entire grounds of the mansion, a half square mile by his guess, were made of steel and glass. It was home not only to the Imperial family but to the Imperial University, Military College, and The Brotherhood of The Magi. When Michael had come to the Citadel, it had been under cover of night as is custom for its newest initiates. Standing here in the majesty all around him, Michael was even more eager to explore the mansion's grounds than the city. However, Tiberius's renewed pace towards the spire forced him on with barely a glance in any direction.

They walked a few hundred feet to the grand wooden door at the spire's base where another set of guards were posted. But unlike the first two sentinels who impeded their entry, the guards at the spire let them through without comment. They passed through the heavy door and entered a vast atrium adorned with the banners of the empire against thick steel and glass windows. The atrium was littered with people working all around them.

Mages and wizards were hunched over a nearby wooden desk, furiously debating scrolls written in ancient languages. Officers of the Imperial military stood over a black steel desk discussing intelligence reports from some far-off land. Knights of the various kingdoms were engaged in discussions over different battle tactics and regaling one another with their own heroic exploits in their homelands.

Barely anyone in the atrium paid the pair any mind as they approached the grand spiral staircase in the middle of the room, save a lone single ranger. At the sight of his commander, the ranger leapt to his feet to greet them. He was younger than the men Michael had ridden with the past few days, but still had the dangerous eyes of a man who had fought and lived in the wild.

"Commander Tiberius! I had not expected you in the capital today," the young Ranger declared, greeting his commander with nervous exuberance.

Tiberius smiled at the young ranger, overjoyed at seeing one of his men. He hugged the young Ranger as was the custom in their order and said, "I had not expected to be here, Henry. We rode out from Childers a few nights ago on the direst of errands."

Henry nodded his understanding. If Tiberius had not sent word of his arrival in the capital, it meant he did not want to risk anyone knowing their movements. That meant secrecy was of the utmost importance. "Yes, sir. I understand. Have you come alone, or are there more with you?"

"The men are enjoying a much-needed three-day pass in the city before making movement back home. Since you were not with us and seeing as I'm here to receive any important news from the city, I suggest you join them," Tiberius said, a long, overdue smile on his face.

At his commander's order, the young Ranger bowed and departed, as quick as his feet would carry him, to begin his unexpected holiday in the Imperial City. His first stop being the nearest tavern for an abundant amount of dark beer and fresh mutton.

Tiberius sure is a dichotomy of a man, Michael thought. One minute he holds a stern military commander's presence, and the next greets his men like old friends. This was very uncommon behavior in the Magi and practically unheard of back home in White Fyre. Men in authority barked their orders, and the men under them obeyed unquestioningly.

Time and experience had taught Tiberius to compartmentalize his actions and emotions. He had learned at a young age that not every person is the same, and no single approach is guaranteed to work. And through years of war, he had learned to control the violence and hate he felt in battle. He knew when to be authoritative and direct, and when to be warm and inviting. When surrounded by peace, he greeted the rangers as friends and companions instead of his subordinates.

Tiberius and Michael continued up the stairs in the room until they reached a wide steel lift that would convey them to the top of the steel and glass spire. When Tiberius cranked a large lever in the corner, the machine sprang to life and begun the ascent.

"Now my young friend, a few words of advice," Tiberius said, turning to Michael. "When we reach the top, you do not say a word. I will introduce us to the assembly, but I will not use your last name. The surname ending in 'born' is widely known throughout the White Kingdom, and I do not wish for them to know where you hail from. Do you understand?"

Michael nodded, his mind beginning to swim.

"Next. I know what you have told me is truthful, but we will be presenting ourselves not only to the emperor and the High Sorcerer but to all ten kings of the empire. And while I know you to be an honest young man, you have not yet learned how to talk to stubborn, stupid men. Do you understand?"

"Sir?" the Mage squeaked, turning to face the Ranger.

"The ten kings gather for His Majesty only once a year, Michael. Some come to air their grievances, and some come to brag to their counterparts how much better their lands are than the others. Some come to seethe and brood. Either way, it would be best that you do not speak to any of them. Your business is not with them, but with the emperor and the High Sorcerer. Do you understand?"

Michael could only nod in response. The hustle and bustle and excitement of the party in the city had quieted his sense of impending doom. Being here with his fate so close at hand, it was all he could do to keep his sparse breakfast from coming back.

Tiberius noticed the look on Michael's young face. "You okay?" he asked.

"No, sir. I'm really not. I know you are an honest and good man, but I'm truly dreading whatever fate I find at the top of this tower." A lump was beginning to grow in his throat.

But Tiberius simply put his hand on the young man's shoulder and said, "Do not worry young one. You are with me, and there is no safer place in the whole empire or beyond, than by my side."

Michael nodded at him, still unsure of the fate that would greet him at the top. Worst case, he would be expelled from the Magi and return to White Fyre, a failure and disgrace. Back to his family to toil the fields and fish the streams until he died penniless and alone. Best case, he would be executed. Neither option sat well with him. Nevertheless, he swallowed hard and prepared his spirit for what was to come.

After a few minutes, they reached the top. The doors of the lift flew open into a grand circular chamber with a magnificent round table that consumed almost the room's entirety. The steel room walls were covered with large rocks and pebbles of many colors that sparkled in the sunlight pouring in from an enormous window at the rear of the chamber.

Seated around the table in high steel chairs sat the ten kings of the empire, each with their counselors standing behind them. They each wore their kingdom's colors proudly, some in chainmail and armor, and others in silken fabrics of multiple colors. Some of these men had seen too many seasons in their lives, others too few to know the power and majesty of their rule. Beyond the table, standing on a slightly raised platform in front of the grand window, stood the emperor himself with the High Sorcerer close by.

In contrast to the ten kings, the emperor wore a simple black and grey clothing more akin to the rangers and sentinels than the ten's frivolous clothing. His cropped haircut with flecks of grey and a trimmed white beard were mute evidence of his age. The lids of his eyes were dark, but his eyes were bright blue-grey and vibrating with life. Like the sentinels, he wore no adornment to mark his authority, for indeed, he needed none. He was the ruler of the Axton Empire, and no proclamation of his authority or stature was required.

All commotion and chatter in the chamber ceased immediately at the sound of their arrival, and twenty-two pairs of eyes immediately shot to the two new people in the room. Undaunted, Tiberius strode in with all the confidence of a proud warrior and leader. It was all Michael could do to keep his feet from collapsing under him as he stood frozen in the lift.

Tiberius circled the table making his way to the platform, and declared, "Hail, Luke Alexander Axton! Supreme Marshall, protector, leader, and steward of the Axton Empire! I, Tiberius, Commander of your Imperial Rangers, and my companion request your immediate attention and counsel!" He stopped at the platform's foot and looked upon the emperor, humble but proud, paying no mind to the ten men behind him.

Silence fell upon the chamber, and the temperature from the men behind him raised a few degrees. Tiberius's gaze never left the man in front of him. Finally, a voice from behind spoke angrily, "I see one Ranger come to interrupt us, but no companion. Has your time in the wild dulled your mind, boy?"

This apparent anger was from King White, ruler of the lands that bore his namesake. A tall, rail-thin man with balding hair and a long flowing red beard. The man was known throughout the empire to have an unmatched temper equaled only by his unmatched impatience. His pristine armor's all-white showed proudly; he was indeed the most majestically dressed in armor in the room. If not the only one whose armor was unblemished.

But at the king's question, Tiberius turned, looking past the assemblage to the lift beyond and said, "My companion is apprentice to the Brotherhood of the Magi. Michael, step forward, and present yourself!"

At the sound of his own name, Michael mustered what little strength he had and lightly stepped out of the lift and bowed to the assembled majesty before him. But King White's patience began to run thinner than usual.

"A wild ranger and a baby wizard have come to interrupt our affairs!? Mage! Declare your king so that he may punish you in the manner you deserve for this offense!" King White spat, his pale face turning shades of red and purple.

"Oh, will you shut your mouth!" Another king dressed in fine black silks spat. "If Commander Tiberius has deemed their presence worthy of this interruption, then it must be of most dire need."

"I will ask that King Black shut his mouth and hold his tongue lest he faces my steel!"

"And I will kindly remind King White, and all our fellow kings, that his sword has never even been unsheathed from its scabbard! Perhaps he should first learn how to properly draw it before threatening another man in anger."

Michael's eyes shot between the two men. He, along with everyone else in their empire, had known of the intense rivalry between the Kings of White and Black. But to see it in person, nearly buckled his legs. From the head of the table, another man stood. Younger than the rest and adorned in well-worn red and blue armor and mail. By his colors, Michael knew he was King Alexander of Zelinka.

"My Lords, please! Should it not be for His Majesty the emperor to deem, who is worthy of his audience?" the young king said.

"Nay," another, older voice spoke, forcing Michael's wide eyes to swing to the table's other side. "We have ventured far for the festivals and our audience with Emperor Axton! We have much to discuss, and the hour grows late."

The voice belonged to an aged man, dressed in beautiful orange and yellow clothes framed with gold and ruby necklaces. His garb's beauty and splendor were recognized at once as belonging to King Dabmanu of the Clastifet Kingdom. "Mage! Who is your King?" the ancient king proclaimed.

Michael's eyes snapped forward as he shot a pleading look at the Ranger who declared, "This Mage is my honored companion and is under my protection! By my authority, which is derived from the emperor and the emperor alone, he shall meet the same judgment as myself." His eyes never left Michael's as he spoke. His words were firm, but his eyes were comforting and protective.

Tiberius beckoned him to the foot of the emperor's platform. The Mage scurried as fast as his young feet would carry him around the large table to join Tiberius's side. At the foot of the pedestal, he met the emperor's impassive gaze. He immediately fell to one knee to echo Tiberius's words. "Hail, Emperor Axton! I, Michael of the Magi, have come to seek your attention and counsel."

At these words, another man dressed deep greens and bright-blues flew to his feet, his steel chair scraping the floor beneath him. "This is an outrage! We have traveled far, and left our homes to treat with the emperor, and this is how we are met!? I demand an answer to these trespasses! I demand these men to state their business to us at once!"

A raucous noise boomed from the ten men behind the companions. Each man shouting and raging against one another in hopes of winning their arguments. Some threatened to draw swords and duel. Others were content enough to simply rage at one another. But the emperor, calm and collected, simply raised his hand bringing the roar of the room to an instant conclusion.

"No," the emperor said, "You will take your seat and regain your senses in this room. This man is my Ranger, and under Imperial decree, his companion is now under my judgment and mine alone."

The emperor lowered his hand and addressed the assemblage, "Now then. My Kings and Lords, I beg you return tonight where we will continue our discussions and possibly begin a new one depending on what these men have to say. Until then, please enjoy the splendors of our city! That will be all."

At his words, each of the men stood and bowed to the emperor. Each, of course, except for King White.

"Something to add, Forval?" the emperor asked, growing agitated.

The King of White burned holes into the Ranger and Mage before standing and rendering a halfhearted bow. The ten and their counselors entered the lift in silence and quickly departed the chamber.

A heavy silence hung in the room. The emperor stood impassively, examining the pair below him before turning to the sorcerer and asking, "Do you know this Mage, Damian?"

"I do, yes. This young man is one of our order's newest members," the sorcerer responded with a chuckle.

"I see," the emperor replied, before turning his full attention to Tiberius.

While his face remained expressionless, his eyes were focused and searching as if trying to read Tiberius's mind. "Do you fully trust your companion, Commander?" the emperor finally asked.

"I do," Tiberius responded.

Oh, gods, this is it, isn't it? Michael thought, holding his breath in anticipation of the swift judgment that was sure to come.

Silence as thick as ice permeated the hall when suddenly loud, boisterous laughter cut through like a bolt of lightning, causing Michael to jump. There was no judgment or anger for their untimely outburst. Instead, the other three men in the room burst into uncontrollable laughter as the emperor and Tiberius moved to hug each other on the platform's steps.

Michael was dumbstruck. Surely, he had passed out and was now living in some sort of vivid dream. But it was not a dream. Before him, the two men were embraced in such boisterous laughter. He could barely hear the echoes reverberating in the chamber.

"Did you really have to do that?" the emperor said, all decorum and sternness in his voice replaced by pure joy and merriment. "Let me see you," and pulled himself back to inspect Tiberius.

"Those men are puffed-up idiots," Tiberius responded, smiling wider than he had in years. "And King White, with his fancy white and grey armor that's never seen combat. I thought I was going to lose all control when King Black called him out!"

"You look good, Ti," the Emperor said, looking him over. "Though I imagine you and your friend didn't come all this way just to see a pair of old men."

"We aren't that old, my friend," Damian said, moving to pour himself a cup of ale.

Michael turned his head frantically, trying to reconcile what was unfolding before him. In all his time at the Citadel, he had never imagined the High Sorcerer himself being anything other than a wise old scholarly person. Still, he had come to learn of late, the truth of people is often reserved for the trusted and familiar, and not for the everyday person.

Tiberius sobered. "Unfortunately, no, we did not. We ran into some trouble up in northern Childers and rode here immediately for your counsel." He began to remove his cloak and poured himself a glass of warm mead.

"So serious that you interrupted my Imperial summit by sauntering in here and putting arrogant royals in their place?" the emperor asked, joining Tiberius at a seat on the round table.

Michael stood in place, frozen and perplexed and slightly agitated as if some great prank was being played on him, and he didn't know why.

"Excuse me! I'm very confused here," Michael interrupted.

"What are you confused about, my boy?" Damian said, downing his cup and moving to pour a second helping. "Didn't Ti tell you he was the emperor's son?"

CHAPTER 8

THE AXTON FAMILY

Michael stared wide-eyed at the three men for what felt like ages. His mouth had unconsciously dropped at the news that his savior and commander, the grim yet kind, the firm but gentle Ranger Commander, was the emperor's son! His eyes darted back and forth between them, searching for some clue that would make this seem possible to him. Their faces were indeed of similar shape. They both had identical beards in fullness and color. They were about the same height and build, and both had the same wide toothy smile. But it was their eyes that caught his attention. Bright and vibrant, but severe and stern at the same time. Surely this is some trick, he thought, shaking his head.

"This is no trick, my friend," the emperor said with a smile as if reading his mind. "I'm sure my son didn't tell you before because, well, no one but our family knows." His face relaxed, and to Michael's eyes, it was more apparent than ever.

"But, the Sorcerer," Michael began.

"I'm the emperor's closest advisor and counselor," the sorcerer cut in, and moving to join Tiberius at the table. "And before that, I was his and my predecessor's bodyguard when I was a Battle-Mage. There's scarcely anything in this empire I don't know," he finished, patting Tiberius's knee.

Tiberius nodded. "Forgive the deception, my young friend. But like I told you on the road, 'We have no secrets between us, but the secrets that bind us together.'" He raised his gloved hand, inviting Michael to join them at the table.

Michael took a seat next to them, and cautiously asked, "If you are the emperor's son, doesn't that make you the heir to the Axton Empire?"

"Aye, yes, it does. One day, many years from now, gods bless us."

"Why are you leading the Rangers instead of, well I don't know, what else someone would be doing in your position?"

The emperor chuckled. "My dear Mage, I too was once the rangers' commander, as was my father, and my grandfather stretching all the way back to Alexander himself. Our family founded the rangers over six hundred years ago with the idea that they needed to be warriors in our land who served the people. Warriors who owed no allegiance to any crown but would fight and die to guard all the people of the land."

He looked deep into Michael's eyes, willing his words to resonate in his mind. "It was the rangers who first resisted the Narzethian invasion five hundred years ago. It was the rangers who first departed our shores to contend with them in their homeland. And to this day, it is the rangers who wander our lands and defend all of our people."

"That's all well and good, Your Majesty. But why? Why risk your lives before ascending to the throne?"

"Because we believe that before one can rule, one must serve. That a leader will never know what it truly means to serve the people if they have never served them before. It has been our family's practice going back before the empire was founded, and it shall be our way until the unmaking of our world."

Michael's head was spinning with all he had learned in such a short amount of time.

"Now, Ti, what is so damned important you had to come all this way?" the emperor asked, turning his attention to Tiberius.

At his father's question, Tiberius's face turned back to the seriousness he wore when he first entered the chamber. The sudden change in demeanor sobered Damian and the emperor, and they both sat upright to hear the story. Tiberius leaned back in the steel wrought chair, poured himself a new cup of mead, and began his tale in full. Michael wished he had whatever the sorcerer was drinking.

The hours stretched on as Tiberius talked. Though the city below began to darken with the waning day, the music and dancing from the festival continued to echo and travel up to the spire's top. Lanterns began to appear at taverns and inns around the city. Street workers were fast at work, lighting the lamps that lined the cobble and stone streets as more and more people filled the squares to take in the nighttime entertainment.

An hour after the sun sunk over the western sky, Tiberius finished his tale and sat back to help himself to a large mug of beer.

"May the Spirit of The Warrior always be with you, brothers," the emperor muttered after Tiberius finished his story.

"May the Spirit of The Warrior always be with you, indeed," Tiberius echoed, his voice somber.

The four sat in silence for a moment before the emperor stood and began pacing the chamber's length. He held his hands folded in the small of his back, his head down, lost in some internal discussion and thought. Damian sat for a few minutes before pouring his third mug of ale, which the Sorcerer downed in one gulp. Michael watched all this happening, unsure of what to say or do. Tiberius hung his head, inspecting the dark, foamy beer inside his steel mug.

When the heavy silence was more than he could take, Michael dared to speak up. "I take it that you knew of our mission, Your Majesty?"

"Yes, I knew," the emperor admitted without halting his stride. "Why do you think you had a company of rangers so close to where your Magi brothers were encamped?"

As if anticipating Michael's questions, Tiberius interjected, "No, we didn't know about your mission, or about the disappearing magic until that morning in the inn. When necromancy was outlawed six years ago, numerous practitioners flew to the farthest northern kingdoms of the empire. After the war was over, we were ordered to continue enforcing the ban. That's why we were ordered to commence our ranging in Childers."

"Tiberius and his rangers did not know, young Mage," the Emperor added. "Damian shared his fears with me and me alone, in our council. And while I was bound by his secret to not openly act, I could ensure that a group of my rangers, the finest warrior in the empire, were close at hand. It would seem my slight deception paid off, luckily. As for what the purpose of excavating a dwarven outpost was, only Damian knows. And even that, he would not share with me."

The companions now turned to Damian, who had lit a pipe and was also lost in deep thought.

"Why didn't you tell my father what your purpose in finding the outpost was?" Tiberius demanded.

The sorcerer sat, blowing smoke rings absentmindedly. "I did not want to give you father, undue hope."

"Undue hope?"

"Aye, undue hope. What if all this was rumor and legend, and there was nothing there at all, Ti? I could not promise answers to your father and my emperor, and then crush his hope."

"Well, forget hope and speak plainly to us! If the outpost is real, what were you hoping to learn?" Tiberius demanded.

"If the outpost is real, I hoped to learn some history, my dear boy," Damian began. "The dwarves were a fascinating race of people. Secretive and mysterious, but fascinating, nonetheless. The scrolls in our Citadel say they had such a deep understanding of the nature of the world and magic. That they could conjure it as easily as you or I draw breath."

The sorcerer stood, moved behind the high steel chair he had sat upon, and continued. "The dwarves were enslaved by the Narzeth for an untold number of years before we freed them. In their captivity, they were forced to build great and terrible weapons, and to abandon magic lest they were killed. Then we freed them and brought them back to our country. They and the Magi built this city, and this very spire we stand in. After that, they ventured into the Land Beyond. And with them went many of their secrets, including the nature of magic as they understood it. With all that's going on, I felt it prudent we seek out all the information we could."

"And what of the outpost?" Tiberius pressed.

"The legends say that they were escorted by Matthew Axton, then the commander of the rangers. Upon his return, he passed word that the dwarves had intended to build a new home for themselves beyond the mountains. And if the stories of their heartiness and skill are to be believed, then they surely succeeded."

"And you think they would have left some information there concerning magic?"

Damian nodded in agreement. "Aye. I do believe they would have, Ti. And for that reason, and that reason alone, I felt the risk of sending the Magi there was worth it."

"As do I, my friend," the emperor cut in, ceasing his incessant pacing and turning to face his son. "But this time, the Magi will not go. You, my son, will take up the venture north starting tomorrow."

Michael looked at the men, confused. Tiberius remained impassive, trying to hide his emotions from his father's Sight. His mind began to race, mentally checking what would need to happen to marshal his forces. He would have to reassemble his rangers first, and that would delay their journey back north.

"You will not be taking your rangers, Ti," as if reading his son's mind. "A group that size will draw undue attention. Suppose people are actively trying to oppose our reaching that outpost. In that case, we'll have to rely on stealth to achieve our goals," the emperor finished. He knew his son's mind well enough; he needn't use his Sight on him. Tiberius's first thought would be of his rangers and how best to use them.

"I am their commander, my place is with them," he said, anger and confusion flaring in his voice.

"You have many capable leaders in your ranks. They can lead in your stead," the emperor responded, more authoritative than Michael had heard him speak to his son. "This mission to find the outpost is our chief concern, and I need my best warrior to lead it. And Damian, I respectfully request young Michael here to continue this journey with my son. He's proven quite capable for someone so young, and I feel that he has more of a part to play in what is to come."

Damian nodded his approval. "You're the emperor, Sire. You can command whoever you want to do whatever bidding you require. But yes, I think we can spare young Michael. After all, he's been through, I feel that he's owed some answers. Besides, the further away from King White the better for us all."

"Then it's settled. Michael, spend tonight in the Citadel. Collect whatever you need and report to the docks outside the mansion tomorrow morning."

Damian downed his remaining ale, offered a low bow, and motioned for Michael to follow him out of the chamber. Michael stared at Tiberius for guidance. This was the first time they would be separated since that morning in the inn. But Tiberius nodded his approval for him to depart. Michael needed to sleep in the comfort of his own room and to prepare for the return journey to the north. Slowly, Michael stood and rendered his own bow before departing with the Sorcerer.

"You had better sleep too, son. We have much to discuss tomorrow before your departure," the emperor said, rubbing sleep from his eyes. The long days were taking their toll on him, but he was resolved in his decision. "And I still have to deal with these bickering fools tonight, gods bless me."

"You don't have to deal with any of them if you so wish. Like Damian said, you're the emperor."

"If only it were that easy," his father replied melancholic. "But you know our ways. The ways of Alexander Axton."

"All too well," he said with a smile. "I learned from the best teacher in the empire, after all."

"Flattery and laughter were always your way of hiding your true thoughts. What troubles you?"

"Father, I know you are burdened with all of these matters, and I know your decision to send me without my rangers with me is the right move. I just worry. With all that is going on, my men will need me if something happens while I'm away," Tiberius said, standing. "Magic disappearing doesn't just mean Michael and the rest of the Magi cannot summon fire to their hands or conjure rain during a drought. It's at the very core of our nation's defense. If our enemies were to learn of this, things could get terrible very quickly."

"Let me handle the burden of keeping our country safe. The weight of these issues is the curse of being the Emperor, Ti. One day, you will be the ruler of this country, and the responsibility of leadership will fall to you. I pray to the gods of all the kingdoms that you make a far better ruler than I."

"I never wanted to be emperor, you know this," Tiberius replied.

"I know, son. Truth be told, neither did I. Neither did your grandfather or your great grandfather for that matter. But that is not a decision we can unmake. We carry our duties as rangers to protect the people of the empire. That duty extends to being emperor as well."

Tiberius approached his father, placed a hand on his shoulder, and said, "I wish we had more time. There never seems to be enough time."

But instead of more debating or arguing, the emperor grabbed his son and hugged him. The years of war and death melted off them both. The horrors and sights they had both witnessed in their long lives vanished, and, in the end, it was just a father hugging his son.

After a minute of silence, the emperor broke their embrace and said, "I love you, Ti. I love you more than all the gold and power in the entire world. You are my greatest treasure, and when I'm dead and buried, I want you to only remember me as a good father."

For the first time in a year, Tiberius cried at his father's words and hugged him tighter. He knew tomorrow would be another farewell and a journey into the unknown dangers. But tonight, he was just a scared little boy who wanted to feel his father's embrace one more time. Outside, the music and cheering flew higher into the sky. Fireworks in the distance exploded in streaking stars of many colors. The world around them spun on, while atop the Unity Spire, all time seemed to stop for their loving embrace.

CHAPTER 9

THE LAST NIGHT

Michael sat at a simple wooden table within his chambers inside the Citadel for hours. His mind raced, reflecting on all that had transpired in such a short amount of time. In the span of a few days, he had encountered undead soldiers, been stabbed, healed himself, journeyed to meet the emperor who turned out to be his companion's father, and was now tasked with journeying back north. And, he would be traveling with the legendary ranger, and heir to the Axton Empire, Tiberius!

He looked around his room, trying to decide what would be best to take on his journey. The whole room was made of grey stone with a simple wooden framed bed, bookcase, trunk, and desk. It was plainer than any other bedroom he had slept in but at the same time contained more knowledge and wonderment than there was in a lifetime. In this room, he had first read about the practice of magic instead of just hearing the tales. It was here he first brewed potions. It was here he had first conjured a flame to his hands, months ahead of his peers. It was here that he had finally felt at home.

But looking around the room now, he felt like a child again. A child who had returned to their boyhood bedroom after years away from home. There were many fond memories and lessons learned here. But they were just that, memories. His life had been irrevocably changed in such a short amount of time, and a growing voice in his head assured him that more was in store for him yet.

He paced his stone room, looking over his things, trying and failing to decide what to take with him on his journey. He had outgrown his old robes and cloaks. He had virtually memorized all of his books. He had no weapon to take.

Should I buy a weapon? He thought. With what money? My parents wouldn't send me any money. They wouldn't even believe me if I told them I needed one in the first place. Besides, what would the Magi think of me taking a weapon!?

Exasperated from all this thinking in circles, he collapsed on his bed, defeated and tired. He felt altogether unprepared for his trip when a sudden knock came to his door. But when he answered the door, he was greeted by a smiling and somewhat inebriated High Sorcerer. He stumbled into his meager room, accompanied, to Michael's surprise, by one of the dragon knights he had seen earlier.

The knight was clad in deep green and grey armor adorned with reptilian scales, and a dragon-shaped helm pulled down over their face. Michael stared wide-eyed at the dragoon, who seemed to tower over him. They bore a mighty black and grey spear with intricate designs laid into its thick wooden shaft in their right hand. The grip of the spear appeared to be wrapped in some kind of red cloth.

No, not red, Michael realized. It's blood. Stained and caked blood.

"Evening, Michael," Damian said with a hiccup, "Don't mind my companion here. The emperor has been having some of the dragoons shadow us as bodyguards. Glad to see you're packed." In truth, no bags were packed, and the room looked quite tidy.

"Seeing as you'll be off tomorrow morning and seeing as your journey with Ti is going to be somewhat of a secret, I thought I'd come visit you tonight to convey some parting advice."

As they entered his room, Michael stared at them dumbfounded before extending his hand to the dragoon and offering his introductions, "Michael Deerborn of the Magi. It's a pleasure to meet one of the dragon knights of Narzeth." But instead, the dragoon stared at him from behind their helm. Michael felt a bit embarrassed, afraid he might have said something to offend the dragoon.

"Don't take it personally, Michael. The dragoons do not take kindly to mention of their former captors," he said with a hearty laugh. "Besides, it's not their custom to shake hands with strangers. Only with their trusted companions and friends. But enough of that, more to the point of me calling on you during your packing."

Michael stared at the sorcerer, unsure of what advice was about to be laid on him. "Oh, yes, sir. Please, sir. Anything you can give me will be of great value."

The sorcerer sat down on the bed and removed a small flask from deep inside his robes while the dragon knight leaned against the nearby wall, spear in hand. "Well, I don't think I have to tell you the seriousness of this mission. Magic is not only at the center of our order, but it is a part of the very fabric of our society and our countries defense."

He took a deep swig of his flask and continued, "It's helped our country thrive during times of great strife whether in battle or in times of drought and famine. Since the birth of the empire, it has been our chief source of strength and salvation. All that to say, it is paramount that we discover what has happened to our ability to harness it. As I told you in the council room, this expedition to the dwarven outpost may yield nothing of value. But even the slightest chance that it could help us regain the use of magic is worth the trip alone."

"I just wish I had the wits and strength to better represent the order in this undertaking," Michael replied. "I'm not a warrior like Master Tiberius or the dragoon here. Even as an apprentice, I'm barely versed in the usage of magic. But I promise at the very least, I will not bring shame or dishonor to the Magi."

Damian nodded in approval and stood to put his flask away. "I know you will do us proud. There is no ill will or malice in your heart. But as I said, I came to give you advice, so here it is."

His smile melted away in an instant, and his voice grew grim. In an instant, the jovial High Sorcerer was gone, and in his place was the famed Imperial Battle-Mage he had been in his youth. "Pay attention to everything you see and hear while on the road. Listen to Tiberius in his commands. He may be a ranger, but he is well versed in not just magic but in all manners of lore and history. A finer companion you will never have in this world. Carry an open mind in your investigations. The things you've read and learned here are the starting point of your journey, and new knowledge is always being discovered. You've read the writings of scholarly men, now's your chance to add to those writings with what you learn."

Michael blushed at the praise his master bestowed on him, especially in front of the warrior who accompanied his master. It was one thing to show humility and embarrassment in front of his Magi brothers, but another to show it in front of warriors who could leap a hundred feet into the air. But at any rate, all apprehensions he had before his guest's arrival were now forgotten. A renewed sense of purpose and excitement overtook him, and he bowed low before his master.

"You do me a great honor with your words and trust, sir."

The sorcerer motioned for his bodyguard to get the door and began to exit the room when he quickly turned back to face the Mage. "Oh, I almost forgot. It's dangerous out in the world, take this," and from deep within his flowing robes, he produced the last thing Michael had ever thought he'd see in his own chambers. An ebony and ivory wand.

Michael stared at the wand, dumbstruck! A wand! A real-life magical wand right here in his stone bedroom. He stammered, trying to summon the best words to use. "But sir, I'm just an apprentice. I haven't earned this yet."

"Nonsense, boy! You faced fifty reanimated heathen soldiers and lived to tell about it. You healed yourself unaided and with great effort, and journeyed home to tell about it. You have more than earned this."

"But, isn't it customary for one to make their own wand once they become a full mage?"

"Yes, but we haven't made new wands in over a year. So, I had to search all over Cycret's chambers to find one."

"But...but," Michael started. But he was cut off before any more words of protest could escape him.

"But nothing! Apprentices have done far less to earn a wand and the right to be elevated to the rank of mage. Take it. And with it, I formally elevate you to Brother Mage. May the Father and Mother of Creation guide you and protect you in this life and in the next."

Slowly Michael reached out and gripped the wand. It was heavier than he imagined. The shaft was made of a wood Michael had never seen before and colored in midnight black. The grip was made of steel and stone woven together, with a curious symbol engraved on the bottom. Fresh tears began to form in his eyes.

Damian placed his rough hand on Michael's shoulder and said almost in a whisper, said, "Remember, wands are tools. Tools for greater understanding and tools for aid. When magic returns properly to our world, I hope you and this wand will accomplish great things in the coming years." The High Sorcerer bowed low to the new Mage and closed the door behind him.

Michael stared at the wand in utter awe, mesmerized by its beauty and craftsmanship. A broad smile broke his face.

"Oh, and before I forget," Damian announced, bursting through the door again. "My bodyguard will be accompanying you two on your journey."

Michael's mouth fell open like a weight hitting the floor. "The dragoon? With us?" he stammered to the sorcerer's hearty laughter.

"Yes, the dragoon. But don't worry, she and Tiberius are well acquainted and should get along splendidly."

"She?" Michael squeaked, his eyes threatening to burst from his head.

As if right on cue, the dragoon removed their helmet, and a woman with long flowing black hair, deep olive tanned skin over sharp bone structure, and deep black eyes stood before him. He felt dumbstruck to see such a beautiful woman clad in armor standing before him.

Damian burst into wild, raucous laughter at Michael's expression. "Yes, she. This is Shayla Rider, First Knight of the Imperial Dragon Knights, and she will be your companion along with Tiberius."

Michael examined the knight again. It was true she was a beautiful, striking woman, but in her eyes, he saw a quiet fury. Above her brow, a few cuts that were probably at one point deep and life-threatening, and a small burn on her right ear. She had seen a fight or two in her day, he knew. But none of those imperfections detracted in the slightest from her beauty.

"Well, I best be off. Do try and pack light, my boy," he said, bowing low and leaving Michael at last.

Michael stared at the closed door for a while, thinking over his newest companion, the beautiful and dangerous Shayla Rider, First Knight of the Dragon Knights. Whatever that meant, he wondered. Perhaps she is like Tiberius, and is the leader or commander or whatever of the dragoons? But how wise is it to trust a Narzethian on this trip? But in all this questioning, he suddenly became acutely aware of the weighted object he held in his hand, his very own magic wand.

Michael stared at the black and white wand for a long time. Never in his life would he have ever imagined that he, the son of a poor fisherman from White Fyre, would ever receive the title of Mage. Let alone with his own beautiful wand. He pondered Damian's words that he had searched through his predecessor's chambers to find a wand to present him. Why Cycret would hide such a beautiful wand in his bed chambers was curious indeed. But Cycret had always been a little eccentric, even amongst the Magi.

Tiberius strolled the bustling city night, taking in all the wonders it had to offer. He and his father talked for a while until he was summoned to continue his council with the ten. Not wanting to impose any more on his father's duties, Tiberius snuck down the stairs behind the vast lift they had first arrived in. Not knowing what to do with himself until morning, he decided he would see the city and take it all in before his journey north with Michael.

Now that he was out and among the people, he was desperate to hold on to this night for as long as possible. All the activities and music he had seen during his march to the spire continued despite the sun's disappearance a few hours before. The war's ending had transformed the whole empire from being on pins and needles with stress and anxiety into a complete state of harmony and prosperity.

He stopped and leaned against a large lamp post as performers from the Black Kingdom began a traditional dance from their homeland. The small square they had assembled was surrounded by tall, wooden and steel inns and pubs. People were bursting out of the windows overhead to get a better view of the show below them. He looked between the dancers and the people around him, all dressed in different clothes reflecting the kingdoms they hailed from. This is what it's all about, isn't it, he thought as he watched the performers. The people of our empire. All from different kingdoms and from different cultures brought together by his family five centuries before. He smiled to himself, despite his own reservations at leaving his rangers.

I'm not a spy or assassin, I'm a ranger. My duty is with my men, yet I am honor-bound to follow my father's orders. His smile faded, and he grew grim at these thoughts. He knew he had to trust his father's wisdom and orders, he realized. That was how he could keep the people safe now.

The performers finished their furious, beautiful dance with a grand flourish. The crowd around them erupted into mighty cheers and applause. Tiberius smiled again and joined in the clapping and cries of "Bravo!" He lingered near the post before deciding he should join his men in the one place he was sure they would all congregate on their night off in the city, Nock Arrows pub. He tossed a few coins into the dancer's open case and strolled away from the square as another group emerged to begin their own dance.

He followed the cobblestone and steel roads around the maze-like city, astonished at the people that seemed to burst from every corner of the city. In his long time as a ranger, he had ventured to all their kingdoms on one errand or another. But to see all these people, hear all their competing accents and manners of speech at once? His heart grew full and proud.

A few minutes later, he found himself at the entrance of Nock Arrows. A sizeable wooden pub lined with flags from each kingdom outside with the Imperial banner held the highest. He entered the pub and took it all in. Several of his rangers were drinking and singing along with the house band to some old tune about gallant warriors traipsing around and righting the wrongs of a long-gone era. He had been coming to Arrows since he first joined the Imperial army. It had become the rangers' favorite hangout whenever they had the opportunity to visit the city. The walls were covered in crude painting and tapestries depicting victories over the Narzeth and dragons from long ago. The wood paneling was chipping and in need of repair, but it added a unique quality and ambiance to the place.

In the corner, he saw his three friends engaged in some debate, no doubt about who slew how many enemies in the war. It was a morbid point of honor between Timothy and Zachary as to how many of the Narzeth they slew in battle. Tiberius and the other senior rangers never understood their strange fascination with this. War and killing wasn't a game, but if it brought some levity to his men, he would allow it. But their conversation ended as soon as Timothy met eyes with his commander.

The archer burst to his feet and roared over the room, "Hail! Tiberius!" A great echo rang over the place as every person present, ranger or otherwise, returned his call.

Tiberius laughed and replied, "Hail, and well met! Rangers of the Axton Empire!" He had always made it a point to return greetings from his men, another lesson from his father. Soldiers of lower offices and ranks yearn to be acknowledged and praised by their commanders, and Tiberius never missed an opportunity to dole out his admiration.

He made his way through the jam-packed pub, stopping here and there to exchange quick words with many of his men till he finally made his way to his three companions. He exchanged quick handshakes with the two young Rangers before they returned their debate. He held his handshake with Trevin just a little longer than what was allowed, but no one seemed to notice with everything going on around them. Or care.

"Glad you could join us, sir. We were wondering how long His Majesty would keep you. Where is our young Mage?" Trevin said, returning back to formality. He, like his lover, yearned for more time together alone. But with the men around, he dared not betray his duty and feelings.

Tiberius grabbed a fresh beer from the bar nearby and settled into his chair. "Not too terribly long, considering everything we had to say. Everything okay with the men?"

"Nothing too out of the ordinary. These two idiots have been debating tactics and body counts, a few of the females broke some poor idiot's nose who didn't believe they were rangers. The other men have been singing and dancing like fools all night," Trevin reported.

"Oh! You should have seen the look on his face! Amanda was just enjoying her drink, and this fool dared to tell her she shouldn't be bothering us. That she was too ugly and bald to be a proper wench, and she was better suited for his company than ours," Zachary exclaimed, holding his side from laughter. "Quick as an arrow she, Freya, and Sara were on their feet and in his face with some choice words I had never heard a lady utter in my life. Next thing you know, WAM! An elbow right in his snout! He fell over bleeding like a pig and ran out with his tail between his legs!"

Timothy downed what had to be his tenth beer judging by the flagons that were piled near him. "They aren't ladies. They are Imperial Rangers with an honor greater than any other 'man'!" He stood quickly and mounted his chair, towering over the assembled crowd. "Citizens of the empire! Raise your glasses high for Amanda, Freya, and Sara! Warriors, protectors, and true ladies of the rangers! HAIL!"

Shouts of praise echoed around the room as all those seated shot to their feet again with raised glasses and returned the cry of, "Hail!" The three women remained standing and bowed to Timothy in response, a lasting gaze between the youngest, Freya, and Timothy.

"How long have you been dying to do that?" Zachary asked as Timothy returned to his seat.

"Spur of the moment. Grand gestures and all that."

"You know fraternizing is forbidden, right?" Zachary reminded him. Tiberius and Trevin quickly turned eyes to each other at these words. Fraternizing between the junior enlisted and the sergeants was indeed forbidden. But the attraction between comrades was a natural thing. Long nights in the wild and the uncertainty of death draws people together in strange ways indeed.

"I know, I know. And I would never do anything. But still…" he trailed off, lost in some secret thought.

"Anyways, what came of your audience with the emperor?" Trevin asked, changing the subject.

Tiberius grew quiet at Trevin's question, thinking best how to break the news to not only his sergeants but to his friends and his lover. "It wasn't just the emperor, Trevin. Damian was there too."

"The High Sorcerer was there?" Timothy said with a raised eyebrow. The mention of such a powerful and magical person was enough to draw his attention away from comparing body counts and staring at Freya to hear what had happened.

"Yes. We told them what had happened in Childers. They were very shocked to hear what had happened to be sure, but in the end, they decided we needed to go back and continue searching for this supposed dwarven outpost."

"Brilliant!" Timothy exclaimed. "When do we leave?"

Tiberius took a deep drink of his dark beer. "That's the problem, my friend. The rangers are not going. Just me. Me and Michael and one other that the emperor has yet to choose."

His comrades looked defeated and were beginning to start volunteering when Tiberius raised his hand. "Don't protest. This order is straight from His Majesty. A whole contingent of rangers traveling north would cause a lot of undue attention. He feels that I should be the one to go with Michael on this expedition. Besides, you all will have to continue your patrols in the wild."

Trevin stared at Tiberius for many heavy moments, not wanting to give away his concern and growing sorrow. At last, he asked, "When do you leave, sir?"

"Tomorrow morning, my friends. We depart from the docks shortly after sunrise."

The silence between the four men was louder than all the noise of the crowded tavern. None of the men made eye contact with one another except for Trevin. He stared long and deep into Tiberius's eyes, searching his soul and mind for some reassurance. He didn't need to use his Sight to realize all Tiberius spoke was true, he just didn't want to believe it.

He and Tiberius had never been separated for longer than a few days since their service to the rangers had begun. In his heart, he knew he was bound to Tiberius and Tiberius to him. And while that thought gave him some comfort, he feared for him alone out in the wild. His emotions were growing stronger than he anticipated and he quickly broke the silence, "What will you have us do, sir?"

Tiberius eyed Trevin with a knowing look. "After the men's three-day pass is over, make for the garrison. We must continue recruiting and training and get back to our normal patrolling as soon as possible. I fear there is some evil conspiring against our empire, and we must stand ready to fight it once it is known."

"Very well, sir. You can count on the three of us to see it done."

"I know I can, First Sergeant. You and these two idiots are the best men I have. I know you will all make me proud in my absence."

Tiberius ordered another beer and decided to get up and visit with his men around the room. Many of them were delighted to be in the presence of their fabled commander, especially in such an informal and relaxed setting. Some of the newer ones remained hesitant to engage their leader in conversation, still stuck in their ways from service in the Imperial Military. Nevertheless, Tiberius made his way to each table and spent time with them.

He stopped when he reached the ladies' table near the back of the bar. The three women were on their feet to greet their commander, who raised a hand to have them sit down. "There's no need for that, ladies. I wanted to come hear what you all thought of our little company."

"I am beyond honored to be here, sir," Amanda answered. Though her head was as shaved as the rest, her youth and beauty shined through, nevertheless. "I saw how the men fought during the war and was envious of their skill. But when I heard you had opened your ranks up to us, I was the first to volunteer."

"Nay! Hold your tongue, lest the gods strike you dead!" Freya exclaimed, her hazel sharp eyes growing wild and angry. "I was the first to volunteer for commander Tiberius! And I challenge any man or woman here who dare call me a liar!"

Tiberius laughed hard and loud at her threats. "Peace, daughter! Peace!" he said in the words of her home kingdom. "No one shall question thine honor!"

Freya gave a hearty laugh in reply before toasting her own mug of dark beer with Tiberius and downing it in one gulp. I can see why Timothy is so taken with her, he thought. She is fire turned human. He stood from their table, bowed, and left to continue his visits around the room.

As the night wore on, more and more of the rangers began leaving the pub and heading for the Imperial Army barracks they occupied when they were in the city. Timothy and Zachary remained passed out at the table, as usual, without a bother to the pub owners. Only Tiberius and Trevin stayed awake, chatting about what to do with the rangers while Tiberius was away. Though they longed to say more to each other, they dared not speak their thoughts aloud.

Love is the death of duty; Tiberius had heard someone much smarter than him say long ago. It was true then, and it held true today.

After many hours, a small beam of light began to shine through the windows of the pub. The morning was here at last. With a smile, Tiberius slammed his hand hard on the table and jolted the pair of sleeping rangers awake. "Time to get up, you lazy asses!" he said, laughing at their shocked, tired expressions. "Don't sleep away your time off! Get up and go have some fun that doesn't involve drinking and women."

"What kind of fun is that?" Timothy asked, rubbing his eyes and stretching. "Are you leaving us?"

"I think I need to," Tiberius replied. "I have to meet with the emperor and Michael soon, and I need to clear my head before then."

Timothy and Zachary stood and hugged their commander. No matter their rank and position, they were brothers first and foremost, and they desired to bid their commander farewell and good luck. Trevin, however, remained seated, staring off into the distance. Tiberius felt a little hurt that he had not risen to see him off. He knew Trevin was as hurt and sad as he was at their departure but wished more than anything to feel his lover's embrace one last time.

He pushed these thoughts down and said to the two Rangers before him, "If fortune favors us, I'll see you all at the garrison before long. Farewell!" And with that, Tiberius left the pub.

He walked slowly, thinking about how Trevin had disregarded him. Perhaps the pain was too much? Or maybe he was shutting him off out of fear of losing him? Either way, a sharp pang of sadness sprung up in his heart.

"Ti, wait!" a familiar voice called out from behind. The sudden informal use of his name made him turn at once and saw Trevin jogging towards him. He had never heard Trevin call him anything other than sir or commander. Rarely did he use his full name, and he had never used his abbreviated name. Trevin rushed to him and embraced him as he had never embraced someone before.

Tiberius stood shocked for a moment before closing his eyes and returning the hug. It was sweet oblivion, and one he never wanted to escape from. All the hurt and sadness he had felt mere moments before were gone now, replaced by a deep yearning to put aside his duty and stay here forever. After a moment, Trevin pulled away and placed Tiberius's hand on his chest.

"I had not the courage to tell you this before, but hear me now," he said, tears forming in the corners of his eyes. "I am yours now and always. Until the seas dry and the skies fall. Until the gods of creation come to wipe us away."

Those were the words of Trevin's home in the Zelinka Kingdom. Words spoken between the betrothed, and the only words he had ever wanted to say to Tiberius since the first time they laid eyes on each other.

As was the custom in Zelinka, Tiberius placed his hand behind Trevin's neck, pulled their foreheads together, and said, "I am yours. Now and until the strength of our empire collapses. Until the seas wash us away, and we join The Warrior in all his glory." These were the words of the empire. These were his words, and he meant every one of them.

They stood in the street, heads pressed against one another, chuckling to themselves. After a few moments, Tiberius said, "When this is over, and we are no longer bound to our duty, I'm going to buy you a cottage. A grand cottage with a grander garden that we can lie around in and reflect back on this moment."

"I would like that very much, Ti."

Somewhere in the distance, bells started to chime. It was time for the city to reawaken and begin the festivities anew. They broke their grasp but continued to stare at each other until, at last, they spoke the only words that mattered in the whole world to them. The only words men like them needed to hear at the start of a journey. The words of their people.

"The Spirit of The Warrior will always be with you," they said in quiet unison. And with that, Tiberius turned and departed his lover.

Trevin lingered on, watching Tiberius until he disappeared around the corner at the end of the street. He turned to see Zachary and Timothy standing at the tavern's doors, hands over their hearts like adolescent girls, great fake sobs emitting from their throats.

"Oh, my gods! That was so adorable!" Timothy exclaimed.

"Why didn't you tell that poor soul you love him?" Zachary asked in between great fits of laughter. "I love you with all my heart! If I don't see you soon, I'm going to die!"

Trevin could only reply, "Shut up and buy me a damn drink."

The two men burst into great cheers at Trevin's words. Now was the time for revelry and relaxation. Now, it was the time to enjoy their downtime the only way three seasoned veterans of the Imperial army knew how. The three reentered Nock Arrows and began their second day of leave with beer and mead and flowing wine.

CHAPTER 10

THE JOURNEY NORTH

Tiberius began to steel his mind and heart from the distractions of love as he walked to the docks. His parting time with Trevin had done much to raise his spirits in the face of the impending journey north. Now that the hour was here, his training and discipline compelled him to bury the memory deep. As he walked, he began formulating a plan for their journey north. He knew their road north would be a long one, and perhaps random to anyone watching for their departure. But that would be the whole point and would serve a greater purpose in concealing their journey.

He arrived at the docks near the mansion shortly after eight. There he found his young companion sitting alone half asleep with his meagerly packed bag nearby. *Guess he decided to go out and drink the night away as well,* Tiberius thought, with a small chuckle. *He'll acclimate quickly to the lack of sleep, just as all men pressed upon a mission do.* He lightly kicked Michael's foot, rousing the Mage from whatever deep sleep he might have been in.

Michael shot awake and covered the rising sun with his hands. "Good morning, my friend. I take it you had a late night of merriment?" Tiberius asked, sitting next to the Mage and retrieving his pipe.

Michael rubbed his sleepy eyes and began to stand. "For me, no, sir. Though you smell a little like you had a long night for yourself."

"Not too much, I'm afraid," Tiberius replied with a smile. "But I had to spend some time with my men before I'm off on this damned journey. How about you, what were you doing if not enjoying some last comforts before we take to the road?"

"I spent the night in the Citadel agonizing over what to bring for the trip. In the end, I just threw some clothes and a few books in my bag. I couldn't sleep even if I wanted to."

"Why is that? A young man like yourself on the eve of a journey in the wild should have gotten all the sleep you could stand."

"Master Nightowl promoted me to Mage last night," Michael replied, the memory drawing renewed energy into his tired body. "And, he gave me this." slowly, he pulled out the ebony and ivory wand from within his robes to Tiberius's astonishment.

Tiberius rejoiced and clapped Michael's back at the news of his advancement to full mage. Michael then began recounting the whole of last night's events in his small stone room to Tiberius, who sat back enjoying the pipe and the excitement that poured out of the Mage like a waterfall. He examined the wand with much of his own wonder when he asked to see it, and chuckled at the thought of drunken Damian Nightowl offering advice to the impressionable young boy.

"I also found out who will accompany us on our journey," Michael added, placing his heavy wand back within his robes. "The Dragon Knight, Shayla."

Tiberius's eyes lit up. "That is fantastic news, Michael! I can think of no better companion for us in our mission than her."

"Begging your pardon, sir, and I pray you to excuse my ignorance, by why? Would it not be prudent to keep our secret mission just between us?"

Tiberius thought on how best to answer the Mage's well-intentioned question. After a few small puffs from his pipe, said, "Secrecy is paramount, I do agree. However, Shayla is one of the finest and most powerful warriors in our empire. Maybe in the world. If my father and Damian didn't think she would make a fine companion, she would not be going with us. Besides, she will hold any oaths of silence as much as you or I."

"Do you trust her, sir?"

Tiberius eyed the young Mage for a moment before responding. "Aye, Michael. I trust her with my life. For one, because she is the leader of her order just as I am the leader of the rangers. And, I was the one that freed her and her people. She and her sisters hold this empire near and dear to their hearts and will not break their loyalty to it."

"Her sisters?" Michael asked, perplexed but curious.

"Aye," Tiberius replied with a smile. "All those that call themselves Dragon Knights are women."

They chatted for another half-hour until just beyond the docks, a small company of sentinels turned into view. The companions slowly stood to their feet and bowed as the emperor, and High Sorcerer with three attendants in tow approached. They were dressed much as they were the night before, though each bore a tired look. Undoubtedly, the emperor had continued his meetings with the ten late into the night, while Damian was fighting a raging headache from his overindulgence in beer.

The emperor motioned for the sentinels to withdraw and turned a beckoning hand towards an anchored boat alongside the docks. After the four men were aboard, the emperor himself took the great oar and began pushing their party downstream. Once they were about a hundred feet from the dock, did the emperor break the silence. "On your mission, I have nothing to give you that will be of aid. Instead, I must reiterate the need for caution and stealth. Once we reach the city's western shore, I and all my powers to protect you will be limited. Limited, but not gone."

"You will have nothing to worry about, father," Tiberius replied, his eyes scanning the approaching shore. "I know the lands we venture to well."

"I do not doubt that, Ti. However, I will advise you to take the road less traveled on your quest. There is almost certainly an enemy moving against us in the wild. Hopefully, they will be focused on the main roads out of the city and not the path you are intended upon."

"Yes but let us pray to the gods above that they have not anticipated this minor subterfuge of ours."

"You may pray, Ti. I will trust in your skill in the wild. But, yes. It would be most troubling indeed, if our unknown enemy has eyes and ears on all the roads of our realm," the emperor responded grimly.

No one else spoke the rest of the boat ride, each lost in their own thoughts on what was to come. They reached the western shore of Kings Lake about ten minutes later. Standing tall and firm to greet them was Shayla, a tall black warhorse and smaller but no less stout brown paint reigned into her sides.

The two departed the boat in silence and, before long, were mounted and ready to be off before Damian produced a small satchel. "Take these on your trip. Recently brewed provisions from our finest potioneers. You might find need for such things before long, I expect."

"Thank you, sir," Michael replied with a bow and placed the leather bag behind him in the saddle.

The emperor approached Tiberius with a slender leather-wrapped package in hand. "This is for you, my son," he said, solemn and despondent.

Tiberius looked confused at his father for a moment before unwrapping the package. Once it was open, he recoiled in shock. In his hands was his father's own sword, the sword of the Axton Emperors. He examined the black scabbard with its deep black handle and grey cross guard. Around the end of the hilt sat a circle with ten steel lines moving away from the center, the symbol of the Axton Empire. His father had carried this sword after he ascended to rule their land. Just as his grandfather had and so on back until the first Axton was named emperor of the realm.

After a moment of confused contemplation, he looked at his father and asked, "Why are you giving me this?"

"A good warrior needs good steel if he is to do good things in the world," the emperor replied.

"Father, I already have a sword, and a good one at that. Besides if things are going the way we fear, you might have more need of this than I do."

The emperor stood next to his son and gripped his hand. "My days in the field are over Ti. You are an Axton, and you are my son. With this sword, you will be carrying the authority and honor and power of our family with you."

A sudden realization dawned on Tiberius. He, as a ranger, could not do much in the wide-open world. But with the emperor's own weapon in hand, that was a different matter. He looked at his father and nodded. He replaced his own sword with this black and grey sword and handed his ranger sword to his father. "Just in case," he said with a smile.

Finally, the emperor backed away and surveyed the three companions. After a moment, he raised his hands and declared, "I bid you all a well and prosperous journey! May you find knowledge and peace in your travels and return home in time for mead and merriment! May the spirit of the unseen guide you, Mage! May the fire of the dragon never leave your body, Dragon Knight! The Spirit of The Warrior will always be with Ranger!" he said, combining the creeds of the Ranger, Magi, and Dragon Knights. In turn, the three companions bowed to their emperor before turning down the stone road behind the western shore and into the west.

The three traveled on in silence for another hour or so, none knowing quite what to say. Atop the magnificent black horse, Tiberius never took his eyes off the wide stone road adorned with beautiful orange and red flowers. The Dragoon walked beside them with her head held high. She carried her ornated dragon faced helm under her left arm, and her mighty black spear strapped to her back. Michael followed behind them, and though he should have been paying attention to the road, found himself staring every now and then at the dragon knight.

As if sensing his eyes on her, Shayla asked, "Is there something I can help you with, Mage?"

Her accent was strange and thick to Michael's ears, which were burning bright red now. "I was just wondering, do you not require a horse, sir...ma'am...? I'm sorry, how should I address you?"

"I do not require a steed to travel upon, Mage," she replied without turning to face him. "The power of the dragon gives us unmatched speed and endurance, and we can travel many days unaided and without rest if needed." 0"I think you can drop the tough act now, Shayla. Your master is well outside of earshot," Tiberius said from the front of their group, a sly smile creeping on his face.

Her stern face began to turn into a broad, beautiful smile, and she laughed heartily and loud. "Force of habit, Tiberius. And you, Michael, may address me as Shayla. But my people prefer to be called by what we are, dragoons. Dragon Knights."

Michael pushed his horse alongside her and met her eyes. Though he was atop the brown and white beast, he and the Dragoon were the same height. He met her deep brown eyes and said, "Well met, Shayla. Forgive my ignorance. I'm learning that there is much I have yet to learn."

"Think nothing of it, Mage. You are young and curious as all children are."

"I am already sixteen years old, ma'am. Hardly a child."

At his words, the Dragoon let out another burst of laughter. "My child, sixteen of your years, is but still a babe to my sisters and me. Though I must admit, you are much smarter and well-mannered than other children I have met."

"And just how old are you, ma'am? If you do not mind me asking?"

It was Tiberius now who let out a loud laugh. He slowed his own pace to ride side by side with his two companions. "Now, that is not a polite question to ask at all, my friend."

"What do you mean, sir?"

"What he means," Shayla cut in, "is you should never ask a lady her age."

Michael looked down, embarrassed. "I'm sorry to offend you, ma'am."

"Oh, I'm not offended, young one. I'm simply answering as Tiberius would have. But, as well-intentioned as his guidance was, it is misplaced on me. We dragoons are used to speaking freely with one another. I find it refreshing to have someone speak so with me again, even if it is out of curiosity. And to answer your question, I am close to eighty years old by your Imperial reckoning."

Michael shot her a look of amazement. "Eighty!? How is that possible?"

"Now that," she said with a soft smile. "Is not a polite question to ask a Dragoon, for it is a matter we hold close to ourselves. Perhaps one day, we will talk on this again."

All talk between the three ceased at her words. Once the sun had reached its zenith, Tiberius called a stop to their journey for lunch. They pulled off the road into a small field of the orange and red flowers they had seen lining the rode they journeyed upon. Tiberius and Michael dug into a few tiny morsels of food stowed for them by the emperor's attendants while Shayla stood watch against the road.

After a few pensive moments, Michael looked at the Ranger and said, "I hope I did not offend our companion."

"Hardly," Tiberius replied, taking a small bite of bread and mutton. "If you had truly offended her, your head would no longer be attached to your shoulders. But I must caution you against indulging in your curious mind."

"Sir?"

"Some things that are of interest to you are secret to others. And though your mind will wander, as is natural of a young and curious mage, it is best to keep it to yourself. All will be revealed in time if you have but the eyes to see and the ears to hear."

Michael's mind flashed back to Zachary and Timothy in the dark field. The two had inadvertently revealed the rangers possessed a blessing they referred to as the *Sight.* Though they should not have, according to Tiberius. *Maybe whatever power the dragoons possess is of a similar, secret nature,* Michael thought. He nodded at Tiberius's guidance and resumed eating his lunch in silence.

An hour later, they were back on the road. Here and there, they met small groups of travelers, adorned in the orange and red dress of the Clastifet, making their way to the Imperial City for the festival. Their carts were laden down with all manner of food and baggage, clearly meaning to stay in the city for some time. After all, he had seen the night before, Tiberius wondered how the city could continue to accommodate so many people arriving.

The sun was starting to sink in front of them when Tiberius headed off the stone road into the dense forest to the north. They trudged on slow and steady in the thick woods until the stars began to twinkle through the closing light of day. After another hour of slow going in the forest, Tiberius called a halt to their travels.

They unpacked their horses in silence and created a small discreet camp inside the thickest part of the wood they could find. Neither of the three said a word all through the night. Tiberius, the ever-watchful protector, stood leaning against a tree, peering out into the darkness. Shayla stood on the opposite side of their camp from Tiberius, also keeping watch into the darkening wood. Michael lay wide awake for several hours in his bedroll near their low burning fire, looking at the stars. He wondered how long it would take them to reach the Forgotten Mountains and traverse its peaks into the Land Beyond.

He rolled over to face Tiberius. The man was stoic and relaxed as ever as he continued to peer out into the dark wood. He wondered if the Ranger's gift could even penetrate the dense blackness that seemed to envelop them. He had thought to ask but quickly decided against it. Tiberius would speak on these things in due time, he realized. Same with Shayla, he supposed.

He turned to face the Dragoon and was struck by the quiet intensity she gave off. Whereas Tiberius always appeared to be a mask of calm and collect, Shayla seemed to always be at a low boil. Anger and the will to fight just brewing below the surface of her tanned face. She would smile every now and then at some sight on the road, but it was all a mask. In her eyes, Michael could see she was alert and ready for battle. He could see the pain in her smile as if she hadn't smiled in years and was slowly learning to do so again.

He rolled onto his back again and let his mind wander on the days ahead. He had no sense of direction in these woods and had no idea how long their journey would take. He wondered what the fabled Forgotten Mountains would actually look like and how they would traverse them. He wondered how their journey would take and prayed that no searching eyes would be upon them.

He wondered what would be found on the other side of the mountains. What wonders or horrors would await them once they crossed to the other side. He wondered if the stars above him would look different on the other side. If they shined the same as they did here, or if they were as cold and dead as he knew the Land Beyond would be. He decided to start naming the star, a game he had done on nights aboard his father's meager fishing boat. But, after a few short minutes of naming the different stars, he closed his eyes and was fast asleep.

CHAPTER 11

THE ATTACK

Michael awoke in the blue dusk of morning. Far off in the sky, he could see the last vestiges of stars being washed out by the oncoming sun. All around him, he could hear the birds and beasts of the land on the hunt for their morning meal. He sat up from his bedroll, rubbed his eyes, and saw his companions still rooted where he left them the night before. He stood from his bed and moved to Tiberius's side.

"Good morning, Michael," Tiberius said as the Mage approached.

Michael stopped in his tracks, trying to collect his thoughts before answering. "Good morning, sir," he stammered. "Uneventful evening?"

"Quiet. Shayla and I did manage to catch a deer during the night, so we should be well-fed for a few days."

Michael felt his stomach growl in avarice. "I could use some breakfast."

Tiberius left his tree and escorted the Mage to a small burning fire on the other side of their camp where Shayla sat cooking a few rabbit haunches. Before long, they were mounted on their respective steeds and resumed their trek through the thick forest. The route they trudged upon was barely visible to the young Mage's eye. There was no road, or proper footpath that marked their way, yet Tiberius seemed to direct them where to go without any effort. Michael was astonished at the skill with which the Ranger traversed Clastifet's unknown forests, before reminding himself that he was the best warrior in the empire. And how fortunate he was to have him at his side.

The sun had now risen in the sky when Michael finally broke the silence between the three of them. "So, are we just going to travel the whole way in silence? At least tell me what our path back north is, sir."

"I was wondering the same thing, young Mage," Shayla said from his side. "This is my first time abroad in your empire, and all I have seen of it is trees and roads. Except for your sprawling capital city."

"My young Mage, would you care to tell our companion where we are at present?"

"Well, our empire comprises ten kingdoms with ten kings, my good dragon knight," Michael began. "Presently, we are in the Kingdom of Clastifet, to the city's immediate west."

"Very good," Tiberius added, his eyes scanning the trees and wood line around them. "Our path is to roughly make a large semi-circle around the country until we arrive in the northern part of the empire, in the Kingdom of Childers."

"So, you mean to take us through the White Kingdom?" Michael asked. The memory of King White in the emperor's chamber hanging heavy on him.

"In another hour, we'll be crossing the Snow River and be well into your homeland," Tiberius replied with a chuckle. "Relax, my friend. King White is still in the capital, no doubt giving my father an earful about the rude interruption we gave them."

"I hope so, Master Ranger," Michael replied.

"White King, Black King. Orange King, peach king. Such a strange empire you Axtons have with your ten kingdoms and ten kings and one empire. In Narzeth, there is one ruler and one alone," Shayla replied. "And the rule of the one is unmatched and unchecked, and all are subservient to him."

"And who is the ruler of the Narzeth now, Shayla?" the Ranger asked.

"There is no ruler now, Tiberius. You know this better than most. But as for my new home, it is strange compared to what we were raised in."

"Yes, I suppose it is a little odd," Michael replied. "Once upon a time, the rulers of this land were greedy and vengeful and warred for years untold over control of their little slivers of land. They had no mind for friendship or peace or unity. But after the Narzeth invaded and swept through our country unchecked, one mighty warrior banded all the generals of the warring clans together and forced their combined armies to repel the conquests. When it was over, the generals wanted to install him as High King of the land. But he was a wise man, and instead united all the kingdoms under one unified empire. In that way, each kingdom could retain their identities and cultures and lands but would be bound together always."

"A King of Kings would do much in keeping all under control," the Dragon Knight replied. "One King above all who would direct and lead as they saw fit."

To someone not born in our county, that would make the most sense," Tiberius added. "But that kind of rule would not last. The clans that controlled our country each had their own ways with their own customs and beliefs and ways of wishing to live. To force them all to conform and give up their identities would have driven them to revolt. Instead, the empire rules above them. Protects them from harm and allows the Ten Kingdoms relative sovereignty within their borders. In this way, the ten could remain as they had in the days long gone, while owing tribute to the true ruler above."

"He must have been a very wise and respected warrior to accomplish that," Shayla replied. To her people, the strength of one's character and arms meant everything.

"They say he was one of the most cunning warriors in the world and one of the best commanders of soldiers. And his loyalty to the people was unmatched. He was Tiberius's ancestor, Alexander Axton, may his name never be forgotten," Michael said with reverence.

Shayla turned to see Tiberius upon his horse. In her mind, she pictured him as his ancestor had been. "That was his sword then?" she asked.

"Aye. He carried this sword himself when he first established the Rangers. After the founding of our empire, it was said to have been reforged by the dwarves as a parting gift when they left the capital," he replied.

"There were actual dwarves in the capital?" she asked, surprised.

"So they say. They were freed from Narzeth along with the Magi, just as you and your sisters. And as thanks for their liberation, they built the Imperial City and taught our smiths all they knew."

"This Alexander Axton sounds like a well-respected man. It is no wonder you and your father are the men you are."

"Why do you say that?" Michael asked.

"In the year that I have known them, I have known them both to be strong in body, spirit, and mind. They have a heart for peace, but a mind for war. They have respect for all people of this world, but fiercely guard their countrymen and the lands of their dominion. Most men upon the earth seek to gain only power and wish to dominate all those they see as lesser. The gods have truly blessed my sisters with mercy to be here and not there."

Michael thought about this while Shayla continued asking Tiberius about the history of the empire. The Axton Emperors had indeed led their realm through years of building and war. It was true they met their enemies with unforgiving wrath, and their submitted foes with unconditional mercy. It was hard for Michael to imagine any other way to live. He felt blessed to have been born in this way of life and at this time than any other.

They traveled on through the woods for many hours before stopping for the night. They settled into a small clearing alongside a small stream they had been following for some time. Tiberius had said this stream flowed from the Forgotten Mountains, and it was the surest way to know their direction in such dense and dark forestry.

"We will hold our path along this stream for another ten days. Before long, it will lead to the base of the mountains," Tiberius said. "From there, we will skirt the mountain's foot until we reach the Ice Steps far in the White Kingdom's northwest."

"Are we in White now, sir?" Michael asked.

"Aye," Tiberius responded, dismounting his horse to begin preparing their camp. "How does it feel to be home again?"

Michael thought about how he felt for some time before saying, "The White Kingdom hasn't been my home for many years, sir. Though, if I'm honest, it is somewhat strange to be back here."

After a blazing fire was lit, Michael prepared something a little substantial for them to eat with their relatively fresh deer meat. But even with the fire burning bright, Michael found it hard to see almost anything outside the ring of light. The shadows in this forest seemed to him to be somehow deeper and appeared as if no light could penetrate their darkness. It was almost as if the night was fighting against the invasion of light in its midst.

I must just be more tired than I thought, he reasoned. At least there is a nice breeze to cool us.

After they ate, Michael settled into his bedroll silently and observed his companions. Shayla leaning on a tree, her black and grey spear nestled between her folded arms. Ever the shepherd, Tiberius, sat off to the side of their camp, his pipe in mouth, and sword in hand for cleaning. The man always seemed alert to what was going on around them. As if he were somehow a part of the world and yet present at all times.

"Do you ever sleep, sir?" Michael asked. It was true enough that Tiberius hadn't appeared to sleep the night before. Or when he had been on the road days ago with all the rangers.

Tiberius and Shayla both chuckled at the Mage's question. "I only sleep soundly when I'm in my bed," Tiberius said. "Years of war and battle and command have helped me learn how to sleep lightly and still be aware of all around me. I'd imagine Shayla is much the same way."

"Indeed," she responded. "We dragoons don't sleep unless we are safely tucked into our beds behind high walls."

"And as for seeing in this darkness, our gift of *Sight* penetrates almost any patch of darkness. Though to be fair, it does seem darker than most nights," Tiberius finished.

"It does indeed, doesn't it?" Shayla chimed in, moving to stand next to Tiberius. "Perhaps some storm is brewing off in the distance."

"I don't think so, Shayla. The air around us is still and calm, and the forest smells are still as they were when we arrived."

"The forest smells?" Michael asked from his small pallet on the ground.

"Aye, the forest smells. If you spend enough time in the wilderness as I have, you come to see the oncoming storms not just from the clouds and winds, but also from the change in smell around you. Those of us with a mind for it can smell the rain and snow coming before they arrive."

"I suppose I should start becoming more aware of these things if I'm to be out in the wild much longer."

Tiberius laughed at the boy's words. "Indeed, you should. Before long, you will be a ranger yourself! Now, sleep, my friend."

Michael nodded and stretched out in his pallet, staring at the fire in their camp. Beyond the burning embers, his companions again stood facing out into the woods. Continually searching for some unseen threat. Whatever tense feelings he had been feeling upon their departure from the capital were dissolved. He turned over and let the wind's sound through the branches slowly rock him to a deep peacefulness.

The sound of the rustling leaves grew louder and louder throughout the night. He tossed and turned and tried to pull more cover to his face expecting a cold wind to rip through at any moment.

But the wind never came.

And the sound of rustling leaves only grew louder and louder.

"Michael, get behind me!" Tiberius bellowed, jarring the Mage awake.

Michael shot up and stared around, bewildered. "What's happening?"

"No questions, behind me, now!" Tiberius yelled again, sword in hand.

Michael bolted up and sprinted behind Tiberius. Shayla was at his side in an instant, her dragon head helm over her face, spear at her side, and legs bent. They both stood silent in the forest, eyes drawn to some unseen force moving in the night. Michael finally regained his senses and heard the loud rustling.

He looked around, frantic and scared, while Tiberius's face had changed from the happiness and joviality he had seen hours earlier to blankness and determination. Then all at once, the noise ceased, and the forest became as quiet as a graveyard. No sound could be heard in any direction, save for Michael's own rapid panting, which turned into a high-pitched wail as dark figures burst through the tree line in front of them.

At least seven of them, dressed all in white armor with swords drawn, rushed faster than a bolt of lightning towards the two warriors. Tiberius was taken aback for a moment at the sight of them. Not for the armor they wore, nor for the sudden violent attack. It was their eyes, burning fire bright against the darkness around them. His mind raced back to that night in the Childers Kingdom. To thoughts of a worn-out beggar, and his fiery hollow eyes.

Oh, no, Tiberius thought, refocusing his mind.

Without speaking, Shayla sprang forward with such swiftness the dirt underneath her was kicked up in great heaps. With a swipe of her spear, all seven of the enchanted attackers were pushed onto their backs. Tiberius sprinted to the left of their flank and sliced through two of them on the ground before they could regain their composure. Shayla turned to the right side and swiped broad again, this time with the blade end of her spear. Two of the attackers were sliced clean open, their insides falling out of their armor as they dropped dead to the ground.

Two more of the attackers charged the Ranger and Dragoon. One tried to swing his sword down on Tiberius with as much force as his limbs could handle, but he was no match for the veteran ranger. Tiberius easily parried his violent swing, ducked to the other side of his assailant, and sliced upwards. The steel of his father's sword cut through the white armor like butter, sending a light spray of red-hot blood to the ground.

Shayla jumped in the air over the head of her approaching foe. The momentum of his thrust against her sent him tumbling down. She landed behind him, and with a mighty thrust of her spear, skewered the man in the back of his neck. She gave a violent twist of her spear, breaking the bones in the attacker's neck with a loud crack.

It was over in less than a minute, and they were finally left face to face with their last attacker. They stood side by side, poised to meet his assault. But it never came. In his bright white armor, the enchanted soldier stood rooted against the pair, a blank expression on his face. The fire in his eyes burned low, but all of a sudden, grew brighter and brighter. A blood-curdling scream rang out over the woods, forcing the companions to fall to their knees and cover their ears. In an instant, the man's body was turned to dust.

Tiberius and Shayla, the two warriors who had long ago witnessed the power of magic at Vermillion Pass, looked on in horror as the man's armor and broadsword fell heavy to the ground as the last of his body evaporated. The screaming rang out over the woods for a moment before abruptly ending without an echo.

Tiberius was on his feet first, his eyes scanning the darkness for signs of another attack. Shayla leapt from her crouched position fifty feet into a grand pine tree to do the same. Michael, who had finally stopped his screaming, stood and made his way to Tiberius. But the Ranger held out a hand for the Mage to stop, his eyes never leaving the darkened woods in front of them.

"I see no one else, Ranger," Shayla called from atop the trees.

"Neither do I. But stay on the lookout while I pack our camp. We need to leave this place now."

Tiberius sheathed his sword and turned towards the camp. He began to pack various items left about, snuffed their campfire out, and readied the horses all in silence. Michael stood watching him, scared and confused at what had just happened. He tried to conjure some measure of understanding, but nothing came to him. Though short-lived, the battle was more intense and frightening than anything the young Mage had ever experienced. It was, after all, the first battle he had ever seen.

It's nothing like the books, Michael thought. The screams and smells and blood...

"Mage!" Tiberius barked, drawing Michael out of his daze. "Get your bedroll packed and your horse saddled. We leave at once!"

"But, sir, what was—"

"Questions later! Bedroll and saddle. Now!"

Michael was in motion at Tiberius's orders. His meager bed was rolled and stowed in a few short minutes, his saddle placed upon his brown and white horse, and they were off. Tiberius gave out a high-pitched whistle, and a mighty thud sounded from behind them. Shayla had joined her companions, who rode hard along the stream as fast as the beasts that carried them could go. They rode on through the rest of the deep black night in silence, the two warriors continually scanning their surroundings, and the Mage lost in confusion.

The landscapes began to slowly change as they rode on. The thick, green forest slowly melted away into more open fields. The air had dropped several degrees, sending thick steam from their mouths. Despite the drastic change in temperature, neither of the three moved to warm themselves. Their combined fear and anger over the abrupt attack compelled them on unbothered.

It well after dawn before Tiberius called a halt to their relentless ride. The horses were panting hard in the brisk morning air, foam beginning to form in their mouths from dehydration. Even after their stop, Tiberius did not move from his saddle. He looked in every direction, extending his *Sight* as far as he could.

Dark clouds seemed to hover over them, yet the familiar smell of rain could not be found in the air. His uneasiness grew more and more with each passing second. The strangeness of the weather around them gave him a moment of paus, deciding if they should continue on throughout the day. He looked beyond them, seeking for any sign of threat to their desperate flight.

In the distance, he could see birds and beasts out freely in the woods. No tracks save the ones their horses had left could be seen in any direction. He took it all in, and after a few contemplative moments, decided to put his worries aside. For now, anyway. They had endured a hard ride from the woods and needed some respite.

After a moment of surveilling the landscapes, Tiberius removed himself from his horse and began to guide it to the edge of the stream they had been following. Michael followed suit, unsure of what to say, if anything at all. Shayla again bounded high into the only large tree around some one hundred yards from where they had stopped. After the horses were watered, Tiberius guided them without reins to a small stone off the stream in a patch of thick grass and deadwood. Michael followed his companion, frustration growing in his mind.

Michael disembarked from his horse and looked around at the clearing where they now found themselves. Though it was a few hours after daybreak, it still seemed to him that the dusk of night had followed them on into the morning. He looked around as best he could in the haze but could not decide if a storm were approaching them or not. He had thought to maybe make a new fire to fight against the encroaching dark but did not want to risk giving themselves away.

His head was still swimming after all that had transpired when he dared to break the silence. "What were those things?"

The Ranger removed his sword and began wiping frozen blood from its blade. "Those things were men, Michael. Enchanted just as the beggar was when I fought the undead."

The memories of their fiery eyes flashed across the young Mage's mind. He had read about the power of enchanting someone. But having seen it in person now, a shiver went up his spine. "What do you think it means?"

Tiberius pondered his question for a moment before responding. "I think our journey from the city has been revealed, Michael. I think there is indeed an unseen foe conspiring against our journey north. And I think you should some sleep if you can. We cannot linger here long."

"Where will we go? We can't possibly turn back."

"No, we cannot and will not turn back," Tiberius responded, casing his sword. "I will think about what to do next while you sleep."

Michael wondered how he could sleep after what had just happened but knew there was no point in arguing with the leader of their small party. He didn't even bother unpacking his bedroll or searching for a pack for food. He slumped against a wide rock, closed his eyes, and quieted the voices in his head. He trusted his companions with all his heart and knew they would not lead them to danger if they could avoid it. In a few minutes, his mind at ease, the Mage fell fast asleep.

The Ranger let out another whistle, followed at once by the thud of Shayla landing nearby. She strolled to where the two had stopped, removing her dragon-shaped helm to breathe in the fresh air.

"Nothing is following us," she reported. "But the clouds give me some pause."

"Me too, Shayla. But the boy and the beasts need some rest."

"Aye, that they do. I cannot imagine the shock the young one must have felt."

"How about the shock you and I must have felt?" Tiberius asked, looking deep into her deep brown eyes. "What would the commander of the dragoons take last night's folly to mean?" He had already drawn his conclusions but was curious to see what this stranger to their empire would have to say on the matter.

"I would say that we have an enemy on our heels. But not a normal enemy. From what you told me about your encounter with the undead Narzeth, and from what we saw last night, I would say our enemy is a magician of some kind."

Tiberius winced at the word "magician" but knew the dragon knight meant no offense. In the Axton Empire, a magician was a child's entertainer, not a wielder of real magic. He decided to let it go, reminding himself to educate her some other time. For the moment, he concluded that she spoke true. A person who could wield magic was resisting their attempts to reach the outpost. The most troubling thought though, and one he did not share with Shayla, was that their unseen enemy could wield magic at all.

"Did Michael say anything about the men who attacked us?" Shayla asked, settling in next to Tiberius.

"You mean about their armor?"

Shayla nodded. "Is he not from this White Kingdom?"

"Aye, he is, Shayla. But, no. He didn't say anything about the men. Either he didn't notice, or he doesn't have the words in him yet to talk about it. And I will not be the one to talk about things unless he brings them up."

"Why is that?" the Dragoon asked, stretching out on the ground next to him.

"He is trying to find his way in the world. Best he comes to things in his own time untainted by our cynicism."

Shayla nodded in understanding. She closed her eyes and began slowly humming a strange and beautiful tune Tiberius vaguely recognized. It comforted him to hear her voice in such turbulent times. He lit his pipe and settled against the weather-worn stone, lost in his own thoughts. He needed a new approach to getting through the White Kingdom, and he needed the answer before Michael woke from his sleep. But the intensity of the past few days began to weigh on the veteran Ranger.

The clouds above began to grow darker, blotting out the morning sun. He felt his eyes becoming heavy, something he had not experienced in many years. He rested his head against the stone, a feeling of drowsiness overcoming him. All the worry and stress of the past few hours melted off of him. Peace and tranquility washed over him, and for the first time in days, he closed his eyes and fell fast asleep.

CHAPTER 12

THE WAR RETURNS

He opened his eyes.

Red dirt crunched and crumbled beneath his worn black leather boots. The hot air was filled with burning sand that penetrated every corner of his body and stung his dried eyes. Every breath he took was torture. Every move he made felt like it would be his last. But his mind and his spirit only knew rage.

Rage against himself for failing his men. Rage against the folly of the last five centuries that brought them thousands of miles from home. Rage against the Narzeth, slaughtering his rangers. And that rage is what carried him through a dead sprint over the featureless red desert to kill as many of the heathen enemies as he could.

At his back, he had nearly two hundred of the empire's finest soldiers and knights. Each of the brave men and women were ready to fight and die wherever he may lead them. He had brought them from their encampment to reinforce his own men on the western flank of Vermillion Pass. Halfway on their march, he saw the advancing Narzeth. The war made had made his *Sight* almost supernatural in its clarity and power.

He saw them overtake his men, and his legs were in motion.

A predator moving in for his kill.

Make haste! he had said. Our brothers are in battle!

His pace was relentless. His speed unmatched. Every one of the two hundred trained and battle-tested warriors endeavored to keep his stride. Every one of the two hundred trained and battle-tested warriors could not keep up with him, such was the anger and desperation that drove him forward.

He had been five hundred yards off when he saw his men take contact from the enemy. Their ancient foe had used the cover of nearby red and orange canyons to conceal their attack.

He was two hundred yards away when he heard the screaming through the furious dust storm that swirled around them. Lighting split through the swirling dust, sending large hails of glass tumbling down to the red earth.

He was one hundred yards away when he could see the Narzeth overwhelming his men. Their crimson cloaks were covered in the blood of his rangers, who continued to fight on.

At fifty yards, he could smell death emitting from the mass of bodies in front of him. It churned his stomach and reinforced his resolve as he flew into the sea of death in front of him.

His sword was lead weight in his hand. That didn't stop him from swiping broad at the enemy's back, cutting down six Narzeth in one stroke. Their armor, as tough as it was, was nothing compared to Imperial steel.

His shield was a thousand pounds heavier than his sword. He bashed it against the advancing enemy with such force their armor caved in on their chest. His screams of anger pierced the sounds of battle.

Rangers! he had said. I am with you!

At their commander's cries, his battered men regrouped and fought back. They were surrounded and outmanned, but that didn't stop them from pushing back with all they had left. They would either live through the day or die and join The Warrior in the afterlife. Their momentum began to slow. More of his rangers died, hacked down by axes, and bludgeoned by maces.

Fight back against these bastards or be shamed to our Emperor!

They heard trumpets sound over the storm and battle. The soldiers who had followed him were now encircled around the melee, destroying all the remaining Narzeth. In a matter of moments, it was over. The living rangers, covered in blood and shaking from anger, stood panting and coughing violently in the dust storm. Fifty strong and loyal rangers who would never see the sunrise over their country again laid dead at their feet.

He hung his head in despair and closed his eyes.

"What in the hell is that!?" Michael shouted over the screeching.

He and Tiberius galloped hard through the dense forest heading atop the black warhorse, bound for some safe haven he hoped would come soon. His own beautiful brown and white horse had been engulfed by the shadows that seemed to be clawing out from every direction to swallow them up. Shayla sprinted alongside them, barely breaking a sweat, but nonetheless infuriated.

"It doesn't matter! Press that damned beast till its legs give out!"

They had thought it was an oncoming storm by the swiftness the dark clouds had overtaken them. By the time Shayla knew what was happening, it was too late. The darkness they had mistaken for storm clouds had descended from the sky to engulf them. She was on her feet in a flash and saw the darkness around them swirl and converge into one large swirling black void. From inside the void, she could see a thousand hungry eyes peering out at them, and a thousand hungry mouths salivating at their intended prey.

The horses started wailing against the void, when a thick black cloud shot from within it, grabbed Michael's horse, and pulled it screaming into black nothingness. Panic and fear overtook them at the sight of such monstrous power. Suddenly, a blade of black mist shot out from the void, trying to pierce whatever it could.

She had leapt to the trees overhead out of instinct, but far below on the forest floor came the screams of agony as Tiberius was struck square in his chest. To his credit, Michael had been on his feet at the sound of his companion's cries. He had no weapon of his own but had brandished his heavy ebony and ivory wand. At his roars of anger, the black void broke apart in a blast that shook the ground beneath them.

She returned to the ground and threw her companions onto the remaining horse. Michael could barely do anything but hold on for dear life as the beast bolted away from their camp. Shayla dared not stand and fight something this strong, especially with defenseless Michael alone in the woods. She heard a great screeching behind her and turned her head as she ran to see the black void following them, groping arms and hungry mouths and the thousand eyes yearning to consume them. Shayla and Michael shouted at the top of their lungs to their leader, but Tiberius could not hear them. All he could do was cry out in great agony and close his eyes.

He opened his eyes.

He was walking the dusty desert floor, tears dried on his face. At his feet were the remains of over one hundred of the empire's soldiers. Their bodies broken, blood pooled around their corpses, eyes blank and staring at the featureless desert sky.

One hundred men died, and for nothing, he heard Trevin say over his shoulder.

They did their duty, Sergeant, he replied, hollow and numb. In truth, he didn't believe his own words.

Forget duty, sir. This was a fool's errand, and now these men are dead.

Trevin was right, he knew. This had been a fool's errand, made by the fools directing this war in his father's stead. He surveyed the massive stone building they had called a library. Its worn and weathered ornate markings would have made it beautiful in its day. In his mind's eye, he could envision thousands of Magi living in such a grand place. Now, like all things in Narzeth, it lay in ruins. He prayed to the invisible gods above that this war would be over soon.

But the gods of the empire were far away back home. The gods of their realm had no business in Narzeth.

How long must we linger in this place, sir?

Until High Sorcerer Cycret arrives to inspect it.

Trevin looked all around him, inspect the dead and broken things that littered their surroundings. The desert winds had worn the once majestic place down to almost nothing. The once vibrant and beautiful colors and tapestries that had adorned the massive stone walls were faded and cracking.

Such is the way in this place and death and evil. Such is the way of all things in time.

Gods damn this war. Gods damn this land. And gods damn the Narzeth, Trevin had said.

A swift dust storm rose up out of the east. The land itself seemed to be trying to repel the empire from its shores. Tiberius hung his head against the oncoming sand and closed his eyes.

He hung his head against the oncoming dust storm and closed his eyes.

The screeching around them had ceased, yet the impenetrable darkness hung heavy around them as they pressed on through the dense, black woods. Their unknown path twisted and turned around large frozen boulders and gnarled dead trees that seemed to be clawing out for them. A mighty terror filled their hearts as they flew to some new haven far away from the evil levied against them.

All of a sudden, the dark clouds around them rushed together and converged into a thick black wall, and the demonic screeching returned louder than before. Michael, try as he might, couldn't rein in the horse fast enough. The mighty beast let out a horrible cry of pain as it crashed hard into the thick black veil ejecting the Mage and Ranger from the saddle. While the warhorse had collapsed on the spot, Michael and Tiberius seemed to shoot through it. Shayla leapt into the sky, twisting and turning in the air like a trained dancer, landing where the others had fallen.

Michael let out a cry of terror as the void retook shape in front of them. Shayla pulled her lance to her chest and crouched low as a thousand eyes took form inside the swirling cloudy mass. She didn't know what good it would do against the foul beast of blackness, but she was a dragon knight. She had faced down untold numbers of enemies alongside her sisters in arms. She was proud and mighty. And she would die fighting with her spear in hand.

Michael scrambled to cover his unconscious companion. "You will not have him, monster!" he shouted at the void.

A shrill high laugh pierced their ears, forcing the Mage to cover his head in pain. Though in pain herself, the dragoon kept her eyes fixated upon the demonic beast in front of her. The void began moving slowly towards them, a shark stalking its weakened prey. The evil creature expanded its cloudy form in all directions, obscuring their vision of the forest around them. Out of the center of its black body emerged small lesser dark clouds. Michael had recovered his wits and fumbled around in his cloak for the wand. Though he knew no magic would come from it, he was determined to not die against such a beast without it in his hands.

The smaller clouds slowly twisted and folded in on themselves until the figures of several large black wolves took shape. No eyes filled their sockets, just impermeable nothingness. Their twisted ethereal mouths twitched open to reveal smaller swirling black masses in place of where their tongues and teeth should have been. The wolves crouched low, eye to eye with Michael.

The first wolf lunged at him but was met midair by Shayla's violent spear thrust to its head. Just as quickly as it lunged, the black wolf returned to smoke and dissipated. Another wolf lunged at the downed man, and another wolf was quickly cut down by the Dragoon's swift attack.

Two more wolves moved towards Michael. Shayla flew at them and swiped their bodies back into clouds before turning to face the last wolf. Black sockets stared back at her. The opened mouth of the beast closed and slowly curled into an evil, human smile. Neither side moved as they stared at each other for many heavy moments.

The shrieking ceased as the void seemed to retreat in on itself. Shayla stood from her crouched pose, unsure of what had just happened, but glad that it was over. In an instant the void expanded back out to its fullest, emitting a powerful force that knocked Shayla off her impossibly powerful legs and onto the frozen ground.

Out of the shrieking void a dozen or more of the ethereal black wolves slowly emerged. Shayla staggered to her feet and began to pull her dragon-shaped helm over her face. Michael continued fumbling for his wand. Tiberius was shaking and crying out loud, adding to the cacophony of noise around them.

—

He opened his eyes.

He stood on a high orange-colored mountain, surveying the red dust bowl beneath him. A vast encampment of all the assembled Imperial forces was laid out before him in the plain leading up to the pass. The grey and black banners of the empire were blowing hard and strong in the hot filthy wind.

Upon a jagged ridge to his left, he saw his men pouring over maps of the valley below and sharpening their swords. He saw the sentinels to his right, staring silent and unmoving at some unknown thing in the distance. They did not know if they were to enter the fray tomorrow but would be ready to fight and die for their emperor all the same.

We attack at dawn, his father's voice had said from behind him.

He turned.

His father looked to have aged more than the five years that had passed since the last time they saw each other on Zelinka's shores. Five years since he had sailed across the ocean with his rangers to meet their country's eternal foes in battle. He had despaired countless times over the years in the face of such hardship. But being with his father here and now and in this place brought him great comfort. That same comfort extended to all the men and women of the Imperial Army. Their spirits were renewed. Their will to win reinvigorated.

We'll be ready, he assured his father.

I know, his father had said. I expect tomorrow will be the last battle of this god's forsaken war.

He embraced his father atop that rocky death filled hilltop. Abandoned were all formality and respect of their stations. He was a scared little boy again in need of his father's love. Neither of them broke their embrace. They placed their hands on one another's shoulders.

I am glad you are with me, he told his father, here at what might be the end of all things.

I am too, Ti, his father replied. Tomorrow will either be the last day for them or for us.

His father hung his head for a moment. When he looked up, he had tears in his eyes, something Tiberius had not seen since his mother passed. His father breathed hard.

You are my greatest accomplishment, son. And not for your soldiering or for your duty, but for the man you have become. If we make it home, I pray to the gods that you will become a better leader than I could ever be.

They broke their grasp and bowed to each other. Tiberius smiled, the first in a long time. He turned again to study the valley, wondering what would come tomorrow. He closed his eyes and drew in a deep breath.

The wolves were slowly advancing on them now, eager to savor the fear emanating from their prey. The screaming around them was deafening and continued to push Shayla down to one knee. Michael imagined the hot breath he would have felt if the wolves had been real beasts of nature and not some demon's apparitions, but all he felt was cold. He continued searching for the wand even though he didn't know why he was drawn to it at this moment. It would be pointless to even try and use magic. His mind was screaming at him to take cover from the oncoming assault, but his body persisted in its search.

The screaming from the void slowly morphed into the high squealing laughter. *This is it,* Michael thought.

The wolves hunched down in unison, and their wide nothing mouths opening impossibly wide.

Here it comes! Michael yelled at himself.

Suddenly, he felt it. The wood as hard as the most rigid iron, the cold metal handled grip. He grasped the wand and thrust it from his cloak, bellowing a last defiant scream against death's black void. But as the wand burst from his robes, a surge of brilliant light strobed out in waves, illuminating the darkness that surrounded them.

Brighter than the sun but not blinding to the eyes, the light flung the wolves away from the companions and back into the void. The brilliant ephemeral light continued to strobe, pulsing wave after wave of energy from its tip. Shayla stared at the beautiful light in wonder. In her long life she had never beheld such a wonderous and comforting sight. She could feel her spirit being renewed by its presence and began to slowly sit up again.

Michael struggled to his feet with his wand held aloft and shuffled towards the void. The light spurted out like a violent fire yet burned nothing but the inky black hole assaulting them. Shayla finally found the strength to stand, and rushed to Tiberius's side to shield him from whatever was to come next. The void began to scream again, but this was no scream of victory or taunting. This was the scream of agony and defeat. A cry of pain not felt in ages past, at the power the young Mage now held against it. It was a scream of death.

As the blaring screeching reached its ear-shattering crescendo, the void collapsed in on itself to a small black ball and shot into the sky away from them. Michael dropped the wand from his hand and fell to his knees. As he did, the dazzling light dissipated, and the morning sunshine rained down on them. Behind him, he heard Tiberius moan and writhe around on the ground.

Retrieving the wand, he rushed to join Shayla at the Ranger's side. Their companion and leader began to violently seize and convulse on the ground. He was screaming inanely to an unseen force around him as if locked in the throes of death. Michael and Shayla looked at each other, unsure of what to do next. The void, in all its demonic evil, was gone. But their leader and friend was in agony beyond all comprehension. Michael dropped to his knees, defeated. He closed his eyes and began to sob.

He opened his eyes.

He saw death. Everywhere he turned, everywhere he looked, death and destruction met his waking eyes.

Bodies, broken, and bleeding littered the ground at his feet. To his left, he saw his own men cutting through the enemy without abandon. He saw the soldiers and knights of the empire being crushed under heavy axes and hammers to his right. The empire and Narzeth were locked in a bitter, furious final battle in the valley of Vermillion Pass. The warriors of the realm were determined to press on to their unseen destination.

No. Not a destination, he thought. A goal. A goal to kill every last one of their enemies where they stood.

Good.

He looked and studied his shield and sword, and after a few solemn moments of contemplation, decided to drop his shield in the red sand. He would not need it where he was going. It would slow him down anyways. He would either die with his sword in his hand or stand victorious amongst his countrymen.

His eyes focused.

He took one last heavy breath into his worn out body as he charged into the fray.

Flaming arrows crashed down on them from every direction from both the Imperial archers and the Narzeth's bowmen. He swung his sword in all directions without regard for friend or foe. He trusted his men to stay out of his way. He danced around the oncoming assault and lashed out violently at all within arm's length. His body pushed through the throng of warriors in the field.

He had danced this dance his whole life. He had felt the music of battle resonate in his heart and soul since he was a small boy. But now, so far from the woods and streams and mountains of the empire, it was a different kind of tune. Not one of honor and respect. Nor of passion and love. Here, on the far side of the world, this was the music of anger and frustration. Of death and anger. Of murderous intent made real.

He ducked an axe swing from one of his enemies and cut his legs out from underneath him. He sidestepped a great sword's killing blow and stabbed the attacker square in his chest, piercing his red armor. Thick hot blood rained from his dead body onto the sand.

A lancer charged him. He took careful aim and threw his sword, slicing his attacker's face open. Even with all the chaos around him, he heard the small weak bones crunch and break in his enemy's face. He rushed forward, rolled to avoid the swipe of another sword, retrieved his own from the dirt, and brought it up hard, relieving his adversary of his arm. The man screamed in agony at Tiberius' strike. He studied the man for a moment before relieving him of his head too.

He grasped the enemy's lance in his hands, swung it in great, violent circles, cutting a swath into their ranks. At his back were his rangers like a sea of black death slowly creeping their way through the melee. They shielded themselves on all sides, and with their free hands, cut and stabbed countless of the heathen enemies.

He heard a deep horn bellow and the sound of drums. The symphony of war. The march of death.

Hulking, massive, Imperial Berserkers ran through the throng, their wild screams of blood lust echoing throughout the canyon. Their maces crushed their enemies flat. Their axes splintered the enemy shields. One Berserker dragged a Narzeth to the ground and was pulling him apart with his bare hands.

He heard a lone voice, loudly singing a beautiful song that penetrated the furious battle's noise. Many of the assembled men on both sides of the struggle stopped their attacks, searching for the source of the beautiful melody. The voice was joined by a mighty chorus that drowned out all the noise in the pass. Tiberius looked atop a nearby ridge as a thin cloud covered the blood-red sun. He pushed his *Sight* towards the cloud, and a smile burst onto his blood-soaked face.

The dragoons were entering the fight at last.

Shayla was in front, her dragon armor shining brightly against the sun. They landed with such force that hundreds of the enemy were knocked flat on their backs. The dragoons huddled together and began to sing again. Then, like a flurry of arrows, they leapt from their formation. Jumping and hurdling around the battle, stabbing and sweeping the enemy in all directions.

Shayla let out a high-pitched scream that pierced his ears. She was answered with a chorus of singing. He saw her kick off the chest of one of the advancing Narzeth with such force his chest bone was pushed out of his back, sending his spine falling to the sand and dirt ground. All who witnessed such power fled from her wrath, but more dragoons fell from the sky on to them, crushing them under their legs.

He heard thunder crack the featureless sky as dark clouds gathered out of nowhere. Lightning shot from the heavens onto the battlefield. Blocks of ice the size of carriages dropped like ripe apples onto them.

The Battle-Mages had been loosed into the fray.

Many were out amongst the men shielding the Imperials from the attacks from the sky. Wizards were out in force now, healing the wounded as they went. They hurled massive bolts of lightning and balls of blazing fire from their wands as they went. The smell of searing flesh from magical fire stung his nose. A smell he would never forget as long as he lived.

Sudden cries of cheer went up over the Imperials in the field. The sentinels were in the field, clearing a path through the Narzeth. His father had come to battle.

He saw his father in his black and grey armor moving like a great lion amid the battle. Age had slowed him from his former might, but he was The Spirit of the Warrior. Leading his men from the front like their ancestors had for hundreds of years. They met in the middle of the fight, locked arms, and bowed their foreheads together. If they were to die today, they would die together, the last of the Axtons. They would die where all warriors and servants of the empire should die. In battle and in service to their country.

They were back to back, striking down all the Narzeth that dared approach as sheep into the mouths of ravenous beasts. Word of the emperor's presence in the battle quickly filled the air. All of the assembled enemies rushed them, eager to claim the glory of killing their real enemy. All who came within striking distance were dispatched with vengeful haste by the two Axtons.

The lightning ceased. Thunder the sound of a million explosions cracked overhead. The temperature in that desert wasteland dropped to just above freezing. A deep, evil roar boomed over Vermillion Pass as all the fighters went silent.

Fire emerged from the sky, flying in all directions to form a wide circle over the valley. Fire from the ring began joining together, creating an enormous flaming disc that hovered above the battlefield. Another deafening crack of thunder rang out. The fire slowly turned a bright green, the flames in the middle a deep black. The black of night. In the black, he saw stars.

Stars that now began to move towards the earth below.

Beasts of legend were now pouring out of a flaming green ring in droves. Dragon fire rained down in all directions. Balrogs, with their massive bodies of shadow and enormous flaming wings, ran their hands over the embattled Narzeth. Frozen leviathans larger than the Unity Tower slithered around the chasms, freezing the enemy archers on their posts.

The smell of burning flesh and the sound of crunching bone filled his senses. He was frozen on the spot as he stared bewildered at the monstrosities that surrounded the field. Overhead, a great and terrible black dragon reared its head back and shot forth a steady flow of fire that obliterated the enemy encampment beyond the valley.

Then all at once, the terrible beasts turned into a translucent light and were gone. He fell on the ground from the shock, unable to move or think.

Those of the enemy that had not perished regrouped to begin their attack anew when, without warning, they froze on the spot as if time itself had stopped. They each began to scream a deep blood-curdling cry as each one of the remaining enemies in the field slowly turned to ash where they stood. He stared dumbstruck until a soft breeze penetrated the valley and blew all the ashen Narzeth away into oblivion.

A cacophony of cheering and screaming erupted over the pass. He laughed uncontrollably until his laughter changed into great tears of fear that began to roll down his bloodied face. He fell to the ground, and all around him went quiet. He shut his eyes, hoping to erase all he had seen. But the sights still lingered in his mind's eye, seared into his memory from now until forever.

CHAPTER 13

THE PATH FORWARD

He forced his eyes open to the daylight streaming upon his worn and tired face. The faint sounds of birds out for their morning breakfast chirped through the straw roof. He tried to blink, but each attempt felt like the weight of the world was forcing his eyes closed. Yet every time his eyes closed memories of the war's final battle flashed in his mind. The smells of dead flesh hung fresh in his nose. The sounds of the dying and the screams of horror from those spared kept ringing in his ears.

He tried to move his body, but every muscle in his body screamed at him in protest.

"Best lie still, King's Son," a stone-hard voice said.

He tilted his head to see a robed man sitting beside him. The man's eyes were dark blue and deeper than an ocean's gulf. His arms were the size of small oak trees, even under his dark green and brown robes. His long flowing red beard almost brushed the ground, and his head was shaved closer than a ranger's. The most curious sight though was this his perfectly shaved head was adorned with tattoos of some ancient forgotten language.

"Where am I?" Tiberius whispered.

"You're in my home, boy," the stranger replied. "Our scouts found you on the edge of our borders two days ago now. Against my better judgment, they brought you to us for aid."

Tiberius tried to speak about all he had encountered, but the words were lost on him. To him, he had just been on the plains of Vermilion Pass. He had just fought and killed countless Narzeth in the sweltering dust bowl on the other side of the world. The memory of the sulfur and the feel of coarse dust was still fresh in his mind. The sounds of the beasts from the sky still echoed in his ears. For him, he had just remembered the worst days of his life.

No, not remembered, he thought. I was there again. Living it again, just as I had before.

"Where are my friends?" Tiberius asked.

"Resting. They spent the better part of two days listening to you wail and scream."

How could I have been out for two whole days? But at least my companions are alive.

"Who are you, sir?" Tiberius asked, his throat hoarse and scratchy.

The man let out a chuckle that shook the stone room. "I am the shaman of this village. And it is only by my great knowledge and power that ye are healed," he replied before standing to leave.

A great shock rattled through Tiberius now that he saw the man standing. Though he was powerfully built and looked as though a man of the forest would look, he was at least a foot and a half shorter than young Michael. His long flowing red beard almost brushed the ground and a pronounced nose extended beyond his mustache. His cheekbones and forehead were stern and looked as though they were carved out of thick granite centuries ago. A sudden realization dawned on the weary ranger's mind.

"You're a dwarf!" he exclaimed.

The man stopped in his tracks and turned to face Tiberius. To the Ranger, he looked familiar and yet so strange at the same time. Now that he knew what to look for, it was unmistakable. His mind flashed to the stories he had read often as a youth, tales of the Magi and Dwarves who built the Imperial City. The dwarves who could summon magic without a wand or staff. Dwarves who had left the empire for the Land Beyond for peace and rest after years of imprisonment and turmoil

The shaman's stone cut face melted away and was replaced by a look of deep sadness and regret. Tiberius could see at once that he had struck a nerve with the dwarf and felt ashamed for whatever offense he might have caused.

"Aye. Once upon a time, we were called dwarves," the shaman whispered.

He turned to see the pained Ranger, and his face reset to its sternness. "Sleep, boy. You will leave today, gods be damned!"

He slammed the heavy stone door as he left, leaving Tiberius alone in the hut.

A dwarf, he thought, before falling fast asleep again. *How about that?*

The Ranger awoke just after midday. His head and muscles were not as sore as they had been that morning, but it was still a great effort to stand. His movements were strained, and every step threatened to make him collapse. Once or twice he had to stop mid-stride to steady himself on wobbly legs. But he pressed on, determined to reunite with his friends.

After a few minutes of painful dressing, he exited the shaman's hut and found himself in a vast open space in the forest. Sprinkled around the wooded area were more small stone buildings and houses with their thatched roofs. He studied the sides of the hut he had emerged from and saw it bored the same runic language tattooed on the shaman's head. However, the closer he looked at the foreign runes carved into the building's sides, he could almost start to hear the words of some ancient language taking form in his mind.

Though his eyes could not understand the harsh shapes and figures, his mind seemed to interpret them just the same. Words such as "Brusgrik" and "Blessing" sprung to him immediately. He stared at the shapes, confused as to how he could understand their writing, let alone what they meant. There was no recording of the dwarven language in the Citadel. Nor in any library on either side of the world. Yet now, he could understand their meanings as though he had known language his whole life.

He looked away from the strange words to inspect the buildings. To his eyes, he could see no seams nor any brick and mortar to hold them up. Instead, all were just a smooth stone face as if some great and powerful person had shaved them down into their shapes. The dwarven power in building and molding things to their use was indeed real, even in such barren and remote environments. It was no wonder they had created such magnificent structures as the Unity Spire and the Imperial City.

The sudden smell of cooking meat drew his attention away from the foreign language and architecture he had studied. He snapped his head around, eager to find the source of the wonderful smelling food, until he saw smoke rising from the center of the small village. As he began shuffling through the snow-covered stone village towards the rising smoke, many dwarven children stopped to stare at him.

He, too, stopped after a few moments to stare and inspect them. He knew they were children right away, despite them all being the same height as the Shaman. Their faces were somehow younger and not as weather-worn. Their eyes were brighter and shined out happier than even some humans. Especially telling was that the children lacked the telltale beard associated with the dwarves of history and legend. A group of dwarven women came to shoo the children away, and Tiberius was further shocked to see the women, like the shaman, were also bearded. Not as full and flowing, but still longer than his own black and greying beard. Many of them stopped to stare at him, too, before heeding their own advice to disperse.

He started to hobble on through the snow for a few minutes until he arrived at the village center, where a small bonfire was burning bright. There, he found another small crowd of young dwarves laughing loudly into the frigid afternoon air. The dwarves were huddled around someone speaking in the middle, enraptured with whatever they were saying.

"And when they looked down at his ugly face, they saw a fire in his eyes. Fire. In. His. Eyes! Clearly, the man had been enchanted. Even being enchanted, there was no way he could have raised so many of the undead soldiers," Michael was saying, reveling in the attention of his audience of dwarves.

A pained smile crept onto Tiberius's disheveled face at the sight of his companions. Like the children, Michael was an odd spectacle indeed, seeing as he seemed to almost tower over them. Behind the crowd of onlookers, he could see Shayla, staff still in hand, but relaxed and smiling back at Michael. She looked past the crowd and met Tiberius's eyes, her small smile growing large. She nodded at her companion and began to walk around the group to meet him.

"What happened next, wizard?" one dwarf child asked Michael, eager to hear more about his misadventures the days prior.

"I told you, Guronin, I am a Mage! But what happened next, you ask? My friend reached down to touch him… and he turned to dust in his hands!" he said with a flourish and a gasp of shock from the children.

"What next!? What next!?" another child asked.

"Then my handsome and brave companion saved my butt from certain death using only his wits and good looks," Tiberius cut in above the exuberant children.

Michael jumped with a start and turned to see his friend and companion hobbled over but smiling at the sight before him. Without hesitation, he cut through the crowd of dwarves and hugged his friend with such vigor it almost knocked Tiberius off his already shaky feet. The days of fear and despair washed away, replaced by a flood of pure joy and relief.

"How're you feeling, sir?" Michael asked after breaking their long embrace.

"Like I've been stepped on by a herd of wild horses, my friend," Tiberius replied.

"I am sorry for your pain, but I am glad to see you about so soon, sir," Shayla said, joining her companions. She placed her hand on the Ranger's shoulder and said, "Blessings of Kazduhl above, you are still with us."

"Blessing to your dragon king that you were here to lead in my stead," Tiberius said, touching her hand on his shoulder.

Michael rummaged in his bag. "I was waiting for you to wake, sir. But here," and in his hands materialized the potions Damian had given them the day they departed.

"Potions? Where did these come from?"

"The High Sorceror gave them to me the day we left the city. I had thought to use them sooner, but that Shaman had said it would have been no use till you overcame what afflicted you."

Tiberius winced. "The Shaman was surely right in saying that. But as for Damian, I could kiss that drunken fool!"

He took the small purple potion from Michael and, in one large gulp, downed it all. The taste of peppermint and elderberry filled his mouth as a warm sensation filled his body. His legs began to feel warm and alive. His chest and arms began to tingle, and his mind seemed to emerge from a foggy haze. His swollen eyes relaxed, and he felt himself begin to stand erect and firm.

"Gods above!" he exclaimed.

A broad smile formed on the young Mage's face. "Better?"

"Indeed! I dare say I feel like I am in my prime!"

"Good!" a booming, throaty voice exclaimed. "Now, take your comrades and get!"

The crowd turned to see the Shaman, armed crossed, from across the bonfire. His red beard looked like twinkling fire against the snowy village and his stern face showing.

"But, sir," Michael began.

"But nothing, boy!" the Shaman cut in. "I told the King's Son that you all would be off as soon as he was better! Well, here he is as energetic as a rabbit in heat! Now be off our lands before I..."

"Thrakeluhm!" a louder voice cut above him, shaking the trees loose of snow.

Stillness covered the village at once. The sound, which had been like thunder, continued to reverberate around them. Slowly, another dwarf emerged from where the sound had come from. All the people close by bowed their heads low in respect at the presence of this new dwarf. All except the three companions. The three were shocked to see that the thunderous voice of command had come from such a small creature.

The closer this new dwarf got to them, the more unlike the Shaman it appeared. The new dwarf was thinner, perhaps, but curvier at the hips and waist. The dwarf brandished its own blond beard that was shorter than the Shaman's, with a bright fair complexion that shown out from its whiskers. Deep smoldering kind blue eyes looked out at them over great bushy eyebrows and a pronounced forehead.

"Pay him no mind, sir," a fair voice said from the bushel of blond beard in front of them. "He only pretends to run my village, but he has surely forgotten his manners. And his place"

"You're a...a...lady?" Michael stammered.

"Are ladies a mythical species to you as well?" she said with a laugh and gesture for the surrounding dwarves to rise and depart.

"Forgive my friend," Tiberius said. "It's just that, up until recently, we didn't even know dwarves still roamed these lands much less imagined that a lady dwarf would...well, you know."

She chuckled at what Tiberius meant. "Aye, son. We dwarf women would look like our mates to your eyes. Though, to be honest, our disposition is much more tempered than theirs. Now, who are you gentlemen and your lady companion?"

"She is Shayla Rider, Dragon Knight of the Axton Empire. This young fellow is Michael Deerborn, Mage of the Magi Brotherhood. And I--,"

"We know who you are, King's Son," she interrupted with a raised hand and a broad toothy smile. "Even if you looked nothing like him, which you do, you carry the sword of Alexander Axton. And we would recognize that blade anywhere"

"How do you know that this sword is his?" Tiberius asked. It was not widely known, even in the empire, that the emperor's sword had been Alexander's own weapon.

"Which dwarf do you think reforged it for him, King's Son?" she asked, beckoning him to show her the blade.

He unbuckled his weapon, unsure what the lady dwarf would do with it, and gently handed it to her. She took a moment to inspect the scabbard before unsheathing it. Not a single detail went unnoticed by her keen fair eyes. The blade still looked new and unused though it had seen far more bloodshed and war than any other weapon in the whole of the empire. She smiled again at Tiberius and knelt in front of him, extending the sword over her head.

Slowly Tiberius reached out and reclaimed his sword and sheathed it again. The dwarf stood and placed her hand on his chest. "The Father has indeed blessed us to be amongst the Axton emperors again."

"I'm not the emperor yet, my lady," he replied stoically.

"No, my boy, not yet. But his blood flows through you. You carry his face and you wield his sword. You command all who enter your presence with firmness and kindness." In a soft, steady voice, she lowered her head and said, "You are The Spirit of The Warrior, boy. Made flesh and returned amongst us."

Something profound stirred in his soul. Like ancient locks opening for the first time in a thousand years, he knelt to face the dwarf and said, "The Spirit of The Warrior will always be with you, my lady."

"Excuse me. I'm terribly confused," Michael interrupted.

"We first spoke these words to Alexander the day he freed us from our bondage, and it pleases us to see that the bonds of brotherhood and commitment to justice and duty have not been abandoned by his descendants. The Spirit of The Warrior roams the world beyond with his vast host of heroes. He is the keeper of order and the champion of the oppressed. It was by his intervention in the matters of our mortal realm that he came down to free us from slavery so many years ago."

"That is a beautiful belief, my lady. But what does it mean exactly?" Shayla asked. She had heard the rangers of the empire repeat it to one another since she had arrived in their homeland a year ago, yet she still had no idea what meaning its words invoked.

"We dwarves believe in the spirits of old, young lady," the woman said as a mother instructing her child. "The Spirits of the Water and Ground that bring forth bountiful harvests. The Spirits of the Sky who were created by the Father Frijigzah to shape and mold our world. And the Spirit of the Warrior is the one who brought order to the chaos of the world. The one who protects and champions the defenseless."

Tiberius bowed at the honor. Though the rangers had long passed this greeting to one another, hearing it recited from the one who first taught it to his ancestors brought an overwhelming sense of pride and humility to him.

"Please, come, my young friends," she said, motioning for the companions to join her by the fire.

The three companions turned to follow her to the now-empty bonfire, Michael slowly shuffling along lost in thought.

"Pardon, me ma'am," Michael said, taking a seat, "But what is your name?"

"Catherine," she replied. "Catherine Stonefoot."

"Tis a fair name," Michael said respectfully.

"Many names I've been called, young one, but fair is not one of them," she said with a laugh. "Now, before you leave, I must ask where it is you are going that has brought you so far north and attracted the demons of the world to waylay you."

The companions looked to one another before Tiberius explained the gravity of their mission and what they were hoping to find at the dwarven ruin. At the mention of the beast that attacked them on their journey, a deep booming noise echoed throughout the village. The three companions turned to see the Shaman, still rooted in place.

"We do not speak of such things here, boy!" the Shaman exclaimed.

"Brusgrik! Shame on ye, for your inhospitality!" Catherine shouted at her fellow dwarf.

"Damn, inhospitality, Stonefoot! These three have brought a plague upon us!"

"Thrakeluhm!" Catherine roared. "Rodeul eiinos! Where is this plague you speak so boldly of!? Hold your tongue, Brusgrik!"

The Shaman glared at the companions before hurrying off out of sight. The three companions watched him go before turning their attention back to Catherine. Her stern face melted, and a warm smile reappeared on her face.

"I must apologize for Brusgrik. He means well, but unfortunately, is not as sensitive to the plights of outsiders as I am. As for what is going on in the world outside, I am deeply sorry for your troubles. There is little advice I can give you on your way forward except to say the path you seek is indeed the right one."

"So, the outpost is real," Michael said.

"Yes, it is young one. Our people were compelled by the Father's will to travel there, and to build."

"What else did you build there?" Shayla asked, her innate distrust betraying her calm, calculated exterior.

"We toiled and built many things there over the years. We thought it would be our new home, away from the troubles and wars of the world. But after a time, we felt the whispers of the Father upon our spirits. He bid us turn our attention to building something else. Something wonderful and terrible though we did not know its purpose. We only felt the need to complete it. And to use it."

"What was it?" The Mage asked wide-eyed.

"It was a machine," the dwarf replied in reverence, "one that we believed would allow us to communicate with our Father. But alas, it was not so.

"We had not heard of a machine there. What did it do?" Tiberius asked.

She thought for a moment, measuring her answers. Then after many heavy moments of silence said, "It took us somewhere beyond this world. To a place that our people call The Deep. A place where dwarves are free to build and learn and discover and thrive undying forever. But the term 'Deep' doesn't really describe this place at all."

The companions looked amongst each other again, not quite sure of how to take her cryptic words. They had never heard of 'The Deep' before, but they felt they understood her meaning well enough.

"If you go there and turn on the machine, you'll see these things for yourselves. But if you choose to return, you won't clearly recall it all. To us who have gone and returned, it felt more like a dream. A vivid, wonderful dream, but still a dream."

"We not seek a machine, ma'am," Tiberius said. "We only seek answers to the mystery of magic."

"Then I must say your quest for knowledge will be in vain, son of Alexander. We took all of our books and scrolls with us into The Deep."

"If this place was so wonderful, then why did you and your people return?" Shayla asked.

"Not all of us did," a sad, familiar voice uttered.

They all turned to see the Shaman had rejoined them, standing just outside the ring in which they communed. "Many of our people stayed in that place. But the rest of us," he paused, trying to conjure the words, "just as strongly as we were compelled to venture to the realm of the undying, we were compelled to return and settle here."

"We built many things when we returned," Catherine continued. "We sent our creations out into the world so that they may be used by all who sought out justice and peace. We forged the first wands for the Magi in secret and delivered them to the first High Sorcerer. We spread our knowledge of craft and brewing to all who would seek it."

"You created the first wands for the Magi?" Michael asked, his voice growing excited.

"Aye, lad. We did. When we returned from The Deep, we found new knowledge and new desires to build had been placed in us by the Father himself. The wands, a way for the Magi to make magic real, was the first thing we created."

"You created the first wands for the Magi" Michael asked, his voice growing excited.

"Aye, lad. We did indeed. When we returned from The Deep, we found new knowledge and new desires to build inside of us. The wands, and way for the Magi to make magic real, were the first things we created. When we came to these shores, the Magi only had the wands and staves they had brought with them. As clever as they were, they had not the mind or knowledge for creating new ones. Alas, all the knowledge of building new wands they left in their library across the sea."

A sudden idea struck Michael. "Ma'am, if I may, did you make this wand?" he asked, producing the ebony and ivory wand from his cloak.

The two dwarves stared, frozen in shock and amazement. Not at all the reaction Michael or his companions would have imagined they would have received at seeing the wand. The Shaman reached for the wand, which Michael gently handed over. He turned it over several times in his rough hands. He brought it close to his ears as if listening to some hidden symphony. A small smile formed on his hard mouth, and he closed his eyes in pure joy.

After a moment, he handed the wand over to Catherine, who mimicked his same movements. When she spoke, at last, it was whispered and solemn. "This wand, my young friend, was not made by our hands. But it is the nearest and dearest creation in the whole world to us."

A frown grew on the Mage's young face. "If you did not make this wand, then who did? Where did it come from?"

"This wand," the Shaman started before a lump grew in his throat. "This wand was made by the Father himself. When we awoke in the deep caverns of the north, I held this very wand in my hands. I could feel the

Father's presence in the wand, and I could hear the music of his halls in the wood."

"Brusgrik and I toiled for nigh on ten years to reproduce its splendor, but were unable to even match it," Catherine added. "How did you come by this?"

"The High Sorcerer of the Magi gave it to me before we departed," Michael replied, confused. "He said he found it amongst his predecessors belongings."

"Curious that such a thing would be left unattended. Other wands were fashioned in the same manner, but none carried the true blessings of The Father as this one was."

"If you awoke with this wand, then why send it away?" Tiberius cut in. "Such a thing should be held as a token of your people."

More sadness grew on the two dwarf's faces. "As in all things, we follow the will of the Father," Catherine explained. "The Father bid us send this wand to the Magi. After all, we dwarves have no need for such things to summon magic. It flows through us like a river that we can reach in and draw out at will."

"Ma'am, if I be so bold. Could magic still be used with it!" Michael exclaimed.

"That would explain how you were able to repel the beast that attacked you in the woods."

She handed the wand back to Michael who stared at it reverently. "I don't know if I am worthy to carry such a thing," he said after some contemplation. "By all rights, this wand belongs to your people. I am but a lowly mage."

"I do not know how the fates conspired for it be placed in your care, but it was brought to you nonetheless. It is a treasure above all others in the world. It is yours to wield. And wield it well."

Michael slowly took the heavy wand in his hands and bowed his head at the woman's words. The burden of carrying something fashioned by The Father himself began to weigh on him. Not to mention possessing the only wand capable of drawing magic.

"Lady Stonefoot, our aim is to find the outpost that your people built," Tiberius said. "Will you journey with us to that place?"

"Alas, King's Son, but we cannot," the dwarf replied.

"Why can't you?" Shayla asked. "Your people were the ones who built it. You should be able to look on your own works again."

"Once we left the place our people now dwell, we were forbidden from ever returning. Now we remain here, the last of the dwarves," the Shaman answered.

A great sadness took hold of Michael, such as he had never experienced. The thought that these were the last people of the ancient and mythical race of dwarves moved him to tears.

"Do not cry, young Mage," Catherine said, wiping his tears away. "I have given you knowledge to aid you in your journey, and now a gift for you that I hope will be of use."

She motioned the Shaman to come closer, and from within his deep billowing robes, he produced a massive leather-bound tome. He gently handed it to Michael, who stared blankly at the large book.

"This is the history of our people, young one," Catherine said. "From when we first awoke in the deep mountains of Narzeth to today. This book has passed through many hands and traveled thousands of miles, and now it is yours. I pray to the Father that you use it wisely and keep it as a token of our people. You have all you need to see your venture through to the end."

Michael looked at the dwarves, his face hardening with resolve. "I shall carry this the rest of my days. You and your people will never be forgotten in the empire."

"We thank you, child," Catherine said. "Though I would venture to say that our paths might cross again."

"Why do you say that?" Tiberius asked.

"There are things in motion that you cannot perceive with your human eyes, but we are able to see with our own. The will of the Father is stirring, and where his will leads, we will follow," she replied before standing. The companions followed suit, unsure of what was to come next.

"Now, it is time for you all to depart our home."

"But I have many more questions to ask of you," Michael started but was quieted by Catherine's raised hand.

"You have all lingered long enough," she said. Without another word, she and the Shaman began to walk away from the ring they all had conversed, the companions moving quickly to keep up.

Small dwarven faces peered out of the stone huts as the companions walked, some smiling happily, others sad at their departure. Sorrow overtook Michael at the thought of never seeing these smiling dwarven children again, but a renewed purpose drove him to complete their journey.

After a brief walk, they arrived at the village's edge to find their belongings stacked neatly against a grey stone hut. Once they were laden with their belongings, Tiberius bowed low and said, "Thank you for all you've done for us, Catherine Stonefoot. I pray that whatever conflict is brewing in the world does not come to you and your people."

"Thank you, King's Son," she replied, returning her own bow. "I hope for that as well, but I have a small notion that we will be drawn into whatever events are moving in the world abroad. We dwarves are closer to magic than any other creature that walks the world. Now, please be off and do not falter in your path. Whatever evils may be brewing outside, it is not time yet for you to engage them."

"I wish it were an easy thing to put them out of my mind," Tiberius admitted. "But I know sooner or later I will be called to answer the threats looming in the empire."

"You very well might find that those threats lie upon the road that you and your companions travel," she replied with a wry smile. "For now, whatever you do, do not abandon your path."

"And how do you know that?" Tiberius asked, surprised.

"I don't know, but call it a feeling," she replied, her smile never abandoning her face.

Tiberius bowed his head in reverence to her wisdom and turned to lead his companions out into the wild once again. The sun was quickly setting at their backs, and they would have many miles to put between them and their hosts before making camp for the night. But as they left, they each turned to look on the dwarven village one last time, each silently acknowledging this was perhaps the last time they would look on this place of comfort and knowledge.

Chapter 14

The Companions

Their pace was slow as they moved through the frozen woods in silence. The wood was heavy with an unnatural stillness, appropriate for the weight that each of them bore. The sun was setting low to their left, the last few rays of welcoming light were creeping lower and lower while dim stars were beginning to shine over them. In a few hours, their journey would be marred in thick blackness. They didn't know what to say after all they had learned during their brief respite in the dwarven village. Even if the three companions had the words to say, they dared not speak them for fear of being called a coward.

Michael's thoughts strayed between his desires to reach the outpost with his longing to remain in the village's comfort. So far, life on the road had not been all that he imagined it would be, and the opportunity for a continued lull pulled heavy on his heart. Not to mention the chance to study and interact with real dwarves. Their race was already shrouded in myth and secrecy, and the prospect of being unable to examine them saddened the young Mage.

Shayla reflected on the strange and turbulent paths her life has followed. She was raised a warrior of the dragoons. A spear maiden from a long noble line of dragon knights, only to be imprisoned by the Narzeth until the empire came to liberate her and her sisters. The dragoons swore undying fealty to Emperor Axton and all who followed him. It was the emperor who elevated her to First Knight of the Dragoons. She would not let her oaths abandoned and made in vain. She would see the journey through to end, be it on the Mage's path or the Ranger's. Though if the dwarven woman's words were any indication, both directions would lead to the same outcome. Deep in her bones she knew that battle and hardship awaited them no matter what they chose.

Tiberius alone felt the most significant struggle on his heart. He had always felt sure in his path, yet a sinking feeling had begun to grow in his heart. He began to suspect that the loss of magic wasn't just an act of nature or the gods' will but as a plot by their unknown enemy. He had never been a believer in coincidence. He had seen too much evil and plotting in his time to know that everything meaningful in life was by design.

It was not happenstance that a group of mages were waylaid in their pilgrimage to the Land Beyond, nor that his father had directed him there to save Michael from undead soldiers. It wasn't bad luck that had sent an evil beast to attack them shortly after taking up their quest. Yet whatever, or whomever, was conspiring against them he had did not know. He knew beyond any doubt that it was all by design. Yet whatever, or whomever, was conspiring against them remained shrouded in secrecy. For now.

In this dark uncertainty, he felt a pull to be with his father and with his men. He was positive they would need him for the fights to come. He began to feel as though his father was becoming encircled by enemies disguised as friends, and conflict would come that would threaten all the people in its path creating untold destruction.

The greatest test of a warrior isn't on the calm battlefield, but in the chaos of their hearts, his father had said. And his father, for whatever minor faults he had, was seldom wrong in his council.

Two hours into their journey, they stopped for rest amongst a thicket of dead trees in the frozen forest. The sun was beginning to set, and the stars above were already shining through a cloudless sky. The bleak landscape conjured up uneasy feelings from the young Mage. Images of the undead flashed inside his mind's eye, like a picture show from the traveling scientists. Sensing his fear, Tiberius reached out and patted the young man on his shoulders like a comforting brother.

"Do not be afraid," he told the Mage. "We are with you, and no manner of beast or demon or ill-intended man will cause us any bother."

"Aye," Shayla added, a wicked glimmer in her dark brown eyes. "The most dangerous and fearsome creatures in the woods tonight are me and the Ranger at your side."

Michael smiled for the first time since departing the village. His companions were indeed a welcome comfort to him. Though they were but a few days out from the journey, they had made many great strides north, and returning to the cold and dark had caused him anxiety. He knew his companions would be able to match whatever evil may come. Tiberius had bested the undead, and he and Shayla had faced down a demon. Together, all three were of a heartier build than ever.

The sun set an hour after their stop amongst the dead trees as they dug into the supper, the dwarves had been gracious enough to pack for them. Michael raised his head and turned from side to side as if examining some unseen point in the night.

"What is the next destination?" he asked.

"We will hold this course another day or so before breaking due north," Tiberius responded.

But at his words, his companions didn't answer, instead returning worried and thoughtful looks. He met their gaze's before realizing his voice betrayed him. Instead of the calm and caring demeanor he wished to portray, his voice was shrouded in doubt and fear. A sound neither of his companions had ever heard come from him.

"What troubles you, my friend?" Shayla asked.

He set aside his plate of mutton and bread and thought for a moment on how best to answer. He knew they would both detect any effort to conceal or deflect, and in the end, decided to be as honest with them as he would be to his men.

"My friends, I am sorry. My body is here, but my thoughts and spirit are on my father," he admitted. "I am honor-bound and ordered to escort you to the outpost, and I aim to see it through. But my heart and my spirit are many miles back in the capital."

"Your father is wise, and pardon the expression, the most powerful man in the world," Shayla replied. "He is well protected atop his tower, and commands the mightiest military the world has ever seen."

"While that may be true, I fear he has many enemies concealed to him."

Michael's brow furrowed. "The emperor is the most loved man in our realm. He has the loyalty of everyone who dwells within our borders. From a lowly stonemason to the mightiest wizard and solder. Even those within our borders who would buck against his rule would never dare out of respect to him."

"Thank you for your kindness," Tiberius replied with a solemn nod. "But if all were indeed true as you say, then you must also concede that there is indeed a plot beset against us. And by extension, upon my father and the empire."

"Coincidence is the way of fools," Shayla said.

"Aye, my thoughts exactly. With all that has befallen us in a short amount of time, I am certain someone is plotting against our mission. I would even go as far as to say someone is behind the disappearance of magic in our world."

Michael put his food aside and leaned in close. "In my first few years at the Citadel, I learned about the nature of magic. Or, how to perceive magic. From all that I was taught, there is no one in the world that can stop the flow of magic. It is simply not possible. And why do you think there would be a conspiracy at all?"

"What is magic then?" the Dragoon asked.

"I think the dwarves spoke rightly enough. They said they can wield magic as if it were water you can draw with your hand. Those of us attuned to the power of magic have always felt as though it were a part of this world. Just as the air blows through the trees, and the streams water the crops. It just is. But, sir, as I said before, why do you think there is a conspiracy?"

Tiberius lit his pipe, took in a deep drag of tobacco, and said, "I understand magic just as you do, Michael. My own apprenticeship with the Battle-Mages taught me much in the manner of magic. Yet, despite all you have said, magic is leaving our world. Someone knows this and is eager to prevent us from reaching the outpost. They fear the knowledge that could be gained there, and are eager to prevent us from reaching it. Twice have expeditions to reach the Land Beyond been attacked. If that is not a clear indication to you that a plot against us is in motion, then you are a fool."

Silence filled their camp as thick as the blackness surrounding them. None knew what else to say to help ease their leader's conflict. Michael had leaned back, letting Tiberius's words wash over him, conceding that his leader's assessment was indeed correct. A shudder went up his back at the thought of a traitor in the empire.

Not just a traitor to the empire, but someone who wished magic itself to leave the world, he realized.

Finally, Shayla broke the heavy silence. "I cannot begin to fathom the burdens you carry, but this mission was ordered by the emperor himself, and Catherine warned against straying from our path. In Narzeth, they had said the dwarves' wisdom extended beyond the present and past but dwelt somewhere ahead of them. As if they could perceive the proper course of action."

"They could see the future?" Michael asked.

"No, of course not," she replied with a slight smile. "There is no power under the sun on any side of the world that could do that. More so, they could assess everything around them and knew instinctively what the right thing to always do was. As though an unseen guide walked beside."

"They did speak of The Father as guiding them. Whispering to them on how to proceed in life. Though, I must admit, it sounds crazy to me," Michael said.

"Sounds like fairy tales, to me," Tiberius added.

Shayla cocked her head at the Ranger's words. In all her long life, she had never heard the words 'fairy tales' and began to wonder what they were.

"You okay, ma'am?" Michael asked after a few quiet moments.

"Oh, yes," she replied flustered. "My mind was turning to the previous few days, and to the beast."

"What beast?"

"The black screeching one that waylaid us and led to us being here in the first place."

Michael thought for a moment, remembering the terror that had filled them. The ethereal smoke and blackness that tried to devour them. "I do not know, ma'am. I have studied many books on beasts, both real and mystical, in the Citadel. To my recollection, I have never read or heard of such a thing before."

The silence fell harder than a boulder. The three companions had all been secretly wishing to speak about what had happened to them two nights ago, yet not even the brave Ranger or the bold Dragoon could muster the courage to talk about it. Fear had taken hold them, such as neither of the three had ever felt. The power it wielded was unreal and never seen before by them. Tiberius, however, knew. He knew the second he regained his senses as to what had attacked them.

At length, the Ranger broke the silence as he whispered, "It was a Revenant. An ancient evil that has long plagued the places of our world that men have not yet ventured to."

"Have you ever encountered one before it attacked you?" Michael asked.

"I have not, no. Though I know them to be very real, and very dangerous."

"How do you know of these things then, sir?"

"There are stories you hear about strange sighting in the more ancient corners of our realm. Stories of people and animals disappearing after a thick blackness overcomes the land. Stories of screaming that haunts the memories of those who lost their loved ones."

He took a moment to collect himself, for he knew what was to come next would be particularly painful to recall. "And I saw them myself across the ocean during the war. The day after the battle... we saw them."

"What is it then?" Shayla asked, turning to face her leader.

"I do not rightly know," the Ranger began, "The wisest men I know speak of them as souls that are chained to a place in the world. Evil black souls who are unwelcomed in the halls of their ancestors, who linger and fester and grow in power to torment the living."

Michael's face changed to pure surprise in an instant. "How did you learn of such creatures?"

"When I was apprenticed to the Battle-Mages in my youth. There was..." he said, pausing. A lump had begun to unexpectedly form in his throat. Memories long suppressed were starting to reemerge, and hot tears were threatening to fall from the corners of his eyes.

"There was a boy I was apprenticed with who fell in his trials to such a beast. They sent him and his master out to investigate a simple disappearance of livestock. Only his master returned. The boy was never seen again."

"What was this boy's name, sir?" Michael whispered.

Tiberius pushed all the emotion he could out of his heart. He refused to give in to his feelings right now when his guard must be at its highest.

"Noah," he said with a small break in his voice. "Noah Bright."

"I see," Michael said, fully understanding the pain behind Tiberius's words. "He was close to you, wasn't he?"

"Aye. That he was," the Ranger replied as the tears began to flow down his frozen cheeks.

"I think it would best to turn in, my friends," Tiberius said, after another long silence. "I'll take the watch tonight. Don't suspect I'd get much sleep anyhow."

After a few pensive moments, Michael and Shayla moved away from where they sat to settle in for the night. Michael inside his worn and patched bedroll, his eyes heavy but focused on the dancing fire in front of him. Shayla rested just outside the ring alongside a tree, her spear beside her, ready to sing into the night. Tiberius had perched himself opposite Shayla, his pipe between his pursed lips and his eyes looking beyond, piercing the veil of darkness. He brooded on his thoughts throughout the night, weighing all the things they had spoken of.

They were back on the road just after daybreak. A quick, silent breakfast had been devoured before departing into a grey featureless day. The cold woods offered no direction to Michael and Shayla, yet they continued to follow Tiberius. What little sleep Michael and Shayla had the night before did nothing to provide them rest from their troubles. Tiberius had found neither rest nor sleep but relied on his disciplined training to sustain him throughout the night.

They pressed on northwest through the White Kingdom, passing through the Georgian Wood and over winding frozen paths flecked with large boulders iced over from the frigid weather that existed in that part of their country. Whatever had lived here once upon a time was now long dead and preserved as if behind a snow globe, forever dead but never gone into time and memory.

Michael had tried to read the dwarf's book to pass the time. There was much knowledge in there to be sure, but nothing that would help them in their present mission. A stiff wind cut through the path they walked, sending shivers through their bodies.

Michael eyed the Dragoon in her green armor. "That armor cannot be good warmth, Shayla."

"Under normal circumstances, no, it is not," she conceded. "But the fire of the dragon keeps us warm when needed, even in these cold dead lands." She turned and observed the bleakness of the terrain, hoping to see some sign of life other than the occasional fox or squirrel that would scurry in the distance. "Does anyone live in such a barren place?"

"Mainly hunters and trappers this far north," Michael replied. "My father would take us here often to trade our fish for pelts."

"I forget you are from this part of the empire. This must be more like home than the city did."

"It is familiar, yes. But not as comforting as being amongst the Magi. I certainly didn't miss the snow!"

Shayla gave out a low chuckle. "There is no snow across the sea, only the heat and sands as far as our eyes can see."

"What about the Dragon Garden?" Michael asked in return. "Is it not without sand and scorching sun?"

"We do not speak of the garden, young one," Shayla snapped back. "It was our home long ago, but it is lost to us now and forever."

Michael bowed his head, acknowledging his misstep. "I mean no offense, Mistress Knight."

"How is it you know of the garden anyhow? I did not think a young Mage on the other side of the world would have ever heard of it?"

Michael held the book away from his chest. "It's in their book, ma'am. Or the parts I can read anyhow. Half of the book is written in their language, and I do not know how to translate it."

Tiberius began to listen closer to their conversation. Fresh memories of runes carved into steel homes flashing in his mind, and strange words deciphering in his mind.

"The dwarves writing goes back far, yet there are no dates when it was inscribed," Michael continued. "They mentioned the garden as a holy place to the dragon's worshipers, though they admitted themselves to having never seen it for themselves."

Shayla nodded at his words. "The dwarves speak true. It was the most sacred place to us until our sundering from it and Lord Kazduhl long ago. And if it pleases you, we will not speak of it again."

Michael nodded at her, acknowledging her request and dropped any further talk of the Dragon Garden, though his mind wandered as to what it was and what had happened to the dragons long ago. Perhaps, he thought, the answer is inside the dwarves' massive book. If only he could read it. He grew frustrated, and not wanting to continue their journey in complete silence, placed the heavy book into his pack.

"Well, as for this place," Michael continued on. "It is said this land was where the elves made their arrival into our world. This place used to be lush green lands, almost like a jungle! But when they came, their magic was so great and powerful that the ground seized up and retreated. The sky turned grey, and the cold pierced every inch of it."

"Well, whatever these elves are, they could have at least returned some beauty to this place when they left," she replied, again scanning the terrain. Yet every way to she looked inside the thick dead forest was more gnarled frozen trees. "This is the most dreadful place I've ever seen in my life!"

"Many good people still dwell in these lands," Tiberius offered, the first he had spoken since last night.

"Ah! He speaks at last!" Shayla exclaimed in jest. "So good of you to join us this merry morning! Perhaps you could pray to your elves for a little bit of warmth! And while you're at it, tell us how much longer till we find it on our own."

Tiberius smiled softly to himself. "I thought Lord Kazduhl's fire would keep you warm?"

"It does, Ranger," she said with an air of sarcasm. "But if it's all the same, I wish the sun would come to visit us soon."

"The sun just might if we are lucky. But as to our destination, we are about ten leagues from the Ice Steps that lead to the Forgotten Mountains. Before we reach them, there is a decent-sized village about five leagues away. We will stop and rest there for the night, and possibly tomorrow before we ascend the steps. We keep a small garrison there to keep watch over the northern realms, and I am eager to hear any news from the capital."

"A most excellent idea," Michael said. Though a part of him wondered if their brief reprieve was more for Tiberius's peace of mind. The Ranger he had met a few days ago would have driven them on through the snow, yet now wished to spend a night in a village.

His soul must truly be conflicted if he wished to expose our journey to the outside world, Michael thought.

"And as to elves," Tiberius continue. "We don't pray to them. They aren't gods of ours or anybody's people. They are just fairy tales the children hear at bedtime."

"There! That phrase again, 'fairy tales,' yet I do not know what that is," Shayla cut in.

Tiberius thought on how to answer that, remembering that Shayla was not of the empire and most likely had never heard of them before. "Fairy tales are myths or legends that people take and turn into children's stories, usually to teach a lesson or a moral."

"So, you tell children lies to teach them morals? Seems silly to me," she replied. "In Narzeth, we hear stories of great battles and heroes of yesteryear."

"We have those too," Michael said. "Along with loads more stories about all kinds of things! Fairies, sprites, gnomes. Valiant knights and disgusting slime covered ogres. Kidnapped princesses and the brave knights who come to save her! I shall have to recite some to you when we make camp."

"I really wish you wouldn't," Shayla replied. "I am a dragoon. A fearless warrior who has slain many foes in battle. And I'm old enough to be your parents' parent. I do not need to have children's stories recited to me. What I need is warmth and comfort!"

Michael and Tiberius exchange mischievous smiles to one another, and spent the rest of that recounting their childhood stories to a bewildered Shayla. After a few hours, she began to pay attention to the stories themselves, the incessant chattering taking her mind off the bitter cold. The whole notion of make-believe morality tales was strange to her, if not somewhat amusing and sad. Though she was enthralled with their strange and silly stories, she could not help but feel melancholic over a childhood she had never had. Her childhood had been one of constant battle until enslavement. Yet now, in this new country, she could see the opportunity for others to grow up in the peace and happiness that she and her sisters were denied.

The snow-covered woods slowly gave way to more and more open yet featureless frozen plains. In a few short miles, they would no longer have the cover of dead trees and limbs to conceal their movements north. Instead, they would have to contend with a wide-open tundra, the first they had left the cover of woods since setting out from the Imperial City. Shortly before the end of the woods, Tiberius called a halt to their march for a brief lunch and rest. Over the horizon, small wisps of smoke were rising into the cold air, welcoming them to a night of rest and comfort.

"Is that the village?" Shayla asked, rubbing life back into her arms.

"Aye," Tiberius responded, after a long gulp of much-needed water. "The Village of Rogers. Our garrison is just inside the town, and beyond that is the inn."

"If I remember rightly enough, Master Rogers was himself a fantastic cook," Michael added. "He often cooks for whatever guests turn up in his village."

"Well, I hope this 'Master Rogers' has something other than mutton on the menu," Shayla replied, digging into the boiled meat from the night before.

"He was a soldier in the Imperial Army," Tiberius replied. "A berserker on the front lines. He ought to know how to feed an army with all he's endured in his long life."

Michael stared, bewildered. "Master Rogers was a berserker!?" he exclaimed.

Tiberius nodded. "Aye, many years ago, when I was a young ranger. The man has seen his fair share of war and bloodshed. And in the end, decided it was best to walk away with his sanity and take up his family's keep of these lands. The Father's fury had left him, and all that remained was sadness and remorse. Human qualities, to be sure, but not the qualities of a berserker."

"The same Father the dwarf's worship?" Shayla asked.

"The same," he replied. "Father Frijigzah carries many sides to him. Creator, smith, and warrior. The dwarves apparently embraced him as their creator and their god of smithing and building. The berserkers worshiped him as a mighty warrior, fueled by unquenchable rage to his enemies. When loose in battle, the Father's fury consumes them, and they fly into the fray without any regard for themselves."

"I remember these berserkers well. They were most impressive at the pass that day."

"Aye, that they were. Long had we withheld them from the war because of their nature. But my father was determined to press our advantage that day, and we would have needed every weapon and warrior in our ranks to do so."

Michael's head was swimming. "I had only ever known him as a kind old village master. Certainly not a deadly and powerful berserker!"

Tiberius chuckled. "Forgive me, Michael. I forget that you are kin to the people of this kingdom. That kindly old man was his father, Tyndahl Rogers. The master now is his son, Tygahl. A hearty and kind man himself hoping to put behind the horrors of war." Tiberius smiled at the young Mage. "At any rate, in a few hours, you can talk to him yourself."

They finished the rest of their meal enwrapped in talk of the berserkers and the countless battles they had been in over the five hundred years of the empire. Once they were finished, they headed out from the woods and into the northwest's vast frozen plains. They longed for a night in the comfort of a homey village before ascending the mythical Ice Steps beyond.

CHAPTER 15

THE MEN FROM WHITE

The Ranger stood on the edge of the tree line surveying the vast open plain before him. The sun was shining down on their path ahead, and small fresh snowflakes were beginning to fall. He pushed his *Sight* as far as it could reach in all directions yet could see nothing save for more openness and the occasional snowy hill. Though he hoped beyond hope that their journey across the open fields would go unnoticed, his better judgment bid him exercise caution. Too often had hubris been the downfall of many, but such was the dire need of their quest that he refused to give in to his own pride. He readjusted the sword at his side and pulled the brown hood of his cloak down over his head as he continued to examine the fields.

"You worry too much," Michael said, packing away his food tray and the dwarven book.

"I worry just enough to keep us alive, young one," Tiberius replied. "Find anything of value in that book?"

"Unfortunately, no. Most of it is written in dwarvish, and without an understanding of their runes and language structure, I have no way of translating it."

Again, Tiberius remembered the runes in the dwarf's home and how their meaning seemed to spring to his mind. He decided when they made it to the village, he would dare take a quick glimpse at the book. He grew excited at the prospect of reading what the Mage could not and began to wonder how he had this gift at all. He had never seen dwarvish until that morning in the village, nor even knew such runes and symbols existed. Any trace of the dwarf's presence in the empire had long ago been erased.

Only their magnificent works that stood to this day marked that they had ever existed at all. That is until he and his companions met and talked with a whole hidden village of them.

Such a fortunate thing to have come to us amidst all this intrigue we find ourselves in, he thought to himself.

But after a few brief moments of contemplation, he pushed these thoughts aside and focused on the task at hand. Any hope of reading that book, let alone making to the Ice Steps and beyond the mountains, rested on them traversing the open plains without incident.

After a few more minutes of careful observation, Tiberius reasoned it was safe enough to begin their trek and motioned for them to follow him out into the open plain. In the distance, wisps of smoke could be seen rising into the morning sky. Though Rogers' village was still a good way off, the sight of some civilization brought much-needed relief to the group's weary spirits. Warm food and honey mead would dispel the cold that clung to them and renew their will for the journey up the mountain. More than a few creature comforts, Tiberius would not risk a night in the open ground, no matter how tired and cold they may be.

Tiberius continued to swivel his head in all directions, watching the environment around them for any sign of an attack. Twice now, they had been ambushed on their journey, and he dared not risk a third attack in the open as they were. Shayla had taken up the rear guard, her eyes straight and focused, ready to fly into whatever foe would come. However, Michael continued to look down at his feet in the stirrups, lost in thought over their arrival to the village.

Slow rolling frost-touched hills began to appear in the white wilderness around them, a welcomed break from the monotony of the flatness that abounded. Small echoes of birds somewhere in the distant rolled through the quiet open land, raising the young Mage's spirits. A small smile cracked his frozen face as he said, "Perhaps our time with the dwarves threw whatever pursuers we had off of our scent, eh?"

"Perhaps," Shayla responded, her eyes never straying from some unseen target. "Though our arrival to their home, as timely as it was, was less than an ideal way to arrive."

"You speak true," Michael said with a shudder, thoughts of the black monster crashing down on him. The terror and majesty that he felt was almost unfathomable yet still fresh as the snow around them.

"Best not to speak of any of these things until we are safe in the village," Tiberius said from the front of their formation. His words ended the chatter all at once, and the three companions continued their trek in silence.

They let the hours and miles fall off without uttering a word to one another. Though they did not run for fear of sapping whatever energy he and the horse had, Tiberius called no afternoon halt to their march, reasoning they would eat once they arrived in the village. The featureless terrain seemed to never change as they marched on. Only the faint plumes of smoke from the small hamlet were any indication of how far along they were.

The sun was now halfway to the horizon, and the cold that had haunted them since they arrived was now harsher than before. Yet only the Mage made any movement to warm himself as his companion's restraint and focus forced them to continue their vigilance. But as Michael tried to wield life back into his frozen face, a booming scream split the still icy plains.

"Loose!" a mighty voice cried out, followed by high-pitched whistling that cracked the sky open.

Their heads spun in unison to their right where the voice had called from. Just over a nearby hill, a black cloud flew high and into the sky before dropping down sharply onto the village just ahead of them. Screams erupted from the villages. A great commotion was stirred up that even miles off was unmistakable. The three stopped their march at once, and Shayla darted to the front of their party to join Tiberius.

"Loose!" the voice roared again.

Another mass of black flew into the sky before raining down again in the village. More screams and shouts burst from Rogers, and the faint but undeniable smell of fire caught their noses. Deep thunder echoed through the open fields, but no clouds had formed overhead.

The three looked again to the hill and saw twenty leather-clad men on horseback charging hard over the fields. Swords and spears drawn, cries for blood and death screaming from their mouths, each horseman driving their beasts hard towards the village.

"What the in the hells is happening!?" Michael shrieked.

Tiberius was already in motion. His brown cloak was unfastened in one move and dropped to the ground, his sword drawn, shining bright. Shayla had her dragon-shaped helmet over her olive-skinned face, spun her spear, and crouched low beside the Ranger.

"Whoever this is has decided to attack the village!!" Tiberius shouted back above the stampeding.

"What will we do, sir?"

He turned to face the scared young Mage and said, "They have no men of arms in the village! We will take the fight to them! Keep that beast behind us as best you can. If you see an opening to the trees, make a break for it!" And with that, they sprinted hard towards the oncoming battle.

Screams of death sounded out in front of them. Though the village was only a quarter-mile in front of them, and still obscured by the hills and dips, Michael's mind went wild with the possibility of another encounter with death. Tiberius and Shayla's minds focused, trained to snap back to their core selves. As they reached the top of the hill, all they saw was a massacre.

Villagers were running wild to their homes as droves of men atop horses cut through them without abandon. The creams echoed throughout the plain amongst the sounds of absolute slaughter. Slaughter at the hands of men clad head to toe in the color of the very kingdom they battled in. The color of white.

The cavalry was cutting down the people of Rogers without care or mercy. More cries of anguish and death rose up in greater volume, and rage filled them all at the sight of such atrocity. Tiberius broke into a dead sprint, eager to cut through the battle and make some sense of the madness. Shayla carried herself alongside him but, in an instant, jumped high into the air and propelled herself forward. Michael was astonished at the power that drove her. The last time he had seen this was at night when she pursued one of their attackers. In the open field, under a bright sun, it was a magnificent and terrifying sight to behold.

The Dragoon landed hard on two horsemen in the town square, crushing them and their steeds into the cobblestone ground. Her spear swung through the air knocking more men from their horses hard onto the field. Five others rode hard towards her, determined to strike her down.

Again, she leapt into the sky and pushed herself down hard on the earth, cracking the ground under her feet. The shockwave from her small jump knocked her would-be attackers from the mounts, followed by quick surgical strikes to each of their chests.

Another cry went up over the village as twenty Imperial rangers poured out of a nearby wooden shack, cutting and hacking their way through the throng of advancing horsemen. They weaved and twisted in place, avoiding the onslaught with ease and finding their marks against their enemies.

At the sight of the rangers defending their post, Tiberius held his sword aloft and exclaimed, "Rangers! I am with you!"

The rangers looked to the hill. Their hearts renewed at the welcomed, but unexpected sight of their commander charging towards the town. "Tiberius is here! Our commander is with us!" a young voice cried out.

But her voice was silenced by an arrow delivered to her throat. Rage filled Tiberius, and he pressed on harder than he had in a year.

In a minute, Tiberius was in the town square, ducking and weaving around the horsemen like a dancer. His sword swung out, slicing through leather and flesh, cleaving the enemies' spears in half. Another volley of arrows fell into the village, stopping his charge forward for only a moment. Over his shoulder, he heard Michael's horse bellow in pain. Arrows littered its hide, driving the beast hard to the ground and sending Michael hurtling out of his saddle.

Tiberius gave him a quick inspection and saw that the boy was okay after his crash to ground. He turned his attention back to a group of soldiers rushing to meet him. But after a quick swipe of his sword, they all laid dead at his boots.

Michael stared at the ground under him for a moment, confused as to how he got here. Screaming from around him broke his daze, and he sprung to his feet to run after Tiberius. A moment later, he had pushed through the horde of enemy soldiers and broke for a nearby building opposite the village center. A cursory glance of the wooden building revealed that it was the rangers' own garrison as he ducked under a nearby water trough and stared wide-eyed at the battle unfurling in front of him. The young Mage had heard stories of the ferocity and skillfulness of the rangers. But up close, he could not form the words to describe what he witnessed.

Shayla continued to leap in and out of the battle, taking two or three more at a time with her powerful swings and crushing legs. The sudden shock of seeing the mighty dragoon in battle had yet to wear off and Shayla capitalized on their folly. This was her element, and she complete mastery of it.

In a matter of minutes, it was over. Twenty horsemen, and the beasts that had carried them, now laid dead in the village square. Cries for water to douse the burning buildings echoed throughout the town and a host of villagers ran to their nearby wells with buckets. Michael retreated from his hideout to take in all that had happened, wondering if there was something he could do to help these poor people. Tiberius and Shayla however, raced to the field in front of the village, eager to meet any new threat that would come. The young Mage, feeling obligated to remain with his companions, followed them as fast as his young legs would carry him.

The remaining rangers trailed after Tiberius and met him in the field beyond. "Commander! Most fortunate, you and your companion here arrived when you did," one of the rangers said, shaking her leader's arm.

"Well met, Constance. We were meant to stay the night in the village. Had we known there would be foes set against this place, we might have asked for help."

"Either way, we are glad you are here. Did you perchance see what they were wearing? Those who attacked the village, I mean."

Tiberius eyed the young ranger before answering. "Aye. But we will not speak of these things now."

"What do you mean?" the Mage cried. "They were wearing white! They are men from---"

New screams arose from the horizon, cutting Michael off mid-sentence. Tiberius gazed out to the top of the large hill in front of them and witnessed nearly fifty men on foot, racing towards the town. He steadied himself, preparing for the oncoming wave. Shayla crouched low, her spear steady and ready to fly. Michael threw his hands to his head, confused and angry all at once.

"They're going to overrun us!" Michael screamed.

"Courage, boy!" Tiberius replied, the fury in his voice cutting deep into Michael's soul. "Find shelter now!"

"But the villagers---"

"As long as I stand, no more death will be wrought on these people!" the Ranger bellowed.

Tiberius turned away from the frightened Mage, and with Shayla and his fellow rangers, flew headlong into the oncoming battle. Bloodlust and rage were etched onto the enemy's faces, matched only by the fury of Tiberius and the defenders who ran with him. Shayla bounded ahead, and with a mighty war cry, burst headlong into the oncoming wave of soldiers. Her spear was faster than lightning as it snaked and spun around, hacking arms and heads off in one swift motion. The rangers were right behind her, slashing and stabbing at more of the white-clad soldiers.

Michael turned and retreated back to the village, his hands still pressed against his head, and his lips fast in prayer to his gods. He flew beneath a small wooden house on the outskirts of the town. A sudden hotness crept up from inside his robes that ceased his constant praying. Slowly, he reached inside the folds of his cloak to find the handle of his ebony wand. He was shocked to find that even though the wand radiated such immense heat, the ivory metal grip was cold to the touch.

A sudden urge to reveal the wand began to overtake him. Despite knowing that such a thing would be futile right now, his body acted on its own accord. He tried with all his might to will his body into submission. For all his strength, the compulsion was too great to ignore. He felt as though something was controlling him like a puppet on the end of its strings. He knew what his body was trying to do was futile, and wrong. But his body continue on regardless.

Just as he moved to produce the wand a mighty roar boomed out from the village, as though from a beast of legend. The shock of such a sound released Michael from his trance. The furious battle beyond the town had come to an immediate standstill.

The Mage spun his head around underneath the wooden shack, trying to see where the roar had come from when he heard a mighty voice thunder out, "My village!"

Heavy steps rumbled out from a large stone building in the village square. The sound of scraping metal on the cobblestone ground ignited the air, and the mighty voice called out again, "My home!"

Michael broke from his cover to see what was approaching them. In his mind, he imagined an enormous dragon such as he had read about as a child, fire breathing from its mouth, and its forked tail swishing to and fro. When his eyes finally found the source of it they grew ten times their normal size. His mouth dropped in fear and wonder, and he stammered back to his hiding spot under the wooden building. Heavy foot stomps echoed throughout the plain and loosed fresh snow from the town's rooftops. The ground shook under its weight and power. In his terror, Michael finally saw him and was taken aback at the sight of him.

A massive heaving mountain of a man three times as tall and as wide as a normal man shuffled out of the village. His enormous muscular body was adorned with tattoos of the ancient dwarven language that seemed to glow against his body. His eyes had turned fire red with rage, sweat steamed off of him, his teeth gnashed into a twisted snarl, and his powerful muscular arms drug two enormous double-sided axes.

Tygahl Rogers, master of the village that bore his namesake, stared down the white-clad attackers to his home.

The air around him seemed to rise several degrees in an instant. He raised the massive axes over his body and cried out, "My people! You dare attack my people!?"

He was in motion towards the attackers in a flash, a mighty roar escaping his massive body. Faster than the fastest horse Michael had ever seen, this large hulking man sprinted to meet the new enemies head-on. No armor, no shield, no strategy or tactic. Just pure, ancient rage. The power of the Father had filled him again.

He cut through a wide swath of the enemy soldiers, his massive axes cleaving through their torsos as if slicing through a hot piece of bread. In one violent attack, ten of the soldiers lie dead in the snowy field. The occasional arrow or spear would find its mark against his enormous body, but never pierced his skin. The weapons themselves crumpled as paper against his thick skin, more of a nuisance than pain. But a nuisance was not something to cause such a dangerous wild man.

The rest of the soldiers turned in an instant and began to flee back over the hill with the berserker, close behind them. Tiberius and his companions flew after him, trying desperately to reach the Berserker, but there was no hope in keeping up with the man's speed. Once their foes had crested the hill, they spun in place to reengage with the beast of a man. Their screams of anger and cruelty almost matched the thundering roars of the oncoming behemoth.

From on high Shayla landed strong and hard, knocking nearly twenty of the men to the ground and stunning the rest with what had just happened. Her landing, as powerful as it was, did not phase the mountain of a man that charged past.

Rogers spun in place, a tornado of heavy slices that cleaved the men down the middle. He kicked another hard, concaving his chest and sending him flying towards his comrade. A few tried to cut him down, but their weapons merely broke under his steel skin. His eyes focused on the closest one to him, and in an instant, he was picked up by his torso and torn apart by Rogers' mighty hands.

The rangers stood frozen at the shock of Rogers' assault but were shaken from their awe as their commander flew headlong into the battle. His precise, fluid swordplay cut through ten men instantly as he continued to rush through the fray. Shayla sprinted through the formation, her spear tripping others to the ground. Having regained their composure, the rangers followed up her tactic by striking the fallen enemies before they could regain their senses.

Rogers continued to swing his heavy axes to and fro. From the outside, it looked as if a madman had been set loose on the battle. Amid the swirling chaos, it was a ballet of well-choreographed death. Within a few furious minutes, this second melee was over.

The rangers were panting hard, searching around for another attacker to strike down, but the three veterans were still and calm. Tiberius and Shayla regrouped behind Rogers near the hill's bottom, his colossal body trembling in with an unmatched fury.

"Is it over?" one of the young rangers asked.

"Silent, girl," Shayla hissed.

Then the voice cried and broke the silence again. "Loose!"

Another black cloud of arrows sprung into the sky. The fighters in the middle followed its gaze high as the arrows quickly climbed before again turning down onto the field where they stood. Tiberius and the rangers clammed up on the ground, hiding their heads and torsos from the oncoming volley. Shayla turned and knelt, exposing the back of her armor to the storm of arrows.

Rogers raised his axes high into the sky and bellowed defiantly against the storm of death above.

Michael trembled uncontrollably. Terror clouded his senses and rendered him immobile. In an instant, the sharp hot sting from the wand returned from his robes, shaking him loose of his fears and anger. His face hardened, he thrust his hand into the folds of his robe and thrust the ebony wand towards the volley of arrows.

A bright light burst from his wand and carried over the village and fields beyond meeting the arrows mid-flight. In an instant, they dissolved into dust, falling like the snow onto his companions. Tiberius and his defenders looked around in shock, hoping to find the source of the bright light until his gaze fell on to a stream of light rising up from the village. A faint smile broke his stern face as a sense of pride at the young man's resolve crept up inside him.

Again, the voice cried out, "Loose!"

Another volley sprang into the sky, and just as quickly was turned to ash. Tiberius, realizing that Michael's magic would continue to neutralize the enemy's arrows, was on his feet and sprinting towards the top of the hill. Shayla was next to his side as soon as he broke cover, followed by the remaining rangers. The Berserker Rogers stood for a moment, arms still aloft, raging into the bright sky.

When they reached the top of the frost-covered hill, they beheld more than two hundred archers in the fields before them. They were clad in the same white armor and leather as the horsemen who now lay dead in the field. In the middle of their tight formation, seated atop a mighty white steed, was their leader.

"Loose, damn you all! I said loose!" the lone horseman cried.

Back in the village, Michael continued to hold the wand aloft, keeping the bright light over his friends. At the renewed sound of arrows, a resurgence of anger stirred in him. He gave a mighty scream that rattled his young frame, and the light that he held above his friends spread wide over the formation of archers. The defenders on the hill stood wide-eyed at the sudden eruption of magic that met their eyes.

Great bursts of lightning began to shatter the ground where the archers stood, turning whole formations of them to dust. Great spheres of fire formed out of the light and fell on another formation sending bright red and orange flames hurtling all around. A thick green fog started to descend on more of them, causing the archers to choke and spasm.

Their spirits broke with all that had been wrought on them. Many began to break ranks and head for the thick, dead forest behind them. A few had thrown themselves on the ground, pleading to their gods for salvation. Whatever prayer these men uttered went unanswered as the green fog choked them too, and balls of fire set their corpses ablaze.

All at once, the destruction that had rained down on the enemy archers was over. The light that had hung in the sky stretched itself thin and disappeared into nothing. Back in his shelter, Michael dropped the wand and shook his head as sudden exhaustion overtook him. His eyes grew heavy, and his ears rang louder than church bells. Everything seemed to turn in to a haze of nothing as he slumped to the ground motionless.

"Cowards!" the horseman continued barked. "stand and fight you dogs!"

But his words were in vain. The remainder of his men had already fled from their posts, many abandoning their weapons where they stood. He looked around, unsure of what to do next when he noticed Tiberius atop the hill. He drew his sword high and exclaimed, "Long live the King!"

The lone horseman began to charge the hill, aiming straight for the Ranger commander. Unthinking, Tiberius sprinted head on to meet his foe. Though his legs were heavy and his chest on fire, he bid his body onward. But suddenly, a great cry thundered over the plains. Rogers leapt high over the hill and landed a hundred feet in front of the approaching horseman. The power of his arrival cratered the earth underneath him and sent soil and snow flying into the air. He jumped again towards the rider and hurled his massive body against the horse that bore him. The impact crushed the animal's body and threw its rider hard to the ground.

The white clad man staggered to his feet in a daze. His head was swimming and concussed, but still, he remained defiant. The berserker no longer needed to rush into the fray as he walked down the small man with evil purpose.

"Come at thee, ye beast!" the man in white cried.

He yelled a great war cry as he raised his sword in a vain attempt to strike down on Rogers. In a flash, Rogers had hoisted one of his mighty axes high and brought it down hard on the man, crushing him into the ground. He let loose a scream of rage and continued pounding the earth where the man was crushed. Swing after swing of his mighty axes rained down on the spot where the man had stood. Each swing was followed by a howl of anger. Each swing was heavier and more powerful than the last, pummeling the last of the man's blood and organs further and further into the earth.

But as the last swing was about to crash down, Tiberius materialized in front of him, exclaiming, "Son of Frijigzah! I bid you cease your rage!"

The mighty axe stopped a foot from the top of his head. Rogers stared at Tiberius, unsure of whom he was speaking. Tiberius held his sword to his face in a salute and bellowed at the behemoth, "I am Tiberius Alexander Axton! Son of Emperor Luke Alexander Axton! I bid you cease your rage! This battle is won!"

Rogers' hands fell to his side. His once red filled eyes began to clear to reveal the bright blue they had once been. His stiffened body began to slack and almost shrink down into a hunch. He breathed hard and heavy, and his face relaxed and began to turn sad. Tears were streaming down his massive face, and great sobs started to escape his mouth. He crumpled to his knees, his mighty chest raised and lowered as he cried hard at Tiberius.

"The Father has not forgotten you," Tiberius said, kneeling alongside the behemoth. "I bid you return to us now."

Rogers turned his gaze to the Ranger, and in a whisper, asked, "My lord. What have I done?"

Tiberius placed his gloved hand on the sobbing man's massive shoulder as if a small child were trying to comfort an enormous brown bear. "You defended your home with honor, Tygahl. There is no shame to be had in your actions, son of Frijigzah."

"Then why do I feel such shame and anguish, my lord?" Tygahl asked in between sobs.

"Tiberius!" Shayla cut in from the other side of the silent battleground. "Where is the boy? Where is Michael?"

A wave of panic and fear washed over him. His pulse and breath quickened, and a chill ran up him. In all the confusion of the battle, he had forgotten their young companion. Their young friend who had summoned such terrifying magic in their defense and was left left unguarded in the fighting. Without another word, Tiberius burst to his feet and sprinted hard for the village.

CHAPTER 16

THE AFTERMATH

The cold air cut through his chest like a hot knife. His side was screaming at him in pain, and his legs felt like they would fall off his body. But he still sprinted faster than he could have ever imagined himself moving in his whole life. He cursed himself for neglecting their young companion in all the mayhem that had erupted around them. He cursed himself for only being thankful for the Mage's well-timed intervention against the archers over the hill, and he cursed his body for not being fast enough to get back to him. He turned his head to see the Dragoon following a way off, lost in her own thoughts at what could have befallen young Michael.

"Shayla! Get in the village and find him. Quick!" the Ranger exclaimed.

Shayla burst into the sky at once, bounding towards the village. Five minutes later, he came crashing into the village square, heaving lungfuls of sharp cold air. But whatever pain he might have felt was silenced at once as he began to scramble from building to building calling for the boy. Several of the locals stopped to watch the two warriors dash about the village square in search, but none could offer any help. Many of them were still fast at work extinguishing the remaining fires from their homes, and several more just sat upon the cold ground in shock.

"Are you looking for the boy?" an elderly villager asked, herself tending to a few small and scared children of her own.

"Yes," the Ranger replied, rushing to her side. "Have you seen him!?"

She pointed a way off from the village square to the small wooden building at the edge of town. "We saw what happened, Ranger. We saw the magic light up the sky. And it was by that power alone that we are still here."

"Indeed, it is, mother. Thank you," he replied before pushing his *Sight* to where she had pointed. Sure enough, sticking out from behind a broken wooden barrel were a small pair of leather boots.

His legs were in motion at once, as he exclaimed, "Shayla, with me!"

They dashed to the wood building in an instant, and after a few tense moments, found Michael passed out against a large barrel. They laid him flat on the frozen ground and began feeling his body for any sign of a wound. Aside from a few small scratches and bruises, the boy looked altogether unblemished. Yet despite their continued probing and harsh words, he did not stir from his sleep. The two warriors started to grow frantic as they tried to rouse him, terror climbing up within their spirits.

"What evil has befallen him that he does not wake!?" the Dragoon exclaimed while she continued to search him over.

"You saw what I saw," Tiberius answered, regaining his composure. "Someone so small and young conjuring something like that. It must have taken a toll on him."

"What can we do? We do not have the skill to help him!"

"I don't know. But the boy needs a bed and warmth, now!"

He wrapped Michael's body in his arms as if holding a baby at nap and stood, looking around for any shelter that might have afforded them. Beyond the smoldering town square, he spotted the inn that was to be their temporary lodging that night and broke for it in a flash. He burst the flimsy wood and steel doors open and was stopped dead by the sight before him.

A dozen or more people were lying about in various states of pain and agony. Many had arrow wounds from the volleys, while others had been trampled in their desperate attempts to escape the fray. Even more were burned beyond recognition and laid on the massive wooden serving tables in unimaginable pain. He surveyed the room, searching for someone to help them before deciding to move past them and find a place of his own amongst the chaos. Yet everywhere he searched, each bed and table were occupied by the dead or the soon to be dead.

"Sir," a bright voice spoke from the door, cutting through the throes of the dying villagers. "Bring him to our quarters."

He turned to see Constance, the Ranger Captain assigned to the village, just inside the large tavern's sitting room. Without another word, he and Shayla turned and followed the ranger back out into the cold. They moved through the village with all haste they could muster, but everywhere they turned, the screams and crying of the wounded penetrated their ears. They were surrounded by a nightmare they could not escape. For a brief moment, Shayla wondered if she had slipped into a dream as the immeasurable destruction around her brought long-suppressed memories of the war back to her mind.

A moment later, they were at the rangers' black and grey painted barracks back near the village's front. They rushed inside the building and placed Michael onto one of the beds they kept in reserve at the back of the barracks. Shayla removed her helmet, knelt, and studied his young face. Tiberius remained standing, but unmoving behind her.

She took one of his hands in her own and whispered, "When will he wake?"

"I do not know," Tiberius replied. "What he conjured over the field was too great for someone so young. The best we can do is let him rest."

After a moment, Tiberius removed his sword and propped on the wall next to the bed. His gloves he placed on the bedside table and moved to leave the room. Shayla bolted upright at once, unsure of what he intended to do.

"You would leave him!?" she blurted out.

Tiberius didn't turn to meet her angry gaze. "There is nothing we can do but let him wake on his own. But there are people in this village that need our help now."

She stared at his back, a quiet rage rising in her heart. "Go then, Ranger," she said, at last, kneeling next to the boy again. "You may do as you wish, but I will not abandon his side."

Tiberius knew himself well enough that sitting and waiting would drive him mad. He had to be in motion. He had to do something to make sense of all this evil that had been called down on these poor people. He took a deep breath, bowed his head, and departed the barracks.

Shayla did not bother to see him out, all her attention on the unmoving young boy in the bed. For the first time in her long life as a dragoon, she set aside her spear and held Michael's hands tighter. She bowed her head, closed her eyes hard, and began to whisper a prayer for the young Mage.

"Kazduhl, lord and mightiest of all dragons, grant this boy your spirit and your mercy. Grant him the peace and strength to return from beyond to here again. Grant him your favor that he may nevermore lie in the twilight of this world but may walk in the sunlight of today all the days to come."

Her lips began to tremble, and her eyes started to water. "Kazduhl, lord and last of the dragons grant this boy the fire of your spirit. Grant him the honor of living under your great wings. Grant him your protection and love," she paused, unsure of how to finish her prayer until finally saying, "Bring him back to his friends."

Outside the barracks, Tiberius surveyed the overwhelming destruction. The sun was now low in the horizon, signaling nightfall was close at hand. He turned to his rangers and said, "Constance, send word to the capital at once. Tell them all that has transpired today and that I personally request a contingent of rangers reinforce us at once."

Constance nodded and sprinted to the nearest rookery to deliver Tiberius's ill news back to the Imperial City. He then turned to the other men. "I need each of you to help whoever you can. All aid from your stores and your knowledge you will render. And be sure to get them all indoors before the sun sets."

At his command, the rangers departed to retrieve whatever medical supplies they had and begin helping the people of the village. For himself, Tiberius returned to the inn. He stood just outside the door, breathing in the musty smell of death that emanated from within. In his rush to secure a place for Michael, Tiberius had not truly taken in the horrors around him. Now he had to steel his mind and his soul for what was to come. He drew in a deep breath of stinging air and pushed the weak door open.

Inside the inn, he saw more people had arrived since he was there only minutes ago. The cries of suffering had quieted down, but the odor he had smelled outside was now overpowering his senses. A small image of the wounded men during the war flashed in his mind before he quickly pushed it away. Now wasn't the time to think on such dark and painful memories. Now was the time to get to work.

Unsure of where to begin amongst the scared and dead people, he walked around the room in a daze. None of the villagers made eye contact with the ranger, all either busy with their own work or in a trance-like state of shock. The smells of burning meat and the whimpering of children seemed to fill every corner of the wooden inn. Near the back, his eyes fell on a group of children huddled in the corner.

He knelt beside them and asked, "Where are your parents, young ones?"

The oldest of them, a frightened blonde girl no more than twelve, slowly raised her hand and pointed off to a nearby table. He turned and followed her finger to see two unmoving bodies upon a massive dining table. They were almost unrecognizable from the burns that scorched their fair faces.

He turned to the scared children again, bowed his head, and said in a quiet voice, "I am sorry, children." His eyes met theirs again. "Do you know who I am?"

"You're Tiberius, leader of the rangers," the blond girl replied shakily.

"Aye that I am. And on my honor and the honor of my men and the emperor himself, these deeds will not go unpunished. I promise you."

The girl didn't move at his words, holding his gaze for a few solemn moments. "We care nothing of punishment, sir," she replied at last. "We just want our parents back."

Tiberius bowed his head again before standing. I can't bring your parents back, little ones, he thought to himself. But the enemy who wrought this on you will taste my steel, nonetheless.

"Are you truly the ranger leader Tiberius?" another voice asked from behind him.

He turned to find the voice and saw a young woman, barely inside her twenties, tending to three older men, all with arrow wounds to their arms and legs. Her eyes were the bright blue of people common in this part of the country, with bright blond hair that almost appeared white. She was small, barely half his own height, but the way she held down the men writhing in pain on the table told him she was indeed a woman of the northern kingdom. Hearty and strong, fierce and loyal. She was the queen of her own little dominion, and all would bend their will to her in that place.

"I am," the Ranger replied, moving to join her. "My men are out in the village, rendering whatever aid they can. What do you need me to do here?"

"My lord, I cannot ask you to help us," she said, her northern accent thick and almost unintelligible. "You are an Imperial and much above us commoners. Your victory against our attackers is thanks enough."

He studied her fair face, searching for why she felt as she did. He locked onto her fierce blue eyes and asked, "What is your name, daughter of the north?"

"Michelle, my lord. Michelle Bearborn," she replied at once.

"My name is Tiberius," he answered, kneeling to help the three men. "Not 'lord' or 'master.' Just Tiberius. And no one is above or below another in this empire, especially when our people require aid."

"With all due respect, that is not the way in our home. The King of White has made it known time and again that we are inferior to your kind."

Tiberius eyed the woman and his voice grew cold. "I care not for Forval's misguided wisdom. I am here to help in any manner you require. Command me, daughter of White."

She inspected his face probing for any lies in him, but finally, she nodded in acceptance of his aid. "I've torn the linen into bandages," she said, waving her hand to a back room in the inn. "We don't have much in the way of supplies around here for this many injured."

"That's smart thinking, Ms. Bearborn," he replied. "I'll set to work at once. Boil more water and find me some paste and wood."

Michelle hurried off to refill the emptied water basin while Tiberius collected the bandages and other supplies. Together, they worked for hours on end, mending the broken and beaten villagers. Cuts and bruises were dressed, and broken bones set as best they could manage. A few more of the people continued to straggle in throughout the night, thanks to the ranger's diligent efforts. That that didn't require care took up arms with the rangers to watch the village overnight. The others were treated immediately by the two and with as much care that their tired bodies could muster.

It was just after ten that night when they had finally managed to treat all the people inside the inn. Tiberius sat at the bar, surveying the crowded, hot room. Many of them were fast asleep now; others continued staring blankly at the floor, contemplating the horrors that had transpired. These were good, decent folk, far away from the rest of their kingdom's politics and strife. Yet they were now drawn into a conflict they had no business in. And a conflict he himself didn't quite understand. Yet.

Exhausted, Michelle plopped down into a seat next to him and laid her head on the bar. "I think that's all of them, sir," she said, shutting her eyes.

"Aye," he replied. "You did good by these people, Ms. Bearborn. They owe you a great debt."

She sat up and looked around the room. "These are my people, you know. Why would I let them suffer when I can help? More help than the master gave us."

"That's not true," Tiberius said, rubbing his eyes. "He helped us repel the enemy before they could overrun this place. He was at the forefront of the battle."

"Yes, he was. But where was he after when his people needed healing? You yourself were in the thick of fighting and are now here to help. Your rangers are still on duty keeping watch over our home. But our 'master' is nowhere to be found."

Realization dawned on him. It had been several hours since the battle's end, and he had not seen Rogers anywhere in the village. He mustered the strength to stand, and after fetching a cloak near the door, began marching through the dark cold. The moon shone down as he walked over the village's charred ruins and out into the field beyond. He trudged up the snow-covered hill, and still kneeling in the ground beyond was the Berserker. He appeared to have not moved for several hours and kept his chin down to his chest.

The Ranger stalked up behind the Berserker, not daring to alarm him lest the rage overcome him again. There was no telling the last time Master Rogers had felt the rage of the Father, nor if it would reappear again. When he got closer, he could make out tears frozen against the large man's cheeks. He stood over him, contemplating what to say. Even on his knees, his head still reached the bottom of Tiberius's chest. Slowly, he reached out and placed his hand upon Rogers' shoulder.

"You know who I am?" he whispered to the behemoth of a man.

"You are the Ranger Commander Tiberius," a rough voice replied. "You are a hero to the empire, my lord."

"Aye," Tiberius replied, kneeling to come face to face with the man. "I am Tiberius, commander of the Imperial Rangers. But do you *know* who I am?"

Rogers raised his head and stared hard at Tiberius's own. "You carry the blade of our emperor. You fought the enemy unquestioningly. You brought the foreign warrior, and I'm assuming the Mage as well."

A lump formed in his throat that he had to fight through to continue, "You called yourself Tiberius Alexander Axton before. You are the son of His Majesty, aren't you?"

Tiberius nodded his head in reply. "Yes, son of Frijigzah. And while I am not emperor yet, I carry his sword and bare his burdens in the wide world. By chance, we arrived at your home tonight, and I am grateful that we did. Why do you sit in the snow amongst the dead enemy and not in the warm tavern with your people?"

Rogers bowed his head again. "I am ashamed, sir. I had abandoned the Father and his gifts to live a peaceful life in my homeland. I helped them build this village with my own two hands when I was but a boy. And like my father and grandfather, I tended to the people as they needed."

"You have served them well, Master Rogers. Despite the horrors laid upon them, they remain strong in spirit."

He looked at the Ranger again, renewed tears swelling in his eyes. "They know not of my past, nor of who I really am. What would they think of me now?"

"They will think greatly and fairly of you. They know you could not have prevented what happened to them but met the foe headlong in the field. It is by your power and your desire to protect them that they are alive tonight. Your people are up in the village, eager to see you. Come, walk with me."

He stood and extended a hand to the giant man. Rogers grasped the Ranger's small hand and stood, towering over Tiberius like a parent to a child. He studied Tiberius for a moment before nodding in agreement. They both turned and began the walk back to the village.

"What has brought you and your companions to my home, sir?" Rogers asked as they rounded the hilltop.

"We were on our way to the Ice Steps beyond your village. The emperor himself has sent us on a most dire mission that was to take us well into the Land Beyond. Your home was to be our last stop before we entered the unknown tundra ahead."

"I see," Rogers replied, surveying the ice-capped mountains silhouetted against the clear starry night. "Whatever your purpose is in those mountains, it had best be of great importance. No one in living memory has ventured beyond these borders to climb those peaks."

"The dwarves did after the founding of the empire," Tiberius said.

"Aye," Rogers replied, looking down on the young Ranger at his side. "If you believe such tales. All I know is in my long life, I have seen many folks try and climb the steps to explore the peaks beyond. None have returned."

"Maybe they found whatever it is they were looking for that compelled them to venture there. After the war, I heard rumors of many men turning to the north to live in peace and quiet."

"We saw these men you speak of, my lord. When I was a boy, many men growing tired of the wars and battles that have long plagued our country would venture up the Ice Steps. And after the five-year war, well, could you blame them?"

No, I don't blame them at all, the Ranger thought. But to abandon your homes to wallow in grief? What kind of man does this?

"Well, at any rate, I reckon our trip up the mountains will have to be postponed," Tiberius conceded. "This attack by the king ---"

"The King did this!?" Rogers exclaimed, stopping dead in his tracks.

Tiberius turned and saw the great man's chest rising and falling rapidly in the cold, dark night. He held up his hand and said, "Master Rogers! You will maintain your calm tonight, do you understand?"

Rogers closed his eyes and caught his breath. After a minute, he slowly opened them again and said, "I beg your pardon, Master Tiberius. It has been twenty years since I last felt the Father's rage in me. My body isn't used to it as it once was."

Tiberius lowered his hand. "I know it must be difficult. The rage and the power the Father bestows is not something taken lightly. I pray you will not need to use it again."

"Let me try again. How do you know the King of White did this against my people?"

Tiberius stared at the man before taking a knee amongst a group of dead soldiers they had been walking through. When he stood, he held in his hand a heavy wool and linen banner riddled with intricate stitching. In the middle of the flag, stitched in beautiful black and green beads, was the form of a great white bear, standing erect and proud against a snowy forest.

"This is how I know, Tygahl."

The massive man stared dumbstruck at the heavy banner in the Ranger's hands. He reached out and brought it to his face to see it closer. "This has not flown openly in these lands in a very long time," Tygahl said after a few minutes of inspecting the flag.

"No, it has not. Yet here it is at the site of a battle. What would you take this to mean?"

Tygahl dropped the flag to the ground and stared into the bright night sky. His breath started to quicken, and his arms like tree trunks, were shaking with anger. He began to take in large gulps of air to try and steady himself and began jerking his head back and forth in denial.

"The white bear had been the symbol of the White clan long ago in the days before the empire's founding," Tiberius pressed, circling around the huge quaking man. "Once they joined the empire, they adopted new banners to show their unity. But some have held onto the old ways and have wished for things to return as they were before the empire."

"I refuse to believe this, sir," the Berserker whispered, his voice raspy and rushed.

"Flying this flag is a crime in itself, Tygahl. But flying it in battle? And battle against your own people? What does this tell you, Master Rogers!?"

Tygahl looked at the Ranger, his face a mix of anger and sadness. He knew very well what it meant but dared not utter such words lest they become real. He looked around the field at the dead bodies in their pristine white armor. He reexamined the banner, studying the colors and shapes of the bear. He thought on the long history of resentment the kings of White had harbored against the empire. He remembered the anger and ire they felt against being beneath the true lord of their land.

"It means that King White has openly declared insurrection against the empire, sir," the Berserker said at last. This is unheard of in our empire. Why would he dare such a thing?"

Tiberius motioned for Tygahl to continue following him back to the village. "Yes, it is quite insidious of a maneuver on his part," Tiberius agreed. "A few days ago, we ran into a few of his knights that apparently had been enchanted. Shortly after that, we were waylaid by an ancient evil in this part of the world called a Revenant. Then we arrive here to find your home being assailed by the King's men. Too much coincidence."

"I've never believed in coincidence, or chance sir. Things fit together as they will," Tygahl offered, his anger beginning to subside. "However, enchanted knights, a black demon from legend, and now the King's own men assailing us? What will your father say to this? It is unfortunate he is so far south in the capital, and not here to deal with this himself."

"Constance has sent word to the capital and to my men at Kovaiyemarck. Hopefully, they will answer my summons and be here soon enough."

"Why would they not answer their commander's summons? Surely such a thing as massacring your own people would be reason enough for the emperor and your rangers to take action."

"Because things are happening in the outside world, Tygahl. A plot is brewing that we cannot quite yet see. As such, my men may be required elsewhere in the country for another purpose His Majesty has intended. In any case, the summons was sent. Until then, my companions and I shall stay here until you all are back on your feet."

"You do us a great service, sir," Rogers replied. "I would be honored for you and your friends to stay amongst us. But please, do not speak of the evil tidings of King White until we know for certain. I trust you and your judgment and knowledge, but these folks would not take kindly to the news that they were assaulted by their own lord."

Tiberius nodded in agreement. Though he was a man of the empire and swore no allegiance to any of the Kings of the land, he had to respect their sovereignty within their holds. The people loved their monarchs, perhaps more than they loved their emperor. It would be unwise to reveal that their beloved ruler had ordered his men to attack a village on the edge of nowhere.

They walked the rest of the way in silence until, at long last, they reached the inn. Rogers slowly entered the crowded room and was taken aback by the sight before him. He inched his way through the throng until he reached Michelle, fast asleep at the bar where Tiberius had left her.

"Wake up, little one," Rogers whispered sweetly to Michelle.

She began to stir, opening one eye then another. It took her a few moments to realize who was speaking to her, but when she saw the now kind face of the Tygahl, she jumped to her feet and hugged his bear-like neck tight. "Where have you been, you big brave fool!?" she exclaimed.

"Out in the snow acting like a child, when I should have been here with you," he admitted shamefully. "How are our people?"

"They are all banged up and hurt pretty badly, but Master Tiberius here and I mended them as best we could," she replied, breaking her vice like grip on his neck. "I fear if we don't have more help in the next few days, things will begin to turn worse."

"Tiberius here has already sent word to the capital and to his men," Rogers revealed to the young girl. "Help will come, I promise."

"Was there not a Mage amongst us today?" she asked. "Perhaps he could use his magic to heal our people."

"I'm afraid our Mage has fallen into a deep sleep," Tiberius replied, joining them at the bar. "He is still a child, and the effort with which he conjured that magic today has taken its toll on him."

Though true that Michael had passed out from the strain of conjuring such powerful magic, Tiberius dared not reveal more than was needed. Doing so would cause too much worry, and these people had enough to deal with as it was. And he was still unsure who was friend and who was a spy for his unseen enemy. But it was fortunate enough that Michael possessed the Father's wand and could still summon magic. Though now that he thought on it, it too was a coincidence that Michael possessed the wand at all.

His mind flashed to the face of the dwarf Catherine, and her belief that things were in motion that none could see. Though now, with his eyes and mind working again, he felt he could begin to perceive the guiding hand of Frijigzah at work. For it was his wand Michael wielded. It was his children, the dwarves, that had saved them after their encounter with the Revenant. And it was his Berserker that had turned the tide in the battle. But he pushed these thoughts to the back of his mind for later.

"The boy had best sleep, Michelle," Rogers said. "I have seen what becomes of young mages who push themselves too hard too fast, and I would not wish such ills on our young savior."

"You have my word, Ms. Bearborn," Tiberius said, placing an open hand on his chest and bowing his head. "Though we are far from you, the empire has not forgotten you and your people. They will come to help."

She stood and embraced the Ranger with such strength that Tiberius had not felt in a long time. "Thank you, sir," she said. "We are grateful."

They broke their embrace and looked at the people scattered in the inn. After a long while, Rogers spoke again. "It must be after midnight; we should all turn in. I suspect tomorrow will be a long day."

Tiberius bid them farewell and left to check on his men who were standing watch throughout the night. He found them scattered throughout the edges of the village, vigilant as hawks on the hunt, and ready for any sign of danger through the night. Satisfied with their positions and demeanors, he headed back to the barracks to rejoin his friends.

He quietly stepped across the threshold into the ranger's barracks. A few stray villagers had taken up the remaining beds since his absence, but at the back of the room, he found his friends. Young Michael still fast asleep, though his breathing had regulated, and a faint snore was escaping his body. Shayla laid on the floor in a makeshift pallet, her spear just within arm's reach but propped against the wall next to his sword.

He stared at his friends for a long time. In the few short days they had spent together, a great many things had transpired, and yet more was still to come before they reached their final destination somewhere in the mountains beyond. He had grown to care very much for both of them. In fact, they had become equal to him as his own rangers were for his affection and loyalty. He was proud to be with them, and he was happy at long last to realize he was in the company of true friends. He sat in a chair next to them, cautious about making no sound lest he wake them from their much-deserved slumber.

He slouched down and kicked his legs out in front of him before pulling out his pipe. He puffed for a while, ever watchful of any signs of trouble. But after many hours of forced alertness, he closed his eyes and, for the first time in many days, fell fast asleep amongst his companions in the safety of the barracks.

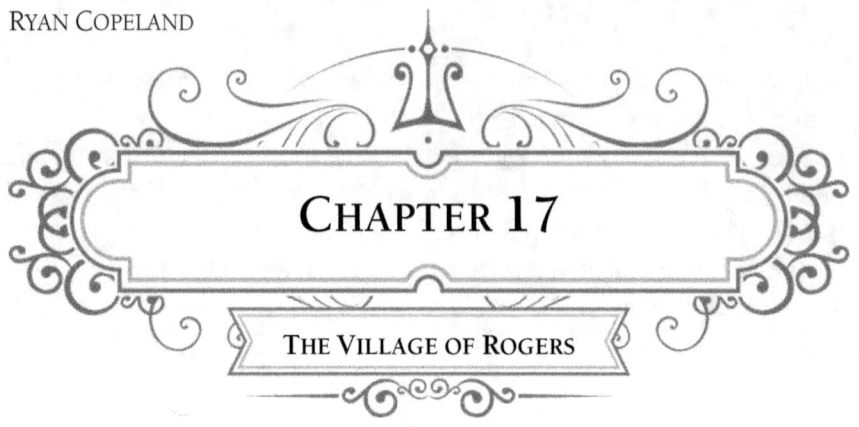

CHAPTER 17

THE VILLAGE OF ROGERS

Tiberius woke to the welcoming smell of crisp bacon and strong bitter coffee. He forced his eyes open and stood from the chair with a great stretch. Michael was still fast asleep in the bed before him, yet Shayla and her spear were absent from where they had lain last night. He retrieved his own weapon and left Michael's room to find the sun beaming down through the windows. In the barrack's central area, he saw many of the villagers had departed from where they had slumbered the night before. Those that remained were awake and appeared to be in good spirits, all things considered. Behind the main area, he found three of his men fast at work preparing breakfast.

"Well met, rangers," he said, the sleep leaving his voice.

"Well met, sir," one of the men, a little younger than the rest, replied. "Your friend the Dragoon left before sunrise to hunt for our breakfast. She did not want to wake you from your sleep."

"I wish she had," Tiberius said. "I am eager to see the aftermath of yesterday's battle before the whole village wakes."

"I don't think that will be an issue, sir," another ranger said, himself busy with frying massive cuts of thick bacon. "Constance and Tygahl have ordered the villagers to stay in the inn lest another attack come today. If they need something from their own dwellings, the Master is escorting them personally."

Tiberius nodded in approval. Constance was new to the rangers but already had the instincts and leadership to make a fine leader within his ranks. He retrieved a small mug of coffee and headed outside to inspect the town but instead was struck with an unexpected surprise. Amongst the tattered village's debris, he found Shayla and the Rogers slowly working through the rubble. Small piles of lumber had been stacked, stones piled up, and anything not reusable was slowly burning in the town square.

"Well met," he said as he neared them.

"Good morning, sir," Rogers replied, hoisting two large beams onto his broad shoulders. Even without the power of the Father flowing through him, the man was just as strong and formidable.

"I trust you slept well?" Shayla asked. Any traces of venom in her voice from their last conversation was gone. In its place was a renewed calm and earnest devotion to her friend and leader.

"Indeed, I did, thank you," he replied with a nod.

"Any word from the capital yet?" Rogers asked, heaving the beams onto a growing pile.

"I have not checked with Constance yet, Master Tygahl. But I suspect not yet."

"Please, sir, do not call me 'Master'," Rogers replied. "I have no dominion over you or your friends, and after yesterday I simply wish to serve and rebuild my home."

Tiberius smiled at the warmth the great man showed him. "As you wish, Tygahl. What time did you and Shayla start this morning?"

"Just before daybreak. Your Dragoon here had already been off for a hunt and brought back much for our breakfast this morning."

"I held my vigil over the boy throughout the night," she added. "The morning sun gave way to renewed purpose. My lord bid me rise and get to work. You helped the people in your way last night. This was the least I could do to help."

"Your skill and power in battle more than enough helped our village, Shayla. We are eternally grateful to you," Tygahl replied with a small bow. "My home is your home for as long as you need it."

"I reckon we will be here for a while," she responded. "At least until Tiberius' friends arrive from the south."

"Aye," Tiberius said, discarding his mug and straightening himself. "We can't very well leave you and yours to fend for yourselves after all that has happened."

"I still don't understand why the King would send his men to attack us," Tygahl said. "What manner of treachery would compel something like that is wholly foreign to me."

Tiberius and Shayla exchanged knowing looks. While Tiberius had confided in Tygahl of their encounter with the enchanted soldiers and the Revenant, he did not reveal all that he thought or imagined preferring to keep such conjecture to himself. Nor had he told their tale to the fullest, but now was as good a time as any he supposed. He beckoned Tygahl to sit with him and, for the next hour, regaled him on all that had happened since their departure from the capital. As to the true purpose of their mission, that he would not dare speak of yet.

When he had finished his tale, Tygahl sat for a moment before leaping to his feet and pacing the length of their work area. Tiberius and Shayla exchanged more looks of worry. Partially over how he would take the news, and somewhat worried that he would succumb to his newly invigorated rage.

"Surely some madness has poisoned the King's mind," Tygahl said at last. "To match might with the empire is folly indeed! In terms of sheer numbers, he does not have them. In terms of battle-tested warriors, he does not have them! By all accounts, he is courting suicide against the emperor!"

"You are right, sir," Shayla said. "I have fought with the empire's armies, and their ferocity and skill in battle were enough to break the Narzeth. That is something that had not happened in all of our recorded histories. What he is hoping to gain, I cannot foresee."

"The kings of the White Kingdom have long held a grudge against the Axtons," Tiberius offered, recalling the history of their shared people. "The Axtons were of Clan White in the days before the empire. Alexander Axton himself was a great general in these lands, revered by all for his skill in battle and his diplomatic and caring nature. The Whites have never forgiven him for assuming the title of emperor. They felt then, as I'm sure they do now, that their own general should have won the glory for them."

"I did not know that," Tygahl admitted, halting in his tracks.

"Very few people outside of our families know that," Tiberius admitted. "The Axtons abandoned all allegiance to its home kingdom, instead swearing fealty to all peoples of the continent. Alexander Axton was a unifier of warring tribes. The Whites saw him as a conqueror and a traitor."

"That is nonsense!" Tygahl declared, spitting the ground in anger. "Your ancestor tamed the leaders of this continent and brought forth the most powerful empire in the world. To say he conquered is completely wrong and a salacious lie! Besides, who could hold a blood feud for five hundred years?"

"I agree, my friend. Alexander didn't win any titles; he unified the people for a common purpose. Then, those same people he led in battle elevated him to emperor. But you northerners are a stubborn lot! And the Kings of White are greedy and have always seen others as beneath them. At any rate, you cannot change someone's view of things. Nor can you reason with someone who has let five hundred years of hatred and resentment fester in their hearts. I would reckon that the latest King White has finally had enough and suffered enough perceived insults that he is claiming what is his."

"Then he will die for his folly and hubris," Tygahl replied.

"It still doesn't explain his actions in laying waste to his own people," Shayla interjected. "Nor, if the Revenant was indeed under his sway somehow. Can a beast such as that be tamed and used for someone's evil purpose?"

"No," Tiberius conceded. "A Revenant is the spirit of the corrupt and evil. It leeches the very power of the land and allows it to grow strong with dark magic. It cannot be tamed. And as to the King's motivations on yesterday's actions, I am at a loss for understanding."

Shayla nodded in agreement before Tiberius continued, "Then do you not also believe it is not chance or luck that we have been rescued thrice all by things tied to the Father Frijigzah?"

Shayla nodded again, conceiting her companion's assessment. "It is true that we have been rescued out of danger by things or people directly tied to him, yes. What would all this tell you?"

"I do not know, my friend. Three times have we come into danger on our quest. Three times we have been rescued by the workings of Frijigzah. Right now, I feel like I'm a pawn in a game being played by something higher than our understanding. To be honest, I'm sick of it."

"The Father has always been a mystery to us," Tygahl added. "We who worshipped him for his might and power were always ignorant to his purpose."

"The dwarves seemed to be fully attuned to him," Shayla replied.

"The dwarves are kin to us through our belief in Him. Yet, we were simply blessed with his power. Both of you should know that the gods and spirits of the world do not bestow their gifts willingly. Each of us carries a portion of their power and have used those gifts for a purpose. Perhaps our purpose has been theirs all along. We have just been stuck in our own mortal understandings; we could not comprehend them."

The Ranger and Dragoon stared at the man, struck in awe of his wisdom and insight. They had never considered their gifts to be for the greater glory and purpose of those who bestowed them. They had always wielded them for their own need. But now, they began to see things differently. Perhaps the Warrior and dragon king did have a stake in the affairs of the mortals below them.

"In any case," the Berserker continued, "I think I will take a walkabout. I need to think on things."

After he departed and was a way off, Shayla turned to the Ranger and asked, "Should we tell the boy of our suspicions when he wakes?"

Tiberius stopped at her question. He surveyed the terrain around them, taking in the beauty of such a cold and desolate world and how it could bring peace to troubled minds. It had been many years since he ventured this far north. But being here amongst these people, and amongst the cold and calm. Amid the woods and mountains in the distance, he could feel as though he were home. As though he were Alexander himself in his native land. Even though he was born in the city way down south and trudged all over their empire in his duties, up here, he finally began to feel home.

His mind flashed to Michael, full of life and smiling around the campfires with him. The dwarven children laughing at his jokes and to how frightened he was that night he faced down the ten kings atop the Unity Tower. How in such a short amount of time he had turned from a scared boy to a man. Life in the wild will do that to anyone, and after all they had faced together, he had started to come into his own. In an instant, he knew the truth.

"Yes, Shayla. We will tell the boy," he said at last. "He has saved our lives twice now, saved this whole village in fact. This whole mission was started because of him, and he has earned the right to be told everything."

"I agree. I was simply seeing if we were on the same page," she replied with a bow. "I think I will go force Tygahl to the inn for some breakfast. A man his size could probably eat a dozen horses and still have room to spare."

Tiberius smiled at her, bowed low, and watched her stroll away back to the Berserker before turning to continue his walk in the village. He stooped here and there to inspect the bodies of the dead soldiers that still littered the ground. Their leather-wrapped armor looked new and untested. Their swords and spears were recently forged and showed no sign of wear and tear. This was a newly fielded army, he realized. And as such, was given all the latest and most modern gear in the kingdom's arsenal, though little good it did them when matched against experience and skill.

What an absolute waste, he thought to himself as he strolled. Their blind devotion to that idiot they call King is what got them killed, and I fear many more of their brothers will fall before his incredible hubris and stupidity is revealed.

An hour later, Tiberius arrived at the inn to check on Michelle and the villagers. To his surprise, instead of the cacophony of pain and anguish that had greeted him the night before, he now heard laughter and merriment from outside the inn. Stepping inside, he found Tygahl and Shayla digging into their breakfast alongside the surviving villagers. Many of the townsfolk had begun to regain their composure and happiness. Many were now offering praise to Tiberius and his companions, while many more had started to offer their services to Tygahl in whatever manner of help he required.

"I'll find some work for everyone to accomplish after we finish our meals," he said in between bites of bacon. "We will all need to pull our weight if we are to rebuild what was taken. But enough of that!" He held a flagon of mead aloft and proclaimed, "Thanks be to the gods of our fathers!"

"Thanks be!" the people replied in unison before toasting their Master.

"And thanks be to the rangers, and the brave Dragoon Shayla, for this much-needed food and comfort!" Tygahl proclaimed again.

"Thanks be!" the people replied again.

Tygahl caught Tiberius's eye from the doorway and stood at once. He raised his large flagon above him and proclaimed in a loud booming voice, "Hail! Commander Tiberius of the Imperial Rangers!"

Cries of "Hail!" sounded out around the room, rattling the wooden building down to its foundations. Tiberius bowed his head in humility to the praise offered by the people. It had been many long years since he had walked amongst the people from the north and he had forgotten their resilience was unmatched by any other kingdom in the Axton Empire. After the cheering died down, he began to move through the crowded inn to take his seat next Shayla at the bar. She offered him a broad smile and leaned close to him.

"Like I said, once the big man had some decent food in him his whole mood changed."

Tiberius chuckled at her words, and said, "You will find northerners often are at their best after a few plates of breakfast, and a few potent cups of coffee, my friend."

He had sat chatting with Shayla and Tygahl for a while when Constance came rushing into the room. All eyes followed her as she quickly approached Tiberius, who rose to greet her.

"Sir, messages just came in," she reported exasperated. "A detachment is on its way here from the capital at all haste."

"Excellent news indeed!" Tiberius said, clasping Tygahl's back. "They will surely bring medicine for these people and reinforcements to protect against—"

"I'm sorry, sir, but there is more," she interrupted, her voice grim. "A red dove arrived at the emperor's rookery last night. A red dove bearing the figure of a white bear against the snowy mountains."

Tiberius's body stiffened at those words. All of time around him seemed to stop, and for a moment, his mind went numb as he tried to process what he had just heard. But then all at once, his heart began to race, his blood boiled, and his stomach turned over. Whatever anger he had held at bay was starting to rekindle inside him.

Shayla stepped towards the Ranger and asked, "What does that mean?"

Tiberius steadied himself, trying to force his anger at bay. "In the days before the empire, the clans of our land would send doves to one another. A white dove meant peace, a blue dove for requesting a parlay. And a red dove---"

"War," Shayla finished for him.

"Best take this outside, my friends. Tygahl join us, please," he whispered before pushing through the throng of people.

Once they emerged from the inn and walked a small distance from the door, Constance continued the message. "The message also said the King's banners have been recalled and his army is marshalled in White Fyre. The city has been completely garrisoned by his forces. The people who lived there have been kicked out of the city and their homes. The King is on his way there to take command."

Tiberius seethed with rage at the news. Shayla, in turn, looked hard at her companion and asked, "Isn't Michael from White Fyre?"

"Aye," he replied, shaking with rage. "That is his home. Or rather, it was his home."

"How did our forces get such information so quickly?" Tygahl asked.

"I would suspect these things have happened since our quest began. Undoubtedly, the emperor was waiting till we made contact with him to reveal all that has happened," Tiberius replied, his mind fast at work.

"Why would the King garrison his men in Michael's home?" Shayla asked.

"White Fyre is the largest port in the empire," Tygahl explained. "If he controls the port, then trade from across the sea is impossible."

"Why would he care about the trade from across the sea when he is marshalling for war?"

"Countries to the west of our empire trade goods with us such as iron ore and golden string. Materials we use in smithing our arms and building our homes," Tiberius said. "He also can't have his army encircled and can make a hasty retreat."

"The King's navy is the largest in our country outside of the Imperial Navy," Tygahl added.

"Before we jump to conclusions, how can we be sure this letter is even real? Who wrote it?" Shayla interjected.

Constance held the letter for Tiberius to read himself. He felt his heart skip a beat as soon as his eyes saw the beautiful and elegant handwriting on the parchment. A faint smell of roses and sunflowers flooded his senses, and dreams of a far off cottage in the woods came crashing on him.

He turned to the Dragon Knight, and with a lump growing in his throat, said, "My First Sergeant Trevin wrote this letter. I would know his handwriting anywhere in the world, and I believe his words to be true."

The four stood in silence for a moment, trying to decide what to do next when Shayla asked, "Did the letter say when this detachment would be here?"

"No, ma'am, it did not," Constance answered. "But if this letter was indeed written by First Sergeant Moore, then he would not openly say what their plans would be."

"The man wants a war," Tiberius uttered without thinking. His whole body shook with anger, and his heart began to pound as if he were in the thick of battle. He looked between the three of them into the square with a clenched jaw and said, "So be it. The man will have war."

"Father preserve," Tygahl muttered.

"There was something else," Constance said.

"Oh, gods bless it, what else?" Shayla exclaimed.

"One of the villagers on guard thought they saw men in the trees early this morning. When we went to investigate, we saw no track or sign of disturbance, but if there are scouts out in the wild, they won't leave much of a trace, even to us."

Tiberius stood still for a minute before turning again to his Ranger. "Take the men and scout wide around the village. When you're done, report back to Master Rogers. Tygahl, I request you give twenty of your most able-bodied men to continue the watch. Until we receive our reinforcements, we will dig in here."

Tygahl placed his hand on his chest and bowed, the Imperial sign of respect. "My lord, me and my people are at your command. We will gladly follow your lead in defending our homes."

Constance and Tygahl bowed at Tiberius's orders and departed to retrieve their men. After they had departed, Tiberius turned to Shayla, his face filled anger and confusion, and said, "I fear our journey must be put on hold, my friend. War and death surround our country."

"Things have indeed changed," Shayla finished. "I am torn though, Tiberius. On the one hand, I would wish to fight against this evil that has infested our home. But on the other, we were charged by your father to see this quest out."

"That we were," he replied. "But what good is rekindling the power of magic if we have no home to come back to?"

"Do you think King White is actually capable of overthrowing the empire?"

"Alone, no. But if he is indeed the machinations that have befallen us so far, then it's not out of the realm of possibility that he could sway others to his cause."

"Surely, his reach and influence has not grown to such an extent. Regardless, should we not continue our quest anyway? Rekindling the power of magic would help sway our favor in whatever war is to come."

Tiberius thought on her wisdom for a moment. He weighed his decisions as a banker weighs money. At length, he answered his companion's question. "True, magic would aid us. But I remember the parting words of Lady Stonefoot. The path we follow will lead us to where we ought to be. It is no coincidence we are here when this has happened. We should stick to the path we are walking now."

She conceded his point and grew silent. Without another word, she turned and headed back to the barracks deciding to resume her vigil on the Mage. Tiberius stood there for a while, contemplating all that he had learned. The weight of an impending war with King White made him seethe with a fury he had not felt since the battle at the Vermillion Pass. Finally, he decided to take a walkabout and examine the village for all that needed to be done.

The sun was beginning to hang low in the sky as he began to trek back to the ridge where they had made their stand against White's soldiers. Large black crows and other birds had gathered in the field to eat away at the dead that littered the area. With their weapons and armor already stripped away by the rangers, the birds were unimpeded in filling their gluttonous bellies. Strangely, the sight of it brought a measure of contentedness to Tiberius. It reminded him of his purpose in life and his duty to the empire. To defend its citizens from harm and evil intent, regardless of the kingdoms of their births. The sight of the dead comforted him mostly because it reminded him of war.

Try as he might to forget the last five years of his life, it dawned on him that fighting the Narzeth was the first time he ever felt truly alive. Being out in the woods and forests with his men and bringing justice to the enemies, both known and unknown, made him feel alive. Cutting down men for a righteous purpose made him feel alive. The realization of this stirred up a great conflict in his soul, for he did not know whether these feelings humanized him or made him a monster.

He stopped at the peak of the hill. He could see the Ice Steps carved into the mountain face in the distance, the only manner of ascending into the frozen tundra that lay beyond. So close to their destination, yet now with all the evil surrounding them, a million miles away. He felt torn between continuing their journey to the Land Beyond and fulfilling his sworn oaths as a ranger to fight the empire's enemies.

He was lost in his thoughts when a faint whiff of smoke caught his attention. He focused on where it came from and extended his *Sight* further out to perceive what it was. But even with all of his power, he could not see anything that would lead him to believe someone was burning a campfire.

He jogged down from the ridge, eager to discover the source of this new smell amongst the rotting corpses. A part of him prayed it was just his imagination at play while the warrior in him prepared itself for battle. Past the field where the archers had fallen, he rushed to the tree line beyond. A sudden curious sight bid him stop just before breaking into the trees.

On the ground lay the dead bodies of the archers who had fled before the might of Michael's magic. Their once pristine white leather armor had now turned a disgusting mix of green and black. He extended his power from where he stood and could plain as day see many of them had been hacked at the waist and knees. Many more had been bludgeoned hard, their skulls and chests concaved as if a large tree had fallen on them. He drew his sword and crept into the woods, his eyes searching deep for any sign of threat.

"Fear not, King's Son," a stern voice whispered from the woods.

He recoiled in shock. It appeared as though the shadows in the forest had begun to move, and slowly dozens of figures began to emerge. At the head, two familiar figures came into focus.

"You will not be alone in your plight," Catherine said, coming into view joined by the dwarf shaman.

"Lady Stonefoot!" Tiberius exclaimed, rushing to greet her. "How is it you are here?"

"A good question that is best answered later," she replied. "For now, you must take us to the Mage."

"Alas, he has fallen into a deep sleep," Tiberius replied. "The strain of conjuring such powerful magic as he used has taken its toll on him."

"Aye, we know this, boy," the shaman said. "And if you don't let us see him, he might never wake from the sleep he's under."

Tiberius furrowed his brow and replied, "I don't rightfully understand."

"I wouldn't expect you to, boy. Yours is the way of the sword; ours is the way of the Father. And the Father's way is the way of magic."

"Please, Tiberius," Catherine interjected. "We have come to help you and your friends by the will of the Father. We have not felt his presence in our hearts for some time, so believe me when I say we are meant to come with aid."

Tiberius knelt to meet their eyes and studied them hard. Her dark blue eyes were deeper than the deepest chasms he had ever seen. Ancient and powerful, but full of love and understanding. In her tender eyes, he saw no sign of dishonesty or treachery. He only saw the will to right the wrongs that had been laid before them. At long last, he bowed his head and placed his hand over his chest.

"I welcome your aid and your counsel, daughter of Frijigzah."

She touched his shoulder with a mother's touch, and when he looked on her again, tears were forming in his eyes. She smiled at him and held his face in her rough stone-like hands. "My boy, I can see there is great anger and sadness within you. But do not be afraid; we will not abandon you in your time of need any longer."

At her words, a dozen more dwarves moved from behind the trees to behind the woman. Tiberius sprang to his feet at once, his hand gripping the hilt of his sword. They were all clad in heavy iron and leather crafted armor, with heavy double-sided axes strapped to their backs. Iron helms were drawn down over their stony faces. Yet, even in the approaching darkness, Tiberius could see their bright blue eyes twinkling in the dusky night. Upon their helmet's metal seams were the same strange runes that he had seen carved into their stone buildings. Their steps were heavy and shook the ground, yet again to the Ranger's astonishment, they left no mark of their walking.

"I take it these are the men my rangers saw wandering in the woods this morning?"

"I am impressed your lot could see them, boy. These twelve hearty dwarves represent the best warriors left in the world, and their years of fighting and surviving have made them undetectable to birds or beasts," the shaman replied.

"Clearly, you underestimate the skill of my rangers. But I had not known there were warriors amongst your people. The tales of dwarves do not ever mention warriors, only builders, and shaman."

"Aye, there are warriors in our people, but only when the need for battle arises," the shaman said. "Yes, we were created by the Father to build and cultivate upon the earth. But we each carry the spirit of the Father in us, for he is also a mighty and cruel warrior."

Tiberius smiled. "I have someone in the village who would be most eager to meet fellow children of the Father."

"We know of Tygahl, son of Tybalt. For it was the power of the Father in him that stirred us," Catherine explained. "We had not felt the Father's presence in our homeland in nigh on four hundred years. A blink of the eye to our people, but a lifetime it has felt to be without his presence. Please, we have lingered long enough in these woods amongst the dead. Lead us to the Mage and to our brother."

Though Tiberius was eager for more news from them, he led them from the darkening woods in silence. The sudden weight of history and myth that was being made right then and there came crashing in on him. Never in a thousand years would anyone in the whole of the Axton Empire ever think that fourteen dwarves would be walking behind an Imperial

Ranger to the defense of a tiny village. More and more, Tiberius began to feel the power of forces unseen moving around him.

They entered the village just after night had descended. Outside of a modest-looking, if not oversized cabin, sat Tygahl. A giant oak pipe hung in his mouth as his thoughts rested somewhere far off in memory. His eyes scanned the village around him as he caught sight of the approaching party. He sprang to his feet in wonder, his pipe falling from his mouth that now hung open in surprise.

The Ranger smiled at the enormous man's dumbfound expression. "My friend, I have brought guests."

Tygahl was rooted where he stood, unable to process the sight before him. "Are these... truly... dwarves!?" he stammered and exclaimed.

"Hail, Tygahl! Son of Tybalt, son of Tygahd!" Catherine exclaimed, walking past Tiberius to Rogers.

Their eyes met, and in an instant, they were connected as two children of Frijigzah reunited for the first time. A lump formed in his throat, and he knelt at once to be closer to her stone-hard face. He examined her eyes again before bowing his head low and saying, "Hail, daughter."

As with Tiberius, she extended her hands and raised his face to meet hers. "Tygahl, child of the Father," she whispered back before embracing his neck with a mother's love.

The twelve dwarves at her back marched to Tygahl, each removing their iron helms and axes. In the dim twilight, Tiberius could see each of their rock-like faces. Their beards were an assortment of colors, and their hair was wild and shaggy. Some were taller and stouter than others, but each of them was still slightly smaller than the young boy asleep in the barracks.

They encircled the large man, each placing their hands on his massive body. Each of the twelve whispering greetings to one of their long-lost brothers. From inside the enormous cabin emerged, Michelle, who squeaked at the sight before her.

"Peace, my love," Tygahl said with a hearty laugh. "As you can see, Master Tiberius has brought us guests! Please, come."

He motioned for her to join the group of dwarfs outside his home, each exchanging greetings to the woman in their own tongue. More of the townsfolk began emerging from their homes at the noise, each staring bewildered at the scene before them. After their initial shock, each of them made their way over at the behest of their Master to greet the new arrivals to the village.

Outside the growing crowd of people, Tiberius stood alongside the Shaman. "Truly amazing," he uttered, if only to himself.

"It is most fortunate we are reunited with our long-lost brethren," the shaman replied. "But enough of this. My business is not with Tygahl, son of Tybalt. Take me to the boy."

Tiberius was stirred from the heartfelt scene in front of him and led the shaman to the ranger barracks. Inside, the assembled rangers were huddled around Constance, receiving their orders for the night ahead. As he entered, they each leapt to their feet to greet their commander but were rendered awestruck at the sight of the dwarf.

Shayla emerged from Michael's room at the commotion, but upon seeing the shaman again, she exclaimed, "Well, the gods bless us indeed! To see these fair folks again in such a perilous and dark time!"

"Where is the Mage?" the dwarf cut in.

They led him to where Michael continued to lay motionless on the bed. The Shaman examined him for a moment with an impassive face before asking, "Where is the wand?"

"Inside his robes," Shayla answered. "Though I dare not retrieve it for you, Master Dwarf. Such a thing is not meant for me to wield, even in passing."

"Aye, you are correct," the dwarf said, searching Michael's robes. At long last, he felt the hilt of the wand and pulled it forth. He examined it hard as he had days before. After careful examination of the wand, the gruff dwarf said, "The conduit is opened. The power from the ocean of magic beyond our world has opened into this wand and flooded this boy. Such a force he could never hope to wield with how young and inexperienced he is. But that is good news for me."

He held the wand to his face. He closed his eyes and began to chant in the language of the dwarves. The air around them grew hot. The light from the candles started to dim, and a burst of light soared from the wand to hang over their heads. The rangers outside fell to their knees, awestruck and terrified at the display of magic in their midst. Tiberius and Shayla remained planted where they stood, their eyes darting between the light, the dwarf, and Michael.

The dwarf chanted louder and faster now, twirling the wand around as if conducting an invisible symphony until suddenly the light collapsed back into the tip of the wand. In an instant, he pressed the wand to Michael's chest, and the light entered his body and illuminated him from the inside out. The jolt of power pushed Michael's back off the cot where he lay, and with a great cough from his throat, he awoke. The candlelight regained its brightness, the air returned to the coolness it was before, and the two warriors rushed to their companion's side, grasping his hands together.

"Michael? Michael, are you okay?" Shayla whispered.

"Speak my friend. Let us know you have returned to us," Tiberius added, rubbing the young Mage's head.

Michael strained to open his eyes, surveying his companion's worried expressions. "Is the village safe?" he asked hoarsely. "Did we win?"

"Yes," Tiberius answered with a smile, "The village is safe, my friend."

Michael nodded in approval before turning on his side to face them and closing his eyes.

"He will need real rest now," the Shaman said, returning the wand to Michael's robes. "He will wake tomorrow refreshed and strengthened. And it is just as well. Now that he has experienced the full might of magic, his body will have adapted to it."

Shayla jumped to her feet and embraced the Shaman, the speed of which shocked him motionless. "Thankee, Master Dwarf!" she exclaimed.

She finally broke her grasp and bowed to the Shaman. He looked confused for a moment before returning the bow and saying, "We shall speak in the morning. For now, I will return to my kin."

He rushed past the rangers outside, each unable to form any kind of word or thought at what they had just witnessed. Tiberius stood and began to explain their brief but impactful encounter with the dwarves the days before and informed them that more were now in the village to help with the defense and rebuilding. The rangers stared dumbfounded at their commander's words before quickly leaving the barracks to greet the remaining dwarves.

Tiberius returned to his friends. Shayla had now resumed her place at Michael's side, one hand in his and the other slowly rubbing his head and face. Tiberius sat on the bed, looking at his young charge with relief. The thought of losing this boy who had bravely helped defend the people of Rogers was too much to bear. Especially after the many miles and many trials they had already faced together.

Tiberius touched Shayla's armored shoulder and said, "Kazduhl's blessing on you, Shayla Rider."

She met his gaze and replied, "Blessing of The Winds and The Hunters, to you."

A smile formed on his face. No one outside of his father and mother had passed the greetings of his gods to him. It was a welcomed, if not small, comfort to have after the past few days. They sat with Michael throughout the night, neither daring to leave his side till morning. The three companions were now reunited, and for a brief moment, all was right in the world around them.

CHAPTER 18

THE STORM

Michael woke before his companions, a rare occurrence given the type of company he kept. He stared around the wooden room at first, trying to figure where he was. Small rays from the coming dawn were peeking through small round windows above him. The smell of pine trees wafted in through the small seams in the wood, and a faint smile cracked his face. For the first time, in a very long time, he felt at peace.

He sat up from the small bed and saw at the foot of his bed Tiberius, fast asleep with his head against the wall. On the floor, curled up like a house cat was Shayla, her armor still secured to her. For Michael, to see his companions alive and well after such a ferocious battle brought great joy to his heart.

He sat in the bed unmoving for a long time, stretching his mind back as far as he could to recall any bit of what had led him here. The last fleeting memories were beginning to slip away from him as if water through clenched fists, but what he could remember was vivid enough that he knew it to be real. Images of conjuring powerful magic from the Father's wand onto a field beyond. The feeling of a deep voracious sleep overcoming him from the strain of his effort. The all-consuming blackness that had swept over him and pulled him down into deep dark slumber.

He rooted around in his robes until he found his wand. He examined it for a minute, unsure of what new thing he might glimpse in it. The ebony shaft retained its high gloss, and its ivory grip shone like the finest pearls in the market. He tried mimicking what Catherine had done before and put it up to his ears to listen. Just as quickly he removed it from his head and back into his robes, feeling altogether foolish for doing so.

If you have but the eyes to see and the ears to hear, Tiberius had said to him that day in the Citadel. Maybe I can't see and hear things yet, but I will one day. I know it.

He shook his head in frustration and then tried to focus on every detail from the day before, willing these thoughts to remain in place and not slip away from his memory. But as he did so, a soft voice like pebbles falling in a quarry echoed in his ears. "Time to wake up, son."

He spun his head around the room, hoping to find the source of the voice until he saw, silhouetted in the door frame, the small familiar sight of the dwarven Shaman. He stood firm and resolute as a stone statue against a clear sky. A slight yellow glow seemed to surround him and fill him, yet he remained wholly undistinguished and plain. Michael's heart leapt, and not wanting to disturb his companions' slumber, pushed the heavy fur blankets away and crept out of the wooden bed towards the door.

Before he could offer any greeting to the dwarf, the Shaman turned and proceeded out of the bedroom door. Michael followed, unsure of his surroundings, but set on accompanying the dwarf, nonetheless. When he reached the barracks' entrance, the dwarf beckoned Michael to open the heavy wood and steel door that led to the village beyond. As the young Mage reached for the steel handle, the door flew open with such a force that pushed Michael back and onto the floor.

An overwhelming frigid air filled his lungs and the air around him, extinguishing all light in the room. Snow began pouring into the room, forcing him to grasp his arms for warmth. He struggled against the hard-blowing snow to his feet again. He looked out the door and could see a mighty swirling storm of snow and rain that appeared to throb, growing and shrinking in rapid succession. But just as quickly as the vortex of snow appeared, the dwarf's shape materialized inside of it.

"Are you coming along, young Mage? Or do you wish to sleep more?" the dwarf asked, his voice calm and impassive.

Michael grew angry and frustrated at the dwarf's cryptic words. "What is this devilry you have brought with you?"

"No devilry, young man, but a path. This is the way forward into enlightenment and understanding. Will you push onward into knowledge, or creep back into ignorance?" The dwarf smiled at the Mage's confounded looks before turning and disappearing into the storm.

Michael was rooted to the floor, confusion, and terror, and anger taking hold of his spirit. Try as he might, he could not reason or understand the sight before him but instead resolved to follow the Shaman. Michael crept toward the door, abandoning all understanding and surrendering himself to the dwarf's summons. He stood on the threshold, the fear within him reaching its zenith in his heart. But before he could turn away in fear and shame, the storm shot through the door and filled the whole room with churning snow and rain.

He shut his eyes in shock at the swiftness that the storm overtook him, but after a moment, he realized that he was altogether safe and unharmed. Instead, he found himself warm and comfortable inside the billowing blizzard that filled the whole of the ranger's barracks. He unshielded his eyes and tried to look around the room but found it had vanished. In its place, he was surrounded on all sides by a raging storm.

Lightning lit up the swirling storm around him, cracking open the sky with the sound of a thousand canons. Sleet and hail fell like arrows in a battle, and the howling wind rolled all around. Beyond the storm, no sunlight or moonlight could be found, just a small dull light that appeared from nowhere but illuminated everything around him.

Terror filled every corner of his body. He reached out reflexively to grab hold of something to steady himself, but looking around, he found nothing at all with which to grasp. He spun in place, terrified of everything that was swirling around him. He looked and found no ground beneath his feet as if he was suspended inside the storm itself. Before a scream could escape his throat, he began to fall.

Through the raging storm, he tumbled straight and hard toward a great churning, violent grey ocean beneath him. No wind or rain whipped against him, nor did his robes unfurl at his descent. In the storm, he could see the vague shapes of fantastic beasts flying in and out of the midnight black clouds. Mighty bellows escaped their mouths and the sound of biting and chomping filled the noise around him. He looked down at the ocean beneath him. The water tossed and rolled this way and that until it began to spin in on itself, creating a swirling mass of black water in its place.

He passed into the swirling water and found himself underneath a blue ocean that churned as violently as the storm above. There he beheld massive creatures swimming to and fro, raging against the storm that flew all around them. Such was their size that it would take nearly a dozen or more of the empire's largest ships to fell them. His wonder at the mammoth-sized beasts was shaken as he realized he had yet to hit the bottom of the massive ocean. He looked below him and saw a thick black circle at the bottom of the vortex. As he gazed on it, he felt a hard pull straight towards the center of the still black mass. Beyond the blackness, faint lights like stars could be seen as he approached the brink.

All at once, he emerged from the storm and sea, through the hole, and found himself suspended inside a deep black void. The storm and oceans had passed away, and no sound could be heard. He turned all around him and saw stars dotted throughout in the distance. But not stars as he saw on the earth: cold, distant, and remote. These stars were vivid, bright with life, and shining as if the sun itself was multiplied and spread across the sky. He slowly studied them, realizing that the celestial bodies before him were arranged in the same clusters and constellations that he had long looked at his whole life.

The stars held his gaze for a brief moment before strange and beautiful words in a somber, elegant language he could not understand began to wash over him. His head jerked from side to side, searching for the source of the strange but sad voices. No matter where he looked, all he continued to see were stars in the sky.

One star to his left began to radiate a dazzling light, pulsing and throbbing as if it were a heart beating inside a chest. He marveled at it as the throbbing started to grow the small star to the size of a great sphere. Michael studied it intently, suddenly realizing it was not an inanimate sphere suspended in nothingness. The shapes of green and blue and red he recognized as the continents and countries and oceans of his world.

A vast storm was raging on the surface of the sphere. In a flash, the planet began to fold in on itself as the ocean had before. He could hear innumerable voices screaming and crying out in fear from within the imploding shape, and after a moment it was gone. In its place, suspended in the black void, was a massive wooden staff.

He examined it for a moment before realizing this staff was fashioned in the same manner as those carried by the most advanced Magi in the empire. Michael could feel untold power vibrating from the mighty staff and reached out to grasp it. But before his fingers could take hold, he was pulled back into the void with such force, the air was knocked from his body.

He crashed to a halt and now beheld dozens of spheres in front of him. Sixty or more similar orbs held his gaze, each a different color and with their own continents and oceans over their surface. Each with a massive storm breaking across them and screams of agony and death to follow. He began to cry at the overwhelming beauty and chaos that held his gaze.

Like before, each of the planets began to swirl as the one that resembled his own world. All at once, they were gone and replaced with gnarled wooden staves themselves. The power they emitted was terrifying and amazing. He felt a stir within him to have them all. He needed them and would kill anyone else who dared try and take them. Again, Michael reached out but could not touch them.

He willed himself to move forward yet found he could not. He tried and failed to push past the oppressive force that kept him in place. He stood on the brink of nothingness, terrified and confused, but consumed with a desire beyond measure. His mind strained to understand all he was seeing, his eyes were wet with tears, and he was forcing his body to move with more vigor than he had ever felt before.

In an instant, he was being pulled back through the black hole and into the swirling vortex of water. He was pulled high and fast through the ocean and into the storm he had passed before. The voices he had heard before returned now, louder and faster and in many different languages. But the words he heard began to morph into the common tongue spoken in the empire, and in the cacophony of noise, he finally understood what the people had been screaming.

Narzeth!

Magi!

White and Black!

Library!

Beaumont!

Life!

Death!

Save us!

Kill us!

His head pounded. His ears burned. The pressure from the force that propelled him pressed hard on his chest, threatening his power to stay conscious. He shut his eyes from the painful strain that was forced against him, and he clutched his ears, willing the voices to leave him. Before he could even begin to readjust his senses, he was hurled back through the barracks door and fell hard on the cold wooden floor.

The voices were gone now, and the only sound around him was the panting that escaped his lungs. His fears and avarice for the power of the staves were gone, replaced by complete confusion. His eyes darted all around, trying to take in this new sight before realizing where he was again.

He shot up at once, determined to find answers, but realized he was not rising from the floor; he was rising from the same wooden bed that he had been fast asleep in. The rush from which he rose forced his companions to burst awake. Tiberius grabbed him hard by his shoulders and examined him all over.

"It's okay, Michael," he said. "We are with you, and you are safe."

Michael looked between him and Shayla, both carrying an expression he had never seen either of the proud and mighty warriors wear before. Fear. He didn't speak at first, trying to steady his breathing and regain his composure.

"What is it, Michael?" Shayla asked.

"I don't rightly know," Michael admitted panting. "I'm not sure if what I saw was a dream or something more. I'm not even sure I'm awake right now."

Tiberius continued to look him over but was stopped still at once. Slowly, he reached the Mages chin and tilted his head up and recoiled at the sight that now held his gaze. Before, Michael's clear blue eyes could have pierced the dark of night. The same eyes he had seen so many days on the road had turned to a deep black with flecks of grey scattered about. Tiberius's eyes narrowed, his voice grew serious and grim.

"Michael, what happened? What did you see in your slumber?"

"If you wish to know what it is you saw, son, you had best come with me," a familiar stone voice called out from the door.

The three companions shot their eyes to the door to find the Shaman standing in the frame just as he had when he first appeared to Michael. Tiberius leapt off the bed and walked down the dwarf who remained unmoved by his advances.

"What did you do to the boy?" he demanded.

"I did nothing to the Mage," the Shaman answered. "I brought him back from a sleep that would have carried on until the end."

Tiberius grew cold and angry at the dwarf's indignation. "Do not lie to me, dwarf! Our friend has slept unmoving for nigh on two days, and when he awakened, he is frightened and confused, with malformed eyes!"

"What's wrong with my eyes?" the Mage whispered to Shayla.

"That is no malformity, King's Son!" the dwarf bellowed. "The boy felt the full power of magic unleashed on him well before he was ready for it. The magic that has long been held in check and dormant by an unseen enemy was released through him. He has seen magic in its most raw and untamed form. He has seen back to the beginning and forwards to the end, and he has returned changed."

Michael's jaw dropped. "You mean to say I saw the future? And the past?"

"No, my boy. You saw magic as it truly is. The violence and beauty of it. You saw magic at the beginning and end of all things, and now it is time for you to truly begin your training."

"What do you mean 'training'?" Shayla asked, rising and joining Tiberius at the door. "The boy has just awoken scared and shaking after two days of slumber, and you speak of training?"

"Things are in motion beyond our understanding, Dragon Knight," the Shaman replied. "This boy has pushed through the block of magic and tapped into it at its source. If he and your quest are to continue, he must learn how to understand it and wield it."

The three grew silent. Shayla continued to stare hard into the dwarf's bearded face as Tiberius backed away and rejoined Michael at the bed. "What do you think, Michael?"

Michael took a moment to gather his thoughts. With all he had seen just a few minutes before, real or unreal, past and future or no, he needed answers. "I will go with him, my friends. If he speaks true, then I must learn all there is to know. You can tell me what I've missed in due time."

The Shaman smiled wide beneath his long flowing beard. "Come then," he beckoned, "you have much to learn, young Mage. And I fear the days have already begun to grow short."

Michael slowly stood out of the wooden bed. He nodded to each of his friends before leaving them in the room. The Mage approached the barracks' outer door again but was frozen on the spot, unsure if another cold blast was to greet him upon leaving the room. He slowly reached out and pushed the door open to see a bright, snowy village against a backdrop of trees and mountains. He took in the somewhat familiar sight before the Shaman pushed past him and headed to the woods beyond.

Michael stood on the brink as he had before, trapped in his own thoughts and fear. In his mind, he pictured all he had seen with great fear and sadness. A growing thirst for understanding and knowledge overwhelmed his dread and compelled him onward. He closed his eyes and extended a foot to the ground outside. The soft familiar sound of snow crunching underfoot met his ears and brought a smile to his face.

He stepped out of the barracks and felt the warm sun greeting his face and the stiff cold air burning his nose. He took a deep breath and smiled, glad to be amongst the real waking world once again. He opened his eyes, a renewed strength and sense of wonder growing inside him. Shutting the door behind him, he followed the dwarf off into the woods.

CHAPTER 19

THE BOY AND THE DWARF

The morning sun was rising over the eastern sky. Fresh frost flecked the ground and the trees that formed a ring around the village. Soft plumes of smoke dotted the village skyline, a sign that the people were tucking into their breakfast for the day. Another long day of building and repair was to be on the agenda, though the arrival of twelve hearty dwarves would undoubtedly bring short work for all of them. In fact, the newly arrived guests to Rogers Village had already begun to pull their weight amongst the work that needed to be done.

During the night, the dwarves removed the bodies of the dead enemies and begun to erase any sign of battle. Now, each of the twelve dwarven warriors set out amongst the small town hauling great lumber here and there and making plans for new huts and shacks to be erected. However, Catherine had spent the night in the company of Tygahl, speaking at great length about their shared connection with the Father. She even went as far as to teach the Berserker how to pray to him in the dwarven manner. In the early morning hustle and bustle, no one paid any notice to the Shaman trotting along in the snow towards the woods beyond. Nor to the young Mage that followed behind him.

The Shaman led him for over half an hour deeper and deeper into the woods behind the village. The fresh snow crunched and cracked under their steps, the cold air pierced their lungs, yet they continued on in silence. Finally, they arrived at a slow running creek surrounded by vibrant blue and white flowers. Michael froze at the sight of them, for in all his journeying in the northern part of the White Kingdom, he had not seen any sign of life amongst the long-dead plant life.

The small dwarf stooped at the creek bed and brought a handful of frigid water to his mouth. A soft smile cracked through his ancient stone set face, the memory of some long-forgotten time and place taking hold of him. He turned and beckoned Michael to join him near the freezing clear water. Michael stared all around, trying to find a path forward before deciding to creep through the field, not wanting to disturb a single flower growing amongst the dead forest.

They stood silently in the glade for several minutes, observing the bright flowers blowing in the morning breeze. The tumultuous days and vision melted off the mage in this place. He breathed in the fresh smells and felt his soul finally be at peace.

At last, the dwarf said, "Brusgrik. In the dwarven language, my name is Brusgrik."

Michael stared searchingly at the dwarf. "That is a fine name, Brusgrik."

The dwarf continued staring motionless at the flowing creek before saying, "In the common tongue of your people, my name is Bruce. Bruce Stonehelm."

"Very well, Bruce Stonehelm. What was your father's name if I may ask?"

The dwarf bowed his head. "Frijigzah is my father, young one. Both in spirit and body." He turned to face Michael and continued, "We older dwarves were not born by earthly means. We were molded and given life by the Father under the stone mountains across the sea. The children born amongst our people are the first truly born dwarves in the world. However, these young beards were not imbued with his divinity and spirit."

"I did not know that," Michael admitted.

"No one outside of our people knows these things, young one. We were born nigh on two thousand years ago, made in his image and willed to his purpose. We had no concept of time when we first awoke in the deep. For many years, we toiled and labored in the mountain halls under Narzeth and built many great and magnificent things. After a time, we ventured to the realm above, and met the Magi tribe."

Michael's face lit up in surprise. "The Magi 'tribe'?"

"Aye. The land was fertile and green then. Not unlike the lands of this country. Magi roamed the outlands of Narzeth, in search of knowledge and understanding. Even then, they could touch magic but did not understand its power or purpose. We helped them build their library in the city of Beaumont so that they may practice their craft in peace."

"We departed from them in peace, having given them all the knowledge we could. We continued to build and prosper, and stretched dwarven kingdom from one end of the continent to the other. As a reward, the Father blessed us with more and more brothers and sisters."

The dwarf paused, a great emotion overtaking him. "Then one day, his will went silent to us, and we became as if children lost to their parents. It wasn't long after that that *they* came and enslaved us into their war against the empire that would one day liberate us."

Michael stood unmoving, unsure of what to say at hearing these words. Instead, Bruce continued, "Thank you for humoring an old dwarf, Michael. Now, I'm sure you have questions. And hopefully, I have answers to satisfy you with."

In truth, Michael had a great many questions to ask the wizened dwarf. Yet each question seemed to collide with another, forming more and more questions. After much debate with himself on where to begin, he settled on asking the most immediate questions he had. "What did I see last night? Was it real or a dream or a vision or a prophecy? And most important of all, how was I able to see it at all?

Bruce sighed and sat down amongst the field. He began to feel the beautiful petals in his hard-worn hands, collecting his own thoughts on how best to answer the young Mage's questions. "Normal wands and staves are as buckets you dip into the river. They can draw magic into them and be used for the wielders purpose. The Father's wand is the dam at the mouth of the river, directly tied to the source of magic itself. When you brandished it in the manner you did, the full force and might of magic flowed into you. Normally, your training with the Magi would have slowly exposed you to it over time. But seeing as your training has ceased as of late, it has been impossible for you to do so."

He eyed Michael hard and continued, "When you used the wand to defend the village, you took on year's worth of magical power in the span of a few short minutes. The result, as you know, was your body fell into a deep unawakening slumber while it tried to readjust and renew itself. Now that you have awakened, your body is now adapted to handling such astounding power. The interesting thing, and most mysterious of all, is after you felt the full power of magic, your mind's eye was opened to all of magic. Both what it is capable of, and what it has done. What you saw in your slumber, I do not know. What I do know was that whatever you did perceive was only by the grace and power of taking on all the power you did and living to wake again."

Michael joined Bruce on the ground, enthralled by all the information the dwarf seemed to possess. "Did magic direct me to those visions? Does it control us somehow?"

"No," the dwarf replied with a chuckle. "No, magic does not control because magic is not a living force. Two thousand years of using and studying the mysteries of the arcane have taught us that. It flows everlasting from the World Beyond. Only by the power and will of mortals can you shape it and direct it to your purpose."

Michael felt lost and stared at the ground beneath him before asking, "What happened to my eyes?"

"What you saw are things only a few others in all the history of the world have ever seen. Knowledge of that kind does not come without a price, young Mage. Be thankful the only payment you had to make was a simple change of the eyes."

"Is that what Catherine meant in the village? 'If you have but the eyes to see and the ears to hear.'"

Bruce let out a hearty laugh that shook the ground around them. "That woman and her words. She loves to give out little hints and riddles while herself knowing everything. Father bless me! She has driven me crazy since we were awoken in the mountain. And Father bless me that she will continue to drive me crazy till we are finally called home."

Michael let out a faint laugh and asked, "Why does she do that then?"

"Because it is her way. If she just told us the answer, we would have never learned the lesson we needed to learn. She cannot tell us where to go and what to do. We would grind against her all-knowing wisdom and change things to ill pursuit. She must guide and let us all come to our purpose on our own. But enough of her, it's not my place to speak on her behalf. What else do you wish to know?"

Michael pulled the wand from his robes and examined it. "Before I faced the Revenant, I felt this wand start to grow hot and burn inside my robes. Then, I felt it again when I conjured the power to stop the arrows."

"I do not rightly know. But if I had to guess, I would say that wand knew it was needed."

"It knew it was needed?" Michael repeated, trying to work out the dwarf's words before pressing on, "How is it that twice now I've been able to conjure magic when I have not even learned to do what I did?"

Bruce shook his head. "I do not know. Instinct perhaps? You had read about the different magical properties, hadn't you? Perhaps you willed the magic to what you wished it to do without realizing it. Or, perhaps, the Father was guiding your hand."

"I did not think the gods and spirits in the beyond could tell us what to do."

"They do not, Mage. Yet, I can offer no other explanations to you. We, as you imperials are prone to say, are in uncharted territory. Even all my knowledge and wisdom is at a loss."

Frustration took hold of Michael, sending him to his feet. "Do you offer any answers for me at all, Shaman? The things I've seen, the things I've been able to do without any training. You've offered no answers! I don't understand how any of it came to be. Nor what it meant!"

Bruce slowly stood and extended his palm to Michael. Michael observed him close before cautiously placing the wand in the dwarf's rough hands. Bruce turned to face the water, and with a small flip of the wand, sent the stream of water flying high in the sky above them. He gave another flick, and the water was sent hurtling across the sky, spinning, and twisting as it went.

Michael's frustrations melted away, and he began to smile at the beautiful display of magic. The sight of such elegant magic always moved him as if lost in the emotion of a lovely ballet. Bruce gave another flick, and the waters changed at once into a raging river of fire. Bruce spun the wand to and fro as if a conductor at the podium. He it above his head, sending the fire streaming further beyond into the mid-morning sky. But just as quickly, he thrust his arms down hard, sending the flames plummeting on top of them.

The fire burst around them, forming a thick eight-foot-tall ring of raging fire. The shock knocked Michael to the ground, as he cried out, "What are you doing? You are going to burn us to death!"

The dwarf smiled mischievously under his beard and, extending his hand, reached out into the fire pulling back a generous handful of roiling flame that sat within his palm. Michael stood, transfixed by this new display of power before him. To his surprise, Bruce began to approach him holding the burning fire out toward him. Once he was near him, the dwarf took hold of Michael's hand and thrust the flaming ball into it.

Michael let out a loud wail before being silenced by the Shaman. "Do not scream if there is no pain, boy. Behold, your hand is unburnt against the flame."

Michael looked at the fire in his hand, and to his surprise, saw that though a great ball of fire was in his palm, there was no pain or injury to him. A hearty excited laugh leapt out of his mouth, and he turned his eager black eyes to the dwarf holding the fireball aloft for him to see. Bruce smiled at the boy and gave another flick of the wand.

The fire that surrounded them now flew up above them. It turned and rolled about in the air until settling into the creek bed. Though the fire continued to burn violently, none of the flowers in the meadow around them were burnt. The fire that licked the petals in the groove seemed to not even move them as the wind had done. Bruce twirled and finally lowered the wand, and all at once, the fire seemed to grow clear and bright. The ferocity that it burned with slowed, and in an instant, the frigid running water had returned to the creek.

Michael remained frozen on the spot, his mind racing as he tried to process all that he had seen. Bruce returned to the creek bed and clutched a fistful of freezing water. He smiled at the Mage's dumfound expression and threw the freezing water hard in the boy's face, snapping him out of his daze. Michael stood blinking in the meadow, wet and frozen but excited and confused all at once.

Bruce extended the wand back to the Mage, who seized it and began to inspect it. To his immense surprise, as he held the wand to his face, a faint humming could be heard emitting from within the wood. He stood rooted in place, unsure of what to do next before asking the dwarf, "When can I begin to learn how to do that?"

The dwarf placed his rough hand on the boy's arm and said, "We began the moment you woke this morning. But for now, I think it would be best that we return to the village. Undoubtedly, your friends would wish to speak with you, and with all you have been through and learned, they deserve to be fully reunited with you."

Michael smiled at the Shaman and finally seized him in a great hug that pushed the air out of his body. The small stout dwarf was built like a boulder, but nevertheless, an incredible feeling of relief and happiness overcame Michael as he said, "Thank you, Bruce."

Their embrace broke, and Bruce nodded in acknowledgment before moving to return to the village. As they walked, they talked about the nature of magic, and what it meant to both of their societies, and how they had long ago learned to harness its potential and bend it to their will. But when Michael asked about where their journey would take them, and what the best way forward to the outpost would be, Bruce grew silent.

"Many things have changed in your empire in such a small amount of time," the dwarf said as they walked through the dead forest. "It is best you and your friends sort out the way forward, for even if you venture there and return, you might you have not a home to return to."

"I saw the soldiers that attacked the village," Michael said. "I saw the colors they wore and the banners that dotted the sky. I know what it means, and I know war is sure to come. But surely, we must press on as the emperor commanded. Solving the mystery of magic must be of paramount importance."

"You wish to obey the emperor's orders because they match your own desires," Bruce replied. "Though you may perceive an end goal, do not forget to observe the road that leads you there."

"But the way forward in discovering what has happened to magic will, in the end, help the empire maintain its power and glory. And, if I'm being completely honest, the opportunity to learn the mysteries of magic and where your people went is too great to not explore."

"The opportunity and knowledge gained from your endeavor could be significant, yes," the dwarf replied with a sigh. "Yet, do you also wish not to stay in this village and continue your training? Many desires cloud your mind, yet you do not have a plan for seeing it done."

"Well, what would you have me do then?" Michael asked.

"I am not your Master, Michael. I cannot, nor would not, command you to do anything that is against your desires. Your will is yours and yours alone. Yet, I would remind you that you are still a child of sixteen living in a world of men. As such, I would caution you against succumbing to your desires and seek patience and counsel with your friends."

"But my friends, as hearty and skilled in battle as they are, have not seen what I have seen. Have not felt what I have felt, and surely cannot begin to understand the loss of magic has to not only our country but to the world itself."

The Shaman stopped in an instant and glared hard at the boy. Michael could feel that he had said something that had upset the dwarf but could not begin to apologize for he had spoken his truth. The dwarf walked in front of the Mage, anger resonating from his gruff voice as he said, "Your companions, though I am loath to admit it, are the finest warriors in this country. The King's Son has fought and killed scores of enemies in his time, and the Dragoon herself has survived the pits of the Narzeth. But more than that, they are leaders. The boy Tiberius has trained and studied to be the emperor of these lands. Has sat at the foot of his father and poured over the history of his people. You will not find a greater warrior and commander of men in the whole world. But a finer companion and leader and counselor for dark and terrible times, there is none as well."

"But magic is…"

"Enough!" the Shaman boomed. "You see magic as a child. The King's Son and Dragoon know magic as men and women. They know magic for what it truly is. More than that, they can see magic as it fits into the wider world. The woman, Shayla, is imbued with the power of Kazduhl! She has walked, unburnt, through pools of fire and death! She has conquered her fate and has charted one for herself. And the King's Son?"

The dwarf held his hands high into the sky and proclaimed, "He is the son of Alexander Axton, may his name never be forgotten! He is the son of the man who freed us from bondage, and he is The Spirit of The Warrior come again!" he lowered his arms, stared hard into Michael's midnight black eyes.

"Do not disregard them because their way is the way of war. You three are bound together by the will of the gods and spirits in the World Beyond. Heed their counsel!"

Once he finished, the dwarf shot past Michael with a renewed pace. Michael stared, dumbfounded and hurt at the dwarf's words, before conceding he was indeed right. *Perhaps I am too young and eager to see the world for what it truly is,* he thought to himself. *Maybe it's time I start growing up.*

Michael walked on in silence, contemplating the dwarf's words and insights into his own mind. He felt ashamed to have used the emperor as a mask for his desire and even greater shame for disregarding his companions. Try as he might rationalize his attitude, he had to admit the dwarf was right. Their fates were intertwined now, and whatever path was to be followed would be followed by all three of them. His eagerness had often flown him from one thing to the next without ever staying put and fully absorbing and doing.

A few minutes later, he emerged from the woods on the edge of the village. Just on the edge of the tree line, Bruce stood waiting for the Mage to catch up. "We will meet again tomorrow in the glade. Come with an open mind and an open heart, and you will learn all you need to know for the days ahead."

"Thank you, sir. I shall meet you just after daybreak. And, please forgive my words. In my youth and ignorance, I spoke of things I did not know."

The dwarf let out a grunt of acknowledgment before heading off to rejoin his fellow dwarves. Michael watched him go in silence, and after a few moments of quiet contemplation, headed off to rejoin his companions at long last. He found them just outside the inn, deep in conversation with the mountain of a man he had seen the days before. Shayla was the first to notice him and rushed to greet him with a great hug. Michael smiled at her embrace, finally feeling reunited with his friends after a few days apart. Tiberius, however, remained alongside Tygahl, examining the Mage for any sign of harm or change. But after a few moments, he decided to join their reunion.

"Well met indeed, Michael!" Shayla exclaimed, breaking her embrace.

"I'm sorry for leaving you all as I did this morning," Michael replied.

"And what answers did the Shaman give you in the deep woods?" Tiberius asked, himself wanting answers to the Shaman's intentions.

"Well, I learned his name is Bruce, and I learned that after I awoke this morning, my body is now greatly adapted to the power of magic."

Tiberius remained skeptical. "And how would 'Bruce' know such things?"

Michael went on for nearly an hour, explaining to his friends why he was affected so much when other magic users before him had not. When pressed to what he saw in his dreams, Michael relayed all that he could recall in as great detail as he was able to muster. At length, Tiberius smiled at his friends and clasped the Mage hard on his shoulder.

"Very strange indeed. I will have to think on what it is you saw. But enough of that. I thank the gods innumerable above that you are okay," he said.

Michael returned the gesture. "Thank you, Master Ranger. But what have I missed in the world since falling into slumber?"

Tiberius brought Michael up to speed on the comings and goings from the village, especially emphasizing the red dove sent from King White to the emperor and the King's occupation of Michael's hometown. At these words, the young Mage grew quiet and sat down on a nearby wood and steel bench. Neither of his companions knew what words of comfort to offer him at the news.

After a few silent moments of deep rumination, Michael whispered, "Has there been any news from White Fyre?"

"None as of yet, I'm afraid. Any messages that might escape the city would surely be intercepted," Tiberius answered grimly. "We are quite far away from everything happening. Any news will take a while to reach us here.

Michael grew silent and contemplative, thinking about the implications of the King's intentions and remembering Bruce's counsel in the woods. His mind raced from one thing to another, trying to sort out his own thoughts but finding it difficult to do so. At last, he decided to ask Tiberius the burning question that had been growing in his mind.

"What are we to do about our mission?"

Tiberius eyed his companions. The time had come to lay bare his decision to both of them, something he had secretly been dreading. Now that it was directly asked of him, renewed purpose filled him. "I have resolved to stay in this village until the detachment from the empire arrives. Depending on the news they bring, or renewed guidance from my father, we will either move on with our quest to the Ice Steps or not."

Michael nodded at the Ranger's words, knowing that what he had decided was indeed the only course of action. He turned to face the Dragoon now and asked. "What of you, Mistress Shayla? What do you feel is the way forward for our party?"

She sat on the bench next to the boy and placed her armored hand on his. Her deep black eyes met his, and a faint smile appeared on her olive tanned face. "I am staying as well, Michael. The empire freed my sisters and me from years of bondage and delivered us into this land. We are sworn knights to the service of the empire, and this treachery to our liberators must be avenged. The people of this village are kind and welcoming and need our protection lest they feel the full wrath of the King."

Michael bowed his head in thought before realizing his mind had already been made up. He had just needed to hear the reassurance from his friends. "Mistress Knight, you speak true. And I shall go wherever you command me to go, sir. I too, wish to stay in this village for a time. Hastening off to the mountains, alone or otherwise, with all that is happening in the world would be most unwise. And if I am to learn more about magic and how to wield it better, then no other teacher than Bruce would do."

Tiberius beamed at the young Mage and nodded at his judgment. Perhaps the wizened dwarf, who shared in the love and connection of magic with the young man, might provide a better mentor than an old soldier ever could. He motioned Tygahl to join them, eager for the village master to finally meet the true hero of the skirmish only days before.

After a few pleasantries were exchanged between the two, Tiberius turned to the Berserker and said, "Tygahl, our party has decided to stay here and help prepare your village from any further threat. However, it is beyond me to take charge of your domain, yet I feel we had best prepare ourselves for any future attack that might come to us."

"My people are yours to command, Lord Tiberius. You need only ask, and it shall happen," Tygahl replied.

Tiberius thanked him and began to lay out his idea for the defense of the people. Walls and barriers needed to be erected. All abled body villagers needed to be trained to take up arms. The rangers and Tygahl's best hunters would start scouting out into the woods and hills at once. Food, water, and supplies needed to be rationed and stored if an extended siege was to come. He spoke plainly and to the point, his years of war breaking through his tired and worn face.

"Who will give instruction to my people?" Tygahl asked. "You can't spare any of the rangers to abandon their watch, and the dwarf warriors, as fierce as they may be, do not all speak the common tongue."

"Shayla and I will conduct their training," Tiberius answered, accompanied by a nod of approval from the Dragoon at his side.

Tygahl, in turn, nodded at Tiberius' counsel and thanked them for humility. "Truly, there would be no greater pair of teachers in the whole of the empire for villagers on the edge of the world," he replied with a hearty laugh that rattled the young Mage's chest. The massive man departed from the three to begin relaying orders to his people at the inn. The companions stood silent for a while, looking around the village as it suddenly burst into motion.

"I guess we had better pitch in, hadn't we?" Shayla asked after a few silent moments.

"Aye, I guess we should," Tiberius responded. "Shayla, take a few people and begin seeking out means for fashioning spears. They will not be of the quality you and your sisters are used to but should serve the villagers well."

Shayla nodded in approval and left to join Tygahl at the inn. Michael, unsure of what to do, turned to the veteran Ranger and asked, "What will you have me do, sir? I might be a Mage, but I grew up in the fields and streams of this kingdom. I know hard work just as well as anyone else."

Tiberius smiled and grasped him again. "I have no doubt to the strength of your body, yet your power lies in your mind and your will. I need you to study and learn as much as you can from the dwarf. If we are to go into a battle, we will need you there with us."

"I intend to do just that, sir. But what about when I am not training with Master Stonehelm?"

"Then you will pitch in where you can. But, for now, find some breakfast, then get to work."

Michael smiled at Tiberius's judgment, and after a quick bow, headed to the inn himself. Tiberius stood there a while longer, observing the flurry of activity that was going on around him. Whether they knew it or not, these people were changing before his eyes. Their allegiance to their king was washing away minute by minute as they hurried to defend their home. He set off to join them in their endeavors, resolute in the belief that he was not commanding a small group of commoners to a task but joining in on the defense and prosperity of the village.

CHAPTER 20

THE LAST NIGHT

The long, laborious days of rebuilding rolled on into weeks of continued training and preparation. All the while, Tiberius and his rangers kept watch for the detachment from the capital yet received no signs of the Imperial reinforcements. Each day was agonizing to the veteran Ranger. His desire for knowledge and news of the wide world gnawed on his spirit. His only respite had become his day to day instruction of the villagers in the manner of combat and strategy, even if the first few days had been rough.

Out of the two hundred able-bodied men from the village who had been delivered unto his and Shayla's charge, barely ten of them had ever held a sword, and none in combat. Perhaps even fifty of the men had even seen professional soldiers at all in their lives. Tiberius persevered, laying out a plan for repelling any attack on them. But as their strategy for attaining victory against any possible incursion came to fruition, the need for archers arose. Fortunately, enough, the people of Rogers were hunters of the highest order, and after some minor convincing and training, their ranks swelled to almost three hundred defenders. Still not as many as Tiberius had hoped, but enough to make a stand if their wills held out. Despite their undermanned ranks, the completed defenses around the village would shield them from whatever manner of attack that would befall them.

The skill and speed at which the dwarves set to work constructing fortifications for the village was shocking to the people. Indeed, their craft lived up to the stories and legends that had been told about them. Within a few short days, lumber and other material had been gathered and shaped into tall, thick barriers. The ends of the tall posts were all sharpened to a precise point, with bundles of sticks fastened together by treated bark and limbs. High in the village's trees, small outlooks had been established for the Rangers and the more skilled archers from the town.

The morning lessons from the Shaman continued on. In the beginning, each day brought a new challenge that frustrated the eager young Mage. But each morning, he grew in determination and in skill. Before long, he had progressed from manipulating the frigid creek water to full-on conjuring and willing the elements to appear out of nothing. Once his insecurities had burned off and his innate aptitude took over, his use of magic astonished the ancient dwarf. In all his long years upon the earth, he had not seen someone so young be so gifted and skilled. By night, Michael continued to try and decipher the runes within the dwarven book. Every so often, he would ask Catherine or Bruce for help in reading the text. But after the first few cryptic smiles and knowing nods, he gave up.

Nearly six weeks had passed since the companions first arrived when any word from the outside world finally reached the village. Early in the frozen pre-dawn hours, a bird whiter than the whitest snow, arrived in their fortified encampment. Constance, ever watchful, had brought the letter attached to its tiny legs to Tiberius with all haste, finding her commander in deep discussion with Shayla over a hot cup of coffee.

He greeted her with trepidation though at the sight of the white bird. She placed the message in his gloved hand, rendered a quick bow, and returned to her outlook again. Tiberius inspected the parchment for a time before bidding Shayla retrieve Michael before his morning lessons with the dwarf were to start. The three companions deserved to read the message together after all they had endured. A few minutes later, Shayla and Michael reappeared with curious looks on their faces.

"A white bird bearing news" Michael said, sitting down beside Tiberius on the heavy wrought iron bench he occupied, "News from White Fyre, I'd imagine."

Tiberius looked between his friends before unravelling the parchment. His eyes narrowed at the letter in his hands, "This is a letter from Arythag."

"Who is Arythag?" the Dragoon asked her companions.

"Chief Marshal of the King's army," Michael replied glumly.

"And former Imperial Ranger," Tiberius added in a whisper.

"Well, go on then," Shayla pleaded. "Best get this over with."

Tiberius hunched over and read aloud:

Commander Tiberius,

At the behest of His Majesty, Telos Amael White VI, I order you to abandon your illegal occupation of the Rogers Village. The King has declared independence from the traitorous and vile Axton Empire, and is set upon removing all remnants of the empire from our land at once.

His Majesty is merciful and will grant you and your Imperial followers safe passage through our lands to the border. He bids you return to the Imperial City and give this message to Emperor Axton: The Kingdom of White is free from the shackles of the unjust and vile laws of the empire.

If you, in your stubbornness and misguided sense of justice, choose to remain in the village we will take it as an act of war. We will arrive at the village before nightfall where we will expect your reply.

Arythag Samborn

Supreme General of His Majesty's Military

P.S.

I implore you, commandeer and comrade, be reasonable and consider the consequences. This village, though of little importance, is still within our sovereign borders. Think of what your men will say if your stubbornness was to draw your country into war? Think of what the emperor would say? I await your reply.

A heavy silence fell between the three. They sat for many solemn moments under the clear morning sun, contemplating the dark times that were sure to fall. Off in the distance, they could hear the joyous sounds of children at play and the laughter from their parents watching close by. They could smell the slow-burning fires from the dwarven camp as they dug into their breakfast. Somewhere further beyond, small birds were chirping and flapping free in the cold air, unbothered by the troubles of the world they flew over.

This is what we are fighting for, Tiberius thought to himself. The King wishes to rule while we wish to maintain peace and happiness. What madness has consumed him to take such bold action?

He handed the letter to Shayla to reread it for herself and sat on the bench, lost in his thoughts. "What will we do, sir?" Michael asked after many quiet moments. "It sounds like 'General Samborn' already knows your mind."

"Aye, he should," Tiberius answered, still lost in thought. "He served alongside me and Trevin for many years before abandoning the empire. For many years we three were inseparable, and the fiercest of companions in battle."

"Then that would explain why he was bid come to this, as he calls it 'village of little importance.' Who better to combat you than your own ranger?" Shayla said. "I know my mind sir, but you are our leader, and will follow your orders. So, what is your decision?"

"Gather everyone here," Tiberius said firmly. "Michael, same with the dwarves. Then you will know my decision."

At his words, they flew into motion, and within minutes Tygahl and the villagers assembled, followed closely by the dwarves. Tiberius stood for a minute, thinking on all that had transpired and what was left to do. His fists clenched, and he stood more erect and majestic than usual. The veil of the Ranger Commander he had cultivated so well was stripped away, and in its place was the image of authority and majesty, the image of one born to rule. The image of the ruler of the Axton Empire stood before them. The Spirit of The Warrior made flesh.

"I received a letter this morning, from General Samborn," he began. "He has ordered that all Imperials within the White Kingdom are to leave immediately, else this village will be razed to the ground. King White has declared this land 'free' of the Axton Empire, and is intent on eradicating all remnants of it from the land."

"Blessings of the Father!" Tygahl exclaimed, "Raze our home to the ground? What madness has come over the King!?"

"I cannot know what has come over the King's mind, Master Rogers. Though I know what has come over mine."

A hush fell over the crowd. Each of the villagers looked to each other with fear etching on to their bright fair faces. "What will you have us do, sir?" Tygahl asked at last, cutting through the impenetrable stillness.

Tiberius beheld each of the faces around him. Half of them appeared to be scared and were prepared to take their families and flee. Though wherever they could possibly go would offer no safe haven against the oncoming storm of death that was bearing down on them. The other half looked determined and brave, ready to fight and die to defend their homes against a ruthless would-be tyrant. The only curious sight amongst the assembled people was Catherine and her brethren, who appeared to remain impassive.

"When we arrived here six weeks ago, men from the King's army were set against wiping your homes from the earth. They came with fire, and they came with arrows, and they came with an unquenchable anger and determination to see you all dead. I do not know why the King has set this place in his sights, but the fact is he has. General Samborn has said they will leave this village in peace if I and my fellow Imperials leave, and I say that his words are a lie. They will raze this land and occupy it for their own intent."

Silence heavier than an anvil penetrated the assembled. Even their breaths were muted in their throats. Tiberius continued to look into their bright eyes before resolve overtook him. "Well I say to you, I will not abandon you. A madman who wields greater power than he can imagine has come to your doorstep. And by my power, I will repel him or die trying!"

Small reassuring smiles came across the group who began speaking on what to do. Others continued to look on in fear. "What are your thoughts, Lady Stonefoot?" Michael asked, cutting through the small chatter.

"We were sent here by the Father for a purpose that was unknown to us," she said, smiling. "And now it is known. We will fight and defend these people, for why else would he lead us out of our homes if not to fulfill his will?"

"Why do you think the King has come for our homes?" Michelle asked from behind the massive Tygahl.

"Your village is at the footsteps of the Ice Steps. It is no coincidence that he has come to this place as Tiberius and his companions have. He means to hold the path leading to the Land Beyond, and eventually go there himself."

"But what can he possibly gain from venturing there?" Michelle asked again. "It is a place of death and ice. There is nothing there for anyone. Why would you seek that place at all Master Tiberius?"

Tiberius and the dwarf woman's eyes met, and he nodded in understanding. He turned to Michelle, and said, "I cannot speak to our intent for crossing into the Land Beyond. I was bid on this quest by Emperor Axton himself, and am sworn to secrecy of our intent. But I will say that if King White is seeking the same goals as I, then it is a most dire situation." He turned and faced the assembled villagers, "I must confess that I have not the words to adequately comfort you. I have been a Ranger of the Axton Empire for nearly twenty years and have resigned myself to the knowledge that I may fall in battle one day. It is our duty to fight and die so that all people who dwell in this realm will never know war or hardship or suffering. Yet, at this moment, I feel as though I have failed you."

"Amongst us, there are only fifteen true warriors who have known war and death. The rest of you have lived in peace and prosperity, far away from the toils of conflict. And that is how it should be! Whatever evil has poisoned the mind of the King, and has driven him to war, is known only to the gods."

"If you all choose to take your families and leave, I will not stop you. I possess no lordship over you, and even if I did, I would not order you to stay. That is not the way of this empire, the way of a free society. One is not controlled by their monarchs for their own purposes but allowed to thrive and live their lives as they see fit!"

He paused for many moments, recalling the faces of his rangers and his father. "Every man, woman, child, and dwarf who dwell here are free. Free to choose their own paths and perils. Free to make their own destiny. Well I say to you all, my destiny and my free will compel me to stay and fight. Though I may be a small stone against the tide, I will break the ocean of evil that travels here nonetheless!"

With a quick motion, he unsheathed his sword and held it aloft. "I carry the sword of Luke Alexander Axton himself! And with his sword, and with all my might and skill, I will meet the King's men in the field, and we will show him and all the free people of White that the empire has not abandoned them! This I swear to you on my honor. Now, will you flee into danger and uncertainty, or stay and defend your homes against the cowards in their white armor!?"

A great cheer went up over the crowd. All the assembled who saw his sword and heard the conviction of his words were shaken out of their fears and driven to action. Though they might fall and be wiped from all memory, they would take as many of the King's thugs with them as they could.

He re-sheathed his sword, and the crowd dispersed at once. Tygahl and Shayla began issuing orders to the villagers to start reinforcing the walls and gates. Constance and her rangers spread into the woods and hills beyond the field to search for any sign of the approaching army. Michelle flew to the children and their families, bidding them gather their food and make for the inn. Tiberius stood in place watching all this, pride growing inside of him.

"Nice speech," Michael whispered to him, breaking him out of his contemplations and laughing hard.

"I'm not one for speeches, my friend," he said with a pat on the Mage's shoulders. "But every now and then, I pull one out of me."

Tiberius turned to the dwarves, who appeared to not have moved. Instead, each of them standing still as stones, smiles etched into their bearded faces. "I hope your Father is with us in our endeavors," he said to Catherine.

"The Father has led us since the sun rose on the world. So too shall he lead us into the sunset. But to you and Michael, I must give counsel," she said, her smile abandoning her face. "We dwarves can feel things in motion around us. Things that would like to remain hidden are revealed to us. I fear this oncoming assault will bring more than just men and horses. Something evil and powerful rides with the King's men. Something that has not been contested against in nigh on five hundred years. And this thing is hungry, not just for us, but for what lies beyond the ice."

"What is it?" Michael asked a deep concern in his voice.

"What it is, we do not know," Bruce said. "But you must steel yourselves nonetheless; for before this night is over, the very ground upon which we stand will shake with wrath never before seen in this realm. Beware."

Catherine turned to her men, and after a few quick words in their language, they hurried off to help throughout the village. Bruce beckoned Michael to join him once again as if part of their usual morning. Catherine joined Tiberius where Michael had just stood and watched the pair dissolve into the woods.

"You're afraid for the boy," Catherine said after they had departed.

"I'm afraid for all of us, Lady Stonefoot," Tiberius admitted. "Though my Rangers and I are resigned to a glorious death, it is not meant for these people. And Michael... Well, after the many miles and misadventures we have gone through, I cannot bear the thought of him falling to such unwanted evil and destruction that now threatens us. He has too much life left to live."

She smiled up at the Ranger and said, "Were you not his age the first time you rode into battle?" Tiberius looked down at her, wondering how she could possibly know when he had first fought in battle.

She smiled at him and placed a rough hand upon his arm. "The boy is stronger than you know. He has learned much in such a short amount of time. Tonight, though, he will truly be put to the test, for the evil that rides with the King's men has come for him."

"The only thing that could contest Michael would be another mage, and so far, he seems to be the only one with the power to wield magic in the empire."

"Aye," she replied. "Though I fear it is no mage that comes hither, yet something of equal power and will. I sense that whatever has cut off the use of magic to the rest of the Magi knows there is one still capable of doing so. And against him, it will seek out and rage."

"Then ascend the steps themselves and seek the outpost as we were intended to do. What has come against us means to seize all of magic themselves, don't they?"

"Aye. That they do."

Tiberius stared at her, searching for any clue in her hardened face. "You do not need to use your powers on me, King's Son," she said with a chuckle. "You know my words are true."

"My apologies, Catherine. I too had begun to feel the timing of White's insurrection was more than happenstance to coincide with our quest. Your words merely confirmed this suspicion of mine."

"Ever since you arrived in our village, we have felt the whispers of the Father in our minds. I do not know how else to explain it more simply than that," she replied. "Just call it a feeling." And with that, she departed Tiberius's company to see to her dwarf's work.

The rest of the day flew by in a flurry of activity. The walls and gates were reinforced with trunks from large and ancient oak trees hewn from the nearby forest. The rangers reported back every few hours with no new updates, save for the unnatural stillness that now seemed to seep into the surrounding lands. The villagers began to fletch more arrows for their archers and fashioning crude leather armor and heavy wooden shields.

Deep in the fields beyond, the dwarves erected long massive barriers of spiked wood and logs and had begun digging vast trenches at a quick pace. Five feet deep or more with small bundlings of wood here and there for a bonfire. They hoped these trenches would force the King's men to abandon their horses and navigate the winding maze of ditches, making them an easier target. The villagers who sat upon the village walls' ramparts marveled at the speed and strength that the dwarfs worked. Especially since they did all of their work tirelessly and still fully laden in the heavy iron armor of their people.

Tiberius walked to and fro throughout the village, inspecting the defenses and stopping here and there to speak to the villagers he and Shayla had spent instructing. In them, he found a renewed sense of purpose and resolve. Such was their rekindled spirit to fight and defend their homes that they, in turn, recruited several of the older boys in their community to come to their aid, swelling their numbers to near three hundred and fifty men.

A small measure of worry crept into his spirit at the thought of such young untrained boys possibly entering the fray. Yet he could not deny them their desires. This was their home, after all, and if they were roused out of fear into action at its defense, he would not raise an objection.

Shayla spent her time with Tygahl, trying to memorize all the terrain around the village for avenues of approach the enemy was sure to take. In her mind, she already imagined the snowy fields filled with the enemy. Her spirit and heart began to stir at the challenge of battle to come. Her long life of fighting had conditioned her to expect and prepare for the inevitable with a cold calculation. The countless deaths she had seen in her time had hardened her to the taking of life. Yet now, on the eve of battle, she felt a sense of eagerness to enter the fray. Maybe it was that she was fighting for the noblest of causes in defense of the defenseless. The thought brought a smile to her tanned olive lips as she refocused her mind on the task before her.

In the woods, Michael spent his time practicing his wand work under Bruce's careful eye. Though he was better adapted to the power he now wielded, and his aptitude to conjuring magic had improved, a growing concern over the unseen force was beginning to stir inside him. Yet every time he tried to broach the subject with the Shaman, he was rebuffed and returned to his practice.

Michael knew Bruce meant well in his counsel to refocus on his training, but for all his skill and his knowledge, he was still after all, a child of sixteen. Despite his youth, Michael had begun to see the world around him in a different and somewhat foreign way. The selfishness of youth was still there, but it had begun to grow quiet. He had started to realize that the world was changing around him. That the time for boyhood desires and impetuousness would have to be cast aside. That it was time to grow up and become a man of the empire.

The sun was starting to set when they returned to the others from their training; Michael returning to his companions while Bruce returned to his fellow dwarves for their daily prayers and communes to the Father. Fresh snow was beginning to fall in small specks. With the sun's last rays, Tiberius and his companions could see dark grey clouds massing beyond the field and forests, a sign of a pending snowstorm sure to follow. The stars beyond the dusky night sky were not shining as they had for so many nights before, instead residing behind a thick unnatural fog that hung just above the trees.

"This is ill weather that comes swiftly upon us," Shayla said as she ran her slender fingers through her straight black hair. "Either by the will of nature or the will of our enemy. For if I were them, I would use this storm as a sign to attack."

Tiberius began to pull on his pipe, his mind focusing on the terrain before him. "As would I. My rangers reported no sign of the enemy, yet these clouds and fog could hasten their arrival. Let us pray they will not come until my father arrives. Though if our luck is any indication, our prayers will be in vain."

"You two are really are putting a damper on things," Michael replied with a shudder. "Come, let's get inside for some warmth."

The three companions retreated to the rangers' barracks, followed soon after by Tygahl. They dug into meals that had been set for them at the rangers' massive table, not daring share their fears of what the weather would bring. Instead, they talked loud and joyfully of long-ago battles and histories of their realm. All at once, silence fell on their group. Throughout their dinner, they each had willfully chosen to ignore the discussion that needed to happen. Yet now, neither of the four dared break it, hoping to live in the joyful memories they had shared just a few moments before. Finally, it was Tygahl, the retired berserker, who broke the quiet.

"If they are to attack, it will surely be tonight," he said heavily. "They will not wait for the clear skies and storms to pass. These are true north men who will march to meet us. They will want to fight in the cold where they feel the strongest."

"Aye, that is what they will do," Tiberius agreed. "But we are as well defended as we can be. It will be our will or theirs that wins the day."

"Beg your pardon, Master Rogers, but will you join us in the field?" Michael asked.

"You will be nowhere near the field," Tiberius cut in. "I know you have grown strong and learned much, but we need you here in the village. Whatever evil that rides with the soldiers will be drawn to you, and if you are amongst us, I cannot keep you protected."

"Begging your pardon, but after all I have learned from Master Stonehelm, I can protect myself," he replied.

"That may be true, but I need to keep you away from the fray as long as possible," Tiberius explained. "The King's men come with fury and madness upon them, and the evil that rides with them has come for you. I must keep you concealed as long as possible."

"But where else would I be safest than with you, sir?" Michael asked in protest. "I would be ashamed if I did not stand and fight for the defense of these people."

"You had best heed his counsel, Michael," Shayla said. "No shame will be wrought on you as you are simply following our leader's command. Furthermore, when the fighting starts it will be furious and confusing. You must stay here where you can be of greater use and better guarded."

"Then I am to cower in here like the women and children? Is that what my friends think I am? A coward!?"

"No, we do not," Tiberius replied. "You were not a coward when you faced down the Revenant, and you were not a coward when you defeated the soldiers on our arrival here. But we must conceal you from the true power that comes with White's men. Do not fear. Before this night is through, I have a feeling you will be called to the defense of these people."

Michael hung his head dejectedly but conceded to his friend's counsel. Sensing his sadness, Tygahl clapped one of his mighty hands upon the young man's back, causing him to jump. "And to answer your question, yes, I will be in the field. My time with my brothers and sister these many weeks has taught me much about the Father. I feel his will upon me too, and I will use it well."

He stood, and after cleaning the food from his beard, said, "Now, I must see to my people and to Michelle. I will meet you all outside after nightfall." And with that, Tygahl departed, leaving the three companions alone.

They sat for many moments in silence, each looking to one another to break the silence. "Do not be scared, Michael," Tiberius said, breaking the tension. "If we fight tonight, then we will fight with all the strength that lies within us. And if we fall, then we fall in service of the empire."

"What would you have me do if not fight with my friends?" Michael asked sadly.

"If it were up to me, I would have dispatched you back to the capital with all haste," Tiberius admitted. "I wish more than anything else to keep you and Shayla safe from the conflict that is sure to come. Yet to tell either of you to do so would be in vain."

"You speak true," Shayla cut in with a laugh. "Dragoons do not run from battle, and Mr. Deerborn is too hardheaded to know what's good for him."

Tiberius chuckled. "As such, I wish for you to remain here and to stay sharp. Though I don't know why I'm leading this defense at all. Your stubbornness and your magic alone would be enough to fell all the enemies in the world."

Michael smiled, the first time all day. Tiberius's words always had that effect on him, and now more so than ever. "I'm sorry, my friends. You have led me so far and through so much turmoil and strife on this fool's errand. And now look at where we have arrived."

Shayla placed her hand on his knee and stared him hard in the eyes. "We were led here by order of our emperor. We continued the path because we believed in you and your mission. And we remain here because as long as evil men continue to seek dominion over the innocent and weak, they must be swiftly cut down. Nothing that has happened to us since we left the city has been by chance. We were meant to be here in this moment. Either by Frijigzah's will or The Warriors will, or even mighty Kazduhl's will. Maybe all three led us here. Either way, we will stand and fight. And if necessary, we will die."

Michael nodded, his spirit reassured, and his mind at ease. An hour or so later, they departed from the barracks. Tiberius and Shayla stood in the village square, observing the villagers running to the inn. Michelle had cleared the larder that lay hidden beneath the floor, and with some help from the dwarves, had made more than enough room for all the villagers who needed guarding against the oncoming battle. Constance and her rangers flew to the trees as silent as shadows. Bow and arrows in hands, beginning to search deep into the woods beyond for any sign of the enemy. Michael had remained in the stone and wood barracks, his young face peering out the windows at all that was transpiring. Tygahl and his newly friended dwarven warriors stood at the gate, his massive chest already expanding in the frigid air

"Arrows will come first as they did before," Tiberius said, at last, a coldness growing in his heart. "Though if the storm persists as I think it might, it will lead their arrows astray."

Shayla nodded in agreement. "Though it will also lead our own volley astray as well," she added.

"Tis true. Though I aim to reserve our archers until the enemy is in the trenches. As we must conceal Michael's power for as long as possible, so too must it be for all the might we shield behind these walls. The enemy will outnumber us, yet we must have them think our numbers are at least equal to their own."

"I agree, my friend," she answered, weighing her dragon fashioned helm in her hand. "Kazduhl has brought me this far, and if I fall in this noblest of efforts, I will be welcomed in his den."

Tiberius nodded in reply and began to focus his mind on the approaching night. After a moment, he patted her shoulder and departed for the ramparts that had been erected atop the walls. There he found the villagers, clad in their homespun leather armor with crude swords and spears. Yet, for the drabness of their garb and arms, their spirits were strong and resolute. In their eyes, he saw the fire of battle and the defiance against tyranny. Shayla flew into the trees behind the village with the rangers, donning her steel helm.

The snow was falling faster and heavier now. In a few short hours, the whole area they stood in would be knee deep with snow, and the harsh cold would start to weigh on them. Great flakes were beginning to hang on Tiberius's cloak and beard, yet he paid them no mind. He pulled his pipe from within his cloak and started to breathe in the much-needed tobacco. He pushed his *Sight* further, scanning the tree line that lay some two hundred yards away from the walls. In the distance he could make out small critters coming and going, seeking shelter from the storm that now threatened to break. Yet nothing else stirred in the deepening night that had come upon them.

CHAPTER 21

THE HIGH SORCERER

Tiberius stood gazing out into the silent forest. His *Sight* extended further than he had used since the war, scanning for any sign of the approaching army. Yet, for all his skill, nothing appeared to him. Perhaps the army from White wouldn't come tonight. Perhaps they had yet to marshal their forces for the push north from White Fyre. Perhaps his father's vanguard had met them on the road and had wiped them out. Despite all these desires, his reasoning and experience in war bid him remain vigilant and reserve.

An hour or more, he stood motionless upon the rampart, sucking in the strong tobacco from his pipe and peering into the night. Another hour or more, he held his vigil when far off in the distance, an unexpected but all too familiar sight surged into the black cloudy sky.

A sickly green light like flames from a hearth burst into the night sky, sending all the forest animals nearby into a frenzy. Shocked cries echoed all around him. The cold air around them seemed to retreat against the strange and evil sight. Tiberius jolted back from the shock so fast he almost fell off the ramparts. In an instant, he heard a faint thud next to where he stood.

"What was that?" Shayla asked in a low, harsh tone.

Tiberius stared at her for a moment, but before he could offer an answer, another green flame burst into the sky. Then another. And another. Before long, the whole of the forest beyond them seemed to be alight with great fiery verdant pillars. His eyes scanned the woods frantically for any sign of what was to come next.

Fear took hold of him as he turned to face the Dragoon again and said, "We saw those flames in the Bradford Woods, Shayla. We saw the flames, and soon after, fought the undead soldiers."

Shayla stared holes into his face. Under her scaled helmet, he could see fear and anger burning bright in her black eyes. "This is the evil that comes forth. A necromancer?" she asked.

"I am no necromancer, heathen!" a voice cried out from the woods, penetrating every corner of the field and the village. As he spoke, the green flames vanished as if for dramatic effect. Even in the darkened barracks of the Imperial rangers, Michael was driven to his feet with shock. For to him, the mighty voice had seemed to come from within the room. After a quick survey, he realized that he was still alone in barracks. He ran to the window and pressed his young face against the frozen glass, eager to see what was going on outside.

Back on the wall, Tiberius and Shayla turned in unison to examine the woods. As if on cue, hundreds of torches illuminated the darkness. In the firelight, Tiberius could see a great host of soldiers, all clad in white armor, marching towards the village. Here and there were many on horseback and more and more carrying bow and arrow. And beyond them, he saw what he feared most of all—the shuffling, disorganized march of the undead.

"Whose voice was that?" Tiberius heard someone amongst the ramparts ask him.

"I do not know," he replied, bewildered.

"Aye, you know that voice," a quiet, calm voice said from behind him in the village square.

He turned and locked eyes with Catherine. She alone stood amongst the empty space behind him. "You know that voice, King's Son. Though time has moved on, and you choose instead to lie to yourself out of fear and disbelief. You know that voice well."

Tiberius stared at her hard until realization crashed on him like a felled tree. He turned again to examine the approaching army. "That's the voice of a dead man, Shayla. A man who summoned the most powerful magic this world has ever seen. A man who called down beasts from legend to smite the Narzeth. A man who turned the entirety of Vermillion Pass into a graveyard."

He turned to face his companion as she shook in her dragon armor. "That is the voice of High Sorcerer Cycret. Yet how he is here now, and with this host of White's men, I do not know."

"Cycret? The wizard who…" Shayla started but was quickly interrupted.

"Do not speak my name, heathen!" the voice said.

In the barracks, Michael continued to press his face against the window to see anything outside. He furiously wiped the windows free of the fog from his breath, not wanting to miss a single detail of the events unfolding around him. Growing frustrated, he threw the door open to the frigid night, the wind from which extinguished all the candles and the mighty fire that had been burning in the hearth.

Tiberius turned to face the trees, his fear becoming replaced by an inconsolable rage. "I do not know how you are here, Cycret," he bellowed out into the night. "But you and this host of traitors you ride with will not come near this village!"

A mighty roar of laughter erupted over the assembled army before them. Slowly, the middle of the formation began to stand aside as a figure dressed in robes of brilliant white glided through them. At his side, clad in simple white leathered armor, was the former ranger, and now Supreme General, Arythag. All whom the figure passed bowed low in reverence as he floated through their formation, coming to a stop in the open field. Tiberius pushed his *Sight* to examine the pair as they strode through the ranks.

The Sorcerer's robes were pristine and unblemished with immaculate stitching and adornment sewed into the hem of his clothes. In his hands, he carried a majestic white staff. But in the hood of his robes, he saw no face he recognized. In the deep black of the white hood, he beheld a mangled mass of concaved and broken bone held together by small slivers and wisps of stretched leathery skin.

Arythag looked the same as ever, save for the long dark hair he had now grown. His bright blue eyes shone out in the night; his own *Sight* focused intently on Tiberius. "I see your stubborn dedication to the emperor is still as strong as ever, Tiberius!"

"I see you have abandoned reason and justice for madness and evil!" Tiberius replied.

"You are a traitor, Ranger! You and the Imperial rats who desecrate His Majesty's dominion! You and your ilk will flee these lands!" the undead voice spoke again.

"Traitor!?" a great voice raged into the darkness. "You dare call us, free people of the empire, traitors!?"

In a flash, Tygahl the Berserker, flew high and over the walls into the field. He stood heaving in the sharp cold air studying the enemy in front of him. The rage of the Father filled his body as if never before, and the urge to kill, to rip this heathen undead sorcerer limb from limb overtook him, and he began to charge. But with a simple wave of his hand, the Sorcerer let loose a powerful wave of wind that hit the behemoth of a man square in the chest and sent him flying several yards back.

The defenders on the wall looked on in shock as Tygahl Rogers, master of their village and berserker of the Imperial army, was knocked unconscious. At once, Tiberius ordered the stoutest men on the wall to retrieve him and bring him back within their defenses. In the distance, he could see a gnarled evil smile creep on the undead man's face.

"This is your last chance, Commander Tiberius," Arythag called out again, drawing his sword. "Flee now, and these people and their homes will be left in peace!"

"You say 'peace' yet draw your sword for battle!? You betray your own words just as you have betrayed these people!"

Shayla looked urgently at Tiberius. "What will you have me do?"

Tiberius looked around him and saw fear on the faces of the villagers. Whatever power had been drawn before them, tonight was more than he had imagined. In his shortsightedness, he began to despair. Whatever forces had conspired to raise this man from the dead had almost certainly granted him the power he had long possessed in life. And that was not a power Tiberius was prepared to contend with here on the edge of the empire.

"Trust in yourself, King's Son," a voice called out.

He turned to the small dwarf in the square. No fear or doubt was shown in her wizened stone face, and instead, she wore a knowing smile that eased his doubtful mind. "No," he said at long last to his companion. "We must temper our aggression. The plan remains the same. But if the opportunity presents itself, do not hesitate to strike against him. Beware! Cycret was the High Sorcerer of the Magi. You saw the power he wielded at the Vermillion Pass, and Arythag will undoubtedly be swift in his attack against us."

Shayla nodded in understanding and flew back to her post amongst the trees. She drew her staff close to her chest and stared at all that was unfolding in front of her. Tiberius's heart and soul hardened at what was sure to come, forcing the fear he had felt to burn low. He withdrew his sword and removed his heavy cloak. In the dim light, he inspected the blade and thought on the countless battles it had been a part of since its forging. He thought of his father wielding this same sword in the war. He thought of his ancestors who had carried this same weapon. In his mind's eye, he could see them all stretching back to Alexander himself. A pained smile broke his face, knowing that their spirits were with him tonight.

He turned his attention back to the field. The knights from White were laughing and smiling in their close ranks beyond. Swarms of the undead were rallying, their twisted, half dissolved faces blank and impassive. "Tiberius!" Arythag called again. "This is your last chance! Flee now with your lives or stand here and die!"

"Easy choice, Arygath," he replied. Tiberius pushed the cold out of his senses and instead stood rooted in place, waiting for the inevitable wave to crash upon them. He steadied his breath and began to brace himself.

"So be it, Ranger," Arygath replied, retreating into the ranks of his army.

Michael began to grow impatient inside the foyer of the barracks. Whatever evil that had come with the King's men had decided to reveal itself early, and the urge to find his companions began to take hold of him. *But Tiberius told me to stay put,* he thought to himself. *Would it not be prudent to listen to one who has fought in more battles than I have even read about?* In the end, he decided to keep pacing and waiting.

Back on the ramparts, Tiberius and the undead Cycret stared at each other from across the field for several heavy minutes. Neither the villagers nor their encroaching foes dared make a move lest it erupted into an all-out battle. Now was not the time to initiate it, Tiberius reasoned, now was the time to wait for their volley. For in his long life of fighting, he had learned that against a superior force, a counterattack was often the best way to achieve victory. Lighting burst over the battlefield, illuminating every corner of the darkened wood. A burst of laughter escaped the hooded sorcerer. He shoved his great staff into the ground and slowly raised his arms as flurries of snow began to pelt the field and wood. Neither side moved in anticipation of what was to come next, the tension so palpable it threatened to break under its own weight.

In one motion, he dropped his arms and the cries of "Loose!" echoed out over the King's army. The distinct sounds of snapping and whistling cut through the storm as thousands upon thousands of white shafted arrows flew high into the night sky. Cries of "Brace!" and "Shield!" were called out over the village as every defender rose their makeshift shields in anticipation of the volley. The whistling grew louder and louder until great thuds echoed around them.

Arrow after arrow rained down on them from all directions. Screams of pain rose up over the crowd of villagers. Some had been too slow to raise their shields and paid the price. Arrows penetrated their arms and legs, tearing bone from muscle and forcing screams of pain throughout the village. More cries of anger rose up to drown out their pain. The will to fight was still strong in the villagers, and by will alone would they fight on.

After more than a minute of constant barraging did the last arrow land amongst them. "Recover," Tiberius ordered. "Archers! Make ready!"

"Nock arrows!" the chief archer called out. "Ready! Loose!"

More breaking and whistling broke out over the village, minuscule in comparison to the King's archers. They flew high into the sky and began to turn down upon the army of invaders when Cycret again raised his hands above him. All at once, the arrows from the villager's dissipated in an instant, turning to snow above them. Tiberius watched as the snow that had just been arrows drifted to the ground in front of him. He stared dumbfounded at the power that was displayed before him as more laughter came from the woods beyond the village.

Michael shook his head in frustration as he continued to pace back and forth within the barracks. He had seen the arrows fall in the village and heard the return fire, but now a thick silence penetrated the town. He wrestled with himself for several tense moments until a powerful hotness began to emerge from within his robes. He had felt it the day he had called down magic against the attackers. Yet this time, he didn't hesitate or ignore it. He thrust his hands deep into folds of his robes, and after grasping the wand by its ebony grip, began to sprint to the wall to join his friends.

More cries of nock and loose erupted over White's army as a thousand more arrows flew high into the sky. Again, the villagers braced for the inevitable impact. More cries of brace were called out, but even more of the villagers were shot down. Many had been frozen with fear, and in their shock, now lie dead or in agony upon the ground.

Michael heard the whistling approaching the sky and ducked under a nearby food cart. The heavy THUNK! from the arrows struck hard against the heavy wooden cart pushing his face down into the snow. He was sure one of the arrows would break through and find its mark on his head. He shut his eyes and clenched the wand tighter in his hands. The heat it gave off threatened to burn him, and the urge to raise it up was overwhelming.

With the simple twist of his wrist, he could turn those arrows into roses or large drops of water. But he was determined to temper his urges, remembering Tiberius's command to remain hidden. The arrows continued raining down upon him. Each strike against the cart forcing his head down further and further into the snow trodden ground.

High in the trees, Shayla stared at the mayhem happening below. She could feel the restlessness of the rangers around her yet continued to force them into patience. Despite her own feeling of helplessness, she remembered Tiberius's words. Their plan would remain the same. Though she hoped, sooner rather than later, the plan would actually start happening. She gripped her spear tightly and continued to peer out at the enemy far in the wood.

This can't be their plan, Tiberius thought under his shield. They can't mean to wait us out and barrage us all night. Why would Cycret reveal himself so soon if they mean to just wear us down with bow and arrow? His mind raced on what to do next. They must mean to draw us out, he finally realized. Yet, for what purpose, he did not know.

He knew he could not wait out the night like this. He needed to take action. He needed to do it now, or else their enemy would continue pressing their strategy. He turned around, inspecting the men trembling under their shields when he caught another glimpse of Catherine. She still stood alone, smiling, in the village square. No shield or protection covered her, yet the mass of arrows appeared to fall around her unbothered.

Unthinking, he jumped from the wall and rushed to her side, holding his shield above him as he went. As he approached her, he found the arrows that had been falling as hard as the snow seemed to fall away in her presence.

"What is this!?" he demanded.

"The Father is here tonight," she said blissfully. "And he is not done with me yet."

He stood and looked around as all of the assembled continued to weather the constant barrage of the enemy volley. Yet here, in her presence, he no longer required his makeshift shield. "What am I to do?" he asked after a moment. "Please, help me!"

She looked up and smiled at him as she was oft to do. "You have all you need to win this day, Son of Luke. They have shown their hand, now show yours. Call for another volley."

"Another volley!? But I can't!" he protested. "It is folly to waste our arrows against them with their power revealed!"

"Call another volley," she repeated.

No trace of fear did he see in her eyes, even as the sky rained with arrows and furious snow. A calm confidence and a strange knowing twinkled out at him from her deep ancient stone eyes. He could not imagine what good another volley from his amateur archers would do. Yet, after a few tense moments, he nodded his head and set off to ready the archers.

After the raining arrows finally ceased, Michael opened his heavy eyes and stared around, bewildered. He eased himself out from under the cart and continued to slog his way through the heavy snow towards the wall where he knew his friends would be. He did not know how much longer he had until the next wave was to fall on him, and the fear of the unknowing spurred him on through the packed snow.

A solemn quiet hung on the defenders at the wall as all eyes turned to their commander. Tiberius offered one fleeting glance to Catherine, who continued to smile broad and knowing. A word in the ancient dwarven tongue escaped her rough lips, and at once, her dwarven brethren had removed the heavy wooden beam from the gate. They lined up behind one another, the Shaman Bruce at the head, and marched out into the open.

Their heavy armor stamped along in the frozen lands, and great flecks of snow were nestled in their long bushy beards. But behind their steel and iron helms, their ancient eyes were focused and determined. Bruce alone wore no armor, just his simple leather clothes and large tunic that scraped the floor as he went.

A burst of hearty, booming laughter echoed around them. "Dwarves, Tiberius?" the dead man's voice rumbled. "You hinge your survival on the broken and useless power of dwarves? Most unexpected that you found them at all, but futile none the less. They too will be slaughtered and studied for their heathen abnormalities!"

"Thrakeluhm!" the Shaman roared in defiance as his band of warriors came to a halt outside the village wall. "Your insults and your evil will be silenced this night, you cursed devil! You have shown your power, and we laugh at it! We laugh at him that raised your filth from the dead! We laugh at your army of misguided wretches! We laugh at you! Thrakeluhm! Aznog no diohm!"

At his words, a mighty roar of laughter like a great avalanche from a frozen mountainside rang out from the twelve armor-clad dwarves. So great and terrible was their laughter that even the raging storm above them was drowned out! "You are the heathen in this world!" Bruce said aloud as his men continued their raucous laughter. "And tonight, the Father is with us!"

In an instant, Tiberius had his archers recovered and preparing to deliver another volley against their enemies. Fear and doubt clouded his mind, yet the confidence of Catherine bade him continue. "Loose!" he boomed out as hundreds of arrows flew to the sky.

They rose into the sky, and at their apex, turned down to fall amongst the soldiers from White. Tiberius bolted for the ramparts, eager to see if this time they would find their mark. But even if they do, it will be a drop in the bucket against such a magnificent assembly.

In the middle of the field, the dead sorcerer again rose his staff, intent to change the arrows into snow as the last ones. But before he could utter a word, Bruce raised his arms and shouted a word in his ancient tongue. A throaty, violent sound boomed out from the small dwarf. Tiberius was rendered speechless as the arrows continued to fall unimpeded. In an instant, each of the hundreds of arrows burst into flame!

Cycret lowered his staff and stepped back in amazement of such brilliant and powerful magic. The arrows had now all been transformed into hundreds of great burning balls of fire that burst brilliantly amongst the invaders. Screams of terror and pain broke out from White's men as hundreds of their cavalry and archers were incinerated by the magic that fell on them.

Tiberius let out a great laugh of excitement that was repeated from the men on the wall. He called for another volley, determined to press the attack. Again, his archers released hundreds of arrows into the sky, and just as they turned downwards upon their targets, they too all burst into giant balls of flame. More screams erupted from the army, who still lay within the forest. Tiberius could see that several men were now running away, abandoning their fight against the village and the magic that now guarded it. Cycret rose his staff high and thrust it hard against the ground. The inhuman sound of moaning and rage crept out of the forest. All at once, droves and droves of undead came storming out from the enemy's ranks heading straight for the camp.

The twelve dwarves in the field fanned out wide to the trench openings they had dug, hunkered low, and brought their axes to the ready. The Shaman alone stood in place as his brethren ran to their positions. He let out a hearty laugh and began to walk towards the undead sorcerer in the field. Across the snow-covered field, the undead Cycret smiled a twisted, gnarled smile in his broken skull face and began to glide to meet Bruce.

Tiberius ordered his people to prepare themselves against the undead's coming onslaught. He called to Shayla to attack when she saw an opening and ordered his archers to continue firing at will against the army. Like a bolt of lightning, the Ranger hurdled the village's walls, followed by the men. With a quick look to make sure all of the defenders were with him, he ordered out to the captains amongst them to secure the trench openings as he ran off to do the same.

Just as he had hoped, the approaching enemy had been funneled into the deep trenches. He stood motionless with one of the dwarves and a few villagers near the largest trench opening, determined to throw himself against them with all his might.

Back in the village, Michael finally reached the square after trying and failing to run through the large mounds of snow that had fallen. Fire illuminated the night sky. Unnatural screams and snarls echoed out from beyond the wall. He spun in place, desperately searching for his friends. He caught a glance of Tiberius just as he hurdled the wall with the rest of his men. Again, he spun in place before he saw a most welcomed sight in the burgeoning bedlam, the only other person alone in the square, the dwarf leader Catherine.

He sprinted towards the dwarf as hard as he could. "Lady Stonefoot," he gasped, "What is happening? What have I missed?"

She remained unmoved at his words. Simply resting a calming hand on his billowing robes before pointing him to the rampart where Tiberius had stood just a few moments before. "Go see, young one."

Michael flew to the wall and was struck still at the sight in front of him. Thousands of undead were swarming through the trenches from across the field. Fire lit up the area and the woods beyond. However, terror and confusion, and anger took root in him at the sight of the white-clad figure gliding towards Bruce. The wand in his hand was burning hotter and hotter. The urge to reveal himself and use his magic to cut down this foe was more overwhelming now than before. He bit his lip and fought to control his shaking hands as he stared on.

"You're a disgusting blight upon my waking eye, you ugly bastard," Bruce shouted to the sorcerer. "Blasphemous and evil!"

The undead Cycret pointed his staff at the Shaman as a great burst of light shot towards him. Bruce remained unfazed as he simply lifted his palm in response. The light burst against his hand as if he wielded an unseen shield and dissipated. Again, and again bolt after bolt were hurled towards the approaching Shaman. And each and every one broke apart and dissolved into faint whips of ethereal smoke. The wraith let out a bloodcurdling scream and began to float faster towards the lone dwarf in the open field.

At the trench, Tiberius stood crouched when one of the undead minions came rushing around the corner. Several of the villagers who stood near recoiled in shock and disgust as the ghoul flew towards the Ranger. In one swift motion, Tiberius raised his father's sword and cleaved the undead man in half. The villagers stared on bewildered.

"See boys, they die just like any other man," Tiberius hollered to the defenders near him.

In turn, they quickly relayed this news to all their fellow villagers at their trenches, eager to pass on this great news. Before long, scores and scores came flowing to them. Tiberius readied himself again, and with a great war cry, hurled himself headlong into the trench, followed by the nearby dwarven warrior and the other villagers.

In the trees, Shayla eyed the approaching enemy, carefully picking the right time to pounce. She was overjoyed to see the volley of arrows turned to fire that rained down on the men from White, for that single change of fortune now drew out the enemy into their trap. She focused her attention now on the dwarf in the field as he marched to meet the undead sorcerer that glided forward. Something inside of her, a voice she had not heard whisper to her in some time, told her that he was the source of tonight's folly. That with him gone from the field, the approaching enemy would be cut down. She prayed to Kazduhl that the honor of vanquishing such a powerful foe would be hers. That she could finally begin to repay the oaths she swore. But she quieted her yearning and continued to focus. No amount of wanting and praying would change anything about this night if she failed to act when the opportunity came.

In the field, the two continued to move unceasingly to one another. "Your power is weak, your evil," the Shaman called as he continued to deflect bolt after bolt from the Sorcerer. "Come, show me what you can really do. I bore of these childish games."

The undead Sorcerer stopped his advancement, and with a great cry of anger, hoisted his staff into the sky. The snow ceased at once, the clouds began to swirl in place as if a great vortex was forming overhead. Lightning was cracking inside the clouds, slow at first, and then more and more with greater frequency until a great stream of lightning broke free and hurtled down on them.

Michael stood frozen as a stream of lightning, more than half a mile wide, fell from the dark heavens above for the Shaman below. The wand was now fiery hot in his hand. His eyes focused hard on the column of light that rocketed towards the ground. He raised the ebony wand to the lightning, closed his eyes, and spun the wand in place.

With a tremendous boom, the lightning came to a complete stop in the sky. Michael twirled the wand again, and the lightning began to turn brighter and brighter and started to coil in on itself as if a great snake poised to strike. The onlookers not engaged in fighting the scores of the undead enemy were frozen in place at the sight above them. In the trees, Shayla let out a great laugh knowing full well her friend and companion had now joined their fight. Even the wraith stopped to ponder this new development above them.

After a few moments, the ball of lightning had finished coiling itself. With a mighty thrust of the wand, Michael sent the ball hurtling towards the undead Sorcerer who stared unmoving in the field below. Those around not engaged in mortal struggle against the undead soldiers looked upon it with amazement, shielding their eyes against the sudden invasion of blinding light. The Sorcerer stood motionless, almost unbothered by the great ball of light that came crashing to him. From across the field, Bruce could see a sly smile cross his mangled face as the undead man opened his arms in almost a childlike embrace to the approaching light.

The sound like a thousand explosions cut through the thick night. The power of the great sphere burst upon Cycret with the power of a million lightning strikes, melting the snow around them and destroying several large trees behind the field. The falling snow was melted into great droplets of rain that evaporated at once, raising up an overwhelming humid air. The blast's force sent several of the advancing army locked in the trenches to their knees, allowing the heroic defenders to cut through them with ease and press their unexpected advantage.

After several blinding moments, the lightning ball was gone, and darkness returned to the earth. The Sorcerer's white robes were all that was left where he stood flapping on the ground in the swift evening wind. His great staff was cloven in two, smoke rising from its insides. A cheer went up over the villagers around despite their continued struggle with the undead.

On the ramparts, Michael fell to one knee breathing hard but feeling relieved. *I did it,* he thought. *Whoever that man was, he's gone now. Surely my friends will be able to...*

A great shrill cry rose up out of the sky, adding to the chorus of screams and steel on flesh that emanated from the battle. The three companions alone felt their blood chill, knowing what the piercing cry meant. Tiberius retreated to the rear of the fight and stretched his *Sight* high into the night. Michael clambered to his feet on the wooden deck of the wall, his blood running colder than the frigid air he sucked in. Even Shayla, the brave and fearless dragoon that she was, threw off her helm where she crouched in the trees.

The sky above them started to move as if the night sky itself had come alive and transformed into a massive swirling vortex. Great black tentacles reached out from the swirling nothingness as if a great beast groping for food. The center ring around them turned darker and darker, becoming blacker than the night sky. The shrill crying turned to laughter, harsh and deafening. Above them, in the night sky, floated the dreadful creature that had attacked the three companions in the woods so many nights ago. The beast that forced brave Tiberius, commander of the rangers, and future emperor, to relive the worst moments in his life. Floating above their furious battle against the undead and traitorous men from White was a great and terrible shadowy Revenant.

Chapter 22

The Battle for the Village

Michael was on his feet in an instant. Fear began to take hold inside him. Memories began flooding back to him, sending great shocks of anger throughout his young body. He tried to speak, to rage and scream against the evil beast that now invaded their midst. Just as the words tried to escape his throat, another horrible evil scream belted out from the Revenant driving everyone below it to their knees in pain. Everyone, that is, save for the sturdy dwarves and the three companions who starred at the magnificent and terrible beast swirling above them.

Its massive black body covered the entirety of the field with enumerable searching tentacles that stretched out even further. So great and hideous was the beast, it made the one they encountered so many weeks ago as if a child barely fresh from the womb.

Tiberius withdrew himself to the mouth of the trench and took stock of his surroundings. Swarms and swarms of the undead continued to press in from the tree line beyond where the remaining men from White now stood cheering. Bruce, the dwarven Shaman, alone stood in the field examining the destroyed fabric and staff from the wraith in the shape of the dead High Sorcerer Cycret. He knew Michael had come to their aid, for he alone could have had the power to destroy such an overwhelming force. Yet for his good intentions, he had unwittingly called forth this latest and perhaps greatest obstacle. Tiberius seethed with rage at their latest predicament and flew to the courtyard within the village walls.

"Shayla! Michael!" he boomed, cutting through the piercing screams, "to me!"

In an instant, the Dragon Knight was at his side, followed quickly by the young Mage. Tiberius was taken aback by the look Michael bore, for though it had been nearly two hours since they last saw one another, he now wore the face of a man touched by the heat of battle. Shayla though, was angry, and her emotions seemed to vibrate off her being. She had been withheld from the action too long while the untested villagers had died by the score. Yet whatever ill will she felt in that moment, she held her tongue out of pure respect for Tiberius' command.

"We need to press the fight, and now!" Tiberius bellowed. "This Revenant seems to be spurring the enemy on faster and fiercer than we can hope to match! And the men from White who haven't fled are still in reserve!"

"What will you have us do, sir?" Michael called out, the burning wand in his hand beckoning to be unleashed again.

Tiberius turned in all directions, taking stock of who was left and what they could hope to accomplish. His eyes fell on what looked to be a small hill in the middle of the yard, causing him to do a double-take. Once he realized what he was looking at, he took off in a sprint till he arrived upon Catherine. She was stooped low, whispering the dwarven tongue to the sleeping berserker. A quick look at the man revealed no wound save for a few scratches, which alone was enough to indicate how powerful a blow the undead sorcerer wielded against him. *At least he is still breathing*, Tiberius thought to himself, squatting next to the dwarven woman.

"Will he wake?" he asked in a hurry.

"Soon, King's Son," she replied sweetly. "Soon."

"Ma'am, we could really use this man sooner than later," Michael spoke, somewhat harsher than he had intended.

"I think Tiberius has other plans for you, young one," she replied, unbothered by the Mage's shortness with her. "Go on, Ranger, tell them your plan while we wait for my brother to stir."

The three companions looked at each other, confused at her words for a moment before Michael asked, "What is your plan, sir?"

Tiberius stood and pulled his friends close so as not to yell. "I'm sick of being on the back foot against this assault. We are going to take the fight to them. Shayla, you will lead my rangers out to the far right and start in on White's men. I'll rally what soldiers we have and do the same on the left. We will meet in the middle. Now go!"

"What will your signal be?" she asked, drawing her helm over her face, readying herself for battle at last.

"Michael will give it to us," Tiberius responded, clasping the boy hard on the shoulders.

Shayla nodded in understanding before departing at once to gather the rangers. *Finally*, she thought, *it's been too long since my blade tasted the blood of the enemy, and no more have deserved to have theirs spilt than these twisted heathens.*

"So," Michael began apprehensively, "I'm going to give the signal?"

"Yes," Tiberius answered, "Get to the field with the Shaman. Your battle lies with the Revenant, and I reckon you will need all the aid you can get against it."

"But," he began but was cut off in an instant.

"You drove the last one off before," Tiberius said, "and you weren't nearly as strong as you are now. With the Shaman's power at your side, you will both prove a worthy foe for that demon."

"If that is your command, I will see it done," Michael answered, "but what of the village? The dead continue to pour through those trenches."

Tiberius glanced down at the dwarf, who continued whispering her language to the sleeping berserker. "Rogers will hold the line here. He and his brothers will not let them enter this place."

Michael nodded and began to sprint through the gate out onto the field to join Bruce.

"And hey!" Tiberius called after the boy, "See if you can thin those ranks of dead men out a little bit!"

Michael, smiling to himself, cut a broad stroke with his wand as he ran past the trenches. From the tip of his wand, a great wave of fire lashed out, burning dozens of the advancing dead, yet not burning a single one of the living villagers. At first, they recoiled, unsure if this was a renewed attack from their living foe or some devilry from the screaming demon overhead. After a quick look at the sprinting Mage, they felt their spirits renewed to press on.

After the Mage was a way off, Tiberius returned his attention to Catherine and the sleeping Rogers. "We're running out of time, ma'am. We need him now, or all we have fought for will be for naught."

She closed her eyes and pressed her head against Rogers and said in the common tongue, "The boy is communing with his Father. Despite my pleas to him, the Father is not done with him."

"Curse you, Rogers," the Ranger whispered. He began to pace the length of the courtyard, waiting for the sleeping Berserker to awaken from his commune.

"Rangers!" Shayla cried as she landed softly on her perch, "Steady your hearts and ready your weapons! Your commander bids us move against the enemy at once!"

"Where is Tiberius?" Constance replied, gathering her arms and gear.

"He's back in the square," Shayla replied. "Quick! We must make all haste to be in position for the oncoming attack!"

"You heard the knight, lads!" Constance called out to her men. "Move your asses! Double time!"

In an instant, they were on the ground and sprinting hard along the side of the raging battle. Outside of the melee, they could finally see the chaos of the fight laid upon them. The rotting smell of the undead enemy was near overwhelming from the charred burned bodies of the King's men who had tried in vain to flee the fiery arrows Michael had wrought down on them. The hardened men of the rangers gagged as they ran. All except Shayla, who alone kept her focus on the task at hand.

Sensing their fear, Shayla shouted from the rear of their formation, "Keep your heads focused, rangers! The enemy before us, and that beast above us, will not see the sunrise!"

"You speak of things you do not know, Dragon Knight," one Ranger called out. "Such evil has never been seen in our empire before!"

"Hold your tongue, child!" Shayla hissed. "You are the one who speaks of things they do not know, for your master and I faced and survived such a beast!"

"How did you defeat it?" another ranger called out, gasping for breath.

"We didn't," she replied. "Our friend the Magi did, and he has grown in strength, skill, and in ways he has yet to know. Now focus on the fight to come! We must arrive with our wits intact, and our hearts strong."

No more words were exchanged amongst them as they ran on, determined to arrive ready for battle before their commander was prepared to give the signal to attack. Shayla, the powerful dragoon, pressed the rangers harder than they had ever been. And for the first time since the battle at the pass, she became alive with thoughts of the oncoming battle.

Fire flew from Michael's wand as he ran for the Shaman in the open field ahead of him. The screaming from the Revenant overhead came in waves now, each one a dagger to his senses. Each scream a painful reminder that he had, inadvertent as it was, unleashed this demon into their midst. Yet now, instead of fear and panic that he had felt that night when they encountered the last one, he felt a strength of spirit that was both foreign and comforting to him at the same time.

A few minutes later, he met the Shaman in the open field. As he approached though, the dwarf did not stir from his examinations of the vanquished wraith's torn white robes and broken stave. "Bruce, we need to get rid of that thing!" Michael called out.

"Is my brother still communing with Father?" the dwarf asked calmly, bringing the broken staff to his eyes.

"Who?" Michael asked confused, now staring hard at the blackness above them.

"Tygahl," the dwarf replied. "Is he still 'asleep' as you think he is?"

"What...yes. He's still asleep in the court," Michael stammered on. "Tiberius and Lady Catherine are with him."

The dwarf nodded and stood, holding the staves in his hands. "What do you make of this?" he asked, thrusting the broken pieces to the Mage's face.

"It's a broken staff," Michael replied impatiently, eager to begin the attack on the Revenant.

"No!" the dwarf cried, grabbing Michael's attention away from the Revenant. "Look! And tell me what you see," he said, thrusting the wood pieces into the Mage's young face again.

Michael stopped and examined the staff. He reached out and brought the broken pieces to his eyes, looking for any sign that might be out of place. He brought it to his ears, listening for some unknown sound until finally, he stared the dwarf hard in the face.

"This isn't a wizard's staff?" he half asked and stated.

"No, it is not."

"This is just a walking stick painted white," Michael continued turning the wood over in his hands. "No magic has been used in this wood, and it shows no sign of wear that Cycret was known to have had on his staff. What does this mean?"

"It means," Bruce started with a smile. "That this was no reincarnated wizard, nor is this the staff he wielded in life. The demon above was shackled to this form. It meant to draw you out to fight, boy."

Michael thought hard for a moment before realization crashed on him. "It meant for me to release him properly, didn't it?"

The dwarf nodded his head. "This demon was chained to the shape of the long-dead Sorcerer. Whoever did this knew that his presence in the battle would stir up feelings amongst you and the King's Son. And only by your power could you release it."

"So, it was a trap," Michael said.

"I would say so, yes. A trap we all sprung."

"Well, what now, sir?"

"Now, my boy," the Shaman replied, turning his attention to the Revenant, "We kill this bloody beast and seek answers when it's over."

Tiberius continued to pace the courtyard, his impatience beginning to boil over. After nearly five minutes, he sprinted to the sleeping mountain and kicked the man hard in his steel-like ribs. "Gods be damned, Rogers! Get your ass up!"

"Your words are in vain," Catherine spoke calmly. "He is with his Father, and nothing will draw him out of that."

Tiberius stopped his futile assault against the sleeping man and instead returned his attention to the trenches beyond the gates. With his *Sight,* he could see the defenders and the dwarven warriors standing their ground yet beginning to tire against the unrelenting enemy. The night was wearing on, and the more the wretched beast above screamed and raged down on them, the lower and lower their spirits would fall. He knew inside of him that they needed to get on the offense. But he also knew that this new strategy he now had formed rested on the sleeping man at his feet to hold off the assault so they could move out.

He turned back to the sleeping man and thought long and hard on what he could do when, like a bolt of lightning, he remembered that day so long ago now that he had calmed the rage within him. He drew his sword, pushed the dwarf woman aside, and held the blade to the Berserker's colossal neck, and called out loud and strong;

"I am Tiberius Axton! Supreme Commander of the Imperial Rangers! Son of Emperor Luke Axton! In his name, and in the name of all Axtons, I command you to return to me now! You will hold your oaths to my family and your home, or I shall remove your head from your neck for your betrayal!"

The large man's sky-blue eyes flew open at the words called out to him by the future emperor. He glanced at the sword at his throat and said in a deep booming voice, "What is your command, master?"

"I mean to press the fight against White's men," Tiberius said, removing his sword from the man's neck and sheathing it back in place. "But your home and your people need you to make your stand here."

"Then here I will stand, My Lord," Rogers said, lumbering to his feet. "I will stand and defend this land as my emperor commands."

"I am not emperor yet," Tiberius said, "But I bid you make your stand here, nonetheless. Your people need their Master, and I require your aid most of all."

Tiberius collected his heavy wooden shield from the ground, offered a curt nod to the man, turned and fled to the blood-soaked trenches beyond the gates. After he left, Tygahl turned to face the dwarven woman and whispered in a language he had never uttered before in his life, "The Father is with us tonight, sister."

His face recoiled at the rumbling words that escaped his mouth, for though he had never learned them before in his life, he now understood them to their fullest. Catherine, the wizened and stone-faced dwarf, nodded sweetly with a knowing smile. "The Father is with us tonight, and every night to come, my brother," she replied in the same guttural language Rogers had just spoken.

He smiled a soft smile of understanding, collected the large, heavy axes that had been knocked back with him, and began to approach the village gates. He looked to the sky and whispered, "Father, thank you for your strength. I call on your name and your blessings one last time to stand against the enemies of the realm." Like a bolt of lightning, his mind went blank, his blue eyes grew darker and darker before turning a fiery crimson. He let out a loud roar, joining in the chorus of mayhem that surrounded them, and leapt hard into the fray.

As Tiberius reached the trenches, he was hit with the renewed screams of the dying men and the demonic screaming from on high. Yet his resolve was strengthened, his plan was set, and he would not allow anything to delay it from happening. "Men of the village!" he called out loud and clear for all to hear, "Withdraw! Withdraw! To me, at once!"

"Are you mad!?" one of the captains of the defense called out, "We cannot retreat against our foe! They will storm the village and raze it to the ground!"

"I did not order a retreat, fool!" Tiberius barked, "I ordered a withdraw! We have a new plan, and we must make all haste if it is to be done!"

At his brief reasoning behind his orders, several of the defenders abandoned their fight and made a hasty exit to where Tiberius stood at the mouths of the trenches. Those not near the openings quickly mounted the trench's edge and clambered out, rolling hard in the snow and slipping here and there. Yet for all those who heeded their commander's call, a few more of the men remained, willfully ignoring his orders. Instead, they chose to continue their struggle against the undead. Tiberius's commands fell on their deaf ears. They had no mind for the obedient nature of taking orders, preferring to give in to their anger at the enemy that now threatened them and their homes. However, these lone insubordinate holdouts weren't long in the trenches.

In their ancient steel and iron armor, the dwarven warriors had wrapped the men in their strong arms and were tossing them out of the trenches against their will as if they were children. Each of the men thrown from the battle landed hard on the snow-white ground with a hard thud and immediately began protesting and cursing the dwarves. One particular dwarf turned to a group of freshly thrown men and said in the voice of a breaking mountain, "Thrakeluhm! Bash-no intrerlor!"

"What the hell does that mean!?" one of the men roared in protest.

"It means fall your ass in line, you idiot! Gods damn your northern stubbornness!" the village captain bellowed at the men, cursing and spitting the ground in anger.

"But sir! What about the village? We cannot abandon our home!" another voice called out.

As if on cue, the roar of the Berserker pierced the night. A heavy thud shook the ground behind them as Tygahl began his furious assault on the undead streaming through the trenches. "The Master will hold the line, boys. Now fall the hell in line!" the Captain called out again.

Once the remaining men were in place, Tiberius turned and began a hard sprint out of the battle. Several men protested in what they perceived to be their retreat from the fight until their formation took a sharp turn to the right. A sudden realization dawned on the men at what Tiberius's plan was now, and several of them exclaimed happily at their new goal.

Tiberius remained unbothered by their chatter and protests. He knew they were not rangers, they were just men and boys defending their homes against an evil that meant to take it all away from them. He knew their discipline was paper-thin, and he knew to be angry at them at this point would not spur them on anymore. All he could do was to lead by example.

He pressed them on harder than any of them had ever been compelled to move in their lives. Barely a man, young or old, could hope to match his pace, and yet not a single one complained. The betrayal by the power-hungry King that wished to destroy and take their homes as a show of strength was enough of a push for them.

"So," Michael began, "how do we kill this damn thing?"

"I was going to ask you that, young Mage," Bruce replied with a quiet chuckle.

"Well, last time we saw this thing, I didn't exactly kill it," Michael admitted, "more like, drove it away."

"I do not think we will be able to drive this beast away tonight," Bruce said, rolling up the long brown sleeves of his robes. "If we truly are to win the night, we must figure out how to vanquish this damn thing once and for all."

Without another word, the Shaman began to spin his mighty arms as if stirring a large pot. His stone-hard eyes never left the swirling beast above them as he started to spin faster and faster before thrusting his arms skyward. A faint whisp as if smoke flew from his hands, aimed towards the center of the Revenant.

"Your magic is wasted, dwarf!" an ethereal voice mocked, "your powers are weak, and I am mighty! Nothing can hu---"

The voice was cut off as the smoke landed against the demon's massive body. Blood-curdling screams of pain called out loud and deafening. Determined to press their attack, Michael gave a quick flip of his wand. A burst of lightning blew from the tip, landing in the center of the Revenant. The light illuminated the darkness around, penetrating the monster and spreading like a spider's web into it.

Renewed screams of agony called out again. Not just cries of agony, but of fear and confusion. The power of the two against the tentacled beast appeared to have caught it off guard and only drove them onwards.

"That's the signal!" Shayla declared loud to the Rangers at her sides. "Fly! Fly and fight with your hearts!"

A great battle cry rose from the rangers as they charged the King's men on the far left of their formation amongst the trees. A few of the nearby men were shocked and fell back at their cry, but soon began to laugh as one of the soldiers called out, "What is this feeble attack against us? Have they run out of tricks and have now grown desperate?"

The soldiers raised the weapons to the oncoming assault, hateful smiles etched into their pale faces. A loud whirring sound broke the laughter as a great spear flew from the group of rangers to land square in the face of the man who spoke. The spear split the man's face in two and exploded his skull and brain on to the ground behind him. His comrades reacted in horror at the violent and sudden attack on their friend and turned to examine his remains. When they returned their attention to the oncoming assault, they were met with a pair of thickly armored dragon scaled boots that kicked them hard in the chest.

Their backs were split open from Shayla's powerful kick, ejecting their organs and bones from their bodies onto the snow-covered ground. She landed with the grace of a trained dancer, removed her spear from the ground, and rose to see another group of soldiers rushing to avenge their fallen comrades. Their battle cry rose high in anger only to be drowned out by the black-clothed rangers who ran past the Dragoon to meet their foes.

"Now, men!" Tiberius cried to the villagers behind him.

He had led the men, unseen, to the far flank of the White's men when Michael's burst of lightning shot up against the floating monster. The exhausted villagers barely had any time to slow to a halt before sprinting hard against the soldiers. A large formation of the enemy was crowded nearby and turned just in time to be met by a large broad stroke of Tiberius's bastard sword. His weapon disemboweled at least five men in one stroke. Without hesitation, he brought his weapon around again and took the arms off another man who dared rush towards him.

Father be with me, Tiberius said to himself before moving forward.

Another group hurried to meet him head-on, but with unnatural speed and grace, he ducked and weaved past their frightened and unfocused strikes, slicing one up the back hard as he rose. The remaining men barely had time to turn to face him before they were overrun by the villagers who had caught up to the battle at last. Many of them stopped to fight the soldiers man-to-man, yet Tiberius never stopped his forward motion. To stop was to die, and he had no intention of dying tonight.

A few soldiers would break ranks to attack the lone ranger, and each and every one of them was dispatched at once. He could see more and more soldiers breaking after him in the distance, but that didn't bother him one bit. He was determined to cut his way to Shayla in the middle of the formation. Then they could turn their attention to the rest of the King's men. Further, in the distance, he could see Tygahl now standing tall against the village's walls. The hulking man continued raging against the undead enemy that poured out of the trenches at him and his dwarf brethren. Hopefully, their legendary stoutness would prove worthy of the match they were up against.

Michael released the lightning blast against the Revenant and stared on for what was to come next. Instead, Bruce again waved his arms, raising a massive orb of snow and ice. He held it aloft for several minutes before it suddenly broke apart and dissolved into a great flowing river that floated along in the air. He turned to face the Mage at his side, and after a brief nod of acknowledgment, sent the flowing water straight up into the blackness.

"Water!" the Revenant boomed out with a laugh. "The Mage brings real power, and you bring water?"

Michael pointed his wand, and the water burst into flames that travelled the length of the floating stream before it too found its mark against the laughing shadow. Another cry of pain reverberated out, shaking the wooden trees below and rattling the village in the distance. Like the lightning before, the flames spread across the vastness of its shadowed body.

After several minutes, the two dropped their arms and watched as the fire spread wide in the sky like the swiftness of the coming dawn. But whatever measure of accomplishment they felt was quickly snuffed out.

"You dare!?" the Revenant called out in fury, "You dare!?"

And in the blink of an eye, great heaps of fire began to fall from the sky to the ground below as if the stars themselves had fallen from their celestial bodies. Unthinking, Michael raised his wand and produced an incorporeal dome around him and the dwarf. The shield blocked several of the fireballs that now fell upon them. They could see many of the fiery spheres had landed in the forest beyond the field, setting it ablaze and spreading amongst the trees. On the other side, they could see the village they had fought to defend was now alight and burning.

"You dare against a power you cannot begin to fathom!" the beast screeched. "I will burn you! I will burn all of you, and only the ashes will remain to bear witness to your death!"

Under their shield, the two stared on in horror as the fire they summoned against their foe hurtled back down around them. The screams of terror rose up from all around them. Thoughts of their friends and the innocents hidden in the village flooded their minds and brought them to their knees.

"What do we do?" Michael bellowed in anger. "What can we do!? Bruce? Bruce!"

But all the Shaman could do, bewilderment and fear imprinted on his stone-hard face, was hang his head in shame. "I do not know, Michael," he whispered. "I do not know." The fire continued to pour as the two crouched in silence and horror.

CHAPTER 23

THE SONG OF KAZDUHL

"What in the hells below is that!?" the village captain exclaimed as the fire fell heavy in the woods. Yet, no sooner had he spoken, a great flaming sphere exploded against his body, crushing his remains deep into the ground.

Tiberius whirled just in time to see the captain burst from the force of the fire that rained down on them. He took several large gasps of air, trying to clear his mind. Several of the villagers had thrown themselves under large tree roots and behind large frozen boulders. Several of the soldiers from White were running from the wood that was now ablaze.

Tiberius turned to the men at his back and yelled, "Flee men! Flee! Get out of the woods! Get out of the woods at once!"

"What about you, sir?" another voice called, already running clear of the forest.

"I'm going to finish this bloody business," Tiberius called back, slaying another two soldiers with ease. "Take these men and get clear of the woods!"

"Gods be with you!" the voice called back.

The fast-rising smoke burned his throat and eyes. The fire licked his face and singed his beard. He was determined to find Shayla in the hell that was wrought around them and kill every single man that bore the White colors. A cruel smile formed on his hardened face as he pressed on through the fire.

"Rangers!" Constance screamed high and clear, "Incoming!"

The fire crashed down on them, scattering the rangers in every direction. Shayla looked up and casually danced around the rain of fire that poured in heaps around them. In the distance, she heard the Revenant boom its hearty death laugh, and a renewed rage grew in her. A group of White's men ducked and weaved around the fire and rushed her and the rangers. But Shayla hopped in the air and slapped her mighty spear on the ground as she landed. A mighty burst of air rushed to meet the soldiers throwing them to their backs. She leapt into the air again, and after three crushing hops onto their bodies, ran forward again.

The rangers were on their feet and sprinted hard to catch up with the Dragoon's inhuman speed. She covered many yards in the blink of an eye, and every soldier she found, fleeing or standing to fight, was met by her spear. The fire fell as relentless as a snowstorm from the mountains, yet the fire bounced off her dragon clad armor without a bother. It was his armor, after all. The armor of the King in his halls of fire and glory. The armor of Kuzduhl.

"Where is the commander?" Constance called out from behind Shayla in between dodges and sword thrusts. Her voice was strained from the smoke, and her movements were beginning to slow from the heat.

"I do not know," Shayla replied, piercing the back of a fleeing soldier. "But we will move on nonetheless."

"This is suicide!" another ranger called out.

"Hold your tongue!" Shayla hissed.

"I will not hold a damn thing, Narzeth!" the ranger yelled back defiantly. "I am a man of the Imperial rangers, and I have followed the orders of a heathen for enough tonight!"

Shayla turned on the spot, and with one mighty leap, kicked the man hard to the ground. Before he could regain his composure, her spear was at his throat. Beneath the dragon helm, her dark eyes burned hot at his words. "You will mind your tongue in my presence, boy! I have sworn my allegiance to your empire and to your commander! I fought and killed scores of Narzeth at the pass! I have walked through pools of fire and communed with dragons! I am a Dragon Knight of Kazduhl!" She removed her spear and turned from the man. "And you are weak and impotent!" she finished before returning to the battle ahead of her.

The ranger stared blankly at his comrades, who returned looks of disgust and contempt at his lack of discipline. The man balled up on the floor of the burning forest, sucking in lungfuls of smoke and debris, and prayed to the gods of his father that the madness around them would stop.

"We can't stay here all night!" Michael shouted from beneath their shield. "Should we try and douse the fire?"

But the Shaman didn't answer. Instead, he continued to look at the destruction that surrounded them. In the distance, he could see the village was ablaze, the Berserker Tygahl silhouetted against the light mauling down the undead that continued to pour in unbothered by the madness of the night.

"Bruce! Help me! In the name of Frijigzah himself, help me!" Michael pleaded.

The name of his Father stirred Bruce from his dark thoughts, and, standing under the shield, said, "We need to kill that thing now. It will be futile to try and extinguish the fire. It pours out as if a waterfall."

"Okay," Michael replied. "How do you propose we do that?"

The Shaman pulled back his sleeves, and as before, began to spin his arms around and around. The ground beneath them started to rumble and crack open. Small alcoves of the earth started to shift, sending loose patches of dirt falling deep into the bowels of the ground. Rocks and debris were now rising into the air. Stones and small tree roots were ripped from the ground and began to float in front of them.

The ground began to shift harder now. Larger cracks and groans filled their ears, and before Michael knew it, enormous sections of the field were suspended in the air about them. Michael gazed all around him, stunned by the raw display of magic that he was witness to. The sheer power it must have taken to break apart the very earth beneath them was staggering to the young Mage.

A few minutes later, no more than a dozen or so large patches of snowy ground filled the sky above them, goaded on by the Shaman's ceaseless turning of his hands. Out of the corner of his eye, Michael saw the dwarf staring at him, and upon meeting his gaze, was given a quick wink from beneath his thick eyebrows. Returning his attention to the Revenant, Bruce turned his arms faster and faster, bidding the suspended earth about them to begin circling around and around.

From beneath his flowing beard, words in his people's harsh, throaty language escaped the dwarf's lips. A final prayer to the Father.

The dwarf slung one of his mighty arms upward, and a piece of earth hurtled towards the beast, finding its mark in the center of its fiery black mass. The Revenant shifted in the night sky and issued a howl of pain. Again, Bruce thrust his arm, and another mound of earth and dirt was sent flying. Small waterfalls of fire began to cease their flow, and the fiery light inside the blackness grew dimmer.

Michael grew excited at the turn of fortune the dwarf's magic had brought on them. More and more pieces of ground were sent tearing through the sky above them. Each landing hard against the shadow's black mass. "It's working!" Michael exclaimed, dropping his enchantment from them.

Bruce lowered his hands as the last piece of earth was sent hurtling into the night. "Aye," he replied out of breath, "But you best start working on how to finish this foe off."

"Keep moving forward, rangers!" Shayla called out, cutting down more and more of the men from White as she went. "Your Lord and Commander are near!"

"You heard the Knight, lads!" Constance belted out, dodging small rainfalls of fire and weaving around the strikes of random soldiers who tried to waylay her and her men. Yet in the fire and confusion, their *Sight* gave them the advantage against the regular foot soldiers of the would-be tyrant King.

The undisciplined soldiers ran towards them, screaming half in terror and half in excitement. Yet their eyes deceived them in the smokey haze, and each of them was dead where they had stood. "Give them no quarter, boys!" Constance called out again. "For they will give us none! Keep pushing! Foll---" but her words never finished in her mouth.

Shayla was more than twenty yards ahead of them when she heard the unnatural sound of groaning and breaking wood. She spun on the spot and saw a large oak, ablaze from the fire, finally give under the strain of the heat and collapse on top of the small squad of rangers. She cursed aloud in the language of her people, and with all the power she could muster, leapt to get them clear of the falling tree, but she was too late.

The tree crashed down on their group with a mighty boom, shifting the burning ground under them and breaking several smaller trees with its weight. The rangers raged against their crashing doom but were quickly silenced. Shayla was there a second too late and began to hunt around the debris for any survivors. Yet none met her searching, anxious eyes. She kicked aside several smaller fallen trees and shattered many large boulders in her search for survivors. Time appeared to stop around her, and all her senses seemed to fail her when a small weak voice called out amongst the cacophony of burning chaos.

"I am here, ma'am," the weak, strained voice of Constance muttered.

Shayla rushed to the trunk of the fallen tree. From beneath it, she could see the Ranger crushed under the enormity of the trunk's weight. Shayla tried to kick at it with the same force she had used in battle, but all of her anger and power was in vain. Overwhelming desperation consumed her as she brought her spear high and thrust it down with all the strength she could. After a few minutes of desperate hacking against the hard iron-like wood, she had neatly cleaved the trunk into several smaller pieces that she sent flying into the night.

She inspected the dying Ranger, and dropping her spear and helm to the ground, knelt beside Constance's body. She began to gently rub the closely shaved head of the dying woman. In the haze, she could see that once upon a time, her head had been a blazing red. In her mind, she could clearly see a young Constance at play in some gladden field. Bright red hair, redder than the fire around them, flowing in the springtime breeze.

"My men?" Constance murmured.

The beautiful image melted from Shayla's thoughts. Even in death, Constance now feared for her men. Shayla bowed her head, determined to hide her tears from the dying woman.

"Do not," Constance said, gasping for air. "Do not cry for me, Dragon Knight. Do not cry for my men. We are servants of the empire. It is our duty, and our honor, to die for our country."

"Aye," Shayla replied, gazing at the woman. "And your duty is now fulfilled."

"Aye. That it is. Now, pick up your spear, Dragon Knight, and fulfill your oaths."

The Ranger closed her eyes and laid her head back. "You," Constance struggled to say, "You are one of us. Now and always. And may... May the Spirit of The Warrior always be with you." And with that, Constance let her spirit go.

Shayla knelt there for a long time, cradling the dead woman's head in her dragon scaled armor. Her heart, once full of rage and sadness, now grew cold. Her tears ceased, her breath steadied, and after reverently placing the Ranger back on the ground, she retrieved her spear and replaced her helmet on her head. She stared at the fire around her and felt a sense of almost joy overcome her.

Her mind was taken back to the flaming pools of Kazduhl. She closed her eyes and beheld the face of the Dragon King. She felt the heat penetrate her armor, and a faint smile draw across her face. She felt at home again. Home in the loving embrace of her lord and king. She placed the helm over her face and retrieved his spear from the ground.

She proudly raised her head, and from her olive-skinned lips, began to sing the song of her people. The music of war and battle. The music of death and life. The song of Kazduhl. The song of dragons. After a few short steps, she burst high into the sky, her voice belting out loud and clear across the woods and echoing off the mountain slopes in the distance.

"What new devilry is this!?" one of the villagers called out.

Tiberius was stopped in his tracks at once. He closed his eyes and felt a small smile creep on his face. He knew that song. It had brought him comfort and terror more than a year ago at Vermillion Pass. He turned to face his men at his back and simply said, "It is the song of the Dragon King, Kazduhl."

"A dragon!? There's a dragon loose now!? What more can that devil above conjure to torment us!?" one of the men exclaimed, dodging a small burst of fire.

"Something worse than a dragon is loose in these fiery woods, men. One of his daughters, and she is angry." He faced his men. In their bewildered faces, he saw fear, but not of the fire or the enemy. Fear of the song that echoed around them. Fear of Shayla and her wrath. "Lady Rider is with us, men! Now fly! Fly to your doom! Fly to glory!"

Renewed in purpose, he drove the men on through the hellscape that engulfed them, determined to meet the Dragoon and join in her song. If not in words, then in deed a resolve. He ran on until, after a short while, he arrived at the center of the woods. He turned to survey the fire around him, extending his power all around him for sign of Shayla. The dragon king's song continued to haunt the burning forest. In the distance, the faint noises of screaming soldiers could be heard before being silenced forever.

He closed his eyes and forced his mind back to that day at the pass, trying to recall the song she and her mighty sisters had risen as they slew their Narzethian captors. The words came to him piece by piece, and though he knew not what they meant in his own tongue, he felt the words and melody come to him. He rose his arms and began to echo her words back into the orange and red night.

The trees rustled and broke, and out of the flames flew Shayla. In the firelight, she looked as a dragon reborn from legend and myth. She landed a few feet apart from him and quickly walked upon him, still singing her beautiful and terrible song. They locked forearms and sang on together as the world burned around them, finally coming to the crescendo.

They locked eyes, and Tiberius, the ranger, and future emperor said, "Hail, Shayla Rider. Dragon Knight of the Axton Empire."

Beneath her helm, her olive lips replied, "Hail, Tiberius Axton. Ranger and heir to Axton Empire. The Spirit of The Warrior brought to life." They broke the lock of their forearms and turned to look amongst the burning forest. "The foes appear to be vanquished."

"Aye, that they do," he replied.

"What shall we do now?"

"I suspect our friend could use some help. And you men," he said before turning to the villagers that had finally caught up, "have fought bravely, but the night is not over. Fly to the village, find any survivors that may be left, and lead them to safety."

"Aye! You heard Tiberius, move out!" a villager called out.

After they departed, the two warriors turned their gaze to the field and the mass of floating rocks beyond. "Shall we?" Shayla asked.

"We shall," Tiberius said before heading off to rejoin his friend.

———

Michael began hurling great bolts of lightning against the Revenant. The fire had stopped raining down from the body of the beast, and darkness returned to the night sky, yet the fire from its wake lit up the field and woods as though it were summer midday. Bruce had tried to stand defiant against the raging monster but fell to the ground in exhaustion.

"Are you alright!?" Michael asked, ceasing his assault to comfort the dwarf.

"A moment, please," the Shaman gasped, trying to steady his breath. "It's been many lifetimes since I've had to use magic such as this."

"You stunted, malformed, runt!" the Revenant bellowed, "You will die for your insolence!" At his words, great tentacles exploded from its shadowed body, flailing in search of its prey. Five of them flew to the ground, determined to seize the dwarf.

Michael was on his feet, his wand wildly hurling blasts of light and fire at the groping arms that now sought them. Each blow from his wand brought out another cry of agony from the beast overhead and a renewed effort to grab hold of them. But with each attack, Michael was there to fend it off. He finally dropped to one knee, still determined to fight off the approaching death.

Without warning, a mass of tentacles landed hard on the ground across from them. They slowly turned and whirled into place before taking the shape of great black wolves such as he and his companions faced before. Their eyes glowed red and murderous under swirling misty eyelids, and their claws stretched forth from their black paws.

Michael stared in disbelief but raised his wand and conjured a spell of daylight, determined to beat them back. His eyes grew heavy from exhaustion, and his arms were like a smith's anvil. He was spent but remained determined to hold the line against the encroaching evil. Despite his valiant attempts at defense, one of the great swirling beasts broke free from his light and leapt furiously at them.

I'm sorry, my friends, Michael thought, still trying to fight back against the wolf. *I wasn't strong enough.*

But in a flash, the beast let out a tremendous demonic howl of pain and turned to smoke before his eyes. Beyond where it had been, buried in the fresh dirt, was a familiar ebony and white spear. He heard a soft thud next to him, and turning his face, saw the green and grey scaled grieves he had seen so many times on the road before. He heard heavy footsteps and the crunching of soil and snow and knew who that was without looking.

"So," Shayla said, bringing the young Mage to his feet, "What did we miss?"

"My friends," Michael said, steadying himself, "I'm glad you are safe and here, but I do not know what help you can provide."

"I reckon we can hold back these beasts long enough for you to kill this thing," Tiberius said with a small twirl of his sword to loosen his wrist. "How's the Shaman?"

"Recovering, King's Son," the dwarf answered, calming his breath.

"Any idea of what to do?" Shayla asked, her eyes fixed on the wolves that stood apart from them, snarling and drooling black liquid upon the ground.

Bruce didn't answer for a moment before closing his eyes and saying, "Yes, Mistress Knight. I know of a way to dispel this evil."

"Then you had best get on with it!" Tiberius exclaimed. "Shayla, with me!" In a flash, the warriors sprinted against the demonic wolves, determined to beat them back as hard as they could.

"Mage," the dwarf said solemnly, "I require your wand."

Michael turned and stared down at the dwarf incredulously. "My wand? What good will that do?"

"Do you trust me?" the dwarf replied, now standing tall and proud.

"Yes, but---"

"Michael Deerborn! Son of Thomas! Brother of the Magi, and servant of the empire!" the dwarf boomed. "Do you trust me!"

Michael examined the stout and hearty dwarf before giving a brief nod and handing his wand over. The dwarf took it and began to look it over as he had in his village so long ago. He brought it to his ears, closed his eyes, and listened to the music only he could hear. A smile cracked his stone-hard face. Calm and happiness engulfed his spirit. He slowly opened his eyes and said in a steady voice, "The Father beckons, my friend. And I go to meet him."

Bruce turned and began to slowly march towards an unseen destination in the field. He raised his burly arms as a child grasping for their mother, holding the ebony wand aloft. Out of his mouth, he began to shout in his people's ancient language against the raging demon. The ethereal wolves continued to bite and claw their way to get him, yet the two warriors continued to beat them off one by one as they approached.

"Come and claim me you vile abomination!" the Shaman exclaimed in the common tongue. "Or have you lost your nerve in the face of your demise!?"

"I have no fear!" the Revenant boomed. "I am fear! I am death!"

A dozen great tentacles burst from its body with such speed, none of them on the ground could react in time. The misty feelers flew past the companions, and in an instant, seized the dwarf and began to pull him into the sky. The great wolves on the ground turned to black smoke and rose to return to their master.

Shrill laughter burst out from the Revenant, triumphant at capturing its prey. "Your folly will mark your downfall! And after you, I will come for the boy! And the heathen woman! And the emperor's son! I will cover this land in a darkness that will last a thousand generations!"

Bruce held the wand aloft, and out of the darkness, a light began to grow from the tip of the ebony shaft. Clearer and more radiant than the sun, the light started to take shape as if the water turned to fire. As if morning breaking the veil of night.

"You will no longer desecrate this land with your evil," the dwarf declared as the light became brighter and brighter. "The Father is with us."

On the ground below, the three companions were now huddled together and shielding their eyes against the growing light. "I hope he knows what he is doing," Shayla said, now covering the Mage with her arm.

"So do I, Shayla," Michael replied, his eyes fixed on the tentacles holding his mentor.

"What is this trickery?" the Revenant said, another burst of laughter escaping its void. "You think light is a match for me? You think your petty power is a match for me?"

"This is no trick, and this is not some petty power called against you," Bruce replied, weakly but firm. "The Father's power flows through this wand. His power and wrath are finally called against you, and you will yield to his majesty."

"Your 'Father' is impotent against me, dwarf! His power is weak and in vain! I will crush you and all of your kin! Wiped clean from this world as you should have been! Then I will travel to the worlds beyond and take him as well!"

"Thrakeluhm!" Bruce shouted in defiance. "Thrakeluhm!"

At his words, the wand exploded in a radiant light brighter than the sun. A shrill scream rang out over the sky, forcing the three below to cover their ears and turn away from the brilliant light that broke the darkness. The light grew on and on until, finally, a sharp crack pierced the sky. The screaming became hoarser, quieter, and the light began to slowly dim. The Revenant that had terrorized the village was gone and all grew still in the frozen land.

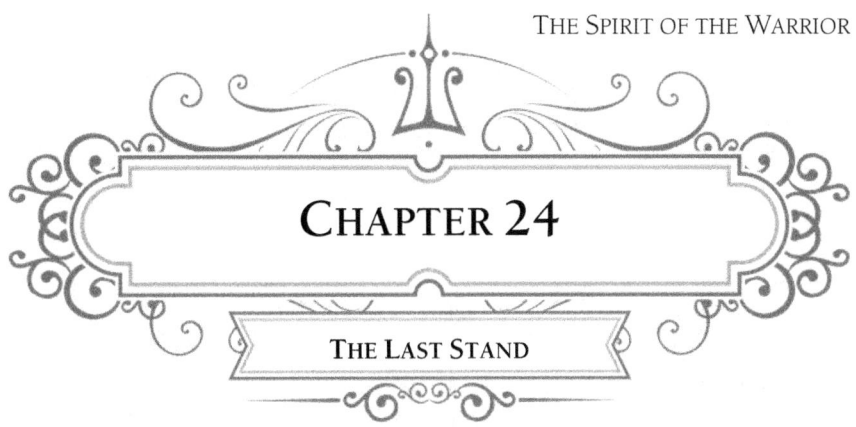

CHAPTER 24

THE LAST STAND

An uneasy silence washed over the northwestern land of the Axton Empire. The fever-pitched battle that had consumed the small village was over now. The only remnants of the mêlée between the outnumbered villagers and the treasonous soldiers of King White were the low burning woods and the same village they had struggled so hard to protect.

The companions removed their hands from their ears and returned their gaze to the black sky above. The once floating mass of the Revenant's shadowed body began to break apart into pieces of black, almost clothlike material that floated to the ground and dissipated into nothingness. The light was growing dimmer, and using his *Sight*, Tiberius could see that the dwarf was no longer suspended in the air. Just the remnants of the beast that was now, finally, vanquished.

"He's gone," the Ranger said flatly.

Michael hung his head, stifling a sob that threatened to form in his throat. *It should have been me*, Michael thought.

"Wait!" Tiberius exclaimed. "I see someone."

"Where? Is it Bruce!?" Michael exclaimed.

The black ring that had occupied the sky was now breaking apart, and sure enough, in the middle of where the mouth of the beast had been, floated a man clad in long flowing red robes. His face was twisted and ancient, his hands shriveled and pale beneath the crimson cuffs of his robe. Shayla stood, able to now see the figure that hung suspended in the sky.

Anger and coldness flashed in her. Her black eyes narrowed. "It's a Narzeth. Bless our lord's name. It's a Narzeth where the beast had been."

"A Narzeth?" Michael asked as he continued fighting back the tears. "How is this possible? How could a Narzeth have conjured this beast or taken its form?"

"They hate magic," Shayla said. "They consider it, and all who use, an evil that flies in the face of their heathen gods. I guess things have changed."

Realization crashed in on Tiberius. Never in the long years of war and struggle against the Narzeth had the empire ever considered their enemy would resort to magic. Long had the empire held command over the powers of magic. It was the backbone of their very society and the ultimate source of their near uncontested might. Yet here, plain as the nose on his face, was a Narzeth adorned in wizard's garb in the middle of where the Revenant had just been.

"We'll figure this out later," the Ranger said finally. "For now, we need to end this before he recovers."

"How are we to do that, sir?" Michael asked. "I do not have my wand, and even Shayla cannot reach him at that height."

Tiberius turned and placed his gloved hand on the Mage's shoulder. "You do not need your wand, Michael."

"Yes, I do!" the boy exclaimed. "It was the Father's wand, and the only way left to reach magic."

"Michael, you do not need the wand to use magic. Do you not remember the night we met? You said you healed yourself with your own hands."

"Yes," Michael answered, "But to fight against another wizard without the wand is futile."

"Do you see a wand or stave in that man's hand? He was able to use magic without it, and so can you."

"But sir---"

Tiberius removed his hand and stared the young boy hard in the face. Drawing himself up to his full height, he said, "Michael Deerborn, I command you in the name of the emperor! Find your strength and ready yourself."

Michael stared at Tiberius, hurt that his friend and companion would invoke the emperor to compel his actions. He stared around the destroyed field for a moment trying to gather his thoughts, when a sudden idea struck him.

After many tense minutes, he nodded back to Tiberius. "I think I have an idea, but I will need Shayla to finish him off if it is to work."

"Then let's get to it, my friend," she replied, crouching low.

Michael took a deep breath and pulled back the sleeves of his robes. He hoped against all hope that he still had strength enough to do this. If this would even work at all.

As the Shaman had done before, he began to slowly circle his arms, slow and broad. He could feel his body straining to pull the magic from the void. He could feel his spirit pulling apart as he focused all his intent and concentration on what he needed to do.

Small pebbles and soil from the destroyed field began to shift under their feet. Loose dirt began to rise into the night air until finally, a small piece of earth was ripped from its place and began to climb into the sky. Michael fell to his knees from the tension but continued to swim his arms in the air, willing the small piece of earth higher and higher.

"Shayla, I don't know how much longer I can keep this up," Michael gasped.

Her heart began to break for the young boy straining with all his might at her side. She would not let his suffering, or the lives lost in this folly, be in vain.

"Kazduhl be with me," she whispered, and with a mighty leap, the Dragoon flew into the sky.

Tiberius joined his companion on the ground and embraced him from behind. "You can do this, my friend," he whispered into the boy's ears.

Michael felt his arms and heard his words, but the exhaustion was threatening to take him over. He continued to press on.

Shayla climbed in the sky higher than she had flown in many long years. Her mighty spear at the ready by her side. Her eyes focused on the piece of earth that hung a hundred feet or more in the sky. With the precision of an expert archer, she landed square on the mark before quickly crouching low again and throwing herself again higher into the sky. Her gaze and spear aimed for the Narzeth wizard's chest.

"She made it!" Tiberius exclaimed. "Let it go!"

At his words, Michael dropped his arms and slumped in Tiberius's embrace, fatigue having overtaken him and sending him into a deep sleep. Tiberius removed his glove and thrust two fingers to the boy's throat, searching and finally finding a pulse. He breathed a sigh of relief before turning his eyes again to the blackened sky.

Shayla cut through the night; her dragon scaled armor shining brilliantly in the emerging moonlight. From above, with the raging fire below, she looked as if she was a dragon emerging victorious from battle.

She thrust her spear forward as she flew, aimed squarely at the wizard's chest.

Her weapon penetrated the wizard's heart. Warm blood gushed from his wound, and his cry rang out. The Narzeth screamed and raged in a tongue never heard before in the Axton Empire. In an instant, the unseen force that had held him in place was gone. His body went limp and began to fall to the waiting ground beneath them. She gripped the spear hard and let his body remove itself from her blade as she began to fall behind the dead wizard.

She knew she was not likely to survive the fall from this height, but that was fine with her. She had promised Constance she would defend their home, and she had fulfilled her oath. For a brief moment, everything was right in the world. She spread her arms wide and looked at the winking stars in the heavens beyond.

She had never taken the time to admire them since coming to her new home. They were prettier here than they were across the sea. Bright and alive and smiling down on the land. She closed her eyes and beheld the face of Kazduhl. Felt his warm dragon fire embrace her and claim her as one of his daughters. Her thoughts shifted to her friends down below, smiling and alive and happy.

Her mind flashed to her sisters, and all they had endured in their long lives. The battles they had won together, and the battles yet to be fought in defense of their adopted country. Her only regret was that she would not be among them, to sing their King's song over the empire as they flew into battle again.

But they would continue on. They would fight, and sing, and win all for the glory of the Axton Empire. For Tiberius and Michael. For Tygahl and Michelle. For all the people of the land that had freed them from bondage and sheltered them from the evils.

A soft smile broke her face. "Mighty Kazduhl. Thank you."

Tiberius was on his feet as the body of the wizard impacted the loose soil near him. But he looked again, and to his horror, saw Shayla right behind him, her back facing the ground, arms spread and welcoming. She landed hard, driven deep into the ground next to where the motionless Narzethian now lie. He was upon her in an instant, and with great effort, pulled her from the crater she had left.

Her armor was crushed in the arms, her helmet cracked and fell apart, revealing her beautiful oval face and fierce black hair that blew in the night wind. As with Michael, he checked her pulse, but could not find one. He grew frantic and began searching again over and over to find a pulse. After many tense minutes of searching, he found one near her jaw.

It was slow, barely registerable to his numb fingers. That brought him no comfort. Alive as she was for the moment, he knew she wouldn't last long. He had not the tools nor the skill to help her out here in the desolate field. And with Michael incapacitated, all hope for saving the beautiful and fierce Dragoon seemed lost.

He stared down at the knight and felt hot tears falling from his cheeks. Great sobs escaped his throat. He threw back his head and wailed into the night. All the fighting they had experienced together. All the long conversations on the road and all the knowledge and laughter they shared would be gone and forgotten.

How can I face her sisters and tell them I failed her? How can I comfort them with the knowledge that she had sacrificed herself for the cause of justice in a frozen land so far from them?

Regaining his composure, he picked her up and walked her slowly to wear Michael lie asleep on the ground. He placed her next to him and crossed her arms. Overcome with grief, the mighty Ranger fell to his knees, bowed his head, and began sobbing to himself until he heard the faint shuffling of feet behind him. He was on his feet, sword drawn and staring down the hulking form of Tygahl.

He was bleeding profusely from deep claw marks. One of his eyes was missing with only a bloody mass in its place. He limped on; his other leg broken in two. Tiberius dropped his sword and rushed to the Berserker's side.

"Did we win, sir?" Tygahl asked weakly.

"Aye," Tiberius said with a nod, "I think we did."

"Good. Help me to your friends, please."

With great effort, Tiberius supported the hulking man as he clambered to where Shayla and Michael lie on the broken ground. Fresh snow was falling into the loose dirt. The cold air was beginning to return now that the fury of the battle was over. The fire from the forest and village started to smolder, rendering the field a dull smoggy pink and orange.

The behemoth of a man fell to both knees and looked over Tiberius's companions. "Father," he whispered into the night, "Do not let these children leave our world yet."

He stood on his good leg, raised his chest and head up into the night. "Father! Hear me! Return these warriors to us! Beat back the dragon and demand he surrenders his daughter to this world! Father! Hear me!" And with a great cry into the night, the Berserker stumbled on his feet and fell to the ground.

His rage was spent. The once fierce red in his remaining eye was gone, replaced by the pure and inviting blue. But in that eye, no life could be seen. He had fulfilled his promise to Tiberius. He had kept his home safe, and now, he went to join his Father in the world beyond theirs.

Tiberius fell to his knees again, bewildered and overcome with grief. Too many lives lost tonight, all for a would-be ruler's evil desires. Such wasteful loss of life, all in the pursuit of power and control.

I'm going to kill him, Tiberius said to himself. I will rip his heart from his chest and watch the light leave his eyes.

But his grief and desire for revenge were cut short by the sudden blasting of horns far in the distance. He turned his head wildly to and fro, hoping to see where it had come from until another louder blast rang out. He looked into the distance and could see horses and white-clad men in armor rushing through the smoldering woods.

Of course. Reserves in case their attack failed. Stupid. I should have planned for this.

He gathered his sword from the broken ground and shambled to his feet. He examined the weapon for a moment, taking the beauty of his ancestor's sacred sword. Much blood had been spilt upon it this night. Much more yet to be shed, he reckoned. He bent low and retrieved Shayla's spear from the ground in his other hand. He adjusted the weight of it in his hands, finding the balance. It was only right that these two weapons be joined in battle one last time.

More horns blasted. The enemy was upon him. He bowed his head, closed his eyes as if in prayer, and whispered, "Warrior, be with me."

After his quick respite, he rushed headlong into the oncoming assault.

Horns blared out clear and bright as more and more soldiers flew out of the burnt woods. Their faces were masked with hate at the sight of their dead comrades. They charged furiously into the open, hoping to exact revenge and fulfill their mad King's desires. Yet, when they caught sight of Tiberius giving charge to them, a great cheer went up over the crowd.

"Tiberius is here!" one of them exclaimed, "The ranger's commander is here! Cut him down! In the name of your King, cut him down!"

Five men on horseback drove hard to meet the Ranger barreling towards them. Their spears were held out, eager to find their mark. Eager to win their victory against the Ranger and earn the adoration of their King.

But to their astonishment, he ducked their spears and, with a great swipe of Shayla's weapon, cut the legs out of their horses. Five quick thrusts from the spear's blade and one swipe for good measure, and all five of the cavalrymen now lay dead and crushed under the weight of their horses.

Knights in brilliant white armor ran to meet him, their broadswords held high above their shoulders. He took careful aim, and with a great effort, sent the spear flying through the air. It landed hard against one of their chests and pierced his armor through. The knight was dead before he hit the ground.

The other knights who had been near him stopped to see what had befallen their comrade. But as they turned again to face Tiberius, they too were met with the fierce strikes of his sword. He twirled and danced between their broad strokes as if moving through a crowded market. He swiped at one, slicing through the mail shirt under his armor, removing the man's arm and leg in one swift motion. Another swung blindly and received the tip of Tiberius's sword through the slit in his armor.

A third knight swung hard for Tiberius's chest, aiming to cleave the Ranger in two. At the last second Tiberius twirled away, avoiding his blade in the nick of time. The knight had put all his strength into the killing blow and threw himself off balance.

With his back exposed, Tiberius thrust hard through the base of his heavy white helm, dropping the man to the ground. The remaining men tried in vain to find their killing stroke against the Ranger, but neither could hope to match his speed and ferocity. And in a few short moments, all five of the armored knights were dead at his feet.

He turned to see more troops plowing in. He took in a deep breath and found it hard to breathe for some reason. A pain he had not felt in many long years began to ache from his body. His hands started to tremble under the weight of the sword at his side. A pain shot from his ribs up to his heart.

He reached his hand to his side and felt the unfamiliar warmth and wetness of fresh blood oozing out his side.

I guess I wasn't fast enough for once, he thought to himself with a chuckle. He fell to one knee and started sucking in gulps of frozen air. *I guess it is fair that I fall here amongst my friends.*

The blood ran steadily from his side, and the frigid air began to sting his lungs. Dozens of them were rushing towards him, eager to swallow him up. His breathing grew shallow and quick. He raised his sword with great effort and readied his spirit for the impending doom that was soon to greet him.

They were a hundred yards away and barreling towards him, determined to avenge their fallen comrades. His eyes narrowed, blackness swarming his peripheral vision.

They were fifty yards away now. He could smell their sweat and hear the whining of the horses.

Forty yards now. He could see their young and angry faces, eager to claim the glory of his demise. He could hear their rage-filled battle cries.

His arms tensed from the struggle of holding the sword, but he would be damned to drop his sword against his foe. Blackness was clouding his vision, and he cursed his human weakness. Their cries grew louder and louder now, the end was at hand.

But all at once, they were replaced with screams of surprise and terror.

He heard louder galloping now from the flanks of the field. He turned his head to see what was happening, but The Warrior's blessing failed him.

He heard new but familiar voices cry out over the battlefield. "To your commander, men! To Tiberius!"

"We are here, sir! We are here!" a beautiful voice called out. The voice, even full of wrath and hate, reminded him of a soft breeze in the trees on a summer morning. His mind flashed to a cottage in a grove surrounded by a vast garden. Of two men sitting amongst the flowers and trees enwrapped in stories of their youth.

He smiled, broad and joyful. Trevin was here.

He dropped his sword and hung his head. *My men. My love. They have come at last.*

"Black banners! Black banners!" one of the White soldiers called out now. "The emperor is here! The emperor is here!"

The man's words cut through Tiberius's haze. He forced his eyes open and turned again to see a mass of horses flood the field. His heart soared as he beheld dozens of great black and grey banners flapping proudly atop massive war horses.

Hundreds of soldiers on horseback and the elite sentinels on foot flew through the woods, overtaking the vanguard of rangers. *Of course, Trevin would have been in the van. He would have demanded it.*

At the head of the formation, atop a midnight black steed, was his father clad in his black leather and fur armor. Above his head, he carried Tiberius' own sword. A fierce battle cry was on his aged lips as his father swung his son's sword to and fro against the enemy.

Age had slowed him, to be sure, but as he continued cutting through them, he appeared to still possess the skill of a veteran ranger himself. Being in the field again seemed to renew his father's vigor, and seeing his dying son spurred him on even more.

In a matter of minutes, it was over. The yelling died out, and in the distance, Tiberius could hear inaudible orders being issued. He felt heavy footsteps reverberate through the ground and felt powerful and familiar arms grab him and hold him close. He looked up through pinpoint eyes and saw the face of his father staring down at him.

He felt like a child again being carried by his father after scraping his knees. He felt weightless and secure in the embrace of the first person who ever loved him. The one person in the entire world who would always be there for him. The one person who would move mountains and slay untold numbers of men to keep him safe.

He heard the beautiful voice call out a few feet away now. "Ti! Ti!"

And then he felt another set of arms envelop him and squeeze him tight. The touch sent fire through his veins, and he felt his heart glow. He breathed in deep the familiar smell and heard the sweet voice of Trevin.

"My son," his father said, cradling his head. "Are you still with us?"

Tiberius smiled. "Aye. Your boy is still here."

"Ti?" Trevin said. "Ti, can you hear us?"

"Of course, I can hear you, my love," Tiberius replied.

"Son?" his father called out, panic and fear in his voice. "Son!"

Tiberius tried to call out again but realized he had made no sound at all. His voice had abandoned him and try as he might to let them know he was still with them he had no strength left within him.

It was harder to breathe now. His once strong and taught body went limp in his father's arms. Out of the needle-sized holes in his eyes, he could see the two men he loved most in the world stare down on him until the darkness finally consumed him.

The two men sat cradling Tiberius in the broken field. The knights and rangers of the empire began to circle around them, eager to provide any small measure of comfort that they could to the grieving men. No one spoke for many heavy minutes, each unsure what to say to their emperor or the Ranger's First Sergeant. The two men's sobs cut through the silence and filled the hard men of the empire with deep sorrow.

CHAPTER 25

THE VIGIL

He awoke to the noise of hushed, urgent voices speaking to one another in the dark. Through heavy eyes, he could almost make out the shape of two men clad in brown and grey leather and fur standing at the foot of whatever it was he was laying on. He tried to speak, but no words were able to escape his mouth. He swallowed hard and tried again to muster some semblance of a tone, but each time, his voice failed him. He decided to lay there instead and listen to what was going on around him the best he could.

"How long have they sat by his side now?" one voice asked from the corner of the room he was in.

"Nigh on two days now," another voice, higher in pitch, answered.

"Two days of unbothered vigilance," the first voice said sadly. "If it were my son or my love, I would do the same."

"Aye," a new voice said, pretty and strong with a strange yet familiar accent to it. "We all would if it were us. I pray both our masters awake soon, rangers. For the sorrow upon us is too heavy to bear."

"Rangers!?" Michael croaked his excitement and eagerness pushing through.

"He's awake! Gods bless us, he's awake!" the young voice cried out.

Michael felt the man sit on his bed, hoist him up, and hug him with such force that his back and neck popped in several places. Something about this man seemed familiar to the Mage. As if he and this man had known and travelled together many moons ago but now had forgotten one another.

"I am so happy to see you again, my friend!" the voice said, coming more into focus to Michael.

In his mind's eye, he could see the shape of a young man with a devilish grin. His bow at one side fitted with a new arrow, and his best friend to his other side, ready to laugh and fight together. Michael struggled to pull this memory out and give it shape until all at once it dawned on him.

"Timothy?" Michael muttered.

"Aye, lad," the archer replied. "I'm here with you. And look, here's Zachary as well."

"Well met, Mage," Zachary called out. "Gave us quite a fright there, but I am glad to see you have managed to elude death once again."

Michael forced his heavy eyes open, and for the first time, could see he was now lying upon a fur-lined cot within a huge leather walled tent. The air was still cold and biting, but now he could see sunlight pouring in through small circular cutouts in the side of the tent wall. All around him were signs and symbols of the rangers and the empire. The emperor's black banners hung to the left and right of a raised wooden chair, weapons wrapped in black and grey leather strips, cloaks of various sizes, and all the color of the woods. He looked between each of the men before pulling them both into a tight hug.

"I am so happy to see you both again," he said as he embraced the two men.

"Aye, lad," Timothy replied. "We are happy to have met again."

Their embrace lasted a few short minutes before being interrupted by a small cough from the corner of the room. The three of them glanced back and, to Michael's surprise, there stood the figure of a tall and beautiful woman clad in a familiar dragon armor. He knew at once it was not his friend and companion, the brave and fearless Dragon Knight Shayla. His companion's armor had been green and grey, in homage to both the dragon lord and the empire. This newest dragoon's armor was bright red as if fire were captured within it. He tried to study it for a moment before his mind raced back to the battle.

"Where are they?" he blurted out. "Shayla and Tiberius, where are they?" he asked, looking between the three warriors who returned worried looks. "Tell me!" Michael demanded, growing impatient with them.

"Mistress Shayla and Master Tiberius are in the tent over, young man," the Dragon Knight replied with a gentle tone that disarmed Michael's growing anger and impatience. "They have hovered between our world and the next for two days now. I fear if they do not wake, the ranger will be amongst his kin and my mistress in the halls of our King."

"King? What King?" Zachary asked his fellow Ranger.

"Kazduhl," Michael answered, astonishing the men and bringing a sweet smile from the Dragoon. "The Dragon King Kazduhl in his halls of fire and glory."

"I see the Mistress has spoken of our King to outsiders," the woman said, though her smile betrayed the sting of her words.

"We aren't outsiders, Dragon Knight," Michael replied, defiant and firm.

The Dragoon continued to smile at Michael. "Beg your pardon, Mage. I meant not to offend. We are still strangers in our new home and have yet to learn our new countrymen's customs. For too long we had no one but ourselves to rely on."

"You Mistress learned quickly then," Michael retorted. "The three of us became comrades in our journeys. No. Not just comrades. Our struggles made us into friends and the closest of companions."

"Speaking of which," Timothy said, standing. "We would like to hear in full the tale of what's transpired since you and our master left the Imperial City. Would you mind resting for a minute while I fetch some people who would show greater interest in your tale?"

"After I see Tiberius and Shayla," Michael said, and judging by the look on his face, the three warriors knew there was no talking him out of it.

Timothy nodded and waved a hand to where Michael's clothes and robes lie. "We'll give you a minute to get dressed then. Meet us outside when you are ready."

The three of them made small bows and left the tent. "Dragon Knight," Michael said after a quick rub of his eyes. "Seeing as you know my name, and I am a friend of your mistress, may I ask who you are?"

The Dragoon stood proud, her fire-red and grey scaled armor glistening in the morning sun. Like Shayla, her hair was raven black, and her face the same oval shape. Her eyes were the same dark brown and set against the same olive skin. Yet her smile drew Michael's attention, and all of a sudden, he felt a pang in his heart he had not expected to feel after all he had endured.

"I am Mychala, Dragon Knight of the Axton Empire," she said with a small bow.

Michael bowed in return. "Well met, Mychala. I am Michael Deerborn, Brother of the Magi."

"Well met, Michael Deerborn, Brother of the Magi," she replied with a smile before turning to follow the two rangers out the tent. Timothy held the flap open for the others to leave and shot a knowing glance and wink to Michael as he left the Mage to get dressed.

Michael felt himself blush, the image of the Dragoon lingering in his mind. But his thoughts betrayed him, and he grew ashamed. How could he think about such a beautiful woman now when his friends hovered on the precipice of death? He forced the thoughts out of his mind, and after steadying himself, slowly stood from the fur cot and began to dress as quickly as his sore and aching body would allow him. After a quick glance in the mirror to adjust his robes over his regular leather clothes, he turned to shuffle out of the tent.

The sun stung his tender eyes as he opened the tent flap. Yet, after a few blinks, he could see he was inside of a vast encampment in the same field they had fought so fiercely only a few days ago. Everywhere he looked, large black banners flying proudly in the soft cold breeze met his eye. Tents of all shapes and sizes were lined up and stretching beyond measure in every direction.

A few knights in their black and grey armor were huddled around a nearby fire talking low, undoubtedly wondering about what had happened here to break the ground beneath them. Beyond them, he could see hundreds of soldiers busy with their daily chores of inspecting and sharpening their swords. The smell of horses caught his nose, and in the distance, he could make out the faint thundering of hooves on snow.

To his right, he could see what appeared to be all the rangers and sentinels in the empire standing guard next to a small brown and green tent. Michael reckoned that's where his friends and those who kept watch over them would be found. From the front of the gaggle of warriors, he could see Timothy beckoning him to come forward. He shambled towards them, a slight limp in his right leg and his eyes still burning after two days' worth of sleep.

However, as he walked along the small lane to the next-door tent, he became aware that all sound ceased as he approached. He could feel hundreds of eyes fixed upon him as he walked on, unsure of what their feelings towards him right now were. He didn't care, though, all his thought and will was bent on seeing his friends again.

The warriors of the empire began to part down the middle, offering Michael a clear path to the tent's entrance. Each of the men clad in leather bowed in reverence as he passed. Some he recognized from his trip to the

Imperial City, and they, in turn, offered a faint smile and a reassuring pat on his shoulders. The sentinels, however, eyed him with a measure of mistrust, as was their nature. They were, after all, the elite guards to the most powerful man in the known world. But what they and anyone else there couldn't know is the unwavering trust and friendship earned by him to their future emperor. How he, just a boy of sixteen, had called fire and lightning down from the sky and helped smote a demon called from legend. They would never know the tears cried for him and the struggle against evil done for his mission.

Just outside the tent opening stood Mychala, she alone of the assembled host smiling broadly at the young Mage. She approached him and placed a heavy dragon scaled hand on his shoulder.

"Do not be afraid," she whispered. "Inside, you will not find a mighty and vengeful emperor, nor a bloodthirsty ranger. Instead, you will find a grieving father and a lover hoping to save the one they love most, and two proud and mighty warriors who hover between this world and the next."

"Which bloodthirsty ranger do you speak of, Mychala?"

"The Ranger's First Sergeant, Trevin Moore."

"But why would he be in there with Tiberius, when ---" but Michael stopped himself. All at once, he understood what the Dragoon was trying to say. Michael's heart broke all over again, now for Trevin as much as for the emperor.

"Who watches over Shayla?"

Mychala removed her hand from his robe and bowed her head. "I had the honor of watching over my mistress, but I can feel our lord stirring the world beyond. I am no longer needed in there; the Son of Axton will be her guardian now."

Michael nodded, not entirely understanding what she meant, but deciding now was not the time for questions. He pulled back the flap and entered the dark and musky tent.

Unlike the one he had awoken in; this tent was shrouded in near darkness. Dozens of candles were arranged in a ring with a giant black banner hanging from the tent's apex. Inside the circle of candlelight, he could see the faint but familiar figures of his friends lying still upon two heavy wooden beds.

They were lying next to each other, only a foot or so apart. Their arms rested at their side as if asleep, and both wore freshly cleaned simple black and white clothes. In the dim light, Michael could see Tiberius' usually shaved head had begun to grow a faint amount of stubble. The Dragoon, beautiful as she was, looked almost peaceful and content with her long black hair sprawled out on the pillow she lay on.

To him, they seemed peacefully asleep, but he had never seen people on the verge of death in a wakeless sleep before. A lump grew in his throat until his eyes looked beyond them. Seated on two small stools, hunched over in thought, sat the two most powerful men in the empire.

"Hail, Luke Alexander Axton," Michael began, the lump throbbing in his throat. "Supreme… Supreme…" he stammered.

The emperor rose, and after two quick strides, rushed to the young Mage and embraced him as if he were his own son. Michael melted in the emperor's arms and began to sob quietly into his fur skinned clothes. Finally, the emperor broke their hug, nodded approvingly at the Mage, and beckoned him to join them by Tiberius' side. Michael then saw Trevin, the valiant and brave First Sergeant. His eyes were bloodshot, and his lips trembled.

"Well met, Brother of the Magi," Trevin croaked.

"Hello, Master Trevin," Michael replied, placing a tender and understanding hand on Trevin's shoulder. Their eyes met, and in the darkness of the tent, they knew the bond between each other for Tiberius was complete. Michael's as a companion and trusted friend. Trevin, as a long unrequited and passionate love.

"Did the Supreme Sorcerer not ride with you, sire?" Michael whispered.

"He did but had thought it best to leave Trevin and me alone in our vigil," the emperor replied, motioning for Michael to sit. "Now. Please tell us what happened, and do not leave out any detail of your journey."

Michael slowly sat on a small wooden stool between the two grieving men. After a moment to collect his thoughts, he began to recount their adventure in full. The two did not interrupt him as he went on and on for long periods. He knew he had been at it for hours when he felt a sudden chill flow up his spine, a sign that the sun was begging to hang low in the sky. When he had finished, he slumped down, exhausted.

The two men stared at the boy for many heavy moments before the emperor stood and began to pace as he was prone to do when in deep thought. Trevin, however, continued to stare, bewildered and confused by what he had heard.

Finally, Trevin cleared his throat and said, "I must confess, I find your tale both amazing and frightening at the same time. The Narzeth conjuring the power of magic is most troubling to my mind. And this talk of dwarves, and Revenants," he thought for a moment, choosing his next words carefully.

"I do not doubt your honesty, nor your integrity, Michael. It's just a little hard to wrap my head around."

"Aye," the emperor said as he paced. "But did we not find a Narzeth in crimson robes when we arrived in the field?"

"We did, Your Majesty. But—"

"And did you see any lie in this young man's face?"

"No. No, I did not. Though my skill with the *Sight* is not as great as yours, it was plain enough that Michael spoke true."

"Curious though that we have not found any of these dwarves. Do you have any idea where they could be, Michael?"

"No, Your Majesty," Michael answered. "The Shaman… Bruce… he sacrificed himself against the Revenant, but by his sacrifice made known the power of the Narzeth. Yet for Catherine and her warriors, I cannot know. Last I knew, they were still in the village and in the trenches with Master Rogers."

"We searched the village when we arrived," Trevin said. "My rangers saw many strange footprints in the snow and soot, but no sign of the villagers nor of dwarves. And Master Rogers's body disappeared shortly after we arrived"

"Disappeared, sir?" Michael asked.

"Aye. The Berserker had fallen near you and the Dragoon. We moved them all into this tent. Yet when we came back inside, his body had vanished."

"What of the Narzethian Wizard?"

"Damian is with him in a tent on the outskirts of our camp, surrounded by one hundred of my best knights," the emperor replied. "He too hovers between our worlds, but gods be damned if he passes before we get some answers from him."

Michael was at a loss for words. To have lost a man as fierce as Tygahl and that their eternal enemy had begun to use magic was more than he could bear. Not to mention that this Narzethian could harness magic while the Magi remained powerless was more disturbing than anything he could have imagined.

Suddenly, his mind turned to Michelle and the villagers they had fought bravely to defend. He thought to ask what had become of them before his logic caught up to his worry. Trevin and the emperor had not said a word on the state of the village because there was nothing left. Tears began welling up in the corner of his eyes. He slumped down further in the stool, overcome with sorrow such as he had not felt in his entire life.

All through the rest of the day and into the night, he sat vigil over his companions. Not once daring to move out of respect for their friendship. It was just after midnight when his stamina began to fail him. He let out a quiet yawn that he stifled at once, hoping he had not offended the two men he sat with. The emperor placed a hand upon his knee with a kindly smile and bid the Mage return to his tent and rest.

"I am sorry I cannot continue, Your Majesty," Michael said.

"Do not apologize, Michael. You fought just as bravely as your comrades. You deserve a little respite. Go."

And after a slow bow and a brief nod to Trevin, Michael slowly exited the tent. A full moon shone down on him. The air was bitterly cold and stung his weary eyes. Yet, now that he was outside the warm tent, he felt awake and rejuvenated. The men guarding the tent were huddled asleep amongst fires in the wide lane in front of the tent. Despite their training and innate distrustfulness, they paid the Mage no bother.

He walked up and down the vast rows of tents, peering inside here and there to see the various soldiers and knights within fast asleep. On the edge of the camp, he could see rangers and archers posted high in the few trees remaining in the forest, keeping watch throughout the night. Those that noticed him offered a reverent nod, while others seemed to look right past him and into the distance.

The sleepiness he had just felt seemed to be washed away from him in the open air, and the sudden urge to walk in the moonlight overcame him. No, not overcame him. Compelled him. He turned and looked upon the burned village awash in the brilliant moonlight. He slowly began to walk towards it, eager to see the destruction that had been wrought upon it with his own eyes.

As he walked, he contemplated the story he had told to the emperor and Trevin. And how, after all he and his companions had been through, they were still no closer to answering the mystery that had started their quest. Nor, for that matter, had they come any closer to ascending the Ice Steps to reach the outpost beyond. To make matters worse, King White seemed bent on open insurrection against the empire. If his evil and malicious fury were to spread, who knows how many other kingdoms would come under his sway?

How can a man's hurt ego and pride lead to the death of so many innocents? Michael thought. Dark thoughts for dark times.

To make matters even worse, the Narzeth had now returned and aligned themselves with the traitorous King. And, apparently, have begun using magic in their evil schemes. Magic, Michael reminded himself, that the empire's own Magi could not seem to use. Mystery upon mystery stacked against them, yet somehow tied together. Had he more wisdom, he might have been able to see the threads that bound their woes together, but for now, his mind was numb to the dangers outside their little slice of the world.

It was a half-hour later when Michael arrived at the burnt wooden wall that had encircled the Village of Rogers. The bodies of the undead enemy littered the ground, all having felt the wrath of Tygahl's rage. The wooden buildings beyond were a mess of burned embers and soot. The once snow-covered square where he had stood with Catherine and Tiberius was now scorched black. He walked amongst the destroyed homes and buildings, a great sorrow welling up inside him.

Had all this been in vain? He thought sadly. Had we, in our hubris and anger at the king, forgotten what we were truly fighting for? Yet if we had not detoured from our path to the Steps, this village would have been waylaid anyhow. What was the point in our delay if the King would sack this village one way or another?

The grief and sorrow overtook him and sitting upon a small bench just outside the square, Michael buried his face in his hands and began to quietly cry to himself. Time seemed to stop around him, and the cold seemed to disappear from his senses. All he was consumed with was the feelings boiling over inside of him. He had no idea how to help his friends, nor how to continue on the journey he still had yet to complete. Hopelessness and grief consumed him, and he cried on unceasingly.

"Do not be sad, young one," a familiar motherly voice said from behind him.

Michael was on his feet in an instant beheld the last person he had expected to see. Bathed in the pale moonlight, small but still powerful and present, stood Catherine Stonefoot. Her face, as always, bore the familiar look of comfort and knowing. Michael's rage reached its peak. No longer able to control himself, he marched towards her as quickly as his hobbled leg would allow him.

"You!?" he growled. "Where in the hells below have you been!? Do you not know what's happened here!? Do you not care!?" He screamed and raged at her, yet her expression never faltered.

"I have been here," she replied. "Waiting for you."

His anger boiled over. "Me? You've been waiting? For me!? What about Tiberius? And Shayla? What about the villagers? We were supposed to protect them! I was supposed to protect them! And you! You and your dwarves were supposed to keep them safe!"

She looked up at him, her face the mask of calm and love. "The villagers are safe, Michael. Miss Bearborn is quite the formidable woman and has led them to safety beyond the glade. They await word to return."

Michael stared at her blankly, letting his rage subside with relief. But still, questions lingered in his mind. "Where have you been?"

"Walk with me," she said, turning to leave the square.

"I lingered here while you and Bruce battled the Revenant. I communed with the Father, asking him to give you and Bruce wisdom and strength," she said as they slowly walked amongst the burned building and out into the unburned woods beyond. "And he did not falter or fail us. Even now, he is locked in battle with the dragon king over the soul of the Dragoon."

"What are you even saying?" Michael asked. "The Father. The Dragon King. The Spirit of The Warrior. How can they even help us in our world? Their realms are beyond us. Their spirits and wills are contested there. We need help here and now."

She stopped and turned to look at the Mage. "You believe in dragons from ages past, yes?" she asked.

"Of course. We have seen their bones, and the books in the Citadel are well stocked in the history of dragons," Michael replied, growing impatient.

"And you know of the Father. And of The Warrior Spirit?" Catherine went on.

Michael was growing impatient now. "I know that you and the berserkers believe in a Father. Just as the rangers believe in The Spirit of The Warrior. But where are they? I don't see them. Do you?"

"Know this, young Mage," Catherine said, firm and resolute. "Gods, demons, spirits. Monsters, dragons, angels. These things are real. Though they no longer walk this world, their spirits endure in the world beyond. Shayla believed in Kazduhl, the dragon king, because he is real. Tygahl believed in the Father because he is real."

"I don't believe, Catherine. How can you believe in things you do not see with your own eyes?"

She smiled and held her palm face up in front of him. She spoke a simple word in her people's language. In an instant, a brilliant flash of light appeared from the nothingness in front of him. He stared dumbstruck at the magic in her hand. Calm and inviting. Warm but not burning. He was mesmerized by the light and struck frozen at the swiftness from which she conjured it.

"You believe in magic, yes? Yet magic was not here before I called it. Magic was not here until you learned to wield your wand. Magic was not here until you made the earth rise with the power of your will alone. So, you see, you believe in the power of the unseen."

Michael was silent. No words of logic or rationale could begin to describe what he felt. For the first time in a long time, he conceded that things beyond his understanding and knowledge were real. She closed her palm and stood, staring him in his face.

"Besides," she said, her smile returning to her face. "You saw the beyond yourself, rather you knew it or not. You saw pure magic. The purest magic resides in the world beyond our world, and only by our mortal wills and determination can we call it down to us."

His mind raced, trying to remember anything of the sort before a great understanding dawned on him. "My dream," he said.

"Aye, your dream," she replied after removing her hand. "You were given a gift, Michael. You saw things no one else has. And it was real. Know that. It was as real as you and I are."

His head was swimming, but he refocused and remembered his friends. "My friends are suffering, Catherine. I need to save them."

"Then you had best go save them, Mage," she replied, with a motherly smile.

"I don't have the wand anymore. Bruce used it to destroy the Revenant, and I fear the wand was destroyed along with him and that beast."

"The wand is a tool. Just as the Ranger wields his sword and the Dragon Knight her lance. They are tools. It is the one that wields those tools that can make them do what they are intended to do."

"Maybe. But I have not the strength to do it without the wand. And even if I did, magic is not as strong in the world as it used to be."

"Aye, you speak true. The wand was made and imbued with the Father's power. It is a direct connection to the river of magic that flows unseen around us."

Michael was growing exasperated at her words. "So, how can I help my friends?"

She smiled again. "Michael Deerborn answer me this and think before you speak. Do you know and believe in the powers beyond at work in the world around us?"

Michael broke her gaze and stared about him. The breeze was gone and rendered the woods still. His mind cleared, and he thought about what he had learned and seen since departing the Imperial City. He thought on Shayla and her tale of how the Dragoons received their blessing. He thought on Tiberius and his power *Sight*. He thought of the Narzethian wizard and the evil power he had wielded.

In his mind's eye, he could see Tygahl standing tall and strong, proclaiming the power of the Father was in him. Could see the magic he had conjured from nothing when he laid dying in the woods so long ago. He saw a great sphere with a raging storm engulfing its surface. And he knew. In an instant, he knew.

"Yes, Catherine Stonehelm," he answered. "I believe."

She sighed in relief. "Good." She bent down and wiped away a mound of snow at their feet. "Then perhaps you had best take this," and as she stood, in her hand, was the black and ivory wand. "It's dangerous to go without it."

The very foundations of Michael's core were shaken at the revelation before him. He stared at the wand for many heavy moments before slowly reaching out and grasping the hard wood and steel handle. He held it to his face and could see no mark or blemish upon it. He closed his eyes and brought the wand to his ears as Bruce was oft to do. A soft smile broke across his face. He opened his eyes and stared at the dwarf, confused and bewildered, before breaking out into uncontrollable laughter.

"Did you know this was here the whole time?" he asked in between loud, gasping laughs.

"Well, I had a feeling," she replied, her knowing and loving face beaming at him in the bright moonlight.

Michael chuckled at her words. "You say that a lot, you know that?"

CHAPTER 26

THE VISION

Michael ran hard through the remains of the ruined village. The snow churned and flew to and fro underneath his feet as he ran. A nearby pack of deer, finally returning to the land after the horrific battle, bolted at the sight of him. His lungs were on fire as he hopped into one of the vast trenches where the snow and ice had not had a chance to pack in. His will and his desire compelled his less than stellar physical ability to rise to their level, and he ran on harder and faster.

He no longer felt the pain in his leg. No longer felt exhausted in his muscles and his soul. No longer felt the pain of sorrow and despair. There was a chance now to save his friends. His friends who had sacrificed so much for him and their country. He would not let their sacrifices be in vain.

The wind whipped through the lanes of tents so hard it made his eyes start to tear up and burn, but he didn't care. He reached the large tent in the center of the formation, startling the slumbering guards outside. He raced inside, bringing the two men inside to their feet with a start. They both had instinctively reached their swords until their eyes adjusted to the shape of the Mage.

"What is it, Michael?" the emperor asked, relaxing at the sight of the Mage.

He didn't answer right away. His gaze had fallen on his slumbering companions on the heavy cots at his feet. After a moment, he turned his attention to the emperor. And out of his robes, revealed his wand for the men to see.

The emperor studied the Mage for a moment and said, "I thought you lost the wand during the battle."

"I did, Your Majesty," Michael replied, bringing the ebony wand down to his side.

Trevin thumbed the hilt of his sword. "Then how is it you have it now?" Trevin asked suspiciously.

But the young Mage grew desperate and frustrated. He didn't have time to explain how he reacquired the wand even to his lord and emperor. Now was the time to put it to work. His friends were on the brink of death, and only he could bring them back.

Michael studied his companions. His mind and heart hardened and focused as it did before the battle. His eyes narrowed, and his breathing slowed. He looked at the two men in front of him and gave and curt nod in response. "My lords. I shall explain everything in due time. But for now, if I may speak plainly, leave me alone."

The finality of his words hit the two men with the power of a warhammer to the chest. They could see the young Mage meant business. That he meant to unleash his power and would do so regardless of their worries or not. After many tense minutes, the emperor nodded and removed his hand from the hilt of his sword.

Michael held the wand away from his chest, and with a simple word, a bright ethereal light burst to the tip of his wand. The two men in the tent recoiled and shielded their eyes from the light. But after a few moments, they could see that Michael had now begun to spin the wand in small circles.

The light started to throb, and each small pulse of light bid the spell to grow larger and larger until it nearly filled the entirety of the tent. Michael continued circling the wand until the light burst out of the tent's seams and small windows. Soldiers and knights from around the vast encampment gathered outside, eager to see the magic within.

After a minute or so, Michael began to utter a quiet incantation. And with a mighty thrust, pointed the wand to the two sleeping figures before him.

The light struck their bodies and grew to immeasurable size and beauty, bathing them all in its radiating power. Michael felt his limbs restored to their former strength, and the dull pain in his leg subside. His spirits soared with happiness. Surely if he felt healed and rejuvenated from the side effects of the spell, then his companions would be completely restored.

The light receded into the tip of his wand, returning the camp to darkness. No one outside the tent, not even the emperor's own bodyguards, dared to move into the tent. The candlelight that had illuminated the tent returned, as the two men stared awestruck at the power such a young man had channeled. They both realized that young Michael, who had been near death in the far north, had grown mighty in his magic. A small fear grew inside Trevin, but it was all for naught as Michael moved to his companion's side in an instant.

"Tiberius," he whispered. "Tiberius, it's me." In the dim light, he could easily see that his wounds were mended, yet he did not wake nor even stir.

He turned to the Dragoon and said, "Shayla? Shayla, it's Michael. Please say something." But just as Tiberius next to her, she made no movement.

Michael rose and held the wand again in front of him. He repeated the words more vigorously than before, twirled the wand faster and longer, growing the light so large it filled the tent completely. He hurled the spell towards them with such force that the tent's flap flew open and sent the emperor and Trevin to the ground. He held the light on them longer than before, hoping that the renewed power would surely be enough. But again, after the intense, fiery light finally dissipated, his friends did not stir.

"Michael," the emperor said softly, standing again. "Perhaps it is best if…"

"No!" Michael cut in. "No! I will not quit! This worked before! It has to work again!"

For a third time, he repeated the healing ritual. However, this time, the spell grew so large and magnificent the tent's walls were ripped apart and sent flying. The warriors of the empire outside staggered backward with their hands held to their eyes. Each startled and confused at the near daylight that seemed to radiate in front of them. A few of the sentinels had regained their senses, and with swords drawn, prepared to advance on the Mage. But they were immediately waved off by the emperor.

Michael continued reciting the incantation as he twirled the wand in larger and larger circles. His voice grew quicker and louder to match his desperation until he found himself shouting at the top of his lungs. The light grew so large it engulfed the entirety of the empire's camp. Such was the power Michael wielded that the wounded who were suffering in their own tents around them were healed and rejuvenated. All as if nothing had happened to them. At last, he directed the power to his friends. A great boom echoed out into the night.

A mighty crack belted out as if a raging storm had burst overhead. The ground beneath them began to rumble and shift. The very air seemed to be sucked out into the night, and Michael felt great heaps of sweat falling down his face and arms. The light in the middle began to slowly shift and swirl in on itself. Michael became fixated on it, determined to see and understand what was happening as he continued to hold it firm over his friends. Slowly, the light started to take the shape of a swirling vortex in front of them. Michael locked eyes with it, somehow knowing he was soon to witness a new vision.

The swirling brightness began to take shape. And, to his mortal mind, Michael appeared to be looking through a window into a beautiful green field against a fiercely blue sky. From within the light, he could see a great man twice the size of the mighty Tygahl locked in a violent struggle with what appeared to be an enormous serpent. His muscles strained and burst out of his body as he wrestled and pummeled the great snake.

No, not a snake, Michael realized. That's a dragon. A gods damned mighty and terrible dragon the size of the Unity Spire.

His mind raced, trying desperately to make sense of what he was seeing. He continued to gaze inside the light watching as this desperate struggle between the man and the dragon raged on.

The mighty beast unfurled its wings and tried to take to the sky in escape. But his foe quickly grabbed hold of his razor-sharp forked tail and swung him back to the ground. The dragon reared its great head in anger and expelled an endless stream of blue fire out of his mouth. The fire engulfed the beautiful green pasture they struggled in, yet nothing in this land seemed to burn.

Michael continued to stare in disbelief. *What is this place? What is going on?*

"Do you believe!?" a powerful voice like an earthquake called out.

Michael turned away from the image, and standing firm and strong in the row of tents behind him was Catherine, the dwarf. She locked eyes with him and began to amble towards Michael. Behind her marched her dwarven warriors, each without the armor they had worn before. They came with smiles on their faces and with hearts full and eyes bright and clear. They formed a semicircle behind Michael. After a brief word from Catherine in their ancient tongue, they held their arms out as if children begging for their parent.

"What is this!?" Michael bellowed over the deafening roar of the spell.

"Do you believe!?" Catherine bellowed in response, her mighty voice adding to the cacophony of noise that pierced his ears.

Michael returned his gaze to the battle. The great man was again wrestling the dragon as hard and as furiously as possible. Still, he appeared to be making no headway in the fight against the winged beast.

Suddenly, from within the flaming image, he heard a horn blast so mightily that it rang out past the sound of the spell. Michael became suddenly aware that all the rangers around him, even the emperor himself, were on their feet. They gazed hard at the moving picture in front of them before each of them, the emperor being the first, had taken a knee in reverence.

From within, Michael saw a tall man dressed in brown and grey leathers seated atop a great war-horse emerge over a distant hill. A vast host of soldiers followed behind him, each clad in armor of assorted colors and designs. The figure approached the battling foes with such regality and majesty that he seemed to exude utter command and authority. He dismounted his horse and strode towards the battle ahead. Michael studied his face, knowing that somehow, he recognized this man though he had never seen him before.

From his waist, the majestic looking warrior drew his sword. Michael's eyes widened, and his mind clicked everything into place. The man was holding Tiberius' sword aloft. The blade of the emperors. It was The Spirit of the Warrior himself. It was Alexander Axton, the founder of the empire. With Catherine's words echoing in his ears, he finally began to understand what he was witnessing.

There was the Dragon King Kazduhl, mighty and terrible to behold. His impossibly large black body and thick neck with scales as sharp as razors locked in mortal strong with the dwarves Father, Frijigzah. The Warrior, the totem and symbol of the Rangers and the Axton bloodline with his mighty sword coming to enter the fray. He was inhumanly fast, weaving in and around the beast's claws and tail just as Tiberius and his rangers were oft to do themselves in the heat of battle. His mighty sword thrust out all over the dragon's body, sending it screaming and thrashing in pain. The Father now pressed his strength on it. Even though he was but a child compared to the size of the dragon, his strength was nearly overpowering to it.

Tears formed in Michael's eyes at the magnificence the three radiated. He thought to look away, wishing to respect the sight of the mighty gods at war. Yet all around him, the faces of men and dwarves and dragoons were staring at the image.

The image began to fade now, growing dimmer and dimmer as the healing spell slowly began to disappear. The crowd around Michael started to draw closer to him, hoping to catch some fleeting glance of the battle inside it. Finally, the light faded, and silence as thick as ice hung in the air. With a quick glance around the camp, Michael could see that all the empire's assembled warriors were crying at what they had just witnessed.

He lowered his wand and looked to the two men standing beyond his companions. Though they were bound in love to Tiberius, they were both men of the rangers. And both of those men were struck still at the sight of The Warrior himself. Michael returned his attention to his companions, dropped his wand in the snow, and rushed to their side.

He knelt between them, closed his eyes, and held both of their hands as hard as his would allow. He began to pray to the gods of his homeland that his spell had worked, and his friends would wake. He began to pray to the Father and to The Warrior, and to the Dragon King to return his friends to the mortal world again. He swore that he would always protect them. That he would never abandon them to darkness and despair. That he would see their quest and oaths fulfilled. That, given the chance, he would lay down his life a hundred times over for theirs. He heard the soft crunching of snow at his side. He knew who it was without having to look.

Catherine bent at the waist and placed a hand on each of his companion's heads. Like Michael, she too began to also pray in the tongue of the dwarves. She prayed that the Father and Warrior would prove victorious against the dragon to release his hold over Shayla. She prayed The Warrior would grant favor to his son Tiberius and allow him to return to battle in his name once again. She prayed the Father would bless this land that had been cursed by evil and bless the sacrifices of his children to defend their adopted homeland.

"You don't have to squeeze so hard," a weak voice whispered.

Michael shot his eyes open. Trevin and the emperor rushed to his side. "Ti?" Michael said shakily.

"Only two people call me Ti," the weak voice replied. "And I love them both more than anything else under the sun or moon."

The emperor fell on his son and began to quietly sob into his chest. Trevin stood where Catherine had and began to slowly run his bare brown hands over his lover's scalp. Michael turned to Shayla now and examined her face. The scars she had born on her olive-skinned face were gone. Her broken bones were mended and strengthened. He heard another quiet crunch of snow and saw Mychala bend down to her fellow Dragoon. She began to run her hand through Shayla's hair and started to quietly hum the song of their people, hoping the tune would lead her back home.

"Shayla," Michael whispered. "Please come back to us, brave knight. Please, daughter of Kazduhl. Please."

He felt her body stir under his hand, and his breath caught in his throat. Slowly her whole body began to shiver, forcing her to gradually roll over to her side and ball up as if a sleeping child. The brave dragon knight opened one eye and looked at the Mage, and a slow smile formed on her beautifully tanned face.

"Thank you, Michael. Thank you." She closed her eyes again and was fast asleep on the cot.

Michael chuckled quietly to himself and slowly removed his robe to drape over her. Mychala continued to slowly stroke her fellow Dragoon's hair, faintly humming the dragon song. She locked eyes with the Mage and smiled softly at him.

"Thank you, Mage. Thank you for returning my sister to us."

He nodded in reply and slowly stood. Suddenly becoming aware of all the people around him, he awkwardly turned and surveyed the empire's assembled men. Each of them wore a broad smile and nodded their heads in approval at the power of his magic. He quickly looked down, embarrassed at the sight of so many strong and hearty men paying respect to him at once.

"Hail, and well met Mage," a deep but loving voice called. "And thank you."

The assembled men turned to find the source of such a powerful voice, but only Michael knew who could have made such a tremendous sound. He pushed through a small throng of people who did not even notice the presence of thirteen dwarves in their midst.

"Thank you for what, ma'am?" Michael asked Catherine.

With a soft touch on his arms, Catherine said, "It has been nigh on four hundred years since we witnessed the majesty of our Father in the beyond. Though his spirit and his will move in our world, our hearts are full to behold him again in all his grandeur."

The dwarven warriors behind her slowly knelt to one knee, and in almost an arranged unison, began to chant in the deep throaty language of their people. The ground seemed to shake under the weight of their words.

The powerful sound was carried out far away from the camp, echoing in the trees outside and deep into the snowcapped mountains.

They ceased their chanting, and the reverberations from their words hung heavy in the air around them. No one in the encampment moved. No one knew what to say after all they had just witnessed and heard until the emperor himself broke the heavy silence. He stood to his fullest height, discarded the heavy fur cloak that hung on his shoulders, and strode towards Catherine. He stood looking down upon her and her kin, examining their hard features for many heavy moments before kneeling to come face to face with her.

"Well met, daughter of Frijigzah," he whispered.

"Well met, Your Majesty," she replied with a small bow that was mirrored by her companions behind her. "I'm sure you have many questions, and I perhaps can give you many answers. But I pray, Your Majesty, sleep and slumber peacefully tonight. My kin and I have matters of our own to attend to tonight. There will be time enough for words before the next cycle in the things to come."

"What do you mean?"

"Things are in motion, your Majesty. Things in this world and in the world beyond. This is but the beginning of what is to come. But take heart, Luke Axton. All is not lost. If we are determined and clever and strong. All is not lost."

She gave a low bow and turned to depart from the encampment with the dwarves at her back. All of the men watched them pass in silence, unsure of what her cryptic words meant but too tired to form any questions.

Before long, quick orders were given to re-erect the tents and get the fires throughout the camp burning again. At his request, Tiberius and Shayla were moved into Michael's own tent. He had felt a longing to be amongst his friends again, even if only to watch them sleep. He had come so close to losing them, he could not bear to be without them close. Besides, after the power he had displayed, everyone reasoned there was no safer place in the whole of the empire than beside Michael right now.

The emperor and Trevin returned to their own quarters and slept harder than they had since arriving at Rogers Village. Michael, now tucked in his own fur-lined cot lie awake in bed for many long hours, exhausted but mind racing at all that had transpired. Questions kept forming in his head, both new and old. And though he was not prone to dwell on things too much lately, old habits die hard.

Time enough for that tomorrow, he reasoned. And with that, he shut his eyes and tried to fall asleep. Yet, images of the great battle he witnesses kept flashing in his memory. Images of great swirling spheres with raging storms on their surface crept in. A great staff being torn asunder. The parting words of Catherine echoing in his mind. The Revenant and Bruce's sacrifice. Tiberius's sword gleaming in the sun. Shayla, clad in her fierce armor, leaping into battle. Mychala and her beautiful face and smile. After an hour or so of tossing and turning, his mind finally gave out under the weight of his racing thoughts, and before long, he fell asleep harder than he had in many long nights.

CHAPTER 27

THE DEPARTED

A strong but familiar voice called out in the darkness. "Michael. Wake up."

Michael slowly forced his eyes to open, and in the dimness of the tent, could see Tiberius, clad in dark furs over his clothes, standing at the foot of his bed. "What are you doing up, sir?" he asked with a yawn.

"We have been summoned," Tiberius said. "Shayla is already out waiting for us. Hurry up."

"Summoned?" Michael asked, with a rub to his weary eyes. "Summoned by whom?"

"By Lady Stonefoot. Now, quickly, get dressed."

Michael blinked a few times, trying to process Tiberius' command before slowly standing out of the bed. He felt drained from the effort of wielding the spell only a few hours prior but dressed as quickly as he could before exiting the tent. The moon was waning in the sky, the sun only a few hours away from breaking the darkness of night. He found Tiberius looking out into the distance. His face was solemn at whatever summons had been placed to them.

After a brief nod to Michael, the pair began to slowly march past the rows of tents as quiet as ghosts. Michael's curiosity was peaked, yet he could not muster the strength to ask any questions.

Catherine had said the dwarves had their own business to attend to tonight. Perhaps this is what she spoke of. How lucky are we to be witness to the business of the dwarves?

Yet as he reached the edge of the camp, far off in the distance at the gates of the village, their eyes fell on a small burning bonfire illuminating the dark night. They continued, unbothered by the small groups of Imperial soldiers that were milling about. The cold had begun to lessen since they first slept, a little comfort in these troubled days they now found themselves.

They eventually came to a stop where Shayla stood outside a soldier's tent on the camp's edge. She turned to them as they approached and quickly seized the young Mage in her strong, lithe arms. Michael stood frozen at her unexpected warmness to him before slowly returning the hug. After a moment, they broke apart, and in unison, the three companions began to march towards the village.

As they approached, they could see that what appeared to them as a small bonfire in the distance was now a mighty burning pyre. Passing through the ruined gates, they could see all the villagers of Rogers and the dwarves assembled on the other side of the fiery mass of wood and kindling. A mighty voice called out into the night. Deep and throaty and powerful was the sound that met their ears, yet their eyes beheld the small figure of Catherine.

Her arms were held high as she was prone to do when in conversation with her Father, clearly embroiled in invoking his name and spirit. Her chant carried on for some time until she dropped her arms. As if on cue, a small shuffling of feet could be heard behind them. Out of the darkness, the dwarf warriors emerged. On their backs, they carried the mighty figure of the berserker Tygahl.

They marched through the throng of people until they arrived at the raging fire in the middle of their circle. It appeared to those gathered around as though they passed into the fire unscathed and brought the massive figure to rest atop the pyre before returning to their leader's side.

"Tiberius, son of Luke," Catherine called out. "What say you to our departed warrior and brother?"

Tiberius looked from one face to another in the crowd. They each bore a mask of sorrow and pain. Several of the villagers remained grim and unmoved, determined to stay strong despite the loss of their master, but it was on Michele Bearborn's face did his eyes finally fall. Her face was set and strong, yet her eyes had heaps of tears rolling down her milky white complexion. He nodded to her from across the courtyard before slowly entering the ring. He brought himself to his full height, removed the furs that hung off his shoulders, and cleared his throat.

"My friends, I have not the words to give at the loss of your master and brother," he began. "Yet, I pray you take comfort in knowing that his sacrifice was not in vain. He died as he lived, fighting to protect those who could not protect themselves. He was a mighty man, yet in the brief time I knew him, I could feel the love and compassion he bore for not only our empire but for each and every one of you."

He shifted where he stood and began to look again at each person individually. "I swear to you, your master's death will not go unavenged. We will not let his memory fade. Nor will we forget the evils that have been brought down upon you by a man bent on usurping power and control for his own selfish gain. A man, not worthy of your loyalty! A man not fit to rule! A man who has forfeited not only his kingdom but his life!"

"You all have known me as a simple ranger. Yet I must confess, I am more than that. I am Tiberius, Son of Luke, the emperor, and ruler of these lands. And by his authority, and the authority of the Axton dynasty, I declare you all true citizens of the Axton Empire! No longer bound to the service of a madman, but eternally protected by the full power of my family! From this day until the end of all days."

The villagers were stifling tears. Never before in their simple lives, on the edge of civilization, could they have ever imagined such a thing would happen to them. That the son of the emperor had been their defender. That they were counted as members of the empire. That their lives, their homes, and their futures would be of such importance to the future emperor.

Tiberius fell to one knee, pressed a fist to his chest, and said bright and clear, "Hear me! Citizens of the empire! Hear the words of my people! Hear me and know my pain! Hear me and know my promises to you!"

He closed his eyes, and in a deep voice, began to sing:
Farewell, my brother, my friend
For where you go, I cannot follow
Farewell Warrior and Soldier
Your battle is over, and at rest, you may be
Long have you struggled and toiled
Long have you resisted the coming end
Long have you waned in darkness and despair
But no more!
No more will ye live in pain
No more will ye wander chains and burdens.
No more will ye be slaved to your struggle and despair
I pray thee will walk in happiness once again.
I pray thee will live in splendor and majesty

I pray thee eternal life in the worlds beyond
Take with thee our prayers and our blessings
Take with thee our love
Take with thee the comfort of your sacrifice
I swear to thee, from this day until the unmaking of the world
We will hold your memory forever and always honor thee
Hail!

A mighty shout of 'Hail!' echoed out in response from the assembled people. And as if a great signal had been given, the flames burst into bright shimmering green. Not the sickly pale a necromancer's, but bright and vivid and powerful. The fire burned bright and powerful for many moments before disappearing all at once, rendering the village into complete blackness. The mighty bonfire itself was gone, transported somewhere beyond their village and beyond their world. Transported into the beyond to be greeted by the Father himself.

Tiberius stood again, turned on the spot, and quickly departed from the village. Shayla followed him as he went, yet Michael continued to linger. He slowly approached the spot where the pyre had once stood and saw that the ground beneath him was completely undisturbed.

He turned to face Catherine. "He is with his Father, isn't he?"

Her sweet smile crept on her stone like face. She turned to face Michael, and said, "Aye, the Father has accepted him into his home. Tygahl will no longer know the pains of war, nor the suffering of mortality. He will run free in the Father's domain, as is the fate of all his children."

"Wow. Thank you for summoning us to see this," Michael replied with a bow.

"You're welcome, young one. It has been nearly four hundred years since anyone outside of our kin have borne witness to our customs," Catherine said.

Michael nodded in understanding. The dwarves had bound themselves to the empire that had liberated them so many years ago. And the act of allowing the people of the empire to see their ancient funeral was indeed a recommitment of themselves and their loyalty to their adopted homeland. Michael knew Tiberius would have figured that out himself when he decided to bring his companions here. Though how Tiberius knew this was happening at all still eluded him.

Come to think of it, where is Tiberius anyhow?

It was hot inside the prisoner's tent. The platoon of knights who stood guard outside had not raised an eye to Tiberius striding into the tent. The Narzeth was seated in the middle of the tent. Heavy chains crisscrossed his body with his hands bound behind the chair he sat upon. To Tiberius, he appeared to be sleeping. But as he approached, a dreadful grin crossed his wrinkled face.

"Welcome, Tiberius," the wizard hissed. His eyes gradually opened, flashing the most intense violet Tiberius had ever seen in his life. "I would pour you a drink, but as you can see," he shrugged his chain-bound body in contempt, "I'm a little preoccupied at the moment."

Tiberius's face remained impassive to the wizard's words. He examined him over, moving closer to sit across. His voice was rather middle-aged, aside from the almost hissing sound he made with each word. But his skin, his skin looked stretched and worn. Heavy wrinkles adorned his brow, and his violet eyes sat back in the skull. He might have been over a hundred by the look of him. His once tanned skin washed of its color, appearing more like a wraith than a man.

"I sense you have many questions for me, Ranger," the wizard spoke as Tiberius finally sat. "But none of the answers I give will bring you any peace."

"I don't know about that, Narzeth," Tiberius replied, removing his pipe and settling in. "There are a great many things I remain ignorant to that you could shed some light on."

The wizard chuckled, seeing past the humble ranger routine Tiberius was trying to employ. "Don't play stupid games with me, Son of Luke. You are no simple foot-soldier that goes running off at his master's whim."

Tiberius remained calm, not even betraying his surprise at the wizard's remark. Though his mind was racing, trying to figure out how this man would know such a highly guarded secret. But the wizard smiled broader now and carried on.

"Yes. I know who you are, boy. Who you truly are, anyhow, Tiberius Axton, heir to the Axton Empire. Long may you reign. So, for the sake of time, let us just assume I know everything about you and your ilk."

"Fair enough, wizard," Tiberius replied. "Then do me the courtesy of telling me your name."

"My name is of no consequence to you," the wizard spat. "The sun rises, and with its coming, I shall depart. My mission is done, and I will be welcomed in sands of all time."

"Unless the King's men are coming to rescue you, I don't think you'll be leaving us anytime soon."

"I do not speak of the King's men," the wizard scoffed. "I speak literally of the sun. I was bound to the demon, and without it, I am powerless. The coming of the sun is the coming of death."

Bound to the demon? Did he mean The Revenant? Tiberius pressed on.

"And what was your mission? To kill me. Clearly, you did not pass the test."

The wizard began to wheeze from laughter in such a horrid way that Tiberius was tempted to put him out of his misery. But he relaxed even more, content to endure this vile creature.

"The vanity of the Axtons! I had heard it was true, but to see it, firsthand! This has been worth it!"

He calmed himself and continued, "No, you stupid boy! I didn't defile my body and soul, learning the heathen magic to come and kill you! What would killing you accomplish? The bastard Luke would just find a new heir. The rangers, a new commander. And all of the Axton Empire would hold you up as a martyr. Brave Tiberius, commander of the legendary Imperial Rangers! What a joke."

Tiberius didn't speak, and why should he? If this fool wanted to spout off, then why stop him? "So then, why come here at all? We beat you at Vermillion…"

The wizard lurched forward, trying to break the chains to get at Tiberius. "How dare you speak that name to me!?"

Now we're getting somewhere, Tiberius thought.

"You didn't 'beat' us. You massacred us! You called down the infernal demons from myth and legend and slaughtered us! And then, as we tried to remove our wounded from the field, your Sorcerer turned them all to dust! Damn you, Tiberius! Damn your Magi! And damn your empire!"

Tiberius did not move. He continued to puff slowly on his wooden pipe, listening to the ramblings he knew were to come. "We didn't start the war, wizard. We didn't invade your country half a millennium ago. Your rulers did that."

"And if they hadn't, there would never have been an Axton Empire. You are here only because of us!"

"Then why did you invade us at all? Why have you continued to antagonize us and war with us for nigh on five hundred years? What compels you on?"

The wizard stared dumbfounded at Tiberius, wondering how he could not know why the Narzeth had waged their eternal war against the Axton's. But after a moment, he retracted in his seat and leveled his bright violet eyes at the ranger across from him.

"Go to hell, Ranger."

Damn. He wanted to tell me. I know he did. But so be it. It doesn't matter anyhow. What matters is the future.

Now Tiberius leaned forward. "I will not compel you to tell me. I suspect it wouldn't do much good anyway to torture you. So, tell me, Narzeth, how and why did you come this time?"

The wizard was silent for many moments, choosing his words as carefully as he could.

"How do you destroy an enemy that is mightier than you?" the wizard began. "After the war, many of us rebelled against our leaders. They had led us into ruin and despair, trying to match might with the empire. But that is the way of the Narzeth, strength above all. Against a foe who is stronger than you? We had to find another way."

"So, you turned to magic, didn't you?"

"Yes," the wizard whispered shamefully. "Magic is blasphemy to our gods. But we were desperate now. Many of us went to Beaumont and unearthed the library. We delved deep into the lore. And in it, we found a way."

"The magic you used would have taken you longer than a year to learn."

"We couldn't use magic. Try as we might, we just couldn't. Though in our study, we learned the skill of binding ourselves to the shapes of others. Our bodies rendered incorporeal and joined onto another. But then, what shape to take? That was the question."

Tiberius's mind clicked it into place. "You found a Revenant in Narzeth and joined with it."

"Many of us tried. Only I succeeded. And once I had done so, I came across the sea to begin my mission. And I am beyond pleased that I was successful, and your downfall is now at hand."

The wizard smiled broadly as he glanced his eyes to the tent opening behind Tiberius. Faint rays of sunlight were beginning to poke through. The hour of his death had come at last. Tiberius caught his eye and bolted to his feet, seizing the wizard by his withered throat.

"Your mission! What was your mission other than death and chaos!?"

The wizard laughed in between gasps for air. "My mission was chaos! How do you destroy an enemy that is mightier than you? From the inside! You cut their legs out! You dig their roots out! You turn them against one another until they destroy themselves!"

The wizard was practically hysterical now. Small flakes of skin began peeling themselves from his bone and turning to dust under Tiberius's hand. "Your King White! He begged for my help. Pleaded on his hands and knees for my power! My power to destroy you! And I gratefully obliged! Now the fool of a King has found himself in war! More and more of your Kings will turn on you! The people will turn on you! And then, you will burn!"

A swath of skin peeled off in Tiberius's hand, forcing him to release his hold on the wizard's neck. "Do you hear me, Son of Luke!? You will burn! All of you! The Axton Empire will fall! Rejoice!"

Sunlight broke through the flaps that marked the tent wall. The wizard cackled with insane glee. His skin began to fall off in heaps, littering the ground in rotten flesh. Tiberius did not turn away from the sight of melting skin. He watched the wizard dissolve, the hysterical cackling ringing in his ears. And in a few moments, it was all over.

Where there had been a man was now a brittle black colored skeleton underneath flowing red robes. The remains were oozing upon the ground with small steam rising from their remains. Tiberius watched all of this with odd wonder. He stood for a few moments longer, thinking on what the wizard had said in his madness. In his bones, he knew it was true.

He knew that civil war against one kingdom was a delicate matter. He knew the other nine could be swayed against them. He knew that if White remained unchecked, he could persuade the people of his kingdom against the empire. It was then all a slippery slope between fighting the King's men and fighting the innocents. Between being a liberator and being an occupier.

Dark thoughts for dark deeds ahead. After one last fleeting glance at the human sludge on the ground, Tiberius turned and left the tent.

For some time, he wandered around the camp, gathering his thoughts. He knew he had to speak with his father on the way forward, but not yet. He wasn't ready to bring these troubles to his father's already anxious mind. There would be enough time for discussions and plans later. For planning and war. For the hardship and suffering of all that was sure to come. For now, at this moment, he was alive; and he wanted to enjoy it. If only for a brief moment.

CHAPTER 28

THE WAR COUNCIL

Dawn had swiftly risen over the Imperial camp. While many of the soldiers and knights of the empire still slumbered on, it was the rangers who arose first. They were marshalled in a large clearing near where they camped to begin their day as they usually would, with vigorous and intense exercise. Abandoned were their leathers and furs, replaced instead with simple undergarments. A few of the soldiers on guard through the night stared at them in awe. Even the heartiest among them had not the mind for exercise in such cold and unforgiving conditions.

At the head of their formation stood Trevin. His spirits lifted, and his body felt renewed beyond measure. He felt the stiffness in his back and legs from so many hours of constant vigil over Tiberius that he practically begged for exercise to release the tension he felt. Yet as he began to pass out the orders of the morning, his voice caught in his throat, and a sly smile broke the stern face he wore in front of his men.

From behind the mass formation of men and women, Tiberius slowly passed, heading to the front of the assembled group. All chatter was quickly silenced at his arrival, and all eyes in the group were pinpoint focused on him. He strode through them with purpose and vigor in each step. Pride and respect beamed out from his men as he took his place next to Trevin. After a brief nod and smile to one another, they turned to face their men.

He smiled at his men. His beloved and trusted rangers, and simply said, "Hail, Rangers."

"Hail!" they replied exuberantly.

"I must apologize for my absence, but I see First Sergeant has kept you all ready and able for combat, nonetheless. While we have much to discuss on the things to come, this morning cast all doubt and confusion aside. This is a glorious morning to be alive and to be in the service of our country. And I think we could all do with a little morning run."

He walked through the throng, stretching as he went until he led them to a wide path in the woods that he had fought in so many nights ago. He turned to look at each of his men in the face, studying them intently, determined to commit each of their faces to memory. Beyond them, he could see his father standing tall and proud outside of his tent, a smile etched on his face. Tiberius shot him a brief nod before turning away from his men and heading off on a brisk run, the rangers at his back trying desperately to keep his grueling pace.

He led them through the burnt woods and into the wide-open country beyond. Every so often, he would turn to inspect his men. Their faces were stiff and frozen but still bore broad smiles. This is where he belonged. With his rangers, out in the wild doing wild things. He knew this moment would be fleeting in the times to come. But he wanted to hold on to it just a little longer.

An hour later, they returned to the camp. The exercise had done much in terms of clearing and focusing his thoughts. While his own mind was made up, he dared not go against his father and emperor's wishes on what he desired to do next. He could see the way to victory laid before him clearer than the Imperial Road. Though he had not the heart to say it just yet, he knew he would have to leave his rangers again.

"I reckon I'd know that look anywhere," Timothy said with a smile as they walked back to their small section of the camp. "You've got something on your mind, don't you, sir?"

"Of course he does," Zachary said, joining them and placing a large piece of tobacco in his cheek. "Of course, the big mystery is what would be crawling around his brain?"

"He aims to leave, and continue his quest with the Dragoon and Mage," Trevin said solemnly from behind them. The three men spun to see him standing just outside of their circle, his face grim and sad. "Am I right, sir?"

"What makes you say that, Trevin?" Timothy asked, also placing a piece of tobacco in his cheek.

Trevin held his gaze on Tiberius as he answered. "He went to see the prisoner last night. Without the emperor or the High Sorcerer present."

"Sir!" Zachary demanded. "Why would you do that? What if he had some foreign trick up his sleeve."

"He didn't, boys," Tiberius replied, breaking his gaze from Trevin. "His power was bound to the shape of the Revenant. And without it, his body was failing him. He died as the sun rose this morning."

"Well, what did he tell you then?" Zachary asked.

"Things I am not prepared to discuss here."

"But it is true then," Timothy cut in. "You do mean to leave again, don't you?"

Tiberius stared at Trevin, the feeling of heartbreak and love washing over him before he slowly nodded in reply. "The First Sergeant speaks true. I aim to continue on the quest that I had pursued. After all that has transpired, my heart compels me to see it to its end."

They stared at their commander for a few moments, weighing his decision in their minds until Timothy flashed a devilish grin. "Ah, don't worry none, sir. We didn't need your help anyway. Not with Zachary and me around. And old grumpy grump here," he finished, motioning to Trevin.

"I know you don't need my help, boys. That is why my mind is at ease over having to depart. But nevertheless, I do have some parting instruction to pass out."

"What parting instruction, sir?" Trevin asked.

"Watch this," Tiberius replied with a sly smile.

He directed his friends to follow him to a nearby table that he quickly mounted. "Hail, Rangers!" he boomed out over the sea of people. A hearty and thunderous reply returned to him, bringing a broader smile to his face.

"Though I am beyond elated to be amongst you again, I am afraid our reunion will be cut short," he began. "You all know me as a plain and honest man; therefore, I will speak plainly and honestly to all of you. This very day, I will speak to His Majesty regarding the manner of the unfinished mission he dispatched me on. A mission that I aim to see fulfilled."

The Rangers turned and gave each other worried looks. The thought of entering in the fierce fighting they all knew was to come gave them pause, but not fear. Never fear. For the Rangers of the Axton Empire never knew fear in the face of combat. Sensing their apprehensions, Tiberius raised a hand to silence them.

"Take heart, warriors. For though we travel two separate roads, our destinations are the same. And although I will not be able to join you in the glorious battles to come, I do have some departing orders to pass."

He invited his three most trusted friends to join him at the table, much to their surprise. "First, seeing as our ranks have swollen in the past year, I have decided that the need for more First Sergeants is in order. Therefore, let it be known that from this day until the last day, that Zachary Trex and Timothy Shepherd shall both hold the position of First Sergeant of the Imperial Rangers!"

A mighty roar went up over the crowd of rangers. His friends recoiled in surprise at his words before a deep feeling of honor and responsibility crashed on them. He motioned them to return to the ground and now brought Trevin to the front.

"Now, I'm sure many of you are wondering why we would have three First Sergeants. Well, rest assured, we will not," he placed a tender hand on Trevin's muscular shoulder. "All of you know Trevin has been a formidable leader in my absence. Indeed, I would not be out of line to say that he is perhaps the finest ranger in our ranks today."

Another mighty cheer rang out over the crowd before Tiberius continued. "Yet now, we stand on the brink of war against the mad King White. And for this campaign, the rangers will need a commander in the field."

The air was sucked away at his words. "I name Trevin Moore as the acting commander of the Imperial Rangers! I grant him the same authority and power that is due to this title and position. He shall have complete control over the actions of our order and will lead you all to glorious victory! Hail, Trevin Moore! Commander of the Imperial Rangers!"

Thunderous booms of hail and applause exploded from their formation. Each man and woman assembled there held their arms aloft in praise of their new commander. Even though they would have desired Tiberius to be at the head of their formation, they could not imagine anyone more suited for the honor and title than Trevin.

"Commander," Tiberius said, facing Trevin. "Take charge of your men."

Trevin stared at Tiberius hard, his eyes softening from the surprise and elation he had felt to love. After a few moments, he nodded in reply and placed his hand on Tiberius's shoulder. "Thank you for the honor, sir. I will not betray your trust, nor your love," he whispered.

"I know you won't, my love," Tiberius replied, smiling. "Now, take command of your men." He hopped down from the table just as Trevin began issuing orders of the day. Now that his men were sorted, he was eager to speak with his companions.

The rangers bowed low to him as he walked through them. He patted each of them on their arms, wishing them good fortune in the days to come. He hoped to be amongst them again but was content knowing they were safe in the hands of his trusted friends.

He wandered around the camp, taking it all in. He knew that this camp would look small in the coming weeks and months compared to the forces yet to arrive. A force equal to the one that had invaded Narzeth would soon be marshalled; with them would come the full fury and might of the Imperial army. He just wished they would all have the wisdom to know their enemy from their friend when the fighting against their fellow countrymen started.

Before long, he found his companions sitting near a fire tucking into their breakfast when he plopped down in a seat between them.

"Well, that was a little dramatic, wasn't it?" Shayla said.

"What was dramatic?" Tiberius asked sheepishly.

"That little impromptu ceremony with your men just now."

"Oh, you heard that?"

"The whole of the empire heard that ruckus," Michael interjected between mouthfuls of food.

"Cut me some slack. I couldn't just up and leave them," Tiberius replied with a laugh. "And besides, it has been a long time since I have seen my men, and my heart was eager to be with them and lead them again. If only for a moment."

Despite a face full of eggs and bacon, Michael's curiosity spoke for him. "I'm so confused."

"Tiberius turned command over to Trevin," Shayla answered plainly. "He knows that in the battles to come, the rangers will need a true commander at the head of their formation."

"Again, I'm confused. Where will you be if not with your men in battle?"

Tiberius thought for a moment, weighing his choice in words carefully. "I mean to speak with my father this morning. Or rather, I mean all of us to speak with him on what we should do next. And while my mind is already made up, on my honor, I cannot act on it without his blessing."

"Why do you speak so cryptically?" Michael asked.

"He means to continue our quest to the outpost but cannot in good faith ask to do that given the threat of insurrection and war," Shayla replied.

Michael spun his head quickly between his companions. He had assumed that he would continue that journey alone and that Tiberius would wish to continue the fight that had been brought down on them by King White. "Is this true?" he asked finally.

"Aye, young Mage," Tiberius replied. "Shayla speaks true. Before, my heart was torn between being with my father and with my men in the fight. Yet now that I have talked to the Narzethian, I know our quest is of the most importance."

Michael's jaw dropped. "You talked to the Narzethian? Alone!? Well, what did he say?"

"I think it best if you hear what I have to say once we are all in council together."

They sat in silence for a while. Michael lost in his thoughts, and his two companions surveying the scenery around them. After a time, it was Shayla who finally broke their quiet.

"I have had these thoughts too, Tiberius. But like you, I am sworn to the defense of our homeland. Yet, after what you and I went through, what they all saw in Michael's spell, and the Narzethian wizard..." she stopped, thinking hard. "I think the true heart of the struggle lies in the world beyond. And if the dwarves speak true, which I do not doubt they do, then the outpost will hold the answers. And if not the answers, a means of obtaining the answers."

"Well, this is most fortunate then," Michael said after a few moments of contemplation. "As I mean to continue that journey myself."

"I know you did," Tiberius said, standing to stretch. "And we can't very well leave our friend to enter the unknown by himself, can we?"

"I wouldn't hear of it," Shayla said with a small laugh. "The boy may be a strong wizard now, but he's still a boy."

"Hey! I'm sitting right here!" Michael exclaimed.

They laughed at his incredulity before Tiberius said, "Let me in on a secret, young man. We are companions and friends, yes, but we are more than that now. After what we have endured, our very fates are now intertwined. We are bound to each one another in both deed and in trust and honor. So, as you can see, Shayla and I owe allegiance to not only our country but to one another. But we will speak of these things later."

He hopped over his seat and rushed off to his own tent to bathe and change, leaving his Shayla to continue poking fun at the young Mage.

An hour or so later, they sat in the emperor's tent along with the generals of the Imperial army and Trevin. After small pleasantries and courtesies were rendered, Tiberius stood proudly and walked to the middle of the circle they had formed.

"Your Majesty," he began proud and firm. "Generals and Marshalls of our grand army, I have called this war council as is my right as commander of the Imperial Rangers. You all know me to be a prudent and honest man. So as such, I will speak so with you."

All eyes in the room were fixated on him as he spoke. Barely anyone could muster a breath they were so enthralled with his presence and renewed vigor.

"When my companions and I set out from the capital at the behest of our emperor, it was under the most secretive of circumstances. We were bidden to travel north, beyond the Forgotten Mountain, and into the Land Beyond. We were sent in search of the answer to the greatest mystery of our time. A mystery, that if left unanswered, would lead to the greatest change in our country since the very founding of our glorious empire."

"And what, pray to tell, is the mystery you sought to answer, Commander Tiberius?" one of the generals asked.

Tiberius turned to his father, who gave a slight nod in approval before turning to face the general. "My lord, magic is leaving our world."

Silence hung on them as though a great anvil had fallen on each of their chests. Tiberius said nothing to break the tension, instead waiting for the inevitable scoffing and questions he knew were to come.

As if on cue, a flurry of incredulous chatter broke out amongst the generals, each of them swearing in utter disbelief at Tiberius's words. Yet, he continued to stand firm and unmoving as the words flew all-around before slowly dying out. Finally, he turned on the spot surveying the seated men.

"Are you all finished?" he asked with a sly smile.

"Commander Tiberius, we do not mean any disrespect to you or to His Majesty," another general with a fiery red beard piped in. "But how in the name of the heavens do you expect us to believe such a claim?"

"Master Tiberius speaks true!" Michael burst out, standing quickly to his feet. "On my honor as a Brother of the Magi, he speaks true."

The red-bearded general scoffed at Michael's words. "Please! You will have to do better than the word of a boy! Especially when all of us witnessed the magic he wielded last night."

"What about my word?" the emperor asked flatly. All eyes turned to him at once. "I believe both of these men, and I believe the Supreme Sorcerer that rules our city in my stead. I believe them for many reasons, but the most obvious one to me should have been the most obvious to you. Why would Tiberius, the commander of the Imperial Rangers, war hero against the Narzeth, lie?"

No one dared speak in protest to their emperor's words, nor could they argue his logic. Silence fell like a harsh thud in the room until the red-bearded general finally said, "What is your quest then, Commander Tiberius?"

"Our aim is for the dwarven outpost," Tiberius said. "And I aim to depart this afternoon for the Ice Steps as was our goal before. Yet, I am honor-bound to our country's defense, and I am honor-bound to rooting out the traitorous King White. But I am adamant that with all we have seen since leaving the capital, the way forward to victory lies beyond the mountains."

"If that is your aim then, sir, then I am adamant that you take ten of my best men with you!" the red-bearded general declared.

"Nay! Tolenor's men might have proven valiant against White's thugs, but they are no match for my marines! And you may take a whole legion of them!" another general proclaimed.

"Sir! General's Tolenor and Irius' men are indeed hearty fighters, but only the empire's rangers can endure such a journey! Take us!" Trevin said, placing his hand over his chest. He was always honored to offer his commander the utmost support he could, despite already knowing his true intentions.

"Gentlemen! Gentlemen! Peace!" Tiberius said, raising his hands to silence them. "While I would gladly take all of your men, it will be me and my two companions who make the journey. We started this quest together, and we will be the ones to see it to its end. Besides, if I know our emperor like I think I do, he will need all of your best men for what is to come."

"I agree with Commander Tiberius' wisdom," the emperor said, standing to dismiss them. "I intend to take the fight to White myself, and it would be best for Tiberius and his companions to continue their journey alone." He walked to the three companions and motioned for them to exit the tent. "Now, gentlemen, if you will excuse me, I must speak to these three in private before we begin our own planning. I suggest you return to your own men in the meantime and make sure all is in order within your ranks."

The generals and Trevin bowed as the four departed the tent to discuss their own plans. Michael leaned close to Shayla and whispered, "Why would we not know what the emperor's plans are?"

"In case we get captured," Shayla whispered. "Pain and torture can make the strongest of us break, and the emperor will not risk that. If we do not know what their plans are, then the enemy could never know them either."

Michael marveled at the emperor's cunning, realizing that he still had much to learn in the ways of war and strategy. He followed as best he could as the emperor directed the three back to their own tent.

Inside he found the dwarves had all assembled. New garments and an assortment of wares for their journey were laid before them. Michael examined all of the items one by one, a growing eagerness forming in his heart.

"I had anticipated Tiberius' intentions to continue the journey, Mr. Deerborn," the emperor said with a chuckle. "I knew the minute I saw him take off on the run with his men this morning that his mind and his spirit compelled him to continue on with the quest I had directed you on."

"Beg your pardon, Your Majesty. But how could you possibly have known that from a run?"

"It's what I would have done," the emperor admitted. "He is my son after all. And I know he spoke with the prisoner this morning."

All eyes turned to the emperor. A wry smile broke his worn and lined face. He pulled up chairs for Catherine and himself and motioned for the others to sit as well. He readjusted the hem of his simple black and tunic and said, "Now, what do you have to tell us, Ti?"

CHAPTER 29

THE PARTING OF THE WAYS

Tiberius told his tale in full. From the pre-dawn funeral for the fallen Berserker to his interrogation of the Narzethian wizard. Not a single detail was omitted as he spoke, hoping that the wizard's words and intentions would not be lost on any of them. His companions stared on in astonishment. News that the Narzethians had recovered the Library of Beaumont was most troubling. But that they had learned how to bind themselves to creatures as powerful as the Revenant was most worrying. Despite the news, the emperor and the dwarf Catherine remained expressionless at his tale.

Once he finished, he removed himself from his chair to pour a glass of water. No one spoke for a long time until the emperor finally stood. He leaned against the back of his chair and said in a low voice, "What madness has consumed Forval that he would take up with a Narzeth in his plots?"

"I cannot speak to know King White's mind, father," Tiberius said with another sip of water. "I can only tell you what the wizard said. But it all goes to show that White's mind has been bent to this purpose awhile. The long years of resentment his family has harbored against us have finally taken its toll on him."

"Indeed. Mage," the emperor turned to Michael now, "What have you to say? Is it possible the Narzeth have indeed done begun learning magic?"

"Your majesty, I was not there to hear the Narzethian's words. All I can tell you is what I saw that night in the field. When Bruce destroyed the Revenant, there was only the wizard left in its place."

"Then why was Shayla unable to kill him once he was exposed?"

Michael shook his head. "I do not know, sir. Perhaps there was still some lingering power within him that kept him protected? I honestly could not tell you how. But I can tell you that if they have excavated the library, then it is most fortunate that magic is hard to touch."

"Aye. I agree wholeheartedly. I cannot begin to imagine a horde of magic-wielding Narzeth." The emperor turned to the dwarf seated at his side, "Lady Stonefoot, what counsel can you give?"

Her rock-like face remained blank at his words as she said, "My lord, whatever wisdom I could give would be for naught. You and your son have already chosen your paths, regardless of what I might have to say."

"Fair enough. What advice then can you give?"

Her familiar motherly smile stretched across her face. Love beamed off of her, comforting everyone in the tent. "My advice to you, Son of Alexander, is to listen to your hearts. Your son is determined to continue north; you are determined to meet this King White in battle. I would advise you to continue these paths. As the young Mage said, the Narzeth cannot touch magic either. Do not worry about them until the time is right."

"But worry about them, I do. Long have they warred with us. To hear they are abandoning their beliefs tell me they are growing desperate."

"Father, I agree with Lady Stonefoot," Tiberius interjected. "They are a threat, of course. From what the wizard had said, his mission was to help White start his insurrection. And in that, he has succeeded. If we are to contend with the Narzeth in the future, we must quell his rebellion first."

The emperor didn't speak for some time as he considered everyone's words. He looked to each of them, searching them over when his eyes fell on Shayla.

"Mistress Rider, what have you to say?"

Her brown eyes met his look. "If I may speak plainly, one soldier to another, all enemies of our country must die."

The emperor nodded in agreement. Succinct and straight to the point was his best way of talking. "I agree, Dragon Knight. Then we all know what we must do. I suggest you begin packing straight away."

Michael slowly got to his feet and began looking over his own fresh robes.

"I take it you mean for us to depart at once?" Tiberius said.

"Aye, son. I think it would be best for you and your new companions to depart immediately. With as large of a force that we have mustered here,

I do not think any scouts in the open would notice less than twenty people leaving. Especially as long as my banners continue to fly in camp."

"Less than twenty?" Shayla asked before turning to face Catherine and her dwarves, each of them clad again in their heavy iron armor. "You mean to journey with us to the outpost?"

"Aye, daughter of Kazduhl," the dwarf woman said. "We follow the will of the Father, and his will compels us to help you in your quest. Oh! And before I forget," she turned to one of her dwarves, and after speaking in their ancient tongue, three large chests were brought from the back of the room. "A gift for you three before our departure."

Shayla bent to the ground, carefully opened the chest, and recoiled in excitement. She slowly placed her olive-skinned hands into the trunk and produced a familiar dragon-shaped helm. Instead of the normal green and red helm that she had worn her whole life, this one was deep ebony, with fierce stripes of grey and white running in from the eyes over the top and sides.

Shayla stifled a sob before kneeling next to the dwarf, and bowing her head, said, "Thankee, daughter of Frijigzah."

"You are welcome, dragon daughter. It is with gladness that I am honored to have made this for you."

Shayla examined the helm. It was beautiful beyond measure with its deep blacks and intricate white ornamentation. "Lady Stonefoot, if I may be so bold to ask. Can you fashion these for my sisters?"

The dwarf smiled at her and said, "Mychala has one of her own. She will give it to the Imperial smiths in the capital so they may fashion them for your fellow dragoons."

Tears were welling in the corner of the Dragon Knight's eyes that she forced away. "Thank you, ma'am. Where is my sister?"

"She awaits us on the edge of the camp. She will see us off."

Tiberius and Michael now moved to examine their own chests, each finding armor of their own fashioned in the empire's colors. Each pair was stronger than the most splendid knight's armor and as light as their own leather garments. They, in turn, thanked the dwarves for their generosity before quickly donning their new apparel.

After a few moments, Catherine bowed low to the emperor and bid him good fortune in the war to come.

"But take heart, Son of Luke," she warned. "Though our paths take us in separate directions, we are bound together. For the real enemy of this evil will only be truly revealed if we both succeed in our endeavors."

"I agree, Mistress dwarf," the emperor replied, returning the bow. "Take good care of my boy."

"Do not worry about him, Your Majesty," she said with a wry smile. "His friends will do enough protecting on their own. And besides, he is The Spirit of The Warrior." And with that, she and her dwarves departed the tent for the edge of the woods.

The four stood in silence in the tent for a moment before Shayla directed Michael to follow her out, giving father and son some much needed time alone.

"I am sorry to leave you so soon, father," Tiberius said at last.

"Ah, it's okay, Ti. It's like I said, I would have done the exact same thing if it were me," the emperor replied. "Besides, I fear Catherine's words are true. Both of our quests are intertwined more than we think, and I would trust no one to carry out this mission than you and your friends."

"They have proven to be powerful friends to have indeed," Tiberius admitted. "Any parting advice?"

"Son, I don't think you need my advice or counsel anymore. You are more than capable, and one day you will make a fine ruler of our country."

"Hopefully, not for many years to come," Tiberius replied with a laugh.

"Hopefully, indeed. Now, I too must get back to the council. I pray thee good fortune in your quest, Ti. The Spirit of The Warrior will always be with you."

"The Spirit of The Warrior will always be with you too," Tiberius said before embracing his father.

His mind flashed with memories from long ago of time spent with his father. Running the halls of the rangers' garrison of Kovaiyemarck. Hunting and tracking in the woods outside of the city. Sparring in the training square outside of the mansions. Memories he was sure to keep in his mind and his heart for the journey ahead. His father had been his rock his entire life. Always there. Always loving and protecting. He was sad to not be with him now when he would need him the most. But his judgment in appointing Trevin in his place was sound. And the wisdom of continuing the quest he knew to be right.

They broke their embrace, and without a word, both departed the tent to rejoin their respective parties. From inside his father's tent, his eyes locked with Trevin's. In all the haste of the day, he had forgotten to say any departing words to him. Yet on his face, Tiberius could see all was forgiven. There would be time enough for their love when this was all over. To say all the things they had wished they could say. For now, they would have to wait just a little longer. Their duty came first, it would always come first, but that was the sacrifice they knew they had to make for loving one another.

From outside the tent, Tiberius offered a solemn nod to his love before turning away. He couldn't bear to see Trevin a second longer. But he would hold his face and the sound of his voice in his mind for all the long days to come.

Tiberius strode through the tents examining the men, all eager and willing to throw themselves into the fight against White's evil pursuits of power and domination. Some offered bows to him that he gladly returned.

They still see me as a hero, but what they fail to realize is that all of them are heroes. From the lowly squire to the bravest knight. Each and every one of them. Heroes of our country.

A half-hour later, he met his companions and the band of dwarves on the edge of the camp. Ever the worrier, Michael was busying himself with repacking his ruck while Shayla spoke with her dragoon sister.

"I am entrusting you to lead in my stead," Shayla said. "Our homeland is beset by traitorous warmongers. Be brave, sister. And lead well."

Mychala bowed at her leader's words. "I will do my best, sister. We will not abandon our home in its hour of need. I promise."

The two dragoons embraced one another and spoke parting words in their own tongue. After they broke apart, Mychala turned to the Mage and helped him put his heavy pack onto his back.

"Keep her safe, Michael Deerborn. She is more precious to us than you could ever imagine."

Michael blushed and replied, "Begging your pardon, ma'am, but she is very precious to me as well."

Mychala beamed at the Mage's words. "Then please keep yourself safe as well. You too are precious."

Michael's face started to become hotter than before. He quickly bowed low, hoping to hide his change in complexion from the brave and beautiful Dragon Knight. Mychala chuckled, and with a quick bow to Catherine, donned her helm and lept high in the sky.

Michael watched her fly into the sky, bound once in the distance, and then disappear over the horizon.

Till we meet again, Dragoon.

Not wanting to disturb their goodbyes, Tiberius finally stepped forward to join the party. Shayla turned to face him and asked, "Are you ready, sir?"

He turned and beheld the incredible sight of the empires might laid out before him. In the distance, he could see archers sending precise shot after shot at their targets. He looked the other direction and beheld swordsmen and knights clad in their deep black armor, sparring as hard as they could.

Further on, in the woods behind the village, his own rangers were hard at work amongst the trees and giant boulders. He could see Timothy and Zachary issuing instruction and watching every move their men made. He smiled a sly and knowing smile before returning his gaze to his companions.

"Aye. I'm ready," he replied. And with that, they headed out into the burnt woods, bound for the Ice Steps beyond. No one in their party spoke, each lost in their own thoughts about what would await them on the other side. Tiberius alone walked with a light step and heart. Gone was the fear and worry that had burdened him for so long, now replaced with the excitement and thrill of adventure. He smiled again, held his head high, and strode ahead of his companions, eager to meet whatever fate lie in store beyond the mountains.

Epilogue

Smoke was rising from the burned city below him. His fists were shaking with an uncontrollable rage at the sheer destruction that had been wrought on his city. From atop the Emperor's Spire, he could see fires continuing to rage in every direction he looked. He looked down at the dead body that lay at his feet. His anger boiled over, and he spat and cursed the dead would-be assassin at his feet.

"Please tell me you have some good news," he said.

"Reports are still coming in, Your Majesty," the sorcerer said from somewhere behind him. "The enemy has been driven out of the Imperial City, but…" his voice died in his throat.

"But what?" he barked.

"Over half our forces were wiped out in the battle," the sorcerer answered solemnly. "We've heard no word from the rangers or the dragoons. The Imperial marines have finished pushing out the last of the invaders to the sea. The army has rallied itself in the city center and has begun reinforcing the barricades. But the dead and dying… it is beyond anything we could have ever imagined, Your Majesty."

Silence hung heavy at his words, suddenly torn apart by a violent blood-curdling scream that shook the mighty Spire to its base. The sorcerer hung his head and began to quietly sob, lost in his despair.

"What are you going to do, sire?" the sorcerer asked finally.

He turned to face the sorcerer and, after a moment or two, said, "I'm going to find out who is behind this attack. I am going to root them out wherever they may be hiding. And I'm going to kill them all."

ABOUT THE AUTHOR

Ryan Copeland was born in south Texas. His family imbued him with a love for all things artistic and encouraged him to pursue his interests. He joined the United States Army in 2012 and is currently living in Georgia. When he's not busy discovering the world of The Axton Empire, he spends time with his family and smoking excellent meats.

PREVIEW
THE LAND BEYOND
THE AXTON EMPIRE
BOOK TWO

Lightning cracked the featureless black sky. The ground beneath him shuddered, thrusting him awake. He looked around their camp, eager to see the ranger or dragoon come running to his aid. But the camp was deserted, and no help was coming. The wind that had blown high pitched whistles down the mountain the past few nights was gone now. An unnatural stillness came over the woods, sending a sudden jolt of dread through his body. His eyes darted in all directions, but in the cold dark of night, he could see nothing. He staggered to his feet, scared and unsure of what was happening to him.

Another bolt of lightning snapped overhead, this time louder and brighter than the first. He thrust his hands to his ears out of shock and crouched again to the ground. He felt an odd slushiness under his feet, and the faint aroma of metal and copper came to his nose. The earth shook violently, forcing him to his hands and knees. He felt a strange sticky wetness on the cold dirt that made him furrow his brow in confusion. He knew well enough what it was, for he had felt it himself only a few weeks ago on his own body at the start of this whole ordeal.

He shot upright again just as another bolt of lightning rang out. In the flash of light, he could see dead bodies littered around where he stood. He slowly withdrew his wand from deep within his robes, and with a simple flick of his wrist, a dull light appeared around him. But the sight that met his eyes forced him to recoil and retch in shock.

At his feet laid the mangled and deformed body of his friend and leader. His friend and leader who had sacrificed so much to bring him so far and faced the enemy hordes outside the burning village walls. The brave and heroic man who would one day be emperor of this country. At his feet lay the broken body of the Imperial Ranger Tiberius. Hot tears formed in the corners of his eyes. He looked away from the broken body of his comrade but again reacted in utter disbelief. A few feet away from where Tiberius lay was the daring and courageous Imperial Dragon Knight Shayla.

He rushed to her as fast as his young legs would carry him and knelt by her side, gathering her in his tiny young arms. Her brilliant dragon-scaled armor was shattered and broken against her body. Blood and heaps of flesh fell from her face and chest. At her side, her powerful ebony and green spear lay in a dozen pieces as if snapped like a tree limb.

He tried to scream against the carnage before him, but no sound would come. Through sheer will, he forced himself to breathe and pushed air through his body, determined to call out into the night long and loud. But, for some reason, he was rendered totally voiceless. Tears streamed down his face, stinging his black eyes. Another sudden burst of lightning erupted overhead, and in the brightness, he could see that more bodies were strewn about their camp.

Even without the aid of his wand to show him, he immediately knew the remaining bodies belonged to who dwarves that had travelled with them. They too were bound for their outpost in the Land Beyond, determined to help in discovering the mystery of the loss of magic in their world. But now, he was all alone, just a scared boy in the vastness of nothing.

More lightning erupted overhead, constant and strobing. The sound was deafening, forcing him to hold his ears in agony and retreat back to the frozen, bloodied ground. The world seemed to spin around him in a cacophony of light and thunder. In the dim shadows, he could see Shayla's lifeless brown eyes staring back at him, pleading for him to save her. Yet all he could do was curl up on the ground beside her.

At least down here, in the mud and dirt, he was safe. Safe from whatever evil had overtaken his friends. Safe from the oncoming storm that was soon to break overhead. Only now, on his safe patch of ground, the earth began to rumble and shook harder than it had before.

Loud groaning cut through the sound of the explosions overhead as great chasms in the ground burst open around him. The ground began to shift and break apart into giant piles. Fire from within the bowels of the earth began to spew up in large columns. The flames licked the sides of his young face, singed the hem of his robes, and melted the dense snow that had been a fixture of their environment.

In the firelight, he could now see clear as day the mangled bodies of his entire party. They looked as if some unworldly beast had clawed and gnawed them to their bones and ligaments. The earth shifted violently again, broke apart, and pulled the bodies of his dead companions into the seemingly bottomless pit. He tried in vain to save the falling Dragoon as she plummeted into the fiery abyss below, but was too slow to grasp the hem of her armor. He looked past the column of fire at Tiberius, who wore a look of utter remorse upon his cold face. The Ranger's body lingered on the edge of the pit a little longer before he too tumbled below. Michael rolled onto his back and was all alone now atop his own small patch of earth amidst the flames and lightning.

www.ingramcontent.com/pod-product-compliance
Lightning Source LLC
Chambersburg PA
CBHW060403260626
47160CB00006B/2415